THE SOUL CRIER

BECKY GAINES

©Ebook cover, paperback cover, and hardcover dust jacket design by Jenny Zemanek - www.jennyzemanek.com

©Laminated hardcover case design: Franziska Stern - www.coverdungeon.com - Instagram: @coverdungeonrabbit.

Edited by Janeen Ippolito.

Paperback ISBN 979-8-9865432-0-8
Hardback ISBN 979-8-9865432-1-5

Published by Lightning Frog Press
www.beckygaines.com

For those who feel cursed
because of what someone did.
You are not alone.
You are not powerless.
Your curse can be broken.
All it takes is one choice.
Your choice.

DEAR READER

This is not a light tale. Although I have sprinkled moments of hope and joy and love throughout these pages, this story is raw and brutally honest about the darker parts of life. There are things in this book that could be triggering, so I wanted to include a brief note on this book's content.

If this story had a movie rating, it would be high PG-13 for violence, abusive situations, and mild language. There is a relationship in this book that is verbally, emotionally, and physically abusive (but not sexually abusive). There are scenes of child abuse and child death, references to past attempts at self-harm and suicide, moments of PTSD, and a messy journey to healing that is hard and doesn't offer easy answers. Nothing was included without purpose.

I hope this story about a banshee who just wants to save one life and break her curse gives you hope for the journey you are on.

-Becky

The old ones say the soul is like a well, filled with joy and with grief. A place where the embers of our memories collect so we have something to burn on nights of bitter despair, and like inward stars, they keep us from fading into the dark.

But eventually, all wells run dry, time runs out, bones decay into dust. Death is the last thing we draw from the well. Or at least it should be.

How I envy them—those who've never been cursed. They live their simple lives and speak their simple truths, dipping into their souls and drawing themselves closer to their final rest. If the old ones are right, if my soul is indeed a well, then it has no bottom.

Grief is my eternity. And for me, grief always begins with a song.

WRAITH

1

WINTER SMOTHERS my whole world under a thick blanket of white, numbing the sun's heat and chilling the air into icy needles. Each breath is a painful challenge for most people and triggers a desperate chant of *survive, survive, survive.* But I'm nothing like the men and women who scrape a fragile life from the snowfields. They name winter their enemy when they should be worried about me. The cold will kill them slowly, but my voice—*it doesn't matter.* Survival is not a choice I get to make.

With the morning sun at my back, charcoal shadows mar the snow in front of me. One is obviously mine, turning my unbound hair into a rustling crown and mantle, but the others... *You're being followed.* I wait for an appropriate emotion to take hold, but my body might as well be made of ice. There's no creeping sense of danger to chill my skin, no stuttering upbeat to quicken the pace of my limping heart, no shocked widening of my eyes. I'm not preparing to run or to fight.

What follows me only becomes a threat if I sing.

I curl my hand around my silent throat, my stomach twisting, soured by the memory of the last kill I began with a song. The fresh blood cooling on my hands. The new rips in my slate-gray dress from frantic fingers trying to hold on to life. The final note ringing in my head as if I am still there. Watching the woman die. But I'm not. *That song is over.*

I grit my teeth and focus on the present, letting the frigid breeze dry my tears, but escape isn't that easy. There's a clock ticking down in my chest, a promise that can't be broken. *There will always be another victim.*

Predators wouldn't follow me if my voice saved lives.

I glance behind me, my long, wavy hair slipping around my face, but my heartbeat remains calm when I spot them. Six wolves. Heads bent low, tails stiff as they pad after me. Apart from their dark eyes and black noses, their white coats help them disappear against the snow. Where are the rusty stains, the signs of their kills? *Predators shouldn't look so clean.*

My palms grow itchy, but like the wolves' spotless fur, my hands bear no evidence of my crimes. *Blood washes off.* Unlike the guilt or the screams of the dying or the wails of loved ones left behind. All forcing me to face a single admission.

I did this. Bringing death with a simple song.

I draw my hands up, letting the sun hit them, but I feel no warmth. My skin is a soft gray, like a watered-down shadow compared to the deeper ash of the sky or the ebony of the half-buried orchards nearer the city. Blood is the only vibrant color I'm allowed to see in a world of shadowed tones. Everything else appears as a mix of grays, whites, or blacks until a fresh stab wound splatters scarlet across my vision.

At least the wolves kill to survive. I sing to satisfy a monster's lust for human souls.

I force my gaze forward, away from the predators who consider me an ally. The wolves keep pace. They stay so close one good leap would land me face to face with their alpha. *And then what?* They know I will sing again, and when I do, there will be a fresh body for them to scavenge without having to do any work. *I fill their bellies by setting murders in motion.*

Happy thought. I excel at happy thoughts.

I start counting the days I've been silent. The break I'm given between victims varies, but it's never shorter than three days and rarely passes two weeks. My right foot sinks a little deeper into the crusty snow, upsetting my balance as I reach the final number. *Twenty-one days.* It's been three weeks. Three weeks since I've felt the cursed pain stab my heart, since I saw the prophetic wound open in the next victim's chest, since I *sang.*

The wolves are right. *I'll be lucky to last another day before I sing.*

The alpha licks his lips, anticipating the meat I will provide, and the movement, the gleeful hunger in his gaze splits me in two. I face the wolf and stare him down. My fingernails prick my palms as my hands curl into tight fists. The breeze falls still. The snow sparkles. The alpha breathes out, but I breathe in. I lurch forward into a scream, my throat burning, my body trembling as I surrender to a futile plea.

Let my voice serve life instead of death.

Let me be the thing predators fear instead of use.

I empty my lungs, but I don't make a hearable sound.

The alpha doesn't flinch, doesn't even bare his teeth or growl. *Why should he?* I tip over, exhausted and panting, and brace my hands on my thighs. We both know my voice is cursed. I'm the monster people hear just once. And it means one thing.

You're about to die.

Everyone in Riffen is already dying. A slow, bitter death of hope and empty bellies. I'm almost a servant of mercy since the victims of my song are granted one last day to live. A quick death is the sole kindness left for the starving people of Riffen. *Even its name sounds like a curse.* The gray city shoves upward through the deep snowfields like a defiant fist. *Ha!* The cracked stone wall, leaning towers, and rising levels of stacked houses shout at the sky. *We're still here.* Riffen has survived plagues and royal assassinations and a world at war over the power to control the four seasons. But then winter came.

A winter that never ends.

I turn my back on the city and venture deeper into the wasteland of snow, my predatory companions ever behind me. The flutter of wings and croaks of interest add to my burden as a dozen crows join the wolves and circle above us. *At least he's not here yet.* The real predator, the monster I serve. Every step takes me farther from Riffen and the next person who will become his prey, but I'm never far enough. Not from him.

Not from what he makes me do.

He gets his name from the wicked game he forces me to play. *Red*, for the human blood soaking his crimson cape, and *Death*, for his sole purpose. Red Death exists to kill, ending life after life with his curved dagger.

Stabbed through the heart. It's how my songs always end.

But he can't murder them without me. *He needs my voice.* I walk beside his victims on their last day like a ghost, unable to run, unable to intervene, unable to be anything more than what he's made me. A wraith, with a terrible power. *I hear their souls.* Entire lives played from beginning to tragic end. Their choices call to me like notes, demanding I give them life, and even though the notes differ for each victim, one thing remains the same.

Every soul has a song.

I'm the monster who sings them.

Not yet. Today, I am no more dangerous to the living than a ghost. There is no melody to fear out here. Winter demands nothing of my weary soul, and without my song, I can almost believe I'm normal until I look down.

A *normal* young woman would be shivering if she wore the

torn rags of my dress with my arms, neck, and lower legs exposed. Her fingers would be blue, her hot breaths short and puffing desperate clouds of vapor into the air. *She wouldn't be out here.* In the cold and the silence stretching over all four kingdoms. She'd be racing to the city with its promise of fire and shelter and meager rations. While I long to be lost, she'd want to be found.

I can't be found.

I'd doom anyone who tried, for one simple reason. They'd have to be Red Death's next victim to find me. I shake my head, dismissing the wishful notion. *As if anyone would ever be glad I appeared to them.*

The crows fall silent as a familiar scent taints the air. Wood smoke. *No. Please, please, no.* I scan the snowfields, hoping to find nothing, hoping a trick of wind has carried the smoke from the city, but the damaged remains of a wall stick out of the snow thirty feet away. There's a glint of fire, the low hum of voices, and a flapping scrap of cloth stretched between stones, all signs of life. Of a people with nowhere else to go. *Refugees.* They risk the snowy wastes and the wolves to come to Riffen, the last place that still has food.

Built over the heart of the world, the city of Riffen sits where the land's natural magic is at its strongest. The forgemasters use their silver fire to melt away the snow so farmers can harness the soil's energy. Together, they're able to grow and harvest a small variety of root vegetables. The slim rations keep immediate starvation at bay and ensure survival. *For now.*

The wolves *yip* at each other, a sound far too close to joy. I tense, knowing what's coming. They bolt toward the refugees' camp, abandoning me and my promise of a single body for the hope of feasting on several bodies instead. I lunge forward, my fingers straining for the nearest wolf's tail, but they're too fast and I'm—

A savage pain stabs into my chest, skewering my too slow

heart, and my knees buckle. I fall with a crunch into the snow, stars blinking through my vision as I struggle to breathe. *I'm close to the barrier.* A wall of magical energy surrounds Riffen, created by Red Death himself for one purpose—*to ensure I can't escape.* The barrier itself is invisible and harmless to everyone else, but if I cross it, my body will be broken. The pain is a warning, a demand I go back. *I can't leave them.* Not when this is my fault.

I've led the wolves right to their camp.

I heave myself to my feet just as a man steps into sight. The wolves tuck themselves against the wall stones. They sneak toward him, their padded paws making no sound on the snow. Another refugee calls to the man. Distracted, he looks behind him.

"Turn around," I whisper as the alpha hunches low. My right hand fists the threadbare fabric over my heart. Even if I yelled the words, he wouldn't hear me.

The wolf leaps for the man's neck. I shut my eyes.

The muted *thump* as they collide makes me flinch.

Shouts and snarls and screams explode all at once as the pack charges into the camp. I cover my ears, lungs heaving as I fight a swarm of tears, but cutting through the chaos is the thud of wood on bone. The shriek and ring of metal. The roar of courage being summoned. I blink and lower my hands.

They're fighting back. With walking sticks, fry pans, or knives. *Some of them may survive.* A tiny spark of hope kindles in my light-starved soul, but I've walked these snowfields for years. I've seen the abandoned bones of whole bands sticking up through the snow. *There were swords among them.* Those refugees had fought back too, but winter has changed us all.

The wolves don't leave survivors. Not anymore.

I swallow against the sting of bile, but there's no pushing the shame down as I look at my shaking hands. Both empty. Both so useless. *There must be something I can do.* But I lack the freedom to intervene. I have no weapons, no magic to call on, no song to delay the slaughter.

"Help me!"

I wince. That simple plea hooks into my soul and draws my gaze to a young woman who's been separated from the group during the fight. The alpha and another wolf work together, driving her away from the others. She's so close I could reach her in a dozen steps.

I cautiously put my foot forward, without pain, but that's no guarantee. I only get one warning, and since Red Death changes the distance between the city and his barrier after each kill, every step is now dangerous. The space I have left could be five feet or fifty.

I have to try. So I shake off the fear of his punishment and run.

Her cries for help jolt into a shriek as she trips. She manages to stay upright, arms swinging for balance, but the wolves are closing in. She has seconds. I push myself harder, my boots crunching snow in a panicked beat that echoes the chant in my heart—*too late—too late—too late.*

I'm four strides away when the alpha lunges for her throat. *No!* My left knee buckles, pitching me into the snow, and before I can rise, a second wolf snaps at her leg.

She's down. Surrounded. Out of time.

My stomach twists into a sour knot as the wolves' thrashing bites make a quick end to her fight. Two men start yelling as they race for her, but—

She's dead.

Guilt lashes my soul as the wolves rejoin the pack and try to spook another refugee into running. Several more bodies lie across the snow, staining winter's white blanket a garish red. A flood of horror begs me to close my eyes again and block out the battle of survival. More refugees cry out for help, their voices merge with all the pleas of my song's victims. All of them roaring in my face.

HELP ME.

For ten years, all I've wanted to do is help, but my wants are like childhood wishes. Whispered in confidence to the stars but never coming true under the sun. *Maybe if I were free. If I were stronger. If I were good.* Maybe then I could save them. Maybe then I could save myself, but my master is cruel, and I am cursed.

Biting my cheek, I stand. I turn as a coward would from the slaughter, but my knees lock, defiant, until I'm shaking from the war between my heart and my reality. *I don't want to be the girl who runs.* Not when people need help.

A bell gongs from the city behind me. Its bright melody is an answer to the cries of the refugees and a promise. *Help is coming.* But the guiders who protect Riffen and patrol the snowfields might not make it in time.

My fingernails bite into my palms as I dig for the sliver of truth that could be my opening, my chance to intervene. *They're not Red Death's victims.* There is no game at play here, no predefined outcome. I may be invisible to the refugees without my song, but I'm still physically present. My hands may be empty, but they're capable of grabbing wolf fur, gouging wolf eyes, and latching onto wolf tails.

I run about ten steps before I slam into the barrier's wall. Any hope I had of intervening dies as the barrier pins me in place with ten-thousand pricking needles of pain. With a groan, I raise my shaking arms and pit my will against the barrier, shoving as hard as I can.

The refugees' cries sharpen, flung through the air like wobbling knives that will never find their target. Blood splatters the snow. A violent omen of what is to come. Death. I dig my heels in and lean forward, but the barrier becomes a heavy weight, ready to crush me, diverting my energy from breaking through the magical wall into holding it up.

Red Death never plays fair. Never gives me the tiniest chance of beating him.

A child breaks away from the broken wall and a wolf gives chase, running the girl down in seconds. I squeeze my eyelids shut against more tears as her terrified screech cuts up my soul. *I can't do this.* Be the one standing by, ever watching, powerless and unable to change our fate.

My boots slip and slide out from under me. I fight to drag them forward again, thighs trembling as exhaustion burns beneath the skin. I'm going to fall. I'm going to succumb any moment now. But I keep pushing, my groan rising into a yell that tastes of copper rage and salty grief. The air thickens around me, clogging my throat and tempting my lethargic heart to add an extra beat to its half-rhythm. Invisible claws rip into my soul in warning. *Go back.* What have I to go back to except more songs, more victims, more death?

The magic surges, searing my skin as it tries to force me to my knees. Shakes rattle my body as I hold on, but I'm sinking, failing yet again. I have no power to draw on, no strength to help me endure the pain twisting like a hot knife in my heart. I'm unseen, unheard, and utterly alone, and yet I wish for an impossible favor. *Please, let me do one good thing.*

Just one.

But there's no mercy for a wraith like me.

The bones of my fingers spread painfully wide and bend backwards, and despite the cold, beads of sweat sting my eyes. This isn't the first time I've challenged the rules of my curse. What began as a search to find a weakness in Red Death's barrier has twisted over the years, becoming a bitter hope for escape.

Break my neck. Inflict an injury so severe his magic can't fix me.

The barrier has taught me Red Death has no such limit. I've

broken my neck and almost every other bone in my body. *But it never stops.* The curse, my songs, his kills. I'm trapped in his loop of music and murder.

The bones in my hands snap first, painting the world in flashes of livid red agony against my closed eyelids. Then the barrier breaks my legs before seizing my spine.

Red Death's magic claws through my memories, poisoning my soul with the screams of everyone who has died because they heard my voice. I jerk sideways, trying to wrench free, but my past swallows me whole until every victim stands beside me. The men, the women, the children. Their hands grabbing at me. Fingernails scraping my skin. Fists bruising my bones. Faces pale with terror or reddening with hatred. And through the chaos whispers my own voice.

You will never be anything other than a monster's slave.

You will never bring anything good to someone's life.

My heart falters as guilt ignites my soul. I burn and burn, but there is no light in this burning. Only the dark of my true name.

My name is my curse. It ties me to a story told by every generation, but unlike me, those stories are safe. They don't get people killed. *I wish I was just a story.*

I am more *and* nothing else. A *soul crier*, to the friendlier myths —a young woman caught between life and death with the ability to discover who Red Death will murder next. There are other names for my kind, crueler in their tone. None of them captures the whole story. *I don't even know my own.* Who I once was. Where I came from. How I came to be this—*wraith*, who plays Red Death's game and sings his victims' songs.

What happened to me?

A question I can never answer or escape. It's rooted deep in my heart, bound to the name every victim hurls at me in accusation. Their faces, their cries melding together as one voice to condemn me.

Banshee.

Banshee.

BANSHEE.

With a crackle of thunder, the barrier throws me back toward the city where I will remain Red Death's favorite tool.

WRAITH

2

Snow scrapes my exposed skin as I bounce and roll to a stop. My body twitches and arches away from the ground, spine screaming, while hammers of red-hot pain pound along the breaks in my bones. Aches shoot down my jaw as I bite back another useless cry. I keep blinking, but the world remains a blur of glaring white and seeping gray as I take shallow breaths and try not to move.

A cold, healing fire spreads through my body as the magic that hurt me repairs the damage, settling over the broken bones in my hands and legs. Red Death requires me to be physically ready for the next song at any time. *Always protecting my vile purpose.*

I face a sky as gray as my despair. The wolves are still snarling, men swearing, women crying out as children wail. Their voices sow seeds of thorny regret in my already weedy soul.

How many more people will die because of me?

I roll my head to the side, leaking tears and hemorrhaging hope. White dominates. Winter's harsh diamond blanket stretches on and on, broken by nothing, stopped by nothing except the ghost-gray city of Riffen, the ebony cracks of dead orchards, and the smudges of human shapes. *Wait.* Those shapes are moving.

The crunching of snow grows louder. I lift my head, wincing at the protest of my bruised neck, and spot five people, swords drawn and glinting in the sun as they race toward the refugees' camp.

Guiders. The white bears embroidered on their dark tunics become clearer as one raises a horn to his lips. A jolting, thick sound like a rough tenor's voice blares through the chaos, and cheers rise in place of screams. I prop myself up on my elbows, careful of my still healing fingers.

The alpha howls, gathering his pack before baring his teeth in a bloody snarl. *Haven't they killed enough?* But the wolves won't flee. Winter has stripped all sense of normal from their behavior, twisting them into monsters in order to survive.

This pack will fight to the death rather than leave a future meal alive.

Dread fills the pit of my stomach as more than a dozen refugees make a desperate break for the guiders. Four of them have their throats ripped open before the first *twang* of a bow. An arrow embeds itself in the side of a wolf leaping for a cowering girl. The wolf's yelp cracks like a whip, sending the rest of the pack into a frenzy as the guiders arrive. Swords meet flesh. The guiders yell a battle cry while the wolves growl and bark.

The guiders form a weak line, pushing the refugees behind them, but the alpha ducks under their blows. He streaks between them and fixes his sights on another child. The boy runs, the adults near him lashing out at the wolf. The pack cuts them off, snapping at hands and arms.

As the dying cries of two wolves pierce the shouting, the alpha surges after the boy. The nearest guider pivots and swings his sword. Silver steel slices through fur and nothing else as the alpha passes the last obstacle between him and the boy. *He's won.*

No one can stop him. Except me, if I wasn't so broken.

They're almost on top of me when the boy looks behind him. The alpha opens his mouth and lunges, and outrage turns to icy fire in my veins.

Broken as I am, I'm not going to sit here and watch.

I twist onto my feet and throw myself toward them. Splinters of pain burn along the fractures in my shaking legs as they support me. I extend my hands, reaching and hoping I'm not too late. The boy's cape brushes my skin before I feel the tickle of fur. I flex my fingers, snagging a chunk of the wolf's coat, and shift my weight backwards, muscles coiling for a mighty heave, when—

CRACK!

The snow crumbles under our tangling feet, revealing a dark pit framed by warped wood, and we fall. A wooden thud precedes the moment my back hits the ground. The impact jolts my tender bones and rings through my head. I gasp for air, both hands buried in the alpha's fur as I search for the boy.

Clumps of snow litter the straw-covered dirt and reflect the sunlight, but the air is stale and moldy. Wooden boards box us into a space about twelve feet wide. *A storage shed.* Likely buried years ago when the snow levels passed twenty feet. The warped sides bulge inward from the weight of the snowfields pressing against the boards. All the tools are missing from the shelves. Only a plow remains as if the farmer knew the world would soon have very little use for it.

The wolf growls, jerking against my hold, but my throat grows thick, my eyes smarting as my stomach plunges. The boy lies on his belly in a twisted heap under the plow, blood dripping down his cheek.

I've failed him.

The wolf turns on me in a blind rage as I lie flat. I'm pinned beneath his snapping jaws, and for a moment, I debate letting him sink his fangs into my face. Even if I hold him off for a while, fighting only delays the inevitable. *I never win.* And whatever damage the wolf causes, my curse will heal.

The guilt brooding down in the pit of my soul welcomes the punishment of the wolf's snapping teeth. *You deserve this.* My arms buckle as I surrender, but the alpha doesn't get the chance to break my skin. I am saved by a *twang.* The head of an arrow plunges through the wolf's neck, the shaft sticking out above his left shoulder. With a whining bark and a violent shudder, I witness another death. Sorrow tightens my throat and blurs my vision, but this grief is born of envy.

The wolf has died, the weight of his body collapsing over me. The game he plays to survive is over. But I'm still here.

I'll always be here.

Above me, a guider looks down, bow in hand with an arrow fitted to the string. He won't find me. His glance is fleeting, quickly noting two things. The threat is dead, and the boy needs no more defense. He leaves, returning to the fading sounds of battle.

I shove the alpha's carcass off me and settle myself beside the boy, rolling him onto his back. His skin is as pale as steel, his clothes woven with bits of bone around his heart, and his braided hair shaved on the sides of his head. *Northerner.* A boy bred to be a warrior no wolf pack would dare challenge, and yet, here he lies. Dead. All the potential of his future lost to an unlucky fall.

Sorrow scratches at my eyes in a familiar sting. Tears. After watching so many lives end, I should be numb, my heart jaded and callous, but death breaks me every single time. *There shouldn't be anything left to break.* Not after ten years spent enslaved to a murderer.

I sweep my hand over the boy's eyes, shutting them, and I ache for a song that belongs to me. A melody the curse hasn't forced on me to satisfy the hunger of a wicked monster. A song of grief, a song of rage, a song I'm allowed to draw from my own soul. Instead, I croak out two words.

I'm sorry. Sorry I couldn't be more. Sorry for what I am. Sorry that there's nothing I can do but be a witness, or worse, a tool.

I am a *banshee.*

Trying to add anything else, anything more human to that simple fact just makes it harder. My heart retreats into the cold until it's buried behind walls of icy resignation so thick winter would be jealous, but my freshly fed guilt is clever, exposing my wound with a single thought. *This boy wasn't meant to die today.*

I press the heels of my hands to my wet eyes and shake my head, a rough breath scraping my throat as blame sinks my shoulders. *I couldn't save him.* Banshees don't get to save lives. *We're the beginning of someone's end.* None of the old stories ever suggest we would fight to change our victim's fate. They paint us as heartless ghouls who revel in singing people to their deaths.

I hold my breath, waiting for the weak objection of my heart, but the part of me that's still curled around a dying ember of denial doesn't cry out against their lies. Doesn't refute the reputation their stories force upon me. *It used to come so easily.* The cry of *I'm not a monster.* Now there's only silence within my imprisoned soul.

I've sung too many victims to their deaths.

The stories are still wrong. About one thing.

I trace the faint scars showing between the shreds of my sleeves. They run from my palms toward my elbows. *They're not even proper scars.* Instead of puckered or damaged skin which would speak of my struggle to break the curse, these lines are smooth, glinting like pure silver. *Beautiful.* And it turns my stomach.

Instead of being markers of hope, the silver scars remind me how powerless I am. They're born from barrier-broken bones tearing through skin, from wolves biting down out of madness and hunger, and from Red Death's victims lashing out with whatever they had—fists and fingernails, knives and glass, even fire. But nothing they tried was worse than what I did to myself to make this—

Stop.

Bring an end to the game I never win.

I have tried. So many times it would shock those who tell the old banshee stories in Riffen. *It doesn't change what happens.* My curse can't be broken any more than their lives can be saved. It's why I stopped trying.

All I'm good for is death.

Acceptance is the only shield I have left, so I let the truth hollow me out. *I'm so tired.* Weary, deep in my bones, but banshees don't rest. We wait. For the summons, for the pull, for the whisper of another soul's doom.

Murder shouldn't begin with a song. Music should be a guide through pain, a reminder of the good things in life. A tool to uplift the soul, not damn it. But for a wraith like me, music has one purpose. *Mark who's next.* Each melodic phrase weaves a noose around the souls who won't escape Red Death.

Male voices and crunching footsteps jar me from my dark thoughts. Small chunks of snow fall beside me as a rope is tossed into the shed. I wipe my face and scoot away from the dead child. Moments later, a pair of black boots crunch down. A tickle of smoke, leather, and sweat scent the air as a guider bends over the boy. I keep my gaze low. There's no point in seeing the guider's face. He isn't here for me.

The world above has fallen silent, an echo of the boy's unnatural stillness, but the guider removes his gloves and presses his fingers into the child's neck. A ragged sigh streams breathy vapor between us as the guider rocks on his heels. The hand he used as an extension of hope, that searched for life in a boy's lifeless body, now rubs his temples. One hard sniff and he shakes the burden of fresh sorrow from his shoulders. Like me, he's not allowed the proper time to grieve.

The guider gathers the boy in his arms and hands him up to the others. A few seconds later, a woman raises her voice, shattering the calm. She wails, a thousand *no's* ripping from her torn soul. Once again I'm left alone to listen, to witness, but never take part. I pull my knees up and hug them close, wishing music was *my* tool. To sing the comfort of a lullaby from a childhood where I was safe.

As the woman's grief fades into weeping, sunlight glints off silver in the snow speckled with the boy's blood. I lift the necklace and bring it closer. Shaped like an upside-down tear, engraving runs along the length of the thin sliver pendant. *A tree with a four-fold canopy.* The first section of branches on the left has falling leaves. Snowflakes and flowers share the center while tongues of fire fill the right side. It's a familiar image with a story far older than banshees.

The season tree. The old ones believed an ancient tree was the source of winter, spring, summer, and fall. With so many people desperate to restore the natural order, superstition is an easy crutch to latch onto, but the season tree won't save them from winter.

I glance from the engraved tree to the plow. *This used to be a field.* The farmlands of Riffen once stretched for miles around the city, but the fields are failing. For every year winter remains unchallenged, the land's natural magic grows weaker. Riffen's hungry mouths continue to multiply as winter buries us with new layers of snow.

Snow upon snow. Never melting, never ending. Hope itself becoming a myth.

It wasn't supposed to be like this.

There used to be an order to the seasons before their magic

grew wild, provoked by men hungry for power. They came and went in the perfect rhythm of four. Winter, Spring, Summer, Fall. We're trapped in winter because some men were greedy, their crooked season trade eventually leading to war.

Seasons weren't meant to be owned.

Their magic is a gift, entrusted to a single human soul at a time. Embers, we call them, those who nurture the seed of a season's magic within their souls until it's ready to bloom. No one knows why the seasons require a human to carry the spark of their power, but the seasons can't change without an ember.

There are no embers left.

The Season Wars saw to that.

Once the four kingdoms started using the remaining embers as weapons, everything changed. Killing the embers provoked the seasons, driving each season to avenge the humans who'd carried them. The balance we all depended upon for survival shattered. *If only the last ember killed in the war hadn't been winter.*

Spring, summer, even fall are far more survivable.

The rope wiggles and the same guider slides down. *Why would he come back?* I stand and shift closer to the plow as he pulls the arrow from the wolf's neck. Bright red spills along the snow, tainting the air with a metallic stench. I shorten my breaths as I taste the copper tang of blood and watch the guider tie the rope around the wolf. *He's returned for the meat.* Since all of Riffen survives on root vegetables, meat is rare and prized more than gold or jewels. With a tug on the rope, those above start pulling the dead wolf up the warped wall of the shed.

I hold still. Unless the curse chooses his soul, I'm in no danger of being discovered, but there's something ... *wrong.* There's a strange prickling awareness, a subtle charge to the air, a whisper of generated warmth as if two normal people are standing here. Together.

"Are you injured?"

It takes all my strength to continue studying the plow instead of his face. *He's not speaking to me.* He didn't ask *me* a question. But his voice is rich and calm, drawing me in, offering me refuge, and promising help. The perfect tone for a guider. His lower range tenor, steeled with confidence and authority without becoming harsh, whispers of an emotion I've never known.

Safety.

Could I be safe with— I bite my tongue and shrink back. *He can't save you.*

A blur of movement sends cold air rushing over my skin as two things happen at once. The guider steps toward me, his right hand nearing my left arm, and I flinch into the wall, causing a small cascade of snow. The hand that *can't* be reaching for me closes around my arm and pulls me toward him. *This isn't happening.* It can't be happening, and yet we're standing a foot apart, our gazes locked on each other, and—*winter's teeth!*

He *can* see me.

He can.

See me.

"Are you injured?" he asks again.

My heart is so loud in my ears I can't hear him. I can't get enough air. There's nothing solid for me to grasp as my mind spirals. *None of this is real.* Yet the skin of my left arm burns where his hand rests. *I shouldn't feel anything.* I never do. The part of me that was still human enough to be reached, to be touched, to be given a place in this world died long ago. *I'm a wraith.* Wraiths don't exist to ordinary people unless—

No forms on my trembling lips, but the curse locks my voice away in silence. *I'm not ready.* I never am. I don't want to sing their songs. I don't want to watch them die. I don't want to be a banshee.

But a banshee is all I am.

I tear myself from the guider and grab the nearest shelf bolted to the wall. The wood creaks, snow falling from the hole in the roof, but I pull myself up and hope running away will be enough. The shelf *pops*, the wall leaning inward, and I lose my grip. Splinters scrape my fingertips as I flail when two hands grasp my waist. The shock of the guider's attempt to steady me is too much. I twist and kick out, desperate to escape whatever this is, whatever it may soon become. With a final *pop* and groan, the shelf I'm holding onto comes free.

The guider breaks my fall, and we both go down hard. My hands sink into the snow along the guider's hips, my body partially sprawled over his lap as he braces himself with his arms. I'm breathing harder than he is, but my breath doesn't fog the air. Our faces are close enough that the delighted smile spreading across his lips is blinding. *He looks like a boy whose deepest wish just came true.*

I scramble back, too shocked to feel anything else.

No one smiles at a banshee.

No one wishes to meet a banshee.

I curl in on myself, knees under my chin, arms over my eyes. Whatever helps me block him out and make this nightmare end before it truly begins.

"You're safe with me." The guider tries to comfort me like I'm a frightened young woman. He doesn't understand I'm the threat. He hasn't realized what I am. Only Red Death's victims can see me, speak to me, or treat me like an actual human being. *But none ever do.*

A soft thump signals the return of the rope. I peek at the hand the guider still offers. *He wouldn't be so kind if he understood what my presence will cost him.*

"Come," he shifts onto his knee and rises. "We'll climb out together."

There is no together between a banshee and Red Death's next victim. *The curse is choosing this guider.* Changing this from an impossible encounter to a familiar one. I stand on my own and take him in. Starting with his feet.

Black boots, scuffed and scarred and worn soft from years of walking; ash colored trousers crisscrossed with stitches and fresh blood stains; a steel gray tunic with a white standing bear and a lone star behind it; a short sword secured at the waist by a belt; a fur-lined cape, and the curved tip of a bow and its quiver with arrows sticking up over his left shoulder. Every inch of his lean frame, from his confident posture to the wear of his uniform to the heaviness resting on his squared shoulders, screams *soldier*. A guider through and through. His right hand extends toward me, but it's what is missing from his chest that makes me step back.

This is all wrong.

The curse marks the next victim with a chest wound that only Red Death and I can see. A prophecy of blood, growing and bleeding as I get closer to finishing their song. Marking the spot where Red Death's dagger will pierce their heart.

There is no wound in the guider's chest.

I avoid looking at people's faces because there are enough haunting me, but I study his, hoping for an explanation. He has rounded features, stubbled along his jawline and hollowed under his cheekbones, framing sharp eyes and a stern mouth. His dark gaze misses nothing, moving from my torn sleeves to the tatters of my cape. Strips of cloth snapping on an icy breeze. But I'm not shivering.

I'm not cold.

"Here," he unbuckles his cloak and offers it to me. I stare at the fur-lined cloth and his hand. His skin is the soft medium gray of snow clouds, which would likely be a deep tan if I could see more than monochrome shades.

No one's given me anything before. A stone of fear strikes my iron ribs, trying to break through with a weapon that terrifies me. *Kindness.* People aren't kind to wraiths like me.

"Go on." The guider encourages, pushing his cloak a little closer. "Take it."

But I don't take articles of clothing from people. I help take their souls. If this guider knew what kind of monster was standing before him, he'd run me through and leave my body for the crows to pick clean. I focus all my energy on glaring at his chest. Waiting. The curse's bloody sign might be a little late, but it will appear. Then the game will begin.

"Dovan!"

I flinch. An impatient male voice calls him back to the world.

Dovan whirls his rejected cloak over his shoulder and holds an arm out toward the rope. "After you."

Clearly, he won't return without me. A mistake I hope the curse won't make him pay for.

We climb out together, me above, him below. The open sunlight glaring off the snow is blinding as I stumble to my feet while two guiders finish pulling Dovan free of the shed.

The pale-haired guider slaps Dovan on the back. "What'd you do? Find a whole feast down there?"

Dovan brushes him off. Only he and I know that I accounted for the added weight.

The pale-haired guider joins one with a scarred face, and they separate the dead humans from the dead wolves. None of the alpha's pack survived, and I swallow against the sting of grim joy. *They won't kill ever again.* The guiders bind the wolf carcasses in pairs so they'll be easier to drag to the barracks inside the city. Once there, the wolves will be skinned and butchered for lottery rations.

Dovan focuses on the living. I'm grateful he guides them away from the bloodstained snow, but their group is far too small. Counting them is a mistake, and yet I have to know.

Twelve refugees survived.

Twelve, out of at least twenty, maybe more.

The other guiders do what the families can't, searching and stripping the bodies down to their underclothes. Cloaks, mementos, any scrap of food hidden in pockets or satchels—nothing of value gets left behind. When they're finished, the guiders retreat so the refugees can have a moment to say a brief goodbye. The mother of the dead boy clings to his body, refusing to surrender him to winter's keep.

I lower my gaze to the snow as choked sobs and fortifying breaths and broken murmurs play the bitter song of loss. If winter allowed any justice, the fallen would receive a decent burial. But the nervous looks of those who survived and the wary stiffness to the guider's movements whisper of another clock ticking against us.

There's blood in the air, and the snowfields are home to many more wolves.

The guiders gather the survivors again, distributing the bundles taken from the deceased. They move between the refugees, studying the color of their eyes, feeling their skin, asking brief questions. *They're looking for embers.* For specks of fire in their irises, for skin that shimmers different colors when tilted in the light. It's not an exact method. Season magic doesn't always shine through eyes or skin. *Don't they know it's hopeless?* Even if they do, their actions scream they're not ready to give up hope that spring will come.

Hope makes for a poor defense from the inevitable, but it's all they have.

A futility I understand, as I sing my useless songs that condemn more than warn. What the guiders are doing won't change the fact they need a miracle. Soon.

If there's one thing the curse has taught me—*there are no miracles.*

The guiders hurry the refugees toward the safety of the city. I try to break away a dozen times, but Dovan always steps in my way, as if he knows I'm about to run. *I'm trying to save him.* Before the curse activates and decides our future.

When the western wall of Riffen towers into the sky, the snow slopes down into a shallow plane maintained around the city by daily melting and shoveling. Through the stone arch of the gate and the iron teeth of the raised portcullis, I glimpse market stalls decorated with ribbons and wreaths with bare branches and fake fabric flowers. Little mementos of what used to be the happiest night of the year.

Spring Eve.

A closer look reveals the guiders are decorating alone, fighting for a hope their people don't share. Spring isn't coming. Not tonight. Not tomorrow. Not—

The final sign, the answer to how a guider could ever speak with a banshee, strikes me mid-step. Pain slices along my sternum and stabs my heart. I lurch forward, falling into the muddy snow outside the gate as I gasp and blink back tears. No one notices my distress. No one comes to help me. I don't exist to any of them, except—

Dovan.

Someone fresh to the banshee life and to Red Death's game might scream and shout and stand defiant. *I will beat you. Good will win.* But I stay silent. I don't even cry. I don't remember a time where good actually won. I don't remember anything except Red Death's victories. I have no weapons to aid me, no allies to call upon, no lies to mask the truth.

This game won't be any different.

I always lose.

I once wished the curse would choose the cruel and the wicked. Their deaths would be easier to summon, but the curse has a taste for purer souls and stronger hearts. Like the guider who's stopped when no one else will. Stopped because I'm no longer in his sight.

Don't turn around. Don't face me. I don't want to see the mark that matches the pain cutting into my chest. But there's no stopping this now.

Dovan walks in a tight circle toward me. Magic strikes a chord in my soul, resonating into my throat, and a new song is born. Where the stories about banshees fail most is how they describe our singing.

We don't shriek. Not at first. The songs begin as a whisper. A tiny awakening that spreads through our souls with a hunger only the fading tone of the last note can satisfy. The first note is a spark of fire barely caught and still threatened by the wind, fragile and yet unable to be blown out. It's the roll of thunder shaking my bones before falling into prickling silence. It's the embrace of arms that won't let go, followed by the rejection of being shoved away. Then we fall.

I fall into Dovan's song. Deeper and deeper into a single note that means everything and yet it somehow fits inside a simple, four-letter word.

Life.

Dovan's life.

It begins with a low, earthy thrum, pulling my voice down to the bottom of my vocal range. Dovan's first note is the strongest one I've ever sung, weeping through my soul with a melancholy I understand. *He's a guider.* He's seen plenty of death. But where my own melody fractures and becomes lost in sorrow, his is anchored by an iron core. I don't yet know why his brokenness is so different from mine, but I will. The notes will tell me as they form a melody into his song.

We look into each other's eyes. Fate winds around us, connecting the frayed threads of our souls through the power of a single note multiplying into three. The opening, melodic phrase drives a knife through the denial I thought could protect me.

He's the next person to die. Another victim I won't be able to save.

I glance at his chest again. This time the sign is there, dripping the first drops of blood down the white bear on his tunic. The wound won't be real until Red Death stabs him, but it will grow with every hour, every note, bleeding more and more as I add to his song.

"Do you like to dance?"

"What?" I blink, confused, my focus jarred from the cruel future we will share.

"Nobody dances at Spring Eve anymore, but we could change that." He glances away, his gaze heavy with a mix of concern and mischief and sorrow. "We could remind them it's okay to..." He doesn't seem to know how to end his sentence, so he shrugs instead.

"No one likes to dance on an empty stomach." I state coldly. Colder than I should, but I can't help it. Not when he should be running from me instead of proposing we get closer for the purpose of *fun*.

A brilliant and defiant hope shines through Dovan's eyes as he backs through the gate. "Dancing is like music. It feeds the soul."

Except when the melody is cursed. Then it breaks the soul.

Unaware of my dark thoughts, Dovan winks at me—*a soul crier*—a cursed banshee, who has begun his song and summoned his death. "I'll save you the last dance."

Stop. My silent order goes unheard. I rub the heels of my hands against the tears threatening a mutiny against my determination to feel nothing. To be numb. To not care.

The thing is, I do care. I always care. Even when I know better. Dovan, with his ridiculous idea of dancing with me, of a melody that could bring us joy instead of death, he won't be the exception I once hoped for.

He won't survive meeting me.

RED DEATH

3

THE KEY to a truly devastating punch is a lack of self-preservation.

I run my tongue over my teeth, searching for cracks or any loose molars. A dull ache throbs from my sharp cheekbone to my jaw, but I find no defect. Not even a sliver-thin chip or a teensy wiggle. *Still pretty then.* My lips spread into a sizzling taunt of a smile sure to earn me more pain. *If you can call it pain.* I've known decrepit grannies with better right hooks. An impatient sigh sneaks up my throat, giving witness to an old, neglected desire.

To kill someone worthy of me.

Won't be finding that kind of victim here.

I roll my eyes as their cautious voices break into another argument. You see, they have a problem, the two men who *happened* upon my misdeeds. I stifle a dark chuckle. *Happened upon.* There's a joke. More like they walked right into my trap. They don't know what to do with me, but I know exactly what to do with them. It's why I'm not smashing their brainless skulls into a wonderful, bloody mess as I wait for them to get to the bleedin' point.

I am the vision of patience.

The image they cast is far more … *dull.* With their pale-bear tunics and their short swords and their stuffy but dignified posture. *Someone thinks they're better than everyone else.* If their measure is cleanliness, I concede the victory. They threw me down a filthy alley, coating my guider's tunic in worse than mud, but that last puddle. Rolling through its urine-gagging stench was an inspired idea. Their eyes water and their lips quiver and their breaths shorten in disgust every time they move closer to whack me. And I do mean whack. Calling their hits punches would insult real fighters.

You'd think it'd be easy for them, to decide what to do with me. *Winter's Teeth! You're guiders, aren't you?* Their swords remain sheathed, their violence tempered as they glance down the alley. Then they swallow. *Nervous.* An effect my true face has on people, but I'm not wearing my true face. *Pity.* And they didn't choose the best place to confront me, or rather, the guider I'm pretending to be.

This particular alley runs east to west and dead-ends less than thirty feet from the lower market. The buildings, built of grimy stone, divide daylight and shadows in equal parts. This means it's not a great alley to drag a man into and then try to beat what you want out of him. I doubt they could scare a confession out of a mouse. *Would be entertaining to watch though.*

A clear line of sight runs from the foul puddle I'm kneeling in, all the way to the stalls set up in the lower market. The murmur of a few hundred people echoes up the alley, offering moderate cover for my cries. If I were crying. Or calling for help. One I never do, and the other, well, it would take a lot more pain than either of these men look capable of causing. Tearing the skin and flesh from your bones kind of pain.

"Ask him where the rest is." The taller of the two guiders nudges his buddy forward.

Predictable. The shorter man hesitates as I meet his gaze. The pink tones of his skin pale. The fist he must hope will be the brutal leverage needed to crack my secrets wide open shudders in the air. He doesn't have it in him any more than his partner does—to do whatever it takes, to pay whatever price. No, he loves his straight, unbroken fingers and his sure grip and well, his life. They're like arrogant children pretending to be ruthless.

I could educate them. Ruthlessness is breaking your own hand to cave someone's face in. *They don't have the guts.* Or the passion. Or the *rage.* They haven't known that type of pain. It's a hungering, bottomless, black abyss. *Home sweet home.* Once you fall in, there's no climbing out. *I didn't exactly fall in.*

I jumped. Heart first.

Look at them. The two guiders who hold me in this alley and pat my cheekbones with their feeble hits. One quick scan up and down their clean tunics and boots, at how they carefully choose their steps to avoid the filth, at the fact they're here, in the alley plotting to better their own chances of survival instead of helping settle the new influx of refugees—

These aren't good men. They aren't bad men. They are *weak* men. And lacking in brains since it's taken them months to notice the trail I've been leaving for them. *Like I'd get caught if I didn't want to.* Their timid nature is starting to annoy me. Hobbies are supposed to keep boredom at bay. The days or weeks between my kills require entertainment. I'm not like Wraith. She prefers walking outside the city in the cold and snow, separated from everything that reminds her she's still human. *She's a runner.* Hiding from what hurts. Me, well, I like noise, and blood-heated hearts, and desperate souls so ripe they beg to be corrupted.

I *thrive* on pain, and I don't see our game as proof of what we've lost. I see what I've gained. Besides, even killers need hobbies. So, I found a dishonest face and transformed myself for the role of traitorous thief, a smaller but still satisfying game I can play between victims.

Knuckles graze my left cheek, jolting my head to the right and teasing my tongue with the taste of blood. *Things must be getting serious.* They've finally made me bleed.

"Where's the rest of the goods?" Shorty grabs my tunic and hauls me up until a whiff of my urine perfume forces him to let me go. "There's more food missing from the communal stores than what we found in your cellar."

Blah, blah, blah. I don't bother listening to him. How can I? There's another sound far more appealing than his voice. I tip my head so my left ear lines up with his chest, so I can hear it. The *thup-iddy-thump-thump* of his racing heart. *Hello gorgeous.*

Heartbeats are my candy.

They bait the monster I am to come out and play. See who outlasts who. But I always win. I've yet to meet a heart that can best me at my own game.

My vision narrows on the cage of bones protecting his heart that practically screams *don't hurt me.* Might as well send me a personalized invitation saying. Stab. Right. Here.

A wistful rush of breath heats my lips as my eyes close halfway. The crunch of bone beneath my dagger is my second favorite part. Then I get messy, my skin warmed by fresh blood.

Not now. I grit my teeth and force myself to focus before the villain I am overpowers my disguise and ruins our little game. Shorty helps by striking me, and as my head snaps to the left, I forget the tantalizing beat of his heart. Violence is my favorite language, but they don't speak it as fluently as I do.

It's almost my turn.

My fists clench tighter as I pull them apart, testing the rope binding them behind my back. The rope gives but doesn't break. I'm not really trying. *Not yet.* As I level a glare at both men, I feel the ire rising. The dark, hungering power running black as poison through my veins. I'm tired of their cluelessness. I could show them who they're dealing with, but they'd run away screaming and my plan would be shot.

Patience.

Another hit, more blood in my mouth, more asinine questions. I heave forward and spit at their too-clean boots. They recoil, disgusted, and I laugh.

The tall one draws a knife. "You won't be laughing when I stick you."

He's an insult to knives, the way his hand shakes. I spring to my feet with the ease and grace of a snow-panther. *Surprise.* It takes a beating far worse than they have given to keep me down. They flinch backward, shoving each other as they scramble as far away from me as the narrow alley allows. *Damn.* Even with my disguise, some part of them always knows the truth.

I'm a predator no matter what face I wear.

"Let's move on from the theatrics, shall we?" I offer a reassuring half-smile. "Will you join me or not?"

They blink, dumb as any doe-eyed fainting goat.

Fine. I'll spell it out for you. "I can take you to my other food store, but I won't agree to less than seventy percent."

"Of—of what?"

"Come now, gents," I strain to keep the annoyance from my voice. "The food. I keep seventy percent of what we *scavenge.*" I mean steal, but most men prefer to bury their wrongs under a layer of comfortable deniability.

Tall steps forward. "Fifty-fifty, or we drag your hide to guiders court."

I lean in, letting my lips widen into a display of my bloodied canines. "Sixty-five."

They share a begrudging look before Tall gives a nod. "Agreed."

And that's how you destroy a city. By corrupting its incorruptible heart.

I turn so they can cut me free, and with the flick of a knife, we're comrades. The kind you eventually stab in the back. Lucky for them, I stab in the front. Straight. Through. The heart. *I prefer it when they see me coming.* Adds extra flavor to their fear.

We step out of the alley into the light and noise and bustle of the lower market. *I'd still rather kill them than work with them.* If I were free, I'd kill everyone in this cursed city, but my particular skills are slaved to another will. We share the same love for bloodshed. Makes us an unstoppable team. My arm presses close to my side, to the hip where the dagger waits.

It chooses my victims.

It decides when the real game begins, and then I get to do what I enjoy most. Stabbing hearts, ending lives, stealing souls.

Speaking of doomed souls. There she is. My banshee. The dark abyss at the center of my red field of vision. Except Wraith isn't lurking along the wall that's as cracked as a drunk's bloodshot eyes. She's not hiding in the shadows, trying to stay as far from everyone as possible. She's inside the city. Down on the ground— with *them*—the people I intend to destroy. *She doesn't belong here.* Where muddied cobblestone streets descend from the city's upper levels and split into narrow lanes around stalls full of survivalist wares, each path clogging with too many moving bodies.

Wraith stands in the middle of their chaos, her shoulders curled inward, her arms wrapped around her middle. The visual definition of pathetic.

The crowds of refugees and helpers and guiders can't see her or hear her, but if they get too close, they can feel her. It's a terrible fate. Making someone invisible and lost in silence while allowing them the gift of touch. Physical contact becomes a curse when robbed of the other senses. *One of my better ideas.* The game wouldn't be as much fun if I didn't play with Wraith's heart *and* my victims' souls. But...

We were.

A sharp ache throbs along my sternum with a flash of heat and then a stab of cold. I press a hand to the pain. Nothing's broken. There's no memory or reason to explain away those two words or give them a foundation from which to grow. But there's a beginning there, and an ending. I don't admit to having either. Especially not with Wraith.

It takes more effort than it should to tear my gaze from her. The pain sharpens, biting deep, but I crack my neck and roll my shoulders. I've got better things to do than get tripped up by a simple phrase without context. Besides, when has a little pain ever slowed me down?

I lead Tall and Shorty along the back lane of the stalls stocked with blankets, clothing scraps, and rations. It's a dull view. Every face mirrors either exhausted relief or weary strain. *Boring.* So I look up at my oldest friend. The city of Riffen itself. *Friend might not be the right word.* As much as I hate this place, we share a similar master. *Death.*

Riffen rises above the lower market in a pattern of mismatched rings stacked upon each other. Houses made of rough-cut stone or warped wooden shack towers give shape to its sharp skeleton, while chimneys wheeze smoke into the air. The city's gaunt face shares my love of a high perch, looking down on the latest group of refugees through a thousand dark-eyed windowpanes. Their reflective voids whisper of a hunger I know well. A hunger to be filled, or in my case, *fed.*

Shall we gobble them up, then? The refugees and those helping them. The lower market is in chaos, a revolting kind that makes more friends than enemies. Everyone's talking. Everyone's moving. A blur of pale pink faces and rust-smudged human shapes shepherded under open stalls once used by traders from other kingdoms to showcase their wares. Glimmering icicles stab down from the roofs of each stall, an inverted crown here to remind us of which season rules our fates.

Winter, always winter.

The wind turns frigid, snapping the banners over the gate behind me. A small thunder no one notices. If they listened, they'd understand there is no refuge. Not from winter. Not from the hunger. Not from me. Or maybe I should say *us*.

Once again, I'm staring. At her raven-black hair and the shreds of her night-dark cape dancing wildly in the breeze. *Wraith sees it.* The truth of this place. Her shoulders slump inward as she surveys the people and the city. She understands. This city is a tomb. Buildings on top of buildings, coffins, ready and waiting for the still alive. *They will all die here.* If not by my hand or by their own, then by the slow starving of an endless winter.

I draw my dagger as I sniff the air for the scent of my prey. My banshee has left her refuge of snowfields to enter the city, and it means I'm about to have some *real* fun.

Tall and Shorty pester me with questions, jabbing what must be Tall's knife into my back, but I ignore them. The true game has stolen my focus, shrieking through my veins. I lean into the pull of wicked magic and let everything else fade. Silence wraps around me in a cocoon until all I hear are three distinct heartbeats. Mine, Wraith's, and the one I will stop. They drum a triune rhythm, calling me and daring me to play. My muscles twitch and my lips snarl away from my teeth.

I'm so ready.

Tapping my thigh with the flat of my dagger, I watch Wraith. How she moves—in short bursts through split-second gaps between people—and how she breathes. Her shoulders rise and fall. Rapid and tight. Not the deep gut breathing used by a singer of her talent. *Stubborn.* She resists the curse's control every time we play this game. But she *will* sing.

She senses me, searching for me with her soul-black eyes and spotting me within seconds, but her gaze doesn't linger. *What's the matter, Wraith? Don't you recognize me?* To be fair, I look different in my guider's disguise, and then there's the face I'm wearing that isn't mine. But the connection between us is a bond of our souls. We don't need to see each other. We always know when one of us is close.

We were.

I grind my teeth at the pain as it moves from my chest to my head. It drills in, echoing something I don't understand. A truth dependent on two words. *We. Were.* I shove the people around me apart, a physical declaration of what I believe. *No, we* are. *Stick to the present.* Because this is where the game I love most begins.

The dagger grows hot in my hand, sending a pulse of heat up my arm, and my hunger echoes its call. A crashing wave of purpose, need, and skill. Wraith says it's a curse, but to me, it's freedom.

Freedom from an ordinary life. From the entrapping rules of decent society.

I inhale, scenting the salty, wheezy desperation huffing through several hundred hungry mouths. Except for Wraith, everything I see is red. So many different shades. Pale pink stone, burgundy and chartreuse capes, faces as dark as cherries or light as salmon. And rust, corroding every outline and setting people apart from things.

Then I spot him. The victim who is mine. To hunt. To kill.

What a bleedin' eyesore. I squint as the reds of my normal vision clash with the guider's unusual color. An offensive shade of green, he's a crack of vibrant life cutting through a sea of rusty shapes. The man himself is familiar because of the uniform and his soft, *I'm here to help* expression, which might as well be a second uniform for most guiders. My lips recoil from my teeth in distaste.

He's letting a crying old woman cling to him, using his body to part the crowd as he guides her to a cart where she can rest. *Such a hero.* And if the dagger has chosen well, a worthy prey. *We shall see how deep his heroism goes.* Then he'll die like all the others, begging for mercy or pleading for a savior. Two things never in my company.

"Feed me." The command pulses through the dagger's hilt into my hand, my skin, my bones, until our purpose aligns.

It's time to play.

I wince as the corner of a wooden beam digs into my back. Tall and Shorty glower at me, lips tight, pupils narrowed as they pin me against the stall.

"We're tired of waiting." Tall brings his knife to my chin, no doubt expecting me to pull away and tremble in fear. Getting bloody has never frightened me. I lean into the sting of the blade pricking my skin. He withdraws and I sneer.

"Show us now, or …"

I've stopped listening, all my senses focused on a new breeze. In this disguised form, Wraith's song sounds like wind wailing through a crevice, brittle and shrill and devoid of the touch of humanity that makes it a melody instead of just background noise. I glance around, but no one else has noticed.

There is no wind.

Only the first three notes of the guider's soul song. *She's finally begun.* To discover the guider's life story, beginning to delightfully bloody end.

I push off the beam and smooth my disguised cape before leading the guiders who have betrayed their brothers and their city away to their doom. *There is no second food-store.* Betrayers always fall prey to betrayal. The way I'm going to betray them will be spectacular. *Like throwing oil on a fire.* A victory that will tip this city over the edge and into chaos.

It's what I do.

When I'm not stabbing hearts.

As we pass the last stall, the wind—Wraith's singing—grows louder. Dingy daylight winks up at me from dozens of small soul-mirrors hanging from strings. I pause long enough to run a finger over the jewel shaped charms. Refugees press around me, anxious to obtain the comfort of Riffen's oldest lie.

I chuckle as I leave them to the futile hope being pawned by citizens who should know better. Riffen is well-known for being haunted by banshees. Long ago, some enterprising soul decided wearing a small mirror over your heart could protect you from a banshee's death song.

The lie twisted through the years, giving ridiculous fame to these soul-mirrors. Promising to save the wearer by revealing a banshee in its reflection. My chuckle blooms into a riotous laugh, drawing more than a few odd looks. Fathers and mothers have handed down this story to their children for generations. *Oh, I bet they wish it was just a story.*

But this isn't a story they can tell. We—Wraith and I—we live it, playing fate's unfair game over and over, and no tiny mirror has ever stood a chance of getting in our way.

Only one person can see a banshee coming.

Only one person can hear Wraith's song.

My. Next. Victim.

WRAITH

4

THE MORNING SUN climbs toward midday, matching Dovan's relentless pace. *Does he ever rest?* He's led me in hundreds of circles between the gate and the lower market. I've lost track of how many people he's helped in just a few hours. *Where does he find the energy?* To field the same questions about dwindling rations without losing patience, to step into the middle of any conversation that's growing heated without resorting to threats, to be whatever someone needs him to be. A guide. A listener. A giver of advice.

Dovan is a protector. That obvious truth causes a hollow ache in my chest. *He isn't protecting himself from me.* The fact he hasn't tried to kill me yet puts him at odds with most of the victims I've shadowed. *He hasn't looked at me once since we crossed through the gate.* Since he told me he'd save the last dance of Spring Eve for us. I rub my sternum, the place where his ridiculous promise slipped past my defenses and sunk a hook into my heart.

There is no us. Dovan's promise will break.

The ache deepens as I wrap my arms around myself, watching Dovan carry a heavy box for an older stall runner. *He's forgotten I'm here.* Good. He shouldn't waste any time thinking about the banshee who's doomed him with her song.

I hang back until Dovan's two lanes over. As he inserts himself into yet another loud argument, I slump into a welcoming shadow cast by hanging pieces of cloth. The large squares of various patterns sway stiffly on the frigid breeze. They hang in tiers from taut cords stretched between the stall's posts. Patches hold the worn fabric together and knots prevent its threadbare ends from fraying.

I brush my thumb along one with the symbol of autumn, a tree with falling leaves stitched at its center. *So thin.* How can it offer any warmth? Despite the worn state of the cloth being offered, the stall maintains a steady flow of buyers. *Better than nothing, I suppose.* The bitter thought anchors my focus to the cobblestones beneath my feet as my soul sinks into the arms of despair. The magic binding me as a banshee pricks my heart in warning. I stiffen, bracing for the voiceless command I can't resist.

Sing.

I grit my teeth, a small and futile defiance, and the pain bites deeper. *SING.* I wince, humming the first three notes of Dovan's song. The relief is instant as I give the curse what it wants, but my mind tilts over the edge of curiosity.

Dovan's song hasn't grown past the beginning phrase. *I should know a dozen notes by now.* Instead, his melody hangs from my lips like a half-spoken promise. I glance up from the ground, scanning the crowd for his straight posture, which helps him stand out when everyone else shrinks under exhaustion, only to find—

I've lost him!

Darting away from the stall, I collide with a girl with messy braids and a bruise shading the corner of her jaw. Frosty fear prickles my skin as the girl stumbles and drops her lumpy sack.

Potatoes tumble onto the dirty ground. She scrambles after them, hands dodging the boots of the crowd until enough people realize she's there and part around her.

No one offers to help.

I take half a step forward before I remember my place. *She won't see me.* The potatoes I'd gather for her would appear to float in midair, and she'd scream, finding my act of kindness to be a ghostly nightmare. My hands curl by my sides, useless and empty, but the desire, the instinct to serve remains, a haunting echo of whoever I was before the curse.

I'm turning away when a human shadow falls across the girl. A familiar tension fills her small body and she goes eerily still. Her posture mirrors my own whenever I'm near Red Death. She makes herself smaller, head bent low over her chest, elbows tucked close to her sides as she rolls the last potato into the bag. My chin quivers as my eyes burn and my hand drifts toward her, open in an offer I wish I could give.

Let me keep you safe.

A man grabs her arm, wrenching backwards until the strain on the joint makes her whimper. She drops the sack again as he yanks her to her feet. He's shorter than me, most of his size coming from the thickness of his bones, but I'd throw myself at him even if he were a giant. I take a step and stifle a cry as cursed magic stabs into my heart, spreading with each slow beat through my veins until I can't move.

You're not here for her, comes the curse's message, branding my body as its possession.

The girl trembles in the man's grasp. Her gaze stays focused on the ground, her hands buried in her cloak as he spits out two words, "Worthless girl."

Her flinch is worse than a scream, a desperate invitation begging for an answer I can't give. *Someone else will notice.*

Someone will intervene. But the crowd maintains their busy rush of movement, letting this broken child drift nearer to being lost.

The gruff volume of the man's voice buries her rushed apologies. One line stands out among the others, "Why can't you do as you're told?"

As if dropping a sack of potatoes is the worst of crimes. As if it was even her fault. I shudder, lowering my head in shame. *This is my fault.* She wouldn't have dropped the sack if I hadn't bumped into her.

A lump forms in my throat, tears freeze on my cheeks, and a brittle feeling spreads fresh cracks through the hollow in my chest. *I didn't think anyone else knew what it was like.* To be called terrible things. To be handled roughly and treated as a possession instead of a human being. A stab of icy rage pushes me forward, air needling my lungs as I take a deep breath. My voice is my sole weapon.

And so I scream.

I scream. For the girl whose arm is still being twisted and bruised.

My cry makes the man's cloak flap around his shoulders, but rustling his clothes isn't enough to stop him. He snatches the potato sack from the ground and drags her away. I deflate forward, one hand gripping the rough post of the fabric stall.

My glare cuts across the crowd, sunlight flashing in my eyes from the mirrors many have pinned to their chests. Mirrors which are supposed to protect them from banshees. One by one, my fingers curl until my hands are fists, holding back the outrage that burns colder than winter in my veins.

Why do they show more concern about the monsters from stories than the ones among them? The ones like *him,* who cover their cruelty behind a charming smile whenever someone inquires of their health. *Why don't they look twice?* At the tears on the girl's face. Tears that he laughs off because she's a *sensitive* child. *Why are his lies more believable than her pain?*

Why does no one *see* her?

This is why I hate being inside the city. It's easier to think Red Death's the only monster in Riffen until I'm reminded humans can be just as monstrous. I retreat further into shadows, but his magic squeezes my slow heart. A clear threat, leaving bruises on my soul where no one will see them.

I have to find Dovan.

I have to sing his song.

With a shaky breath, I force my emotions down, letting winter chill the ache away. Even when numb, I never forget what it's like to be that little girl. To have no power. To know no one's coming to save you. To spend your wishes on hoping to survive a monster and the next moment of pain. *At least she has a chance to leave her nightmare behind.* One day she'll be older and stronger, and she'll escape. Her survival will become a new song. A melody grown from the journey of finding her true self.

Singing people to their deaths remains my sole future.

I turn in a circle, straining on my tiptoes to peer over the heads of the crowd. *So many faces.* Some hiding monsters underneath. I switch to studying their shoulders, scanning for posture that hasn't been ruined by winter or hunger.

The crowd blurs together. Everyone looks the same when you don't want to really see them. *It's easier this way.* To focus on three repeating notes and the monochrome colors defining my view of the world. Different shades of pewter and smoke for skin, darkening to iron for their clothes and hair, set against a backdrop of pale stone and ebony shadows cast by the crooked maze of houses rising with the city's uneven levels. *I'm still too close.*

If I were on the wall, the distance would fuel my illusion of detachment. Here, I am on their level. I flinch from the brush of their bodies. My nose catches a dozen scents, some salty, some sweet, some sour. My ears ring with the beautiful range of their voices. My eyes note all the ways truth makes a home in their faces, no matter how neutral their expressions. *They're more than three colors.* More than bones and skin wrapped in worn clothes and threadbare hopes.

Whispering emotions twist around their eyes and mouths, telling me far more than their age. I see their stories. Their lives. Their hopes and fears and dying dreams, all sketched across their faces as if their skin has become the canvas for their souls. Tears bud against my eyelids like seeds. Seeds for a sorrow they will never understand.

I'm alone.

They might have used those two words during difficult times, but when they cried, people could hear them. There was a chance someone would recognize they were hurting and then offer comfort for their pain. A chance I will never have as a soul crier.

The curse maintains two barriers for its banshee. One keeps me tied to the city, and the other stands between me and everyone else. I can speak to anyone I want. I can hold their hands, stroke their backs, wrap an arm around their shoulders in an embrace I am starving for, but—

I spin toward the beam of the nearest stall and push my forehead so hard against its weathered wood I anger a host of splinters. They stick my skin, pitiful pricks that won't save me from what's coming. *Don't think about it.* How I'm different. *Why* I'm different. One shaky breath in, and then another, but it's not working.

Some truths never stay buried.

Frigid air scrapes my throat raw as I suck the sorrow back inside. I force my eyelids to close and sever my inward self from the tears I don't need. But the tears form a string, falling one after another, a line of unending regrets and crushed hopes. They burn like ice against my skin, freezing their way to my soul.

Why can't I accept my fate?

I have no memories of being anything other than a banshee, and yet I... *I still hope.* That I was once like them. That I could be like them again. *Free.*

The worst part of a curse is that it lets you feel normal, lets you think all is not lost, and then you discover the cruelty of what's been taken from you.

They never know it's me. Touching them. Speaking to them. The curse wraps my voice in wind and the pressure of my hand in the excuse of anyone near enough to explain away my touch. I sigh it out, all the trickster emotions tempting me to believe in *more.*

Dovan brought me down here. Dovan pulled me from the shadows I use to numb the ache sizzling along every torn shred of my soul. *Why would I risk facing the pain for him?*

A valid question but searching for an answer would mean chasing after false hope. *He's just another victim.* That harsh truth snuffs out my spark of curiosity, but there's a little voice in my soul singing its own deadly banshee song.

Nothing about this game feels *familiar.*

Dovan saw me first.

Before the curse confirmed our link.

He didn't shriek. He didn't run or fight, reactions that make it easier to be a wraith. Dovan saved me from a wolf and then went back to the routine of his life like nothing's changed. Like I haven't destroyed all his hopes and dreams. *Do guiders dream?*

I've followed Dovan for hours within the city's lower market. He's shouldered the burden of being relied on by so many without a moment's hesitation, leaving no time for a brief rest or the escape of a daydream. *Maybe they are his dream.* The people he serves.

I smile, a bittersweet twisting of my lips. *He's a good man.* The kind who holds their broken world together. *He might even see hope for—* I shake my head.

There is no hope for someone like me.

The heaviness of my purpose sinks my heart deeper into the icy tomb of my chest. *Let's get this over with.* I resume my search, listening for the next notes of Dovan's song as I scan the crowd.

A man roars with laughter and shoves his buddies into my path. I avoid them with a quick sidestep and get a whiff of salty iron and wet fur. My stomach twists. Small beads of blood stain their sleeves, guiding my gaze to the still-bleeding sacks they've placed on the rations table. A white wolf head hangs out of each one. I suppress a shudder, glancing away. I hate death, even if it means human survival. And the meat won't last long. It never does in this market. *They'll be lucky if it doesn't start a riot.* The guiders move in as the hunters' celebration attracts more attention.

Leave. Now. A sensible instinct, but my body has other ideas. None of which are sensible. A tremor starts in my hands, rattling up my bones until I'm shaking.

There's a woman haggling for an extra ration on my left. She stops mid-sentence and hurries after the stall runner around its corner, trapping me from behind. Their voices escalate in pitch as they join the hunters and the lead guider, who's trying to maintain calm with promises to divide the meat by the customary lottery.

A normal young woman would speak a polite *excuse me*, pass between them, and continue on her way. *The curse robbed me of everything normal.* I hug my stomach, trying to make myself small enough to slip through them. There will be physical contact, but there's a lovely dark shadow waiting by the wall behind the next lane. Quiet and alone. Two things I desperately need.

I've almost worked up the courage when a dozen children race down the lane. I'm jostled and pushed and jabbed by elbows as the children cause a stampede. Men and women crowd me, the slivers of free space tightening like a noose around my chest until I'm surrounded.

Trapped.

I can't breathe. But my lungs pump as hard as a fighter's fists.

I can't see. But my eyes don't miss any movement.

I can't move. But my body trembles as panic rips ice-cold across my flesh.

The guiders confiscate the meat, a trigger that heightens the tension.

"We don't stand a chance with the lottery!" A man with a ragged beard yells over my shoulder and I flinch.

"You will have the same chance as everyone else." The lead guider puts himself between the people and his men.

"Winter's Teeth. You're talking about a chance in thousands. I can make better odds myself."

The bearded man surges forward, knocking into me from behind. His weight crushes the air from my lungs as I cushion his fall. The beginnings of several cobblestone-shaped bruises throb along my arms and legs as the crowd clamors in confusion. They lean over us, curious and questioning. But the distraction doesn't last long as the guiders try to move the meat. The focus shifts, and Mr. Beard joins the new shouting match. His dirty hands push me against the cobblestones as he gets up. I bite down on a whimper. One boot misses my head, while the other comes down on my right hand. My wall of silence shatters.

I scream, the damage behind my cry running far deeper than the searing pain that burns along the broken edges of my bones.

See me.

Please.

See. *Me.*

But the man doesn't realize I'm here, though his brow wrinkles in momentary confusion at the feel of one boot sitting higher because it's *on* my hand. The curse twists my cry into a wind gust and lashes through his straw-dry hair. I pour every bit of breath I have into the scream. It makes no difference. The people near me simply tuck their arms closer to their bodies, bracing themselves against the raging, frigid breeze that is *my* pain.

Mr. Beard shrugs and moves on as if my flesh and bones are nothing more than rubbish cast off into the street. *Trash.* That's what I am to the uncursed world. Broken scraps not worth the notice. *No harm done.*

The crowd presses closer. I stiffen as prickly nerves sink needle-like fangs across my chilled skin. If I can't pull myself together long enough to escape, he won't be the last person to trample me.

Get up. My body rebels, curling into a ball that won't protect me from them.

Another person, another boot. This one skims my spine, and the woman trips.

I wish I could die.

My shriek withers into a pointless, sobbing plea. I glance from face to face, but no one looks down into the shadows they cast on my broken soul. They just keep coming. *No one cares when I'm hurt.* It'd be a miracle if they did. *Only Red Death's victim knows I exist.*

Red Death.

A twinge of hope sparks to life. We're connected through the magic of his curse. *He'd hear me.* But why would he come? I doubt he'd care if their boots broke every bone I have. *All he cares about is winning the game and killing*—Dovan.

I am truly, completely, alone.

I almost surrender to my fate when a pair of worn black boots plant themselves on either side of me. *I deserve this.* To be trampled by those Red Death preys upon through my voice. The shame of that thought comforts me. If there was a way for me to be the one who bleeds, the one who dies, so this game of death finally ends—*I'd do it.* But nothing I've ever tried has worked.

"Enough!" A strong, male voice cuts through the chaos.

Dovan. The boots I expected to be my punishment are his. He stands over me, left hand resting casually on his sword hilt as he twists to meet every gaze he can. *Why is he trying to spare me?* Preventing my harm has never been a priority for any of Red Death's victims.

"You're better than this." He tells the crowd. "We're all better than this."

One by one, they turn away or hang their heads as they avoid Dovan's intense stare. No one speaks until a woman cradling a child against her chest breaks the silence. "Being better than this won't help us survive longer than—" Her voice becomes too broken to continue as her eyes pool with tears.

Her tear-shined gaze settles on her child, swaddled in a thick wool blanket. The child should bring us all hope. Hope in the fact that life is resilient. Life goes on. But this babe is born into a desperate situation. He probably won't survive long enough to learn how to say *momma.* My heart cringes at the thought. *This isn't right.* But where can she go to get justice for the life she and her child have been robbed of?

Winter answers to no one. It's as relentless as my curse.

Dovan lifts his arms, a gentle request to hold the most precious thing the woman has. Silence falls over the market as she places her baby in Dovan's arms. A grin breaks like dawn across his face. Not the cold kind of mornings we're used to. There is heat to this showing of joy, a calm, expanding warmth that flows through him.

"I named him Lucas, after his father." She caresses her baby's covered head, pausing to look up at Dovan. They hold each other's gaze for a solid moment. A sense of understanding passes between them and she wipes a tear from her cheek, glancing once more at her son. "And I named him Dovan. After the man who tried to save his father's life."

My mouth opens in surprise.

The joy vanishes from Dovan's face, his lips slipping down into a grim line.

"You did your best," the mother's voice draws an echo of agreement from the crowd. "You always do your best."

He swallows and nods before handing the child back to her. For a second, his gaze falls to mine, and I recognize my own ghosts haunting his eyes.

"You have so many scars, Dovan. Each one earned for us," she grips his right forearm.

I stare at his bracers, their leather marked by the bite of teeth and the slash of blades. I study the stains of old blood darkening the deeper cuts and shiver. A desire rises from the dark emptiness of my soul, to rip the bracer from his arm, to tear open the sleeve, to see his scars. To understand such caring. *I didn't know anyone was still capable.* Of the type of sacrifice that has won Dovan the respect of an entire city. *What drives him?*

Love would be the obvious explanation, but there's something deeper. To everyone else, he's the hero they wish to be or the rescuer they call on when they need help, but to me. *I see pain.* Years of sorrow, piled on top of what they either choose to ignore or aren't sensitive enough to notice. But it's there. Black as night. His—

Guilt.

Why? What have you done? Unless... I glance at my bruised hand. The hand that just wants to help but will never be allowed to because I'm cursed. *The weight of what hasn't been done.* That's what darkens Dovan's soul, his regret curling inward and twisting until it mutates into guilt. *What more could he have done?* To save the woman's husband? To help his city? *What more could he owe them?*

The mother is speaking again, jarring me from my thoughts,

"—but sacrifice can't beat what's killing us. Not this time." She turns from Dovan to survey the market.

"We're running out of food." The blunt honesty of her admission wins my respect. "My son needs me to be strong. I can't be strong if I am starving." Her challenge is clear, and yet her lips sag at the corners. She hates what they'll become before winter ends if an ember of spring never appears. She's forced to put her son before her city, to think of herself and her needs first, even if it causes others to suffer, to starve, to die.

I refocus on Dovan, expecting his expression to harden into anger, but the darkness in his eyes deepens into grim understanding. "I won't stand in your way." He raises his voice to address everyone else, "I won't stand in anyone's way."

The other guiders shift, nervous, as people murmur in shock.

Dovan stands just as tall as he did before he admitted he wouldn't stop them from taking what they want. *He's either mad or not finished.* On cue, his chest expands with a full breath, backing his next words with strength. "But where will it end? Will you be satisfied with a handful of wolf meat?"

No rings as loud through the sudden silence as if everyone had shouted it. The market falls so still I sense the thrumming of their hearts in the air. A subtle, soft pulse connecting them with a melody no voice could ever sing.

"The truth is," Dovan's tone softens, "there aren't enough supplies to satisfy everyone's hunger. Not even for a month."

"Dovan," the lead guider warns.

"The truth is, we have survived this long *together*." Dovan points to the city rising behind us. "We're the last hope of a starving world. If we destroy that hope out of selfishness," he glances from the man who stepped on me to the woman with the baby, "if we destroy that hope out of fear, no one will live to see a new spring." He turns, letting his gaze rest for a moment on every face. "And spring. Will. Come."

His mention of spring earns him a few snide chuckles before Mr. Beard directs his own sarcasm at Dovan. "Oh yes, spring will save us. Spring is coming. We've heard that before, *guider*. It's a trick to keep us in line."

"Have I ever said it? Before today?" Dovan matches the man's rigid posture, except he wears confidence rather well. Better than Mr. Beard.

"You must have." Mr. Beard crosses his arms.

"I've never heard Dovan make such a promise," the mother speaks up. Her face is paler when she looks back at Dovan. Once more, a secret they share passes between their locked gazes. *She believes him. Why?*

Dovan breaks their stare first, a subtle quiver of unease twitching around his mouth. "Spring will come and it will come soon. I swear it on my life."

No one expresses doubt over his oath. They're comforted by it because they trust he'll do whatever he can to keep it. *The only way he could would be if he's found an ember of spring.*

"I know you're hungry. So am I," he continues. "But we either survive winter together as a family, or we all die alone as enemies. I know which I prefer. I leave the choice to you."

He's letting them decide? When has that ever turned out well? A leader putting their trust in the goodness of human hearts, *desperate* human hearts.

The selfishness I expect the crowd to act upon doesn't happen. Dovan's challenge, his promise that things will improve, draws a thoughtful calm over everyone. *How?*

I glance at his chest for a clue as to why his words hold so much weight, but there are no stripes on the forelegs of the white bear stitched across his tunic. The number of stripes determines rank among the guiders. Since his bear is unstriped, it means—*he has no authority over anyone.* And yet the refugees, the citizens, and the other guiders seem more than happy to yield to him.

The hunters break the silence first. "We could roast the wolves on spits here in the market. It is Spring Eve."

Dovan gives them a gentle smile as subdued agreement spreads through the crowd. The wolves will make a small feast when shared among so many, but they'll eat together, defying hunger for one more night. *It's almost heartwarming.* If the icy sting of my curse's healing power pooling along my bruises didn't remind me of the truth. The people of Riffen may not be cursed by a murderer, but they are cursed by a winter no one can end. They might have chosen to work together today, to stay a family as Dovan put it, but that's no guarantee for tomorrow.

Dovan won't be there to prevent them from turning on each other.

He'll be dead. By dawn, if not before. The promise he's made to them, of a spring reborn, will break with his last breath, leaving his city without hope. *Why would he be so cruel?* To raise their hopes when he knows he will be their fall? *I hope it's worth it.* Whatever the reason may be, the song of his soul will tell me. Right before Red Death kills him.

The crowd thins as everyone goes about their business. I'm left alone with Dovan. The stiffness of his duty as a peacemaker eases from his body. His shoulders sag and his confident expression cracks with a flicker of exhaustion, revealing his burden has grown no lighter.

"Are you injured?" He asks softly without looking down at me. A wise precaution, since I'm invisible to everyone else. The last thing he needs is for them to think he's losing his mind.

I roll to a sitting position, delaying my answer because the truth tastes bitter as blood on my tongue. *My hurts don't matter.* Confessing them won't keep him alive or change my fate.

New stains soak into my torn dress from being pressed against the muddy cobblestones. *At least it's not blood.* I cringe as a familiar coppery scent fills my nose, followed by a *drip, drip, drip.* The curse's pain slices across my sternum, forcing me to look up and see the place where Red Death will stab Dovan.

The first note of his song wails through my throat even as I try to swallow it into silence. Dovan reaches for me, his hands gripping my arms and pulling me to my feet. The shock of his touch stops my singing.

He'd think nothing of this. His hands bracing me, offering me the help he gives to anyone in need, but my body slowly hardens.

I'm as stiff as a post of iron, unbending to the gentle firmness of his grip until something deep inside me splits open. Softness creeps back into my limbs. I lean into his strength when a rush of cold coats my skin, shoving his heat back. *It doesn't matter. It doesn't mean anything. It doesn't change what you are.* My mind battles for control over my focus, stabbing the ice-hard truth into the center of my heart. *He's going to die.*

Because he sees me.

Because I sing for him.

"Come," his voice makes me flinch, and the tiny grin curling the right corner of his mouth disappears. "I know where you can be safe while I finish the day's work."

I drop my gaze to his hand because he's looking at me like it's his job to protect me. *That's not how this works.* Red Death's victims don't preoccupy themselves with the safety of the banshee who's come to sing them to their deaths.

I was wrong. He doesn't understand what I am.

Dovan lets me go and steps to the side, one hand held out to the left. *He means to guide me.* Like one of his refugees. And I let him even though I know I shouldn't.

Even though I know he won't outlive the night.

WRAITH

5

DOVAN LEADS me deeper into the pulsing rhythm of the lower market. I shiver as we pass an abandoned platform in the center. When the royal twins were killed at the beginning of winter, the old king condemned dozens of members from his own court without evidence or trial and hung them from spikes driven into the platform's wooden crossbeams.

Some people say winter broke the old king, but I suspect it was loss. For years, he has hidden away in his palace, caring nothing for his city or his people, giving the guiders no choice but to take control. *One reason to be grateful for winter.*

Dovan's pace picks up as we near the northern end of the market. I dodge men and women in patched clothing in an off-balanced dance, pushing down the sorrow brought on by every brush of their bodies against mine. The lanes narrow as the crowd thickens, and I search for the dark arms of open shadows. But here, where the stalls have no roofs, sunlight saturates the market. The few shadows I find cling like paper thin wisps to stall beams or pool in quivering puddles around people's feet. *There's no place to hide.*

Panic nips along my skin as I trip over a loose cobblestone. I force a deep breath into my lungs and uncurl my icy fists, fixing my gaze on Dovan's straight spine. But he's stopped and I am once again surrounded.

The bite of my fingernails against my palms anchors me as I search for a distraction. *Remember the game you used to play?* I'd pick a person out of the crowd and let a single thought fill my mind. *That could have been me.*

If I hadn't been cursed.

I'm already looking at Dovan, but he's bound to my deepest regret, so I glance off to his right. *There.* The woman three stalls from me. *I could have been her.* Wrapped in a frayed shawl, hair in a loose braid, she watches the other traders with a sharp eye and whispers secrets to her son.

She's teaching him how to barter. The prize being several spools of wool yarn for a few dried fruits. A rare delicacy she should be careful about showing in the rougher of the three markets. The guiders are always present to deter the bolder crimes, but pickpockets live better than most in this city. Providing they don't get caught and lose both their hands for their theft. *A bit severe.* But in a city where dwindling food stores have replaced the wealth of silver or gold, how else would you deter thieves?

The boy makes his trade, and the woman hugs him tight, planting a light kiss on top of his head. An ache pinches my heart at the love shining through their simple affection.

What do I know of love? I finger a loose strand of black hair, sunlight exposing the silver scars on my forearm. They prove how one-sided my experiences with other people have been. *Has my skin ever felt a touch that didn't leave a mark?* A touch that is safe. A touch that heals, that somehow makes the world right even when it's still a mess.

My chin trembles and I bite my lip to hold the desperation blurring my vision at bay. I study my hair. Soft and pliable, like how I imagined my heart was before the curse. *What if I'm wrong?*

What if I was always this broken?

Maybe that's why Red Death chose me. Because I was already damaged. *I was easy prey.* Easy to control. Easy to use.

A rush of air lifts the stuck strands of my hair from my face. I stiffen as I wait for the next blow to come, for yet another person to deepen my cracks, but no shoulders bump against mine. I'm not tripped or knocked to the ground to be trampled. A few hard blinks clear my vision as I glance up.

Dovan.

Shoulders squared, he stands an arm's length from me. One hand rests on his sword hilt while the other is folded behind him. His stern guider's pose forces the crowd to part as he—the words to describe what he's doing take a moment to form.

He's shielding me.

Before the warmth of that realization reaches my heart, I recoil a half step. I'm unable to reconcile his odd behavior with what I expected. He could whip out his sword and try to kill me any second now. Except both his hand and the weapon it holds are on his left side. The position is relaxed, like the deepest part of him is at peace because he's standing here, between me and everyone else.

"What are you doing?" I cringe at the sound of my voice, so brittle and tight it screams how uncomfortable I am. *You shouldn't even be talking to him.*

"My job." Dovan's answer is as direct as I had expected, his words clipped as if he cut himself off.

"I'm not—" Now I'm holding back, even as the end of that sentence slashes at my heart. *I'm not your job.* He's mine. Vibration tickles my throat as a twinge of pain spasms above my sternum. The fourth note is coming, but a glancing brush of warm fingers along my right arm rescues me from the demand to sing.

When I meet Dovan's gaze, reality gives way to a familiar longing. *Does he see me?* The person underneath the curse. The girl I might have been. The girl I wish I could be. There's no judgement, no fear, no anger in his dark stare, but I don't know him well enough to make anything more of it other than his desire to serve.

"People in need," he says, "are always my job."

I've learned the hard way that what I need is a weapon in someone else's hand. *What if Dovan is trying to charm you to save his life?* It'd be an unusual approach and wouldn't work, but... *It's possible.* I surrender to the new note, using his melody as my shield. *Nothing has changed.* I'm still cursed. He's still fated to die. My voice drops to a wincing murmur as I pull my arm from his touch.

Dovan's eyebrows knit together in a question he doesn't ask. *Good.* I don't want to talk about what neither of us can change. Instead, he leans closer, bringing the scent of leather and wolf fur with him. "I won't go far."

It wouldn't matter if he ran out into the snowfields. There is no distance the curse won't make me overcome.

His eyes brim with yet another futile promise before he nods to the stall on my left. "You'll be safe there."

I'm not the one who needs to be kept safe.

As he passes me, my hand tangles in the length of his fur-lined cape. Or at least that's what I tell myself. I wasn't reaching for him. I wasn't trying to keep him close, pretending to be a normal person who wouldn't think twice about sharing affection with a friend. *We aren't friends. We haven't even introduced ourselves.*

Monsters like me don't need an introduction.

Even if he asked, I have no real name to give him.

Dovan glances over his shoulder at me, proving whatever my hand was doing—*he felt it.* As he stands still in a moving parade of haggling traders, uncertain refugees, and guiders shouting directions, he attracts the wrong kind of attention. They search for what he's looking at, their gazes drifting over me as they try to understand what's holding him to this spot. An empty spot.

The burn of guilt stings my throat. *He's waiting for me to say something.*

I duck below his questioning stare and draw my rebellious hand behind me. A deep breath of winter air seals the cracks in the walls around my slow-beating heart, and then I meet his gaze again. "You should worry about your own safety."

The left corner of his mouth twists upward into a disarming smirk as he bobs his head forward. "I have better things to do."

"Like talking to a girl no one else can see? How ambitious of you." I regret it the moment the words escape. My muscles tense, preparing for the slap or the harsh tirade that's sure to come. *Hate or fear.* Those two emotions are always their response. Every time Red Death's latest victim hears my voice.

Dovan's eyebrows rise, and then, he *laughs.* The hearty, wholesome sound warms the air. More people turn toward us. There's no way for Dovan to avoid raising their suspicions. *Not with* that *smile.* Which is definitely not for my benefit.

He steps forward and I lean back. While he looks over my shoulder, his mouth returns to its firm line. "We both know working for their safety," he flicks his gaze to mine for a bare second, "and for yours, is a better use of what time I have left."

I gape at him, my head whirling his words into a tangle of conflicting emotions. The pieces won't fit together in a pattern that makes sense, because what he said—he couldn't mean it. He doesn't mean it.

I'm not worth the effort.

He backs away a few steps and then spins into the crowd, but he's tall enough that I don't lose track of him. The chords in my throat vibrate as a fifth note rattles through my chest, a mix of respect and shame. *He should be fighting to survive me.* Nothing good will come of treating me with kindness.

Our journey ends in death.

I drift closer to the little stall he insisted will be my safe place and I almost laugh. All the other stalls bear the heavy shadows of our reality, catering to adults, but this one is different. There are no patched clothes, no threadbare blankets, no worn shoes held together with twine. The wares being offered here won't help anyone survive. *Impractical.* And foolish. Like a stubborn guider I know.

People crowd around, offering whatever they have left to trade for rag dollies and wooden toy swords, for child-sized guider's tunics and cloth flower-crowns, for singing Ceana shells and Parvane mirage-pencils, for finger flutes and *are those fliers on strings?*

The stall is run by the cleanest faced children I've ever seen in the dirty lower streets of Riffen. A frowning granny watches over them. Her narrowed gaze examines each customer as if she's weighing the worth of their souls, but it's not driven by greed. It's concern. Concern for the children who look for her approving nod whenever they doubt their own negotiating skills. Which should happen for every purchase. They're terrible at making deals.

They're losing far more than what they gain. Grinning as if their pockets are filling up with the rarest dried fruits and even rarer dried strips of meat. Their pockets lie flat against their thin bodies instead of bulging, as they should be if they were any good at running a stall. *They might as well post a sign that reads "free."*

Their granny does nothing but observe while the citizens and refugees leave with what they want. Some trading pinches of thread pulled from their own clothes. Others sharing a memory that brought them joy.

I step to the right so I'm no longer facing the stall, blinking away a fresh icy sting. *Profit isn't everything.* Neither is survival.

Survival is an empty promise without joy.

A child laughs. I hold on to the warbling sound as it rises like a song, higher and higher, lifting every soul who's close enough to hear.

If spring were a sound, it would be the laugh of a child.

More people flock to this stall, drawn like bees to flowers wearing honeyed diamonds of life-giving nectar. They buzz around, steps lighter, heads held up, eyes rounded and soft, babbling with the children about strapping enough fliers to one's back so you could laugh in gravity's face. Telling stories of the mysteries of mirage-pencils drawing what isn't seen, or seashells holding the songs of sirens. Together, they dream: the adults who know better and the children who refuse to. And it twists my heart, squeezing a few extra thuds from its normal half-rhythm as my skin prickles with a warming desire.

I want to talk nonsense with them. I want to speculate about flying. I want to forget. To lose sight of the truth— *I'm already one of their stories.* Worse, I'm the monster they fear. If the dozens of soul-mirrors pinned to the customer's chests are any sign of how they feel about banshees.

My lips are trembling, an echo of the shiver in my soul, and yes, they were lifting upwards to mirror the happy expressions of those finding refuge at this stall. But I'm—*I'm nothing like them.* I'm not free. I don't even have a memory to trade. Just a blank notion, an insistent idea that stands as alone as I do next to the uncursed.

I haven't seen a flier since...

There's no answer in my memory.

My lips curve downward. *At least they can't see my frown.* I'd hate to be the customer the children fail. I'd rather die than crush the beautiful hope they offer so freely. They're helping people believe in the future again. A future without hunger, where there is no winter burying our souls one frozen flake at a time. *I don't belong here.*

Nothing they have will fix me. I'm too broken, my wounds too deep for their simple offerings of joy to reach the bottom of my soul. There, in the darkness no light can touch, Red Death's magic festers and poisons my voice with a song.

The curse is all I have. My past, my present, my future.

I focus on the fliers before my sorrow drowns the spark of wonder their stall has revived. Made of twigs and whatever fabric scraps available, their diamond design is plain but effective for soaring on the eastern winds. I lift one, slightly, so the movement is unnoticeable. The flier is as long as my torso and twice as wide. Crooked letters stitched to its patched, mottled heart spell out a simple, childish wish.

Fly without wings.

The flier grows heavy in my hands. The inscription demands the impossible of its user, but it's not really talking about joining the birds in the sky. *Making dreams come true is how we soar.* I put the flier down. Its maker never fell prey to a curse. *I stopped believing in the impossible long ago.*

I slip through the crowd to stand in a vacant corner between two stalls, my back pressed to the beam while I search for Dovan. He's in the lane two stalls to the left, hearing a group of women and men complain about current housing shortages. He gives a good show of paying attention, but his eyes keep wandering elsewhere. Often stopping on me. My face, my hair lifting on the breeze, and the ruins of my dress until a woman taps his arm to regain his focus.

I try to smooth the torn pieces of my skirt and fail. It might have been a grand ball gown once. Or maybe that's what I want to see in its frayed embroidery and dangling strips. *At least the underdress is intact.* Otherwise... I let the embarrassing thought fade, fully aware of where Dovan is, of the calming sound of his voice and the weight of his concerned stare. But he's not alone in watching me. My skin tingles from the attention of an unknown observer.

Red Death? I scan the nearest lanes, searching for the flash of crimson, but this—*feels different.* Red Death's notice bites harder and leaves me in no doubt of who's in control. This isn't like that. There's a touch of curiosity and whimsy to it. A child?

There, perched on the far corner of the children's stall, knees bunched up to her chest to support a journal and the frantic scratches of her pencil. Tight braids dark as a raven's wing escape the patterned scarf wrapped around her head and cascade down her shoulders. She's older than the other children running the stall. Probably fifteen or sixteen. And she's staring right at me.

How?

I move right but her eyes don't follow. She doesn't blink either, her focus snared by something nobody else has noticed. It's not me, even if my skin continues to prickle as my stomach knots itself around a misguided hope.

I work my way behind her and look over her shoulder at a strange drawing. With her pencil, she fights the graphite shadows smudged on the page, herding them, stretching them, pushing them into a shape she alone sees. The shape of a gray ghost. I'm reaching for her journal before I realize what I'm doing. The moment my fingers brush the paper, the girl gasps.

The rebellious shadows tame to her will under the weight of my touch. I hold on because I can't believe what I'm seeing. The slender silhouette, the wild hair ruling every breeze, the ripped dress and shredded cape—

It's me.

No artist, no matter how sensitive, should be able to draw a banshee who doesn't sing for them. I focus on her pencil. Pale wood with a dark silver tip. It's not normal graphite but the sap of

Parvane Mirage Trees in its center. *A mirage pencil.* A tool for revealing unseen things. But even with the help of the mirage pencil, she couldn't sketch what it showed her. Not without my touch.

I press as close as I dare, catching my hair before it falls on the girl's shoulder. Dovan's tall form joins mine on the page, recreating the moment before he left me at this stall. Her strokes grow heavier. She tears at the space between me and Dovan, a flurry of dark lines exploding outward—

"You!"

The girl jumps, startled by the young man shoving through the crowd. I dodge left just in time to avoid her crashing into me. Her journal slips from her hands, falling into a half-frozen puddle with a *splat* as she goes stiff.

"You little liar!" He stumbles forward, clothes smelling of refuse as if he's spent the night in a filthy alley. He swings his finger at her and almost loses his balance. "You cheated me!" His hands close into fists and a hateful light burns in his bloodshot eyes. "You won't get away with it."

Whatever she did, she doesn't deserve to be attacked by a hungover young man. I glance around, hoping to spot Dovan or another guider, but no one close by is wearing a white bear.

No one moves to stop him.

They're all frozen while he charges straight for her. I'm the only one close enough, the only one standing in his way.

The only one who can save her.

I kick my leg out to trip him while I pull the girl behind me. His shin knocks against mine, and he whips his arms back to regain his balance. Call it the luck of youthful agility, but he succeeds. If he was furious before, he's livid now, aiming all that rage through me to the girl who remains his target. *He can't honestly blame her for tripping him.*

I tilt forward, wincing as the curse squeezes my heart. My

punishment for intervening. But I quickly hum through the notes of Dovan's song to ease the pain.

The girl's shaky fingers press into my back, exploring left, right, tangling in my hair. I've trapped myself between two people who can't see me. *Now what?* If I move, he'll hurt her. If I stay, I'll get hurt. *I can live with that.*

He lunges. I brace myself, shifting my weight forward to counter his momentum when there's a solid *thunk*. He cries out and falls to the ground where the sour-faced granny pins him with her crutch.

"Ye best be staying put," she warns.

"She stole from me!"

Granny jabs him in the chest, leveraging her weight and position against his, and he's forced to lie flat. "Calm yerself. Nothin' be gained by this nonsense."

"True love isn't nonsense."

Granny leans a little harder on her crutch and he grimaces. "Sanaa be half yer age. Best not say such things ta me face, *boy*."

I glance behind me at the girl, *Sanaa*. She won't look at him as her chin dips toward her chest. All markers of guilt.

The man takes a deep breath and offers the view of his raised, open hands as a sign of surrender.

"Get on up now," Granny instructs, wobbling off balance as she removes her crutch from his chest and wedges it under her left arm. She leans on its sturdy wood, drawing my gaze down its carved length to glimpse her boots peeking out from under her thick skirt. No, I miscounted.

One boot. I try to swallow, but it won't go down as I keep staring at the vacant place where her other foot should be. *She's a* — There's a word for what she's missing. A word that shelters *rip* at its heart. Fitting, since it's so often used to demean someone because they lack something others take for granted. *Like two working feet.* But she stepped forward and knocked some sense into an angry young man when no one with *two* feet would, reminding me of another word inside *cripple*. If it weren't for the *c* in front, people might see them for what they truly are.

Ripples. I grin, because this granny is definitely a wave-maker.

"I mean her no harm," the young man stands and flicks mud off his tunic, "but your charge cheated me of my food."

The crowd gasps and murmurs. It's a crime worthy of maiming, banishment to the snowfields, or even death.

Granny's stern gaze shifts to Sanaa. "Be this true?"

Sanaa's chin falls even further.

"Sanaa promised me a portrait of my beloved. I wanted to surprise my Emalyne. She's been so down of late. I thought, if she could just see how beautiful she still is..." His broken words trail off into silence. He sniffs back tears, and the lines around Granny's mouth tighten as her glare sharpens to knife points aimed at Sanaa. "But when the portrait was delivered—" he breaks off to rummage through his cloak before withdrawing a crumpled piece of paper with a handful of lines. They form a crude stick-figure any toddler could create.

"Is this a trick?" His expression softens with the pain of betrayal when they land on Sanaa. "I've seen your drawings before. They're beyond words."

Granny moves between them. "What price did she ask?"

"Enough to mean I won't be eating dinner again tonight."

"Then ye'll eat with us." Granny rests a hand on his shoulder. "I can't promise ye'll be filled."

He nods. "And swear she'll never draw for anyone else."

"Agreed." Granny accepts his terms.

I feel Sanaa wince. My hand strays closer to hers, a futile offer of comfort, but holding her hand won't make losing her right to draw any easier. I retreat, trying to avoid the tug of understanding dangling like a thread between us. *You know how much this hurts.* When someone else rules your creative soul and decides your fate.

Banshees aren't the only ones living under a curse.

Granny hobbles next to Sanaa, focusing on the disbanding crowd and keeping her voice low, "Do ye want ta die out on the ice?"

Sanaa bends down to reclaim her journal, but Granny's crutch stomps it further under refreezing water.

"Sanaa. I be tryin' ta keep ye safe."

The girl extends to her full height and glares straight into the old woman's face. "I'd rather be dead than never draw again."

"*Sanaa*," Granny speaks her name between grinding teeth.

"I drew Emalyne's portrait just like he asked," Sanaa's dark eyes flash with bitter fire. "It is not *my* fault he didn't get to *see* it."

Granny grabs Sanaa's arm as she leaves. "Be glad he didn't. Or do ye think he'd be satisfied with a meager meal as recompense?"

What did the girl draw? That made the old woman so afraid of what he'd do she exchanged a poor fake for it instead. I glance down at the journal, still held in place by Granny's crutch.

"My art isn't evil." Sanaa wrenches free, nearly costing Granny her balance. She ducks into their stall with a fake smile plastered across her face and offers a finger-flute to a man with a young boy perched on his shoulders.

Granny sighs, shaking her head. "That girl ... "

"Will be the death of you?" Dovan's voice startles me as he appears next to her. He reclaims Sanaa's journal, shakes excess water and ice from it, and tucks it in his belt.

"Where were ye?" Granny thumps his shoulder.

"I know you can take care of yourself, Gran." He gives her a peck on her cheek.

His family title for her makes me look twice at them both. He's a lot taller, his face rounder, his eyes deeper set behind always concerned eyebrows. The shape of his features, the darker coloring of his skin, the curl of his hair, none of it matches hers. *Not all families are born of blood.* Some begin with a choice, but it's hard to imagine the confident guider before me as a frightened orphan.

His *Gran* slaps him away. "This be serious. It can't go on."

Dovan watches Sanaa, picking up on the hurt she buries beneath a smile, and his shoulders sag from their straight line. *He looks so tired.* Weighed down by too many worries.

The desire to help him roars through me, a kindred song to his own, but I can't act on it. *As if a banshee sharing his burdens would make anything better.* He'll still die by dawn. A fact the curse won't let me escape, forcing my lips to fulfill its purpose. Another note is born. Another flinch of pain over my heart. Another promising drip of blood from the prophetic wound in Dovan's chest.

I'm not here to offer my shoulder. I'm here to sing him to his death.

Dovan and his Gran start discussing Sanaa again, but I've stopped listening. There's no reason to hear of another girl having her future decided by other people. I move away, seeking the nearest shadow as black as the chasm in my soul. A place where I can disappear.

Before I've gone very far, a hand wraps around my right elbow. A touch that doesn't seek to guide or to command but to simply tell me Dovan's there. That it's his turn to follow. I blink hard to clear away the rippling horror of where I'm leading him.

"So. Children are your weakness."

I stop and Dovan bumps into me, triggering a flinch. Fresh pain replaces his gentle half smile. He doesn't mouth the words, but *I'm sorry* moistens his eyes, begging me to believe he understands. His misplaced pity sparks a dangerous hope that must be snuffed out. I can't let it burn. I can't let it blaze through my whole soul because I know what follows.

Ashes.

His hand falls from my elbow and he tilts his head left as if he's surveying the market. "Thank you, for helping Sanaa."

"I didn't do anything," my voice sounds raw, but not from thirst. It's a lack of use. *Talking has never helped.*

"I've been watching you all day." His fingers capture an errant strand of my hair and pull it behind my shoulder. "I've seen how the touch of others hurts you. So yes, you did do something." He tips his head forward as if being closer will give his words more meaning. "Something brave."

It's easy to be brave when what needs to happen is something you *can* do. My gaze falls to his chest, to the prophetic wound, as the truth leaves my lips, "I could save her." I bite my tongue before the rest escapes.

But I can't save you.

We're both bound to a cruel fate. Somehow, our bleak future doesn't bother him. *I need to know.* Why he's different. I follow the slope of his shoulder, the line of his neck, the stubbled angle of his jaw, the dip in his cheek just before the bone, and then, the eyes. *What color would they be?* If my vision recognized more than three colors.

Knowing his eye color won't make what will happen any easier to bear or soften the cruel nature of my song.

If I didn't sing, would he still die?

"None of this is your fault," Dovan's voice is too gentle, too kind, twisting guilt's blade deeper into my heart. I slowly meet his gaze. His fingers brush my arm, a whisper of touch awakening the hunger locked deep within my soul.

I want more. More than he can give. More than I deserve.

A twinge of sorrow tightens his mouth as he squeezes my hand. "You don't owe me anything."

I hiss in a breath, his voice drowned out in a roar of blood in my ears. *My heart—* It beats faster than I ever remember. The parts of my hand that were in contact with his tingle. Not the tingle of limbs falling asleep but of those waking up. Not the bite of frost-fanged cold but a timid, flickering warmth. And it doesn't last anywhere near long enough.

I turn my hand over, gaping at my palm and blinking through denial, but the impossible tan cracks in my gray skin are fading, their jagged trails of color blending into the rest of my hand again. I snap my wrist, willing them to return, but my skin remains a stubborn and pallid shade of pewter as if nothing happened. *What does this mean?*

I find Dovan a short walk away. *Who is he?* This young guider who doesn't fear a banshee or hate me for what I'm here to do. Whose touch— *No.* That hope is too painful. *It must have been a trick of the light.*

Another guider has claimed his attention. Dovan throws a strained glance over his shoulder at me before striding after the other guider with controlled haste.

Something has gone wrong.

He doesn't need to wait for me. I will follow, but this time the curse isn't forcing me onward. *I want this.* I want to know who he is. Finding the answer will explain why this game is different. Why he's not running from me.

Why my song hasn't changed him.

RED DEATH

6

Plans are like rules. They're made to be broken.

I'm not surprised we wound up here, in the underground storage rooms beneath the guider barracks. There were two possibilities, and even though this choice is less exciting, it spreads the stain of betrayal from the guiders I corrupted to those who concealed our treason. Either way, I win. I didn't get my public spectacle, but it only takes one wagging tongue to start the fire of outrage. Although a slower and sadly bloodless tactic, gossip will be my ally. Some might say gossip is Riffen's sole hope. What else have they to do but starve and talk?

The slow way it is.

Searing pain flashes bright crimson across my vision, a pulse pounding through several bruised bones—my left leg, right arm, left ribs. Not even going to mention the nose that's sprouted its own twin streams down my face. I spit blood at the hard-packed dirt floor. My busted lips pull away from my teeth in a grim sneer as torchlight winks off the fresh red splatters on the ground. *At last. Someone who knows how to hit.* And she's hung up on the arms of three other guiders.

She snarls and jolts forward, snapping her teeth around a single word, *traitor,* and a chill of delight nips at my skin. It's one of my underrated titles. Most people focus on *murderer, monster,* or *villain* when we're face to face. Understandable. When my dagger is buried six inches deep in their chests, treason hardly compares to my bloodier skills. *I'm a well-rounded monster.*

The pale bear of my accuser's guider tunic has three stripes. *A Second.* Confusing, I know. It should be third, but guiders count backwards. First Rank takes four stripes. They say it used to take thirty years to gain a Second Rank. This woman, no, this *girl,* barely looks eighteen. Skinny, but wild. A different kind of tempting fun if I wasn't already preoccupied. I'm much more impressed with her bloodied fists. They're swelling, possibly broken, and yet she still wants more. More pain. More blood. More *vengeance.* A desire we share. I'm tempted to break my bonds and give her what she needs.

A real fight. To the death.

I'd have to trick her into killing herself, since my dagger chooses its own victims. Torch fire reflects off a stand of chipped pikes leaning against the stone wall to the right. *Perfect.* It'd be easy to bump them, manipulate the fall of one pike, and time it so the head goes right. Through. Her. Chest. *She'd die well.* Unlike the spineless cowards caught with me. Well, *caught* is such an uncomplicated word. It's boring. I'm never that.

"Let go of me!" Her voice slashes like a knife. Even I have to control the wince of the face I borrowed. *Such fire.* "NOW!"

They have no choice but to obey. They stand back as she smooths her tunic, leaving a merlot streak across the pale bear. It's either my blood or Tall's or Shorty's. *I hope it's mine.* I like marking my interests.

"We should wait for Dovan," one of the other guiders cautions her.

"He'll know what to do," another agrees.

Boys, you're digging your own graves.

"I know what to do." She glares at the quivering, wormish-form of Shorty. "Kill them and toss their worthless bodies over the wall. Let the wolves make a decent meal out of them."

I've never been decent and don't plan to start today.

Through my sweat slicked curls, I scan the room for something useful. The place is small, about five strides across. Cold and crumbling earth fills the air with the bite of minerals, rust, and decaying wood. Stone closes in from the sides and the ceiling while barrels and shelves line each wall, filled with weapons more broken than Tall and Shorty. Each of their legs bend in the wrong direction. Mine would be broken too if there wasn't *more* to my blood, than well, *blood*, but where was I? Oh yes, this delightful room.

It's not even a proper place for interrogation. *This is where they store weapons that have tasted their last souls.* My grin widens. Several dozen uses for each one flashes through my mind. I could kill hundreds with what they deem unsound, picking the perfect body part for each damaged blade. What can I say? I like warped things.

I don't like people who beg for what they don't deserve.

People like Tall and Shorty. They shudder. Moaning and sobbing jumbled pleas for mercy, for something to numb the pain. *Really?* My hands coil into fists. I've endured far worse, and I never asked for relief. Pain is a weapon if you know how to use it. Tall and Shorty prefer to be ordinary. They clutch at their legs and arms and sides and heads, moving from one torment to another, while I push myself onto my knees. Ready for more.

But the female guider ignores me. *I'm not the one she hates.* Unlike Tall and Shorty, I confessed our shameful, food-stealing plot. I turned them in, hoping for a trial, and earned a little less wrath. But not the trial.

My sneer stretches wider as she falls right into my trap. *She's making this easy.* Acting out over nothing more than an accusation. One look is enough to spot the budding disagreement in the eyes of the guiders under her command. This is what I wanted. To drive a wedge. It doesn't matter if it's between the guiders and their leaders, or the guiders and the people. In the end, it will be both. She's planted the seeds and waters them with my blood.

I sniff and then spit metallic-tainted saliva from my mouth. *Good souls are so easy to trick.* Spin them a horrifying tale and they won't care about evidence.

Some accusations are too horrible to doubt.

Caring about our innocence or guilt isn't her job. Her duty is to Riffen, to protect the bond between the guiders and the citizens that holds this city back from chaos. It's why she had us brought down here, under the guider's barracks by the west gate instead of their court of justice. No one can find out how thread-thin the bond is growing. How weak the foundation of their peaceful life is becoming.

Every man for himself. The oldest seed of evil.

I've been busy sowing it among the guiders for months. Tall and Shorty were not the first to let it take root, but they were the easiest to harvest. With bleedin' terrific results. *No one's incorruptible.* That's their mistake. The guiders built a reputation for themselves they have no chance of maintaining. Not as supplies continue to dwindle and the meager harvests fail. *Only a matter of time now.* Before need triumphs over duty. Before those who took an oath to protect others decide to protect themselves first.

It will be my masterpiece. Watching Riffen tear itself apart. Watching it burn itself to the ground. *I've already picked out the perfect spot.* Even hid a few stolen snacks. And when the fires of panic and betrayal die, when every man, woman, and child who calls this city home is dead, I will walk over their still smoldering corpses and laugh until I can't breathe. *Who needs an army when you have the selfishness of men's souls to play with?*

Riffen will fall, starting with their precious guiders. My dagger couldn't have picked a better time to choose a guider for our next kill.

Speaking of our next victim. He enters the room with the screech of rusty hinges and the thump of the wooden door slamming into the wall. *Kick it in, why don't you?* I like a good forceful entrance. Lets everyone know who's in charge, who has the power. This—*Dovan*—as they call him. I grimace. Such a soft name, matching his rounded face, and concern-pinched eyes. *Ugh.* His green-tinted presence clashes with the darker red tones of my vision as caring floods off him in sticky-warm waves. I glance away to relieve the sour revolt of my stomach.

He's followed by a younger guider with pale hair and—*Wraith.* She hangs back, clinging to the shadows of the doorway, her posture timid and wary, the same few notes humming through her lips. I relax my face as her gaze skims too quickly over me to notice I'm hiding behind someone else's face. *It's the blood.* Drying under my nose and around my mouth that keeps her examination brief. She's always hated bloodshed.

"Is it true?" Dovan's voice is deeper than I expected, worn ragged by the disgust twisting his expression.

The female guider who didn't want to wait for Dovan tries to ball her hands into fists as she steps forward to report, but her fingers hardly curl. *Definitely broken.* From beating Tall and Shorty and, well, me. *My kind of girl.* I could buy her a drink later, but I'd have to steal a new face or risk getting a glass shoved into one of my traitorous eyes. *And you'll be busy.* Stalking Dovan and Wraith. *Maybe after?*

I shake the idea from my head. Her attractive rage won't last. It's fading as the adrenaline of the moment burns from her blood and awakens her to pain. The pain of a split-second loss of control. Glimmers of horrified tears flash in the corners of her eyes. *She's nothing like me.* Boring, like the rest of them.

"This one," she points at me. I restrain my sneer and bow my head in submission like a repentant little traitor. "Brought their crime to our notice."

Dovan's focus shifts to me, a smothering green heat pressing down on my corrupted soul, but I don't break so easily. I've born burdens far worse than one man's disappointment upon my shoulders. "Speak."

I bristle under his command, but I obey for the sake of my destructive plan, playing my part so well he'll find no flaw. Not in the tears tasting of salty fear, not in the tremors of regret puckering my face, nor in the gusting breaths pleading more for my life than the words I use. Ending with a simple *forgive me.* A request no good man would refuse.

"Have you checked his story?" Dovan asks after a brief pause, his gaze sweeping from guider to guider.

"We've sent men to the place he described, sir, and we checked our stores. Four hundred rations are missing."

Dovan's wince of a breath scrapes a chill through the air. I angle my head to get a better glimpse of his face. *Oh.* All the softness has turned to stone. A mask of terrible duty if ever I saw one. *This should be interesting.*

His gaze settles on the splintered spear that did the most damage to Tall and Shorty's bodies, and then focuses on her, the female guider who outranks him.

She holds her ground against his veiled disapproval. "I gave them less than what they deserved. I'd have killed them if you—"

Dovan waves her off before she finishes. He nudges Tall and Shorty onto their backs with his boot, filling the room with their hissing breaths and feeble moans. Dovan stares down into their faces, his own devoid of any sympathy for the bond of brotherhood they shared, or even a twinge of rage over their selfish actions. *Where's the fun in that?* My plan should have left every persevering bone in his soul shattered. I didn't think he'd be so cold about betrayal.

"Did you steal food from our people?" Dovan's tone remains irritatingly neutral.

Where's the anger? Why is he wasting time on questions meant to determine true guilt? I'd have torn them apart with my bare hands just for being accused of disloyalty.

Tall presses his bloody lips closed and nods. Shorty coughs and sputters a weak apology. It's a partial lie. They *were* going to steal food with me, not that I gave them the chance. Their confessions must be a side-effect of whatever scrap of honor they're trying to reclaim. *Spineless worms.* Can't even take pride in putting themselves before others.

Dovan turns his back on them and everyone else. *Inconvenient.* If, like me, you enjoy watching people fall apart. I wanted to see it in his face, the crumbling of his way of life, the shaking of his moral center. But as the seconds slip away like the failing beats of a pierced heart, the man I will kill holds his spine straight, his shoulders level, his head up. Unafraid, unbroken, unfazed. *Damn.* He's better than I am at controlling temperamental emotions. *Someone should tell him it's more fun to lose it.* To give in to the chaos. To stop thinking and act.

Life is short, after all. Especially for him.

"What should we do, sir?" The guider with pale hair asks. "Take them for trial?"

"If we try them, the whole city will realize they've been betrayed," Broken Hands girl jabs her elbow into Pale Hair's chest. "By *us.*" She looks to Dovan as if waiting for him to decide, and adds, "There's only one thing to be done."

I know that and she knows that, but I doubt he has the—

In one swift movement, Dovan turns around, draws his sword, and drives his blade into Tall's chest and then Shorty's.

Winter's Teeth.

He killed them.

It's what I would have done, eventually. After having some violent fun with them.

As Dovan withdraws his sword, the wet crunch of steal scraping bone sends a tingle down my skin. A sound I love, but hearing violence never compares to performing the act itself. My dagger releases a pulse of heat from my side, a crimson flash of lust for the taste of Dovan's heart, his bones, his flesh and blood. *Soon.*

I study the placement of the wounds left behind by Dovan's blade—*the perfect strikes.* He stabbed them straight through their hearts, while they were down, while they couldn't defend themselves, *before* their guilt was proven. A brutal mercy they didn't deserve. It's a clean kill. As quick and efficient as my own blade work.

Well, someone's full of dark surprises.

I check for any cracks in Dovan's stony facade. No shaking in his hands, no slumping of his shoulders, no sweat on his brow, and no twitching around his lips or his eyes. His stare is as steady as it was before. *No regrets, then.*

He faces me, sword tip stained several inches deep with their blood. "Your honesty has saved your life."

Oh, if only he knew. The edges of my mouth twitch, but I suppress my grin.

"But he's just as guilty." Broken Hands darts to Dovan's side.

"He'll face the ice and the wolves. In chains. Alone *and* unarmed." He presses the tip of his sword against the center of my chest. "One night without his brothers and sisters guarding his back. If he survives, it will cover his debt."

From the doorway, Wraith's voice carries into the room. Frail and aching and heard by me and Dovan alone. "*If* he's even guilty."

She's right. All they have to prove a crime's been committed is my word, which is practically worthless, and the coincidental missing rations. Except, I *am* the coincidence. I know where the rations are, and they'll never find them. Call it my last laugh. Another move made in my *watch Riffen burn* long game.

Wraith's comment about guilt affects Dovan. He lowers his sword and almost looks at her, his brows pinching over his eyes as his shoulders dip in a signal of remorse. *Still not regret, though.* The annoying realization stirs a flicker of respect in my black heart.

"Killing him now would be kinder," Pale Hair breaks the silence.

"He doesn't deserve to live," Broken Hands tries to push around Dovan to get to me, but he holds her back.

"He's earned a chance to redeem himself." Dovan grabs my tunic and hauls me to my feet. "If you *ever* betray us again, I will kill you."

Oh, now I've got chills.

He pushes me into the two guiders who've come behind me. "Get him out of my sight."

It's a shame, really. Leaving him at such a crucial moment of our acquaintance. *Just when we were getting friendly.*

Next time, it won't be so easy for him to send me away.

WRAITH

7

I*T'S NOT* *what it looks like.* My heart's pitiful objection dies with the first full breath of freshly shed blood. The sickening, coppery tang turns my stomach into an ocean of outrage, crying out against the ruthless act the kindest man I've ever met has just committed. *It's not. Dovan's not like*—but everywhere I look, I see red. Spattered on the stone walls, drying on the hands meant to help, and soaking into the ground by the bodies.

His *victims.*

Two words that swing, heavy as a war-hammer, for my heart. A heart no longer protected by a solid wall. *I let him weaken me. I let him tempt me with hope.*

I thought he was good. Good for his people and good for me, when what he's really good at is stabbing people in the chest.

I recoil deeper into the shadowed passageway, but I can't tear my gaze from the two dead guiders. They were still breathing a moment ago. Breathing and in pain and begging for mercy. The gift Dovan gives to anyone whether they deserve it or not. But not here. Not this time. Not with these men.

Why? Why are they not worthy? What makes me any different from them?

Their betrayal made them a threat, but with me, there is no threat, no suspicion. I'm the real danger. And not just to Dovan. I've sung to hundreds and watched them die, and that won't stop after he's dead. I'll keep singing to his people, my voice triggering their murders. *What would he do if he could see the body count of my songs?* They'd be stacked so high we'd have no hope of ever climbing our way out.

You're alone with him.

We're deep under the barracks by the west gate. The other guiders, at Dovan's order, marched the man who survived up the stairs, their thumping steps echoing down the stairwell before fading into silence. Now there's nothing but the slow pulse in my ears and the repetitive notes I'm humming. I've cycled through the same melodic phrase multiple times. *There's no note for murderer.* I bite my lip, unsure, but what other word fits better than the one I hate most?

He killed two men who couldn't fight back, couldn't even get up. I shiver as the air cools between us. *He's not a mur—* I stop myself because there's no prettying up what he's done.

The melody of his soul song dies in my throat. Not even the curse knows how to go on, how to forge the anthem of a good man and a cold-hearted kill together. *How do I make this okay?* Because I am *not* okay with it.

Dovan cleans his blade with the cloak of the taller victim. I flinch at the scrape of metal as he slides his sword into its sheath. He faces me, slowly, and I'm not prepared for the darkness in his eyes. His brows pinch together over his nose as if he's worried about me. Again. *He should be more worried about what I think of him.* If he is, he offers no explanation, no clever excuse to chase away the shadows growing between us like ebony blood stains. *He knows there is no excuse.*

The cost of his violence lands on his shoulders like a lead weight, pulling him down, and yet, he hitches them up higher until they hold a straight line again. *Is killing so easy for him?* How can a couple deep breaths, a pause of a few seconds, be enough to rid himself of the burden of taking life? A burden that should last a lifetime.

Dovan's head tilts down as he approaches me. I squeeze against the passageway, flattening myself so we do not touch, but as he passes by, the lantern light shimmers in his irises. Tiny stars of honest emotion blink through the darkness, hinting at the deeper feelings he locks away. He wore the same guilty look at the market when promising spring would come. *How many lives does he carry on his shoulders?* How many are still living?

How many are dead?

He pauses at the staircase, waiting for me.

My steps are stiff at first, but I join him. He keeps the pace slow, right hand within reach of my left arm as if he fears I might trip and fall. His misplaced concern adds to my confusion. *It doesn't mean anything.* Dovan doesn't care about how deeply violence affects me. He hasn't noticed my hands won't stop shaking or the dampness of sweat beading along my skin. He wouldn't know to look for such little things. All the timid clues of a maelstrom locked inside my chest. A storm that wants to rage. To pin him to the wall and demand he answer for his kills.

I am no one's judge. I couldn't be. Because I'd wind up being judged instead.

Silence is safe.

Silence is better.

After four flights of stairs, after I trip seven times only to be saved by his quick hand, my heart still won't keep quiet. *What if he is a monster?* It would explain why he isn't afraid of a banshee, but not why he's making sure I don't fall and bleed out on the same ground as his victims. *Unless he knows the fall wouldn't kill me.*

He can't. None of the stories mention how the curse heals its banshees of all injuries so Red Death can keep using our voices. We're ghosts to the story tellers of old, and ghosts don't die or heal.

I'm no ghost.

My fingers glide along the sleeve of Dovan's tunic as if to prove I'm really here. His muscles pulse with heat but harden under my touch as he clenches his hand. He stops with each foot on a different step. Ribbons of daylight mingle with the hissing torchlight as the ebb and flow of the city breathes down the stairway. We're close to the ground level. Once he's free of this narrow space, he'll be back to work and out of my reach, but the reason I stopped him goes fuzzy.

What would it be like to have his arm as my barrier? Curled around me, protecting me, reminding me I am still human. Still a girl with dreams. A tiny splatter of blood on his sleeve brings a chill to my face and draws my gaze to the sword belted at his other hip. This arm I wish would be my shield—*it's his sword arm.* The same arm that delivered a killing strike so precise it couldn't be his first or his second, or third, or... I withdraw my hand and he exhales. The sound of air leaving his lungs is louder than it should be, as if he'd been holding his breath, waiting for me to speak.

Ask him. Now. I swallow to moisten my throat, but I'm not brave enough to face him while questioning his character. "You killed them?" As if that could be in question. *You were supposed to ask him why.*

"Come," he starts up the stairs again. "We don't have much time."

A single tear chills my skin as I hesitate, but I feel the pull, the tug on my heart that makes me take a halting step. Then another.

I want him to be different.

I want his kindness to be real instead of a lie, or a clever way to manipulate me, or a mask to hide a cruel nature. *Please don't be like everyone else.*

My thighs burn from the burst of speed as I leave the underground stairwell behind. Dovan's already reached the stairs cut into the looming outer wall of the city. Skipping every other step, he reaches the top by the time I'm only halfway there.

"Wait." I call after him, sliding between the other guiders patrolling the wall, but Dovan's pace never slows.

The wall rises and falls with the hilly terrain of the land, coiling around the city like a serpent. It curves away from the housing quarters and heads due north. Rows of failed, frosted fields replace all signs of life except for the occasional guider.

A mournful howl shatters the calm, raising the hair on my arms. *Wolves.*

I catch up to Dovan and stand beside him, gazing out into the sparkling snowfields. A trio of guiders hurry toward the gate, but they've left a man behind—*oh.* The guider who confessed. He walks in a tight loop, held in place by a chain attached to an iron post.

Pale blurs of movement draw closer and begin to circle. I count at least three wolves, their shapes growing clearer as my eyes adjust to the light of late afternoon. *He doesn't stand a chance.*

Dovan brought me here to watch another man die because of him.

I step back, trembling as the corner of Dovan's mouth settles into an emotionless expression similar to Red— *No. He's not like that. He's not a monster.* But what other title fits a man who spares a life just to watch him be torn to pieces by ravenous wolves? *This is worse than what Dovan did to the others.* At least they won't be eaten alive.

The words I couldn't find earlier settle on my tongue, burning like acid. "I thought you were different."

He ignores me, fiddling with something on his right side that I can't see.

"You're a killer. Just like him."

His jawline flexes as he bites down hard to keep his face neutral, but his eyes betray him, their glassy shine fracturing his stoic mask. Where a true monster would wear my accusation with pride, Dovan's shoulders are heavy, his body rigid. There's no swagger, no sneer, no evidence of enjoyment. Unlike Red Death, Dovan takes no pleasure in his kills.

Another howl jolts us both. With a deep breath, Dovan releases the tension in his shoulders. He lifts a bow from his right side and fits an arrow to the string.

"We don't have much time." I replay his words as he aims, trying to make sense of why he rushed to this spot. *Unless.* He knew the wolves would be close. He knew sending that man out onto the ice was a death sentence as certain as driving his sword through the man's heart. *But he didn't do that.*

The bow twangs and he draws another arrow, releasing it after a breath. I watch as they both streak across the pale gray sky. The first slams into the chest of the wolf closest to the man they want to eat. A perfect kill shot. The other wolves snarl, circling tighter, as the second arrow lodges in the snow near the man's boots. He yanks it free, ready to fight.

"Now he stands a chance." Dovan slides his bow over his shoulder. He doesn't even wait to see the outcome before he leaves.

I raise my voice so it carries over the distance separating us. "You want him to survive."

Dovan slows to a stop. His shoulders heave up and down before he faces me. "I do. Every life we have left is precious."

"But you killed the others."

He stiffens, brows lowering into a hard, defensive line to

protect himself from me, from what *I* think of him. "I did what needed to be done."

"What if they weren't guilty?" I tread closer. "What if you killed two innocent men?"

He matches my slow advance until neither of us can take another step without touching. "What is it you really want to know?"

"Doesn't it bother you?"

He huffs a ragged breath and surveys the dead fields within the wall. "Does it bother *you*?" The muscles along his jaw flex as he fixes me with a stare that burns. "You are a banshee after all. You've seen more people die than I have, I'd wager."

I flinch away from him. The rational part of me says he's lashing out because he's as trapped as I am now. But Dovan's harsh words open new fissures in my walls that won't stop cracking. I'm always breaking but never falling apart, cornered between a curse and a victim.

Run.

From the pain in his eyes. From the accusation of what I am and the pity softening his glare and the notes clawing their way up my throat.

RUN.

I reel back from Dovan and bump into the parapet. The stacked stones come up to my waist, which makes it easy to climb. Even in a dress.

"What are you doing?" His voice still cuts like a knife, but this time panic gives it an edge.

I peer down fifty feet of stone to the bottom where wavelike drifts of snow lap at the wall's side. A deadly fall. With hungry wolves to look forward to if you survive.

"Don't."

I glance down at Dovan, the windswept strands of my hair

acting like bars between us, reminding me he is free while I am not. *I will never be free.* Even this small escape is a lie.

I lean away from him, from the wall, from the city that has become my prison. *Let me fall.* Into the cold and the ice. Into the numb safety of distance. Let winter freeze over my heart as it always does when it's just us. The coldest season and the girl who sings of death. I lift my arms to the side as a frigid breeze snaps through my hair. Gravity shifts, tugging me down, but I'm jolted backward by an even stronger force.

"I've got you." Dovan's hands lock around my left arm, and I choke on my next breath as a surge of heat crackles over my icy skin. "I won't let you fall."

I twist so I can see him. "It'd be better for you if I did." A half-lie. It'd prove to him I am a monster when he watches me rise unbroken from a fall that should kill me.

Dovan responds by jerking me so hard we both fall backwards. He catches me, pulling me against him as our momentum slams him against the parapet. For a moment, neither of us moves. My hand pressed to his chest, where every skin cell throbs with the thunderous heat of his drumming heart. His breath coils in tendrils of gray vapor while his sword arm loops around my waist.

I blink through the needling-shock of his proximity before it persuades me he can in fact breathe fire. *The temperature's dropping.* Turning his exhale into a thin cloud. The first sign of the sun's decline into the west. I focus on one word. The only word that matters. *Time.* And stare at his sternum, at the mark of the curse. The wound is wider and I snatch my hand away before I get his blood on my skin.

Too close. I pull free of his arm, shivering, as cold air replaces his warmth. *You're getting too close.* A warning I don't know how to heed. Everything about Dovan, it—*he* draws me in. He's a doorway to what I've been missing. An answer to a question I forgot how to ask.

"What you said before." He shifts, straightening and then leaning so he's half-sitting on the parapet's edge. "Why would it be better for me if you fell?"

"It was a foolish thing to say."

"No, it was honest." Dovan pushes off the wall to stand beside me, and the temperature of the air rises between us. "The odd thing is, you weren't afraid of falling."

I stare out at the snowfields. Answering his question will earn me pity. A powerless emotion that does more harm than good for someone under the power of a curse.

"I've talked down more than a few people who thought jumping off the wall would end their pain, but," his finger brushes my arm with splinters of heat, "there's always uncertainty in their eyes. I saw none in yours."

My chin sinks lower, giving me a perfect view of snow hard enough to shatter most bones in the human body. *I wish I was like most people.* I'd be dead a dozen times over if I wasn't cursed. *Sometimes living is the worst punishment there is.*

Instead of telling him any of that, I swallow the grief and say what he's already expecting to hear. "I've fallen before."

He does a methodical sweep of my straight posture, searching for bones made crooked by a hopeless jump. "From how high?"

I hold his concerned stare for a moment before finding the bell tower over his left shoulder. It stands a hundred feet high at the heart of Riffen, and I remember the eternity of seconds it took to hit the palace courtyard below. *I didn't even scream.* I knew the fall wouldn't kill me. *I hoped it would damage me enough so I wouldn't be able to sing.*

So one victim could be saved.

If Dovan is horrified by the answer I imply with a glance, he doesn't show it, but when his gaze meets mine, there are no more questions lurking in their depths. He folds his arms across his chest and slumps against the parapet. Before he switches his focus to the snowfields, I glimpse the intense spark of an emotion I didn't expect.

I've seen this dark agony burn through those who've failed to protect someone they cared about from harm. *The loved ones.* The families of my victims expressed the same thing, although they raged out loud where Dovan broods in silence.

"You're angry." The itch to take his hand and ask him why my fall upset him spreads across my palms.

He tucks his chin close to his chest, a boot digging at a loose stone. "I hate..." His voice is so quiet I almost miss what he said.

I hate.

Me? I retreat half a step, my fingers tracing the silver scars on my right forearm. They're all that remains of the victims who came before him.

Dovan picks at his palms before wiping them down his thighs, and then he meets my gaze. "It matters."

"What matters?" I prod, my heart tiptoeing along a foolish clifftop hope. *All I've ever wanted*—was to hear two words. *You matter.* Not because of a talent, not because I am useful, but because I exist. A piece of the world that would be missed if I vanished, if my fall from the bell tower had worked.

"Jarrek and Ivan—the men I killed. It matters if they were guilty or innocent."

My mouth opens but no sound comes out. *He didn't mean me.* I blink quickly before he notices how the sting of disappointment glistens my eyes.

Dovan stands and rubs the back of his neck, pacing a few steps before facing me. "This city is one mistake away from chaos." He sighs, head shaking. "If they lose their trust in us, everything will be lost." He looks at me, dark gaze still haunted. I was wrong about it being born of indifference. It's the darkness of a man resigned to do whatever he must to ensure his people survive, and it offers him no escape from the horror or the guilt of killing two helpless men who might be innocent.

"I can't." Another breath of vapor, another painful twitch of his lips as he rubs his forehead. "I *won't* let that happen." He sniffs hard and straightens his spine, gaze drifting down to mine. "Not on my last day."

I've been punched in the face, kicked in the gut, and stomped on, but those pains were superficial. *But this*—my chin trembles and I turn my back to him. *He's blaming me.* He has every right to. *What's the weight of two more lives on my conscience?* I carry the burden of hundreds. Yet the dread that this is also my fault—that I have darkened Dovan's soul—makes my legs give out.

Dovan is quick to react, holding me up and spinning me so I sit on the parapet, his hands lightly curled around my shoulders. "What's wrong?"

I choke on a laugh that becomes a sob and scrub at the icy tears stinging my cheeks. "Everything."

"Tell me one thing, then."

I take a deep breath and hold it in, but the words build up, suffocating me until I confess. "You killed them because you're running out of time. If I wasn't here, you'd have the time to prove their guilt."

Warm fingers lift my chin, guiding my face toward his. "My death has nothing to do with you. Neither did theirs. They made their choices. So have I."

"You didn't choose this, Dovan. I'm here because I know how you die. A banshee's curse *is* to know, to sing, to...watch."

He pulls back as I expected. Yet even as his expression turns grim, as his eyebrows sink and his stare narrows, fear and disgust remain missing. "There's no stopping my death."

"There's no stopping him."

"*Him?*" Confusion ripples across his brow. "A *man* is going to kill me?"

"How else did you think this worked?" I ease off the parapet and step into the cold air waiting beyond his reach. A tiny sigh of relief slips through my lips, distracting me from the words I meant to say but no longer have the courage to speak. *I'm enslaved to a murderer. That's how this works.*

"The old stories about banshees are short on details, apart from the singing and the dying parts, but," Dovan's tone grows lighter, "they never mentioned you'd be beautiful."

I hold perfectly still as the air warms behind me as he steps closer.

"Or brave."

"I'm not," I slump forward, gritting my teeth. "I'm not brave."

"You have to be brave. You couldn't stand beside me, knowing what's coming, if you weren't."

I don't—*what do I say?* I don't even know what to feel.

Dovan gently turns me around. I focus on his boots, too scared to see whatever emotion caused him to say such things. He lifts his hand and brings his palm to my face. I tense, a self-preserving reflex that's been broken into my bones. His hand stops an inch from my cheek. Dread needles my skin in a painful reminder of what so many other hands have done, but Dovan isn't trying to hurt me.

He's offering me the chance to be touched, to be treated like a human being. A miracle I thought my curse had made impossible. And his hesitation, when he could have laid his hand on my face or any other part of me seconds ago, shows me he understands what no one else has even tried to. *He knows I've been hurt.* So he waits.

He gives me what my curse has taken. A choice.

I grip his wrist and draw his hand the rest of the way, inhaling the moment his skin settles against my cheek. There's a soft hiss that triggers a resounding crack deep in my soul. I'm shaking but I'm not falling apart.

A smile teases his mouth as he leans in. Letting him cup my face is one thing, letting his lips get any closer to mine is another. I tilt my head down, allowing a strip of chilled air to slip between my cheek and his palm.

"You're wrong, you know." Dovan doesn't come any closer, but he doesn't withdraw either. "I'm glad you're here with me."

I look up into his face and find no lie, no malice, no cunning. Nothing to justify the shiver scraping my skin. *He wants me here.* To be with him on his last day. A flush of heat challenges the ice protecting my heart, but something's wrong with Dovan's eyes. His right one is brighter than his left, reflecting a shade of color beyond monochrome. *Almost like—*

The tower bell clangs and he pulls away. I stay where I am, one hand on the cheek he touched, staring into the space where he was standing. *It wasn't a color.* It couldn't be. I don't see color anymore.

Dovan has leapt onto the parapet, scanning the horizon. "They've spotted another band of refugees." He jumps down. "I have to go back."

I meet his gaze, new questions piecing themselves together in my heart, but I don't know how to voice any of them.

Dovan picks up enough clues from my slightly, parted mouth and wet eyes. He takes my hand in his, his thumb caressing my skin in a gesture that's far more intimate than a simple, comforting touch. "Come find me when you're ready."

I lift my hand, too afraid to hope, but for the second time, there are light brown cracks in my gray palm. Cracks of *color* weave jagged paths across the area he rubbed. *It won't last.* It can't last. Unless I'm wrong about the one thing I've always accepted as unbreakable.

What if my curse can be broken?
What if Dovan is the key?

RED DEATH

8

WRAITH IS NEVER *where she should be in this game.*

The guider left. She's staring after him, touching her cheek like some dream-sick child. I straddle the parapet, my cape unfurling in the breeze. I've left a crimson blood trail in the snow and up the wall where I climbed. My trophy chain clinking against the stone should have given me away. *Not this time.* A worrying development.

That guider has stolen the focus of her heart. *Time to get it back.*

The chain whips through the air and lands a few feet from Wraith, tugging a still-warm wolf's head with it. The wet splat of its open mouth on stone, the grinding clank of the skidding chain, Wraith's squeak of a scream as she jumps when the head knocks against her leg—*priceless.* Definitely one of my top ten entrances. Why settle for startling her with my voice—*so ordinary*—when there's a wolf's head lying around? So convenient. I should thank whoever ripped the animal's head from its body.

Wraith retreats several quick steps. She bars her arms over her stomach, which judging by the paling of her face, must be giving an outstanding acrobatic performance.

"You."

There's an accusation somewhere in that single word. Pity it's not meant for the real me. *The face again.* Maybe I should change back to myself. But that would spoil the purpose of this little talk with my disobedient banshee. So, with a disappointed sigh, I lift my other leg over the parapet and land on the wall with a slap of boots on stone and several splatters of fresh blood dripping from my fingers.

I cock a brow, smirking, and lean against the parapet. "I was beginning to think that guider would never leave you alone."

Her glare softens as the shock of my appearance fades. She focuses on my guider's tunic, making the connection. "You?"

I control the urge to roll my eyes. *You'd think she'd have more to say.* After my scheme forced Dovan to kill two guiders and send me to die on the ice. *Or did he?* I finger the bloody arrowhead tucked into my belt. I plucked it from the body of the wolf he shot so I'd have a chance. *He should have just killed me.* Not that he could. The disguise would die, not me. I cast the arrow aside. Wraith flinches as it clatters on the stone.

"But you—" she darts to the side of the wall overlooking the snowfields, searching for the iron post they chained me to and the wolves. Oh, she'll find them all right. What's left of them anyway. *Ten, fifteen pieces?* I lost count because I was having too much fun. My dagger may control which human lives I take and how I end them, but it has no interest in the death of wild beasts. I'm free to kill wolves however and whenever I want.

I duck my chin to hide the smile begging to surface. The wolves should have known better than to attack a predator like me, but the rips in my sleeves reveal the marks of their single bites. *It was only fair they got a taste of the meal they'd never live to enjoy.* I prefer my prey to have a chance. A sentiment both Dovan and I share. Though, I doubt he has the guts to call anyone beneath him *prey.*

Wraith gasps, backing away and tripping over the chain and the wolf head. I catch hold of her arm before she falls and lands face-to-face with its bloody teeth. See, I can be nice.

"How did you escape?" She studies the chain, the very broken manacle. A party trick really. When her gaze settles on my face, she swallows. *Nervous.*

My cape billows around us. The edges flash crimson as the dagger refuses to disguise me from the second soul bent to its will. Her wide eyes flicker with a delightful mix of horror and anger. But not fear.

"It *was* you. This whole time." She pulls from my grasp, getting my blood on her hand, which she hurries to rub off on her ruined dress. *Pity.* Red looks good on her gray skin. A much-needed pop of color. I'd paint her with my own blood if I knew she wouldn't lose her mind.

"Isn't killing Dovan enough for you?"

"What?" I gesture to the pale bear on my chest. "You think this was all for him? You think too highly of the importance of one guider."

Her posture straightens as a flash of fire brightens her dark irises. "You made him a murderer."

"If only that were true." It'd sweeten my victory, but Dovan's protective instincts drove his violence. *How annoying.* What should have been an easy win for me deflates into a bitter draw. He didn't even savor the kills. *Such a waste.*

I back Wraith into the parapet until nothing but a sliver of air stands between us. "Why would you care what I do to him?"

She won't look at me. "I always care."

"Not for a long time you haven't. I broke that out of you." I brush a wavy strand of hair from her cheek and she steps to the side. *Can't let her discomfort rule my actions.* I lean closer, breathing in her scent of sweaty tears and stinging cold.

Her eyelids droop and her lips tremble as I sink my fingers into the thick mass of waves at the base of her skull. The muscles along her shoulders and back stiffen at our minor physical contact. *She hates this.* My touch, my nearness. I don't blame her. There are so many wonderful, brutal things I could do to her. Push her over the wall. Wrench her face toward mine. Break her fingers just to watch them heal and break them again. But using violence against her starves the rage burning in my soul, reinforcing what I've always known.

She's not my prey.

I'm not a danger to her.

But she is a danger to me.

I force the sneer she expects. "If you show any more concern for that guider, I'll have to start calling you sour face." I drag my bloodied thumb along her jaw, leaving a sticky trail of red behind as she whimpers. "Pretty, pretty, sour face." *If you find thin faces drawn tight by fear and made grim by shame attractive.* I go for sharper things. Not soft and caring and powerless. Still, the guider sees something of value in her.

All the more reason to stab his heart.

Multiple times. I'm in that kind of mood.

I slide my fingers from her jaw and step back. "I expect to hear the guider's song in full by midnight, Wraith." That earns a fresh flood of tears. "Don't make me wait." A perfect conversation ender if ever there was one. Except my banshee isn't bowing. She doesn't cringe or beg for mercy or try to flee.

The angle of her chin nears defiance as she stares me down, her glare all but yelling *you're a monster* at me. She can't even stand up to me without her body betraying her. The trembling of her hands, the twitching of her lips, the slight inward curl of her shoulders, all pointing to her true nature. *The cowering girl.* The one who knows how to take a beating but not how to make a stand. *Shall I tell her how unnatural courage looks on her?*

She'll never challenge me.

We both know how that would end.

Still, she's holding my gaze for the first time in years. *That guider is getting to her.* In a way that threatens me, that threatens *us.* Feeding her with lies, telling her she's brave, and treating her like she isn't *my* favorite tool. Well, second only to my dagger.

Good thing I know all her weak spots and the right words guaranteed to shatter the sliver of confidence she's displaying. "Of course I'm a monster, but I'm not the only one here, am I?" I snatch her chin and jerk upwards before she can react. "Did you forget what you are? What I *made* you?" She flinches in my hold, but there's no escaping me or what we've done. "If it wasn't for you, my darling banshee, today wouldn't be his. Last. Day."

Few things are as rewarding as sinking my dagger into a beating heart, but words themselves are another type of blade. I watch mine cut her deep. A physical impact as devastating as ramming my fist into her gut as she stumbles a few steps away. She doubles over, gripping the parapet for balance. *Strange.* How Wraith takes on the sins of others as if they were her own.

You used to make her laugh. I sway on my feet, unnerved by such an idea. A dull pain knocks on my chest, but there's nothing living inside to answer. Joy is for the weak. *I prefer to make Wraith cry.* The next blow that will take out her knees burns on my tongue, but my clenched teeth form a wall.

All warmth flees my skin. There's a reason why I never break her completely, buried under an emotion I will never admit exists.

I. Do. Not. Care.

I kneel, pretending to wiggle a loose stone near her as I clamp down on the disgusting desire to offer her comfort. Her hitching breaths grow as wet as her face, which she hides in her thick hair. A vengeful rage chars my soul. *I hate that sound.*

Wraith is crying, and the answer she needs escapes before I can stop it. "The men the guider killed. They *were* guilty."

She jolts upright. I stand with her, my anger shifting from sympathetic to cruel as the dagger I carry burns with hunger against my hip.

I taught her not to care, to be a queen of ice. I freed her from the tangled web of emotions. *And here she is.* Rejecting my gifts. Moving backwards. Returning to a mere girl, ordinary and forgettable when I made her special. I made her a force to be feared.

Fine. Let her have her little relapse. It won't change anything. The guider will be dead in a few hours and she will once more be mine. Mine alone.

"What did you do?" Her glare cuts across my face and stabs into my eyes. Our little interaction just became fun.

"You heard me. The guider only *thinks* he's guilty of murder." A brilliant tactic, if you ask me. Some of the best ways to destroy a man are no more complex or bloody than a single idea planted in their heads. I cross my arms, lips twitching wider. "The guilt must be eating him alive."

"They were guilty—" Wraith pushes me, "—because of *you*."

Now my grim smirk *is* real. I've missed her righteous outbursts of violence. *Perhaps we're not so different.* "I did help things along."

"You? Help?" She scoffs, turning her back on me as she leaves. "You only know how to help yourself."

I let her go, but not before getting the final word. "You didn't think murder was my only game, did you? I'm always playing more than one."

She spins round and a glint of gold flickers in her irises, wiping the smirk from my face. "*You* are corruption. You ruin everything you touch."

I hardly notice her words. *Gold.* A color I haven't seen since...

Before.

Before her eyes turned black. I shudder as the gold spreads, throbbing through the veins in her skin until she shines with hope. Hope the guider inspired. *You have to stop this—*

Before.

Before what? There's no answer, but that doesn't stop the word *before* from hanging like a threat over me. A promise made, an oath sworn, a defeat I can't allow. I stalk closer to my banshee, hands curling into claws ready to tear into her skin.

"You won't corrupt Dovan." A slight tremor rattles her voice as she retreats. "He's stronger than you."

I grab her by the neck and lift her onto her toes. She doesn't struggle. She knows better than to fight me. Her gaze sharpens with a challenge to match her soul against mine, to finally battle this out between the two of us.

I apply more pressure, grinning at the soft choking sound she makes. "You're probably right about that guider, but we both know it's a different story when it comes to you, my *loyal* banshee. You are not strong enough." I give her a little shove.

She trips and falls, landing hard on her rump, and I bend over her. "All I have to do to defeat you is say one. Little. Word. Shall I?"

Fear of what I will force her to do shreds the hope in her eyes. They've returned to their normal pitch-black shade, empty and subdued. The guider's influence on her is no match for my power. *I'm going to make him beg.* Because he made Wraith long for a different future. A mistake I'll carve into his chest. After all, I don't have to kill him quickly. I can make death linger. Make it hurt worse than anything he's ever known until he's desperate for the end. And it all starts with a single word. A word hissing through my throat, as deadly as a wolf's four-fanged bite.

"*Sing.*"

Wraith inhales, opens her mouth, and does what I command. Like she always does. She sings a growing string of notes as tears stream down her face. They repeat, over and over, through her gritted teeth.

I dig my fingers into her jaw and force her head up, stopping the song. "Now, go find him." I yank her to her feet and point her toward the city. "And finish his song."

"I hate you," she whispers before groaning as my curse takes control of her voice to fulfill what *I* want.

"Maybe, but you'll never act on it," I lean next to her ear. "That's what sets you apart from him. He's a man of action, and you, well. You run away. I told you once running away would have consequences." I push her forward. "Who knew they would be so much fun for me?"

She never looks back, not even once. *I win.*

Wraith is out of sight when the pain hits hard, driving like an iron spike into my chest. I double over as my vision flares blinding hot. The quiet of the snowfields is ripped apart as I'm dragged deeper into my own mind. Someone is screaming. *My voice.* But different. The desperation, the defeated tone marks me as a loser.

Blood pools along a marble floor, thick and dark like wine, and there's a body sprawled in the middle like an island of decaying flesh. *Just one?* I've killed so many the sight of a single body is almost meaningless.

Almost.

My hands start shaking. I clutch my dagger, drawing on its power, but I can't break free of the image. *This kill is old.* A reminder and a warning of the one thing I fear. The failure I sacrificed everything to erase.

This isn't real. But the body was real.

"Who bleedin' cares," I mutter, pushing through the pain as I always do. With a stamp of my boot, the image flickers. The marble floor fades into the muddy stones of Riffen's wall. I blink my vision back to normal red hues without looking at the body's face. Why would it matter who it is? None of my victims have been worth remembering.

I am Red Death. I kill and kill again. I don't grow tired. I don't lose focus. And no one escapes my bloody game once it's begun. A twinge of a sneer pulls at the corner of my mouth as I mark the setting position of the sun.

Won't be long now. Till I end the man who tempts Wraith to hope. When I am done with him—*she'll never hope again.*

WRAITH

9

THE LITTLE BOY clutches a shredded scarf to his chest, his knit cap swallowing his puffy face. Dark stains spot his clothes and taint the air with notes of copper, salt, and urine. I hate the way survival has marked him. Every time the wolves howl, the boy goes pale and wedges himself deeper into the crevice between the wall and a barrel of torch oil.

If no one helps him, grief will become his grave. He's already falling into the silence of shock. I search for a capable comforter, but only guiders stand this close to the open gates after dark. *They should shut them.* At least at night when a clever wolf could sneak in. The safety of the city, of children like him, should matter more than a gesture of hope. I grimace.

When is hope anything more than a gesture?

Lowered voices distract me, shifting my focus a few feet to my left where the wall ends. Brilliant silver light glows through the gate and washes the figures of four men in shadowed tones. Forgemasters lit the bonfires outside the gates at dusk. Unlike normal fire, their burns hotter and brighter and will last all night on a single log, eliminating the risk of tending the flames when the wolves are most active.

Yet another symbol meant to inspire hope. My stomach rolls, knotted and sour. Tonight, the terrified boy I'm watching over joins me in knowing how ineffective light can be against monsters.

"Where did you find him?" Dovan's voice rises above the others as the four of them huddle together for warmth, their breaths creating puffs of cloud.

The shortest guider with a braided beard wraps a bandage around his forearm, wincing as he replies, "The orchards. Due south."

Dovan shakes his head as if that's the worst possible answer. *What is he waiting for?* I've never seen him hesitate or hold back when it comes to rescuing people. My heart sinks further. He'd never stand there if he thought the boy's family might still be alive. "The parents?"

The guider in the middle with an axe perched on his shoulder spits into the snow as the others stiffen. Each of them failing to put whatever bloody scene they came upon into words.

The bearded guider uses his teeth to help tie off his bandage as he speaks. "He's an orphan now." This time they all look at the boy, their gazes slanted down, heavy with pity.

Are you trying to crush him? I step into their line of sight. Not that being the boy's invisible shield will do him any good, but it's the only thing I can do. He curls into himself until he's hardly two feet of skin and bone. I drop to my knee, but my hands stay at my sides. A desire I can't fulfill stabs outward through my chest—to hold him the way no one can ever hold me. *He'd feel it.* The weight of my arms pressing his pieces together. *But he wouldn't understand.* My invisible touch would bring more harm, more fear.

"He might have family in the city," Dovan sounds closer, a tepid wave of his heat brushing my spine.

"There's little hope of that."

Heartless. No other word fits the axe-wielding guider's callous tone and the mumbles of agreement from the other two. I glare at them, but my anger dims as the torch anchored near the gate exposes the cracks in their cold demeanor. Cuts and bruises mar their skin and peek through tears in their clothes. Fresh blood, as crimson as Red Death's cape, speckles the white bears on their tunics, reminding me why they can't indulge their emotions while on duty.

These guiders fought for him. They fought to save a child from the beasts who preyed on his family, and they're preparing to go out there again, dipping fresh torches into the oil and lighting them. Three weary men against savage wolves with the taste for human flesh.

Where are the other members of their patrol? I start counting guiders. Six on the wall above the gate with bows, always facing the snowy landscape and the darkness beyond the bonfires. Two more are stationed on the ground within the arch, spears clutched in their hands, and a dozen monitor the emptying lower market.

"I'll take the boy with me." Dovan catches my eye as he volunteers. "If anyone has news of his family, it'll be Ioana."

The guiders all clasp arms, nodding to each other before separating for their tasks. Dovan stares after them for a while before turning from the gate and the dangers his fellow guiders face outside it.

I move aside. Dovan wraps his cloak around the boy, and then lifts the child's motionless little body into his arms. He cradles the boy against his chest and scans our surroundings.

The citizens and the guiders pack up the rations and the supplies as the lower market closes. The hunters from the morning string their wolves on spits over roaring fires as promised, bringing a touch of merriment to the bitter breeze, but winter's blistering breath thins the crowd. Not even a little roasted meat can tempt them to stay. *Maybe they'll return when the hunters finish cooking.*

Most of the refugees have been settled within the city, leaving a few stragglers behind who gather by the cook fires. Firelight glints off the whites of their eyes and their teeth, but the emotion exposed by the fire isn't fear. It's—*relief.* It's hope. *How can they smile?* Don't they know they haven't been saved?

No one here is safe. Not even the child in Dovan's arms.

He's moving. The deep freeze of shock thawing from the boy's bones. He takes deeper and deeper breaths, his shoulders trembling. Two little hands wriggle through the cloak to curl around the nape of Dovan's neck in an anxious lock. A tiny sob escapes the boy's lips. He holds on so tightly his stubby fingers turn white.

"You're safe," Dovan whispers to him, left hand sweeping along the child's back.

I follow, humming Dovan's song, as he leads us through the lower market. We wind through an alley where the houses' upper stories lean over the path, spilling a deeper darkness, like puddles of black poison, from their sagging windows.

Dovan's boot catches on a loose stone and he stumbles. I reach for his arm, wanting to steady him, but he doesn't need my help. He's already righted himself, his steps sure once more as he shifts the boy closer to his shoulder. My hand falls. I move farther to the left, slipping into blackened shadows and the icy embrace of winter.

How long can he keep going?

The sun fell behind night's inky curtain hours ago, and yet Dovan remains on duty. *He must be starving.* And tired. My legs ache and my head grows heavy from following him. I haven't seen him eat a meal that's more than a half strip of jerky or sit down for longer than a few minutes. I doubt he'd ever be selfish enough to devour a full plate of food, preferably followed by a nap. Not when his sacrifice would make a difference to another frightened, hopeless person. *He needs to keep up his strength.* If he faints from hunger or exhaustion and collapses, he won't be able to help anyone.

A knife made of cold pricks my sternum. *Maybe that's the point.* These are Dovan's last hours. His final chances to do what he loves most. The blade presses deeper, bringing with it a pain I've tried so hard to keep from destroying my heart.

The pain of watching people run out of time.

Plenty of Red Death's victims were selfish with their final hours, indulging in pleasures they'd denied themselves, getting the revenge they'd never pay the consequences for, or burying themselves in busywork. They fought, they ran, they tried to hold on, but Dovan—*he gives and gives and gives.*

This is his way of saying goodbye.

A wail burns my throat, adding another note to his song and bringing us closer to his end. An ending I care more about than I should.

I always care. I grimace, tasting the lie in what I'd said to Red Death.

"Not for a long time you haven't. I broke that out of you." His answer replays in my mind and I suck in a freezing gasp of air. It hurts, stinging deep into my lungs as Dovan glances at me. One broken soul already fills his arms, and yet he still makes room for me. His gentle message clear. *I hear you.*

His kindness pours through my cracks in a flood of warmth, filling them in and trying to make me whole. All while the moon crests over the buildings before us, creeping nearer to midnight, to Red Death's ultimatum.

"Don't make me wait."

How do I tell Dovan he has a few hours left to live? That this boy he carries might be the last person he gets to help?

I shrink into the shadows cast by the houses overhanging the alley. Their numbing chill whispers of what I wish wasn't true. *You will survive him.* My lip trembles and I bite it and hug myself as the tremor spreads into my core. I know what happens once he's gone. Every good thing Dovan has poured into my soul will drain away. Once more I'll be nothing but a wraith, hollow and alone and *hated*. Embracing the role of my curse. I'll be Red Death's banshee, forever haunted by a single question.

If I didn't sing, would they still die?

On cue, Dovan's song whispers through my lips, anchoring my focus on the guider who's made the mistake of thinking I'm worth any of the moments he has left. Once more our eyes lock. His betray genuine concern. Mine—*what does he see?* But a banshee with a banshee's futile choice.

Because I'm singing. *I always sing.*

The alley opens into a broad street that dead ends at a large, chipped-stone house. Four-stories tall and three houses wide, the inn huddles over the half-moon courtyard like a mamma bear gathering up every scrap of space as if the adjacent buildings are her disobedient cubs. Two mermaid statues support the over-hanging upper levels and frame a tear-shaped doorway. Each window glows with warmth and hope, while laughter and music trickle out through the slatted front door.

The Mermaiden. It's a pet name for this place, derived from The Mermaid Inn.

A splintered board serves as a sign and hangs crooked from a chain between the coral-crowned heads of the mermaids, their tail fins twisted up as if beckoning people inside. Faded letters spell out— *Welcome.* My hummed notes fall into melancholy. If there's one thing I've never been wherever I show my face, it is welcome.

Dovan tromps up the steps and pushes through the swinging doors. A blast of firelight and the clamor of voices escape behind him. The beckoning heat coils around my upper body, tightening and tugging me after him, but the moment my foot falls on the first step, I freeze. The creak it emits under my weight nibbles along my skin, tasting me on behalf of an unfamiliar but ravenous fear.

Don't go in.

I hesitate, waiting for an explanation that never comes.

My legs shake under me as I climb the last few steps and cross the landing until I'm pressed against the doors. My mouth opens, the strange and sudden dread giving way to awe.

Pale flames dance in starfish lantern wheels hung like rustic chandeliers from the beamed ceiling, casting out bands of light in flickering rings. Close to a hundred people sit at seashell shaped tables covered in sparkling mosaics, crowd around the pearl-toned bar running the full length of the back wall, or slip into darkened booths along the sides to conduct secret business or exchange the latest rumors.

Sea creatures, carved into the molding that gilds the top of the walls and support pillars in a bit of shine, bare their teeth or offer sly grins at the people who never look up. Another mermaid coils by a stairway that twists up into the darker shadows of the upper floors. A fire roars through the mouth of a great sea serpent to the right of the door, hissing out flames and bristling heat. *Whoever built this place must have come from Ceana.* The land to the east full of salt and lakes and deadly sirens.

There's a raised platform in the left corner where a seahorse-shaped harp sits. It sparkles as the player's fingers dance over the strings. My stomach upends over a wave of dread.

Time to sing.

I tear my gaze from the harp and stumble into the inn, my voice trembling as it tries to cover the harp's twanging notes with Dovan's song. *Find him and get out.* A simple task complicated by the number of people crammed inside this place.

I dodge a man's chair as he leaps to his feet, angry over a lack of potatoes in his stew. I duck under a woman's arm as she points toward the harp and giggles as the boy plucks the wrong notes. He's lost the rhythm of the song and earns a chorus of jeers. I twist through a tangle of men and women speaking in low voices, more than one pale bear reflecting the firelight on their chests.

Spilled *voda* splashes over my boots as the people at the bar clang their tankards together. My lips curl in disgust. *Yet another example of how the old king has failed them.* Allowing root vegetables like carrots or potatoes to be fermented into spirits. *Such a waste when so many are hungry.* Still, there is a partial blessing in drink. Those at the bar wear the easiest grins in the room. *Voda* helps them forget they're all dying one reduced ration at a time.

They tell a dark joke about a child crying over wolves and roar with laughter. My icy fingers curl into fists because I know a boy who's crying, who carries a scarf stained with the blood of his parents. If they're laughing at him—*the coldhearted-cowards.* As one of the men stumbles from the bar, I stick my foot out and let a justified grin take over my face. Not that the fool will see it, for his sneering mouth, which feasts on the tragedy of a little boy, is about to become acquainted with the stone tiles of the floor.

He trips, falling backwards, and his companions reach for him. But the *voda* has worked its magic on their abilities to recover. They tumble across the floor with *moans,* and *oofs,* and half-bitten-off *curses.*

"Remind me never to make you angry."

I hear the smirk in Dovan's voice before I locate him. He's halfway through another set of swing doors, his lips tweaked higher on one side, but his arms are empty. *Where's the boy?* He shouldn't be left alone in such a traumatized state. Dovan jerks his head over his shoulder in answer to my unspoken question, and I follow him into a kitchen.

Salty brine, earthy and pungent with herbs, fills my lungs as I take a deep breath. A massive wood-burning stove takes up the entire wall in front of me. Several young women and young men, all under the watchful instruction of a stooped, old man with bristly whiskers, rush around the stove with pots, spoons, vegetables, and heavy cloths to protect their hands as they check whatever is baking. Hints of cardamom and rare honey turn the hot, salty air sweet. Dovan grasps my arm, guiding me into a narrow hall that runs parallel to the bar. The rowdy laughter is muffled, but my stomach still twists over how cruel some can be.

Small bedrooms open on the right, all plainly furnished and empty. I linger at each doorway, but Dovan pulls me along before I finish looking for the boy's knit cap or any sign he's here. The hall ends in a communal chamber. Mismatched chairs and settees shoved against the walls frame the stairwell to the guest quarters above, while a bright mural of sirens swim-dancing around a crescent-shaped ice floe covers the wall. At the center of the ice stands a pale tree with snowflakes instead of leaves. The symbol of the season everyone else hates. *Do sirens still worship winter?*

Dovan's hand grazes the middle of my back as he guides me further into the room. The little boy sits in a chair with Dovan's cloak draped over his shoulders, his parent's scarf dangling from his curled fingers. Relief eases the tension in my spine. *He's safe.* Far from the wall and the wolves whose howls remind him of the horror he survived. I blink away sudden moisture as I glance at Dovan and find tears present in his eyes as well. *Does he see himself in this child?*

As I study our surroundings with renewed curiosity, I think about our time in the market when Dovan called the sour-faced granny his *Gran*, revealing he was once orphaned. *Was he brought to a place like this?*

A slender older woman kneels before the boy. *She must be Ioana.* The woman Dovan mentioned at the gate. She offers the child a steaming mug with a medicinal smell. *Nightwell tea.* A soothing blend of herbs laced with a pinch of hope, a promise that tomorrow will be better. He doesn't seem convinced as fresh tears stain his flushed-gray cheeks, but the violence of his sobbing has calmed for now.

The woman leans up and kisses the boy's forehead before rising and approaching Dovan. Her skin is the darkest shade of night, pale hair fuzzy and cropped close to her scalp, and her irises glimmer the liquid black of an untamed sea pricked by glimmers of starlight. *Ceanan.* The land of bewitching sirens and deadly songs. *Something we have in common.* I restrain the urge to look for the sparkle of scales peeking over the high collar buttoned around her long neck or the whisper of finned feet under her skirt's hem.

She guides Dovan toward the hall behind me, a clear signal she doesn't want the boy to overhear what she's about to say. "You were right to bring him here. I'll send my runners through the city tomorrow, but," she sighs, shaking her head, "I fear we both know he's alone now."

Dovan crosses his arms, a defensive stance taken against our harsh reality.

The gentleness of Ioana's knowing smile only grows wider. "He reminds me of another boy a different guider brought to my inn."

I shift my gaze between them. *Does she mean Dovan?*

"Your father was a good man, like you. I'm sure this boy will find a family as you did." Ioana squeezes his arm to accent the word *family*. A flicker of pain tightens Dovan's jaw as his eyes darken.

She thinks he should adopt the boy?

Ioana takes both of Dovan's arms, unfolding their crossed line, steadying him even though he is twice her size. "You shouldn't doubt yourself. Years of service as a guider have already taught you how to care for the vulnerable, how to guide them and how to meet their needs. You'll be a great father."

I can't is written all over his sagging expression, but the desire to say yes is there, burning through the tears lining his lower eyelids. He blinks them away before they fall. I retreat into the shadowed hall, arms folding to guard my heart because—*it's me.* I am why he can't.

As if to further illustrate the point, the curse forces me to sing the beginning of his song again. I grit my teeth to lock the notes inside, to hold them to a whisper, but Red Death's magic has never cared about what I wanted.

The volume of my voice rises, growing louder and louder, until everything I want to hide about who I am, about why I exist, is flung into the air for all to hear. A ghostly cry of wind that rips through clothes, topples unsteady furniture, and coaxes out a few shouts from the patrons on the other side of the wall. Dovan's shoulders stiffen. His head moves, turning my way, but our eyes never quite reach each other. For the first time, he shows a twinge of regret over one thing.

Hearing my voice.

There's nothing so painful as being someone's deepest regret.

You don't have to stay here. The curse doesn't care how close I am to Dovan as long as I sing his song. *This was a mistake.* Following a few steps behind him when I should have stayed a hundred steps back. I should have kept my heart encased in ice, safe from hope, safe from him. Because my heart is crumbling, having tasted what it will *never* have.

His—*don't think it*—love. I grimace. The wind screeches down my throat, my gasping breath rushing in, as if I could withdraw such an admission.

The word love conjures up daydreams of romance and happily-ever-afters. I stopped believing in fairytales years before I met Dovan. The only kind of love that could tempt me now wouldn't be based on happiness or frilly feelings or shooting stars. *Can you imagine Dovan ever loving that way?* It's ridiculous. A sip of champagne fading long before dawn. No, the love I crave, the love Dovan offers, is deep and solid and a true gift. Romance has nothing to do with it. His love is a choice.

A choice to be kind, to listen, to guide. A choice to just be there. *He never runs.* But the intentional turning of his back is a clear message. His love is not meant for me. Through the blurring tears and the hollow ache counting down in my chest, I sing.

Our ending has begun.

All the beautiful, hopeful things he made me feel earlier in the day wither into an icy poison. He isn't the cure to what's wrong with me.

I face the wall. Dovan's and Ioana's voices cut through my singing as they discuss her need for a ration delivery. I don't care what they say. I don't care if I never hear Dovan again. I've woken from a dream where there was more to us than a curse and a song. Red Death might play games, but he's never made me believe in something *more*.

"You run away."

I run because there's no reason to stay. *There can never be a reason.* I'm cursed and I bring death to anyone who hears me.

It takes little effort to turn my back and retreat, but even as I leave Dovan behind, his song stays stuck in my throat, an unbreakable knot of sorrow and shame tying us together in all the ways I wish we weren't.

SIX YEARS BEFORE WINTER

SURPRISES WERE THE worst kind of secrets to keep. Had the boy known this before he convinced the girl to brave the city's streets alone with him, he might have thought better of his strategy. Things had cooled between them ever since the Announcement decided their future. Being a creature who craved distance from most people, the boy should have been fine. Except when it came to her, he was never fine. Not if she wasn't by his side.

Weakness. Perhaps, but the one weakness he allowed himself involved her smile, her laugh, her song. A sound so powerful it would change their fate. Only a fool would say she had the voice of a siren. To the boy, sirens were petty creatures best left for dead in the Abrykarran desert. Sirens sang nothing but lies. The girl sang the truth. Her songs were real, not traps built of gilded dreams, and he was determined to make her father understand.

Their father. His hands coiled into fists. With gritted teeth, he kept the curses that man deserved inside. The man had silenced her voice, forbidding her music, forbidding the boy from encouraging her.

"She must be strong."

But what the boy knew and the father failed to see—*there are many kinds of strength.*

The boy had learned that lesson the hard way. His understanding came by pain. A pain he never could outrun. He heard it in the clink of every step, felt it in the rub of metal against his calves and shins, and tasted it in the bitten side of his cheek. But tonight wasn't about him.

This is for her.

The girl who should be singing.

A problem the boy expected his surprise would fix. *Oh, the look on the old man's face when he finds out.* That his most obedient child had defied him and made a public spectacle of herself. Her rebellion wouldn't come without risks, of course, but risk was the true flavor of life.

It's time she had a taste.

WRAITH

10

I BURST through the kitchen's swinging doors into the front room of the Mermaiden, no longer concerned about the whispers behind me.

"Did you see that? The doors moved on their own."

"Must have been the wind again."

I force myself deeper into the crowd. There's less space between people than there was. I ricochet between them, bouncing off their sides, and every bump of their bodies against mine aches deep into my bones. The air grows thick with dozens of conflicting smells. The briny stew melding with sweat, leather, and steel, choking under a heavy layer of pipe-smoke, yeasty *voda*, and unwashed skin. My stomach twists as I wrench through a couple reaching for each other, only to find a solid line of men and women standing in my way.

The door flaps open behind them, letting in a rush of frigid air. To get past them, I'd have to shove my way through, but they're not drunk enough to blame each other for my escape. The curse protects me, but only to a point. If one of them made a grab for me and caught me—I shut my eyes and take a deep, song-free breath. *You can do this.*

It would be easier if Dovan was leading the way.

I sag forward. *I don't want him with me.*

Applause breaks out across the line and spreads through the room, and then silence falls. Even the cowards at the bar have ceased their vile jokes, though their rude slurping of *voda* continues. Everyone's attention has shifted to the platform behind me where tentative fingers stroke the seahorse harp's strings. The notes are as sharp as knives. They stab through my heart and cut into my soul. *Don't turn around. Don't look.*

I'm already turning.

A girl with a braided crown of hair plucks the harp with growing confidence. She never strums a wrong note while a boy near her age fidgets beside her. His thick curls hang in his face. He flicks them back with a jerk of his head, revealing two dimples with his nervous smile. *Just like...*

Their image shifts, warping, as my mind switches the boy to the harp, and the girl becomes the one lacking confidence. The one being asked to perform. My stomach knots as the song they play bows to the melody ringing in my ears. The inn grows darker. The crowd larger. Sweat slicks my skin as the urge to escape pulses through my tingling limbs, but I'm frozen in place.

I was here.

I stood on that stage beside that harp.

And I wasn't alone.

"Go on. Sing." The girl encourages the boy, and he tries. He opens his mouth, but I sing for him. Deep, haunted notes of bitter sorrow, somehow overpowering my curse.

A song to break the hardest heart.

That's what we named it. *We?* Icy-claws rip down my chest and I gasp. Everything goes fuzzy as a pain more wicked than any

I've ever felt burrows under my skin and grips my bones before sinking teeth into my heart. *I can't remember.* Who was with me, why we were wrong to perform, or why the song we chose mattered.

The boy's round face scrunches, confused by how my voice replaced his, when an idiot at the bar shouts, "He sings like a girl!"

Others join him, jeering and laughing until they drown out the harp, and the embarrassed boy runs off the stage.

The girl chases after him. "Come back!"

I flinch because someone shouted the same words at me when I ran.

I didn't want this. A stage or a crowd to entertain.

I wanted—the chilled sting of a tear sliding down my cheek cuts my thought off in the middle. The memory and the melody that escaped my curse fragments into meaningless background noise.

When I turn away, Dovan is standing in front of me, eyebrows drawn together in concern. The understanding behind his worried expression rubs salt in an already stinging wound. *Why does he care?* I've stolen his future with a song. The itch to flee scrapes its icy nails down my spine as tears blind me.

"Don't—"

I can't let him finish. Running away is the only thing that's helped me survive while living under a curse.

Once my right foot hits the tile, propelling me forward, there is no stopping the other. I run through the people in the way. They stumble and break apart, swearing, but I'm already through the door and out into the night.

Red Death was right. I always run, and it doesn't matter where.

I run through alleys thick with shadows and frozen filth, through lantern-lit streets glittering like fool's gold of brighter futures no one will witness, and past the frowning doors of homes that will never open for me. I run from the *caws* of excited crows whipped into a frenzy by my sudden haste, from the throbs of laughter lashing out from tavern doorways, and from the faces that one day might see mine because there is no ending for me.

For what I do.

Every exhale blasts through my throat in full, screeching melody. Dovan's song grips my soul and drags me down until my steps falter.

You can't outrun a curse.

My boot snags on a loose cobblestone. I pitch forward, my hands barely moving fast enough to provide a cushion before my face hits the ground. Everything goes black for a blink or two as silence hisses in my ears. *I've stopped singing.* I press my forehead against the street, grateful for a moment of peace, but the emptiness I had hoped to use as a shield fills with the noise of night.

All the sounds I—*loved.* A strange sense of knowing sparks a weak warmth in my chest. *I loved this city once.*

I close my eyes and listen.

To the chime of the tower bell marking half-past the seventh hour, to the wind rustling through wooden shutters, to the plodding of feet made lighter by thought of a night's revelry. So normal, so peaceful. All the different voices humming together in a symphony that swirls around me.

It's beautiful. And chaotic. Every voice, every sound woven into a single melody. A song that tells the story of survival.

I listen harder, embracing a banshee's ability to hear beyond normal human limits. A trick the curse allows so we can locate our victims anywhere by sound. I grimace, ignoring the pull of magic demanding I face the other direction, and focus on the streets south of me. The ones winding farther away from the inn where I left Dovan behind.

I don't want to find him. I want to hear the heart of my city while it still beats.

I focus on one group of voices at a time. Mothers and fathers telling night-tales to their children. Workers joking and clapping each other's shoulders. Friends and families gathered around meager meals softened by the joy of their company. Guiders giving bits of news and directions as different patrols pass each other. Young couples whispering from the rooftops as they dare to dream under the stars.

I glance up, longing to see what they do, but the sky is blank like my past. The stars are gone, quenched by a dark bank of clouds threatening to strengthen winter's hold on our throats. *Winter always wins.*

Red Death always wins.

Hope never stood a chance.

What was thawing inside me freezes solid as I shuffle onto my knees.

The first snowflake twirls down from the sky, shimmering like silver and pearl lace before it lands on my tattered skirt. I hold my breath, scoop the flake into my palm, and bring it close. *Please melt. Prove I belong here.* But the snowflake's star-shaped fronds remain as pristine as if it had fallen onto ice instead of human skin. I exhale, but my disappointed sigh is too cold to become vapor, to give witness to a warm heart beating inside my chest and hot blood pulsing in my veins.

Neither of which I have anymore.

My heart is sluggish and slow, beating a rhythm that's half of what it should be, and my blood is black, frigid, and thick as tar. It webs along under my pale-gray skin, etching lines like chains that can never be broken. I almost laugh at the irony.

The curse locks me in a half-state, neither fully alive nor dead. It's why I don't need to eat, or sleep, and it's why I don't age. The few times I've glimpsed my face in the glass of a window, or the reflection of those ridiculous banshee-revealing mirrors, I see the same young face. Unaltered by time or deed. With tired eyes and hollow cheeks and lips worn so thin a real smile could break them.

Smiles taste too much like hope. And hope for a banshee is always a cruel trap.

I let the snowflake slip through my fingers when one corner dips, shrinking. *It's melting!* A rush of relief prickles down my arms, right before I recognize the soft steps approaching from behind. The air is growing warmer, not my skin, which means—

Dovan.

He found me.

I shouldn't be surprised since he is a guider. Tracking is one of his strengths. *But he came looking for me.* When no one else would. I blink hard before my tears freeze into ice, keeping my head down.

Dovan kneels on my right in the middle of the street. A wave of heat reaches for me, turning the snow falling between us into a misting rain that glistens my skin and tightens the curl of my hair. I'm tilting towards him, all thoughts of our bleak future erased by the simple gift of his presence. Our shoulders touch, and I lose the battle against sinking into his warmth, against leaning on him.

He regrets you.

I snap my spine straight, breaking the spell. Cold spreads from my core, pushing his heat back and rescuing the snowflakes from a melted death. There's no point in letting this moment linger. Kneeling beside a banshee in the snow is not how Dovan wants to spend his last hours. I lean forward, palms against the cobblestones to help push myself to my feet when he breaks the silence.

"Why did you run?"

I sit on my heels, unsure of how to answer. *What happened back there?* The inn, the children on the stage who woke what must have been a memory, but now—*I don't know.*

I glance at Dovan out of the corner of my eye. His head angles up to the clouds and the dancing snow. Wonder shapes his lips into a soft, upward curve not even the threat of his impending death can overshadow. I mimic his posture, but wonder is a distant memory. All I feel is the icy kiss of winter's unending promise, a slow freezing death.

I look away, picking at the rips in my skirt. "Most of my victims would be happy if I ran from them."

"I am *not* your victim."

Saying that doesn't make it true. "You'll die because of my song."

"I will die, yes," his hand settles over mine, sending a jolt of heat up my arm, "but not because you sing."

I jerk my hand from under his and get up. "What is wrong with you? Are you blind to what I am?" I hold out my arms, displaying the dozens of snowflakes surviving on my skin. "What better proof is there that I am a monster when winter and I are allies?"

He stands up and dares a step closer.

"No. Stop!"

Dovan's wet eyes mirror the sorrow I can't acknowledge, as if he knows what I'm feeling and saw the broken memory I did. *That's nonsense.* How can I make sense to him when I can't even understand myself?

He moves forward again.

"Stay back!" I throw my hands out, retreating as my voice weakens. "You shouldn't even be here."

"Why shouldn't I be here with you?" He takes another step, putting us within reach of each other.

A spark of anger overpowers my more vulnerable emotions. "Why can't you understand?" I heave a breath in and out, scattering snowflakes into his wall of heat where they vaporize. "I'm a banshee! Hearing my voice dooms your soul! You should be running." I flex my fingers to hide their trembling, my gaze drifting down with the snow. "Or trying to kill me."

"I'm not running. And I'd never hurt you."

I've heard that before. But this is the first time I want to believe it as his hand appears next to mine. An open invitation that fills my heart with ice until I am heavy, smothered under a fear that's been my most loyal companion.

I always get hurt.

With a slight twitch, I fist the hand he would hold and try not to shiver from the warmth of his promise, of what it could mean if our circumstances were different. The jagged ache in my chest frames my reply as I look up at him. "Why not?"

Dovan's eyebrows rise, his lips parting at the insinuation I deserve to be harmed. *Why does that shock him?*

I deepen my study. Noting his straight-backed posture, his relaxed shoulders and calm hands. Nothing about the way he's standing identifies me as a threat. "Why aren't you like everyone else?" A telling question that bares too much of my already bruised heart.

Dovan's chin tilts downward, mouth opening and closing around the answer I need as he battles some inward struggle. "Did running or fighting save the others who heard you?"

I try to swallow the rising shame and fail. "No."

"Then ... " he hesitates and rubs the back of his neck before meeting my gaze. The fire burning in his eyes would terrify winter, but I'm not frightened by the intensity of his emotions. I'm holding my breath, waiting for him to speak, to act, to give this bleak moment a glimpse of real hope, but his silence remains unbroken.

Snowflakes land on my shoulders, my collarbones, my arms, creating a quilt of patchwork armor. The bite of their frosty touch hardens over my heart and cages its softness. "I'm not like your refugees, Dovan. I'm not like the orphans you carry to safety, or the people you serve."

His gaze narrows, sharpening into an objection, as if he still sees me as worthy. Worthy of his time. Worthy of the risk. Worthy of him. *Time to shatter that misguided notion.*

"Look at me." I lift my arms out to the side and expose my palms. Dovan's quick to notice the dozens of silver scars revealed by the hanging strips of my sleeves, his expression hardening as my stomach twists. "I am marked by the fear and the hatred of those my voice has doomed. My hands are stained with the blood of hundreds of innocents. I am—" A flood of tears blurs his face, the snow, the street and the houses as I force myself to admit my truth. "I am damaged. I am cursed. A murderer's tool. A city's dread."

The air rises in temperature, heating my skin. I blink several times and find Dovan has cut the distance between us in half. Our boots are almost touching, but I can't give up any ground now. "Every note I sing is a step closer to death. *Your* death. So yes, I am a monster like the stories say. I am as much to blame as—"

Whatever I was going to say disappears as his hands slide around my waist and my breath lodges in my throat. He pulls me toward him. I stumble and shift my head to the right at the last moment to avoid head-butting his chin as the strength of his arms, the firmness of his chest, enfold me in a solid embrace. My mind goes blank, overwhelmed by something so simple and yet so beyond words.

I don't know what to do. So I just let him hold me.

His breath ghosts along my cheek, lifting my hair. One of his hands runs up and down my back, stroking me as innocently as he did with the little boy, but his firm touch carves invisible fissures into my chilled skin, leaving trails of fire in his fingers' wake.

It's been so long since I've been held. My curse made this kind of embrace impossible, and yet Dovan breaks that rule. I shudder through a choked-off sob as I weaken just enough for my right arm to curl loosely against his back. *This is as far as I go.* There's nothing to be gained from falling apart in his arms. *In a few hours, they'll be cold like mine.* I swallow hard, pushing those unhappy thoughts down. I won't be robbed of this moment.

Closing my eyes, I rest my temple on his shoulder and breathe him in. There's a woodsy wildness to his scent, like the great pines to the east that have outlasted all other trees in this cursed winter. *Standing tall, still green and thriving.* There's also something sweet and young hidden under the heavier notes of leather, sweat, and steel. Something that doesn't belong in a land buried in snow.

Dovan's chest expands against mine as he prepares to speak. "Being a banshee doesn't make you a monster."

I stiffen, but he keeps his hold gentle, giving me the option to withdraw.

"When you're trying to save lives, it's not strange for your hands to have more bloodstains than a killer's. Saving lives is messy. You have to put your hands where the wounds are. You get bloody whether you save them or don't, but that doesn't mean their deaths are your fault. Don't carry the guilt of what someone else has done."

His words ache through me. I lift my head, twisting toward his collarbone, but can't bring myself to look at him. *All I carry is guilt.* The spark of hope drowns in the shame of what I am, of what I've helped Red Death do.

I'm never enough.

No matter how many stab wounds I've covered with my palms as I tried to stop the bleeding, I always fail. Dovan paints a noble picture, but how is failure noble? How can ten years of defeat prove I'm not a monster?

Dovan leans back, signaling a desire to finish this conversation face to face, but I press my cheek against his shoulder. He sighs, relenting. The stubble along his jaw tickles my temple as he says, "Every song, every life, has an ending. You shouldn't be punished because you see it coming before we do."

I tilt my neck until the side of his face fills my vision. "I am your punishment." *And you are mine.*

What should have been a devastating blow doesn't even make him flinch. His grip loosens a little, but he doesn't recoil or let me go.

He glances down at me. Our faces are so close and our lips—a fresh rush of cold brings an end to that thought as I jerk my gaze back to his.

Dovan's half-grin makes a dazzling appearance, but it lasts less than a few heartbeats as his mouth forms into a determined line. "I don't believe someone as gentle as you could ever be a punishment." His hand slides up and over my shoulder to cup the side of my face, the heat of his skin stinging against mine. "I'm not here because of a curse."

A nervous spine-twitch clangs like a warning bell through my mind, clouding his strange admission. The way he's holding me, the way our heads settle into the best angle for close study, the way our breaths mingle and become their own form of language. My muscles tense as I realize what we are positioned to do.

This is how couples stand together before they kiss.

But we are *not* a couple, and he's not staring at my mouth. Dovan peers into my soul. Finding me in the dark and the broken mess of where we are and where we're heading. There's a confession building in his eyes as he takes a deep breath, summoning a few snowflakes to melt against his jaw.

"There's no place I'd rather be on my last night, than watching the snow fall with you."

My chin trembles, sinking with my heart as I shake my head. I'm still a banshee, still cursed, and Dovan's still going to die.

"I need to tell you—"

"Stop." I plant my palms on his chest, wincing as the prophetic wound stains my skin with the promise of death. In desperation, I latch onto the horror of the image. The crimson liquid drip, drip, dripping on my thumb.

His blood will always be on my hands.

I push him with all my might, breaking us apart. The frigid air replaces his warmth and gives teeth to my words. "Nothing you say will change what's going to happen. I know what I am even if you refuse to accept it."

He frowns, but I cut him off before he offers me more false hopes.

"I'm not blind to the damage I cause to people like you." I glance over his shoulder in the direction we both came from. "Back at the inn, I saw it."

The darkness that's always lingered in his gaze deepens as his shoulders slump.

"I saw the regret you tried to hide when Ioana suggested you take the boy as your own."

He shifts his weight to his left foot as he clenches his jaw. "I was having regrets, but they were old regrets. Ones I buried years ago. They had *nothing* to do with you."

"I'm the reason you can't adopt him."

"No, you're not." He straightens. "I'm a guider. I gave up the right to be a father the day I joined."

I blink, untouched by the last few words for a second, but when I grasp what they mean, what he's saying, I gape at him in shock. *He has sacrificed everything for his city.* Everything but his life, and soon, that will be taken from him with my help.

"It's not required of us, but I made my choice for the good of my people."

That's all he thinks about. The good of others. How can he help, how can he restore, how can he prolong their hope? We stand in silence. His heart resolute, mine cracking into brittle pieces. A fall is coming for us both. I finger the torn shreds of my sleeve, but escaping reality requires something more powerful than mindless fidgeting.

I move aside. Just a few steps so I'm surrounded by falling snow, but it's not enough to freeze out the grief, and the anger, and the shame. All twisting into a single voice, crying out over the unfairness of it all while a darker voice whispers the truth.

You know how this ends. With a dagger through his heart. If I don't want mine to be pierced with his, I need to create some distance. Fast. Find a shadow, any shadow, and let its dark, wintry chill numb my heart to sleep. I stare down at my unmoving feet, face to face with the frail longing of my soul.

Even knowing how this ends—*I don't want to be anywhere else.*

When I find the courage to look up, the soft light of the street lanterns bathes Dovan's face in gilded shadows, sharpening the hope in his eyes. A hope no truth, no matter how dark, can snuff out. And then I witness the impossible. *Color.* Not the shades of white, black, and gray I'm used to. This color is vivid and vibrant and everything I ever hoped color could be.

Dovan's eyes are green.

A deep, enchanting green like the forest pines. *My favorite.* Except, I don't remember having a favorite color. *I do now.*

Heat crackles up my arm as his rough fingers tighten around mine. "Let's go home."

His words yank me from my open-mouthed staring. One word in particular—*home.* Instead of homes, banshees have city-prisons where we wait for the next victim. I tug my hand back, hoping Dovan lets go, but of course, he doesn't.

"I have no home."

He curls my hand around his arm despite my confession and guides me along the lantern-lit street. *Stubborn.* The corner of my mouth twitches, but I have nothing to smile about. Not as another note finds me, completing half of his soul's song.

It's halfway over.

Behind us the tower bell strikes the eighth hour. *Four hours left.*

Dovan starts walking but I don't budge. *I can't.* Moving forward brings us closer to his death. If I could, I would stay in this moment forever, but I have no power over time. The crisp air drains into my lungs, but nothing can fill the void in my soul or prevent the crime that is coming. After all the people he's comforted and rescued and found shelter for, Dovan deserves to live. *His city needs him.*

My soul rebels against our unchangeable future, replaying every moment we have spent together. Every touch and every word binding into a stake that drives through my heart and exposes how deeply he's affected me. *He makes me believe there's hope even when I know better.* Dovan is a good man, the first man to treat me well, and I—

I need him.

My knees weaken as the curse poisons the moment, forcing me to add three new notes to his song. I'm trembling as I lean into him, and he loops his arm around my waist without saying a word, fingers gripping my left side. He holds me up, lending me his strength, until I reach the end of his unfinished melody.

The truth I should never confess slips free. "I wish I could save you."

"I know you will try." Dovan's chin dips down as he meets my upturned gaze. "Trying is enough."

His words cave in my chest with one savage hit. He means to be kind, but there's a point where kindness becomes cruel. *Trying and never succeeding is the worst part of my curse.*

I straighten my spine and step away from him to create just enough space so we no longer touch. Quiet freezes around us like solid walls of ice, reminding me of the fate we can't escape.

He's to die. I'm to watch. And he is wrong.

Trying has never been enough.

THE GIRL

SIX YEARS BEFORE WINTER

THE IMPATIENT TAP of the boy's foot on the boards of the stage pounded a warning through the girl's head. *They're waiting.* A crowd of strangers packed the inn and blocked the path to the door. Half of them were drunk while the other half were sober enough to scowl at her silence. The girl tugged her bell-shaped sleeves down to hide the bruises from the last time she'd made someone wait too long. *Tonight was supposed to be our escape.*

Everyone stared at her as the boy played the harp and flashed his dimpled grin, repeating the intro when she missed her cue as if it were planned. *He's always trying to save me.* The girl owed him for that and so she filled her lungs. She tried to sing, tried to make the boy and the crowd happy, but the notes felt wrong.

Singing here felt wrong.

"Surprise," the boy had said when he'd led her onto the stage. His *I knew you'd love it* smirk stretched wider than she'd seen in years, but during the months of silence since they'd last spoken, he'd forgotten. What the girl wanted wasn't a chance to perform.

She performed all the time.

The boy had misjudged the reason she'd stopped singing. It had nothing to do with their father's threats. Her songs were the only things she could call her own. The one piece of her heart she wasn't forced to change or to share. Except now she was.

"Sing!" The boy hissed through gritted teeth, starting the melody over with a new flourish of notes.

Joy, when left unsatisfied, had a wicked edge.

An edge that cut into her heart as her failure became refusal. The jubilant atmosphere sharpened, and she became a target. They laughed at her, hurling insults like stones because she wouldn't sing. Not even for the boy who'd brought her to the inn to cheer her up.

He frowned when she ran, his demand she return chasing her up the stairs and into the shadows and down another flight into a room lit by a handful of candles. Children rescued from the war tossed under mismatched blankets, their narrow cots filling the entire room. She walked between them and envied their dreams.

I wish I was one of them. An orphan could choose their future.

The heavy thud and metallic rattle of the boy's steps warned her of his coming. He would take her back to her real stage, where she played the obedient but tortured daughter, but that's when she heard a muffled cry. A tale of kindred sorrow rising into the jagged wail of a shattered soul. The girl waited for an adult to come, waited for another child to rise and offer comfort, but the orphan seemed doomed to cry alone, forsaken by all. *Not by me.*

She found him curled on the floor in a corner.

The boy was older than she expected, older than ten but younger than her thirteen years. *He's so thin.* Proving his journey to this city had been hard. A guider's cloak draped his trembling form while his brown hand held his mouth shut.

When her soft steps betrayed her approach, he quickly faced the wall. Gone, were the signs of his distress. The orphan had made his skin, his expression, like stone. Locking down his grief and whatever nightmare had woken him. A talent the girl envied.

She stopped beside him, but he wouldn't look at her. An ache throbbed through her chest. *How do I help him?* Her hands were empty, and there were no words for this kind of pain.

The girl had nothing to give him.

Nothing but her song. And so she sang.

RED DEATH

11

HOME IS one of those silly words normal humans use to excuse their weakness for comfort. *As if a grouping of walls is enough to keep them safe.* No wall has ever proven capable of keeping the villains of the world out. Especially when we could be anyone. Like a weary old man looking for shelter from the cold. *No threat to see here.* Not in my tattered robe, my stooped posture, or my knotted hands.

A girl, maybe nine, answers my knock, welcoming me with a brilliant smile peeking through a waterfall of curls. *So innocent.* Oblivious to the monster standing in her doorway. The tightness of magic-aged skin limits my grin from becoming the full smirk that would betray my vile purpose for being here.

Did nobody warn her the worst monsters always knock?

Being let in by our victims is half the fun of the game.

She guides me into a bare entry and then struggles to shut the door against winter's screaming wind. If I were a gentle old man,

I'd help her. Instead, I savor the grunts of her continuing struggle as my eyes adjust to the brighter shadows.

Capes hang from hooks to my left. A rainbow of worn red fabrics splashing against the anemic pink of the wall. Below the capes, all sizes of boots sit in haphazard piles. An inscription scrolls over the narrow hall, the words so faded only four are readable. *Truth, hope, peace,* and *love.* My sneer deepens to the point I hear my skin creak.

I've stumbled into a house of fairytales. By the time I leave, it will be a house of horrors. Assuming the guider stays in one place—*this is where he dies.* Preferably not in his sleep, but I suspect he won't be that boring.

A few swords hang between the capes sway from the wind, leather belts creaking. *Who leaves their weapons at the door?* It's rather convenient for monsters like me. The third sword matches the common size and shape of the kind guiders use. The red tones of my vision deepen, flickering with the pulse of the heart I'm hunting. *My prey is here.*

I kick the door closed behind me. The girl loses her balance at the sudden loss of resistance and I snatch her arm before she falls. But it was too fast, too limber, my grip too firm. She backs away from me, rubbing the spot where my fingers were, eyes rounded in the first wise emotion she's shown. *Unease.* That first, blessed whisper of understanding.

I am not who I appear to be.

This time my grin does more than crack my skin; it tears it open. Terror pales the girl's face as hot blood trickles down my cheek. What can I say? I am scary good looking when covered in blood. I bend down and give her a closer look. "This is the part where you run."

With a cry, she vanishes down the hall, giving me an opportunity to fix the damage. I draw my dagger and angle my head so I can see myself in its blade. Gaunt skin and bones and wicked eyes stare up at me. *Still devilishly handsome.* Even with so many wrinkles.

My new face acts like a drape drawn over a razor-sharp skull, concealing my identity while failing to hide the monster underneath. I scrape my dagger across the bleeding tear, down and along my chin, and up my other cheek. Heat stings my skin, erupting in sores no hero will question when they come to face the little girl's monster. They'll find an old man with scary looks who just wants to get warm.

Wood plunks against the floorboards in tandem with a soft step. I hunch my back as the hero appears, but it's not the guider I expected. An old woman, with an expression soured by years of kissing lemons, limps forward, her weight balanced between her sole foot and the wood of her crutch. *Could they make this any easier?*

"What be yer business?" Her glare makes up for the higher pitch to her voice, backing her question with an unspoken threat. *What would she do? Hit me?* If she tried, she'd fall over from the imbalance brought on by such a swing.

As amusing as the picture of her in a heap on the floor is, I maintain my disguise, wrapping my voice in humble desperation. "A little food and shelter if you can spare them."

"Ye be late for eatin', but shelter ye can 'ave."

I bow, acting grateful. "You are most kind."

The end of her crutch jabs my chest, pushing me back. I jerk my head up in mock surprise, and a flicker of triumph lifts the corner of her mouth. She's braced herself with her palm against the wall to balance her weight. My hand twitches, longing to send the old Sour Face flying backward to skid down the hall on her rump. One good shove to her crutch would do it. Lucky for her, she is not my prey.

Patience.

I let her pin me to the door. The wind whistles through a crack near my ear, but it's not Wraith's voice this time. My ever-obedient banshee has stopped singing again. *That will change when I find her.* But to get to Wraith, I must sell my current disguise to the old woman frowning at me.

"If any more of my young'ns be screamin' because of ye," she leans forward, twisting her crutch to cause a flare of pain across my sternum, "ye'll be sleepin' on ice."

I raise my knobby hands, gesturing to the sores on my face. "I'm only frightening to look at."

She drops her crutch, huffing as she settles it under her arm and points a finger at me. "One scream."

"I know, I know. I'll sleep on ice."

She nods and beckons me into the hall. *Victory.* Even when they know I'm a monster, they can't stop themselves from letting me in. *Killers are rather entertaining guests.*

We always brighten things up with a dash of red.

A large room opens on the left, filled with fire and candlelight and stuffed with people. I've cut open pregnant cow stomachs that had more room. All the non-human parts of this housey womb appear sturdy at least. Smudged, plastered walls crowned by the exposed beams of the second floor; a threadbare, stained rug stretched over scuffed wood; a tangle of mismatched chairs, all assembled from the broken pieces of other furniture; and a hearth in the corner, darkened by years of fires weeping rings of soot along its stone. *How very ordinary.*

The people occupying the chairs do nothing to elevate the room above a storage den for unwanted things. They're a mix of ages. Some old, like me, but most are children huddled around the fire on their knees.

The girl who opened the door for me ducks out of my sight behind a pair of older boys. I wink at her when she dares another glance at me, but no one else pays me any attention. A different girl, who's missing her front teeth, whistles as she tells a story from the small space cleared before the hearth. The glint of green beside her snatches my focus. *Dovan.* My prey. He acts out her story, playing the hero who's on a quest to slay a mighty beast but got sidetracked by an adorable—*what?* I can't have heard her right.

An adorable thistle-goat.

With feathered slippers.

And a—a fake beard of smelly cheese to keep the blood-sucking swamp flies away.

Snorts escape several noses as my vision flashes a deeper red. The room is too warm, too full of unrelated people who've become a family. It wouldn't take much to ruin the mood. The girl at the heart of their sickening sentimentality stands within falling distance of the stone hearth. The right push and her skull would crack open against it. A thrilling end to the worst story ever told. The dagger sears my side, a warning to focus. *You're not here for the girl.* I tear my gaze from her dimpled cheeks until all I see is green.

My prey bends in half, unleashing a fit of braying chuckles, and unfortunately for my ears, he's far from alone. The entire room descends into the chaos of pointless joy. Even the old woman beside me loses her immunity to the ridiculous. Her sour-frown reverses into a raspy giggle. But one voice stands out from the rest.

The voice I know better than any other.

The voice I enslaved to death and sorrow.

Wraith. Is *laughing.*

She sits on the hearth, her back to the flames, with the guider I'm looking forward to killing between us. *She can't laugh.* I won't allow it. Not when she has a song to finish. I squeeze the dagger, summoning its hunger and our curse, and I focus on a single word.

Sing.

I prepare my sneer, eager to watch my power break her again

and return her to our cursed roles. I blink. Once, twice, three times, but instead of a melody of death bursting from her lips, I hear a giggle.

SING.

I repeat the command with no success. Wraith laughs harder, and harder, her entire face glowing. My mouth falls open as she transforms. Her skin is no longer sickly gray. Her irises no longer black as night. Pain cuts deep into my chest and I fall against the doorpost, gasping for air.

The old woman asks if I'm well, but I don't answer. I have no words, no thoughts, no reasons for why my legs are shaking. I can't look away from Wraith. From how *right* she looks.

Skin—the creamy brown of a spring day.

Eyes—the pale gold of a candle's flame.

She's beautiful. A radiant young woman capable of doing anything. A heart stealer if ever I saw one.

My hands curl into fists because there is one heart she's tempting from its chest. The guider never turns his back, keeping her in his sight at all times. A clever ruse to hide how often he glances at her. *I'll carve his self-righteous eyes out of his bleedin' head!*

There's a link between them that I don't understand, binding them together in a way that screams of fate or whatever fairytale nonsense people believe. But like all fairytales, their story ends in tragedy.

No matter how many times that guider tempts her to forget —*her voice is still mine.*

A fact that usually tastes like victory, but this time it's sour. Bitter. Like poison.

Everything's gone blurry as a glassy wetness veils my gaze, and there's not enough air to satisfy my lungs. I roll outward so my back is to the wall. I am free of the sight of her, but not from the most dangerous development of all.

Dovan makes her—*happy.*

A savage pain splits my skull. I grip my head as voices I don't recognize roar through my mind. They speak, but their words are lost in the haunting echo of Wraith's laugh. All swirling around a single assumption.

I used to...

The thought hangs unfinished over a cliff. Whatever waits at the bottom isn't enough to tempt me to jump. *What good is happy when you could be safe?* We live in a world where having one will cost you the other.

I grimace, sliding down the wall as my chest throbs from a fearsome ache. My fingers drift along my sternum and come away wet. I give them a lick, tasting—*blood.* The leftovers of some poor soul I butchered bleeding through my disguise.

A tickle in my throat dares me to laugh at myself. *You're going soft.* Killers don't get sentimental over the giggling of one girl. There's a lie somewhere in that phrase. A traitorous whisper that's almost an apology because—*she deserves this.* She deserves more than a flinch of joy stuck between the notes of my cruel game. Not that I care about such things. Only one thing matters.

Killing the guider.

Winning the game.

And when it is over, it won't matter that Wraith might be more to me than just a girl. *I'll have beaten her.* Stolen all the hope, all the laughter, everything that guider represents from her. All she'll have left will be me. Me, and our unending game.

Wood thumps my thigh. "Do ye wish to sleep down there?"

My lips find their natural, sneering state as I meet the old woman's gaze. "Dizzy spell." I gasp and sputter as I fake my struggle to stand. She decides to help, lending an arm for support.

As she points me toward a narrow staircase and gives directions to a room where I can rest, I risk another glance at Wraith. My lips fall from a sneer into the downward embrace of shame. The glow is gone from her skin, smothered by the trembling shape of her ashen mouth. Melody spills through her lips and her once golden irises fade into bitter darkness.

I put it there.

Sooner or later—*I always win.* I take pleasure in that fact, but tonight, the sweet taste of victory melts into acid in my throat. I thought having her under my control and killing people was all I needed to be...*happy.* But I'm hollowed out by one bleedin' sound. *How had I not noticed?* The depth of her loneliness, of her sorrow, seeping cold as ice through every note. The notes that are never hers. I shake my head, but I don't know how to go back. Not after seeing her as she could be.

Yes, I always win, but—another pain stabs into my chest, and I lurch forward, landing hard on my hands and knees on the steps. Drips of blood patter the warped wood, and for each drop, a new word brands my soul, forming a question that should have stayed lost inside the heart I killed long ago.

Who would we be if I didn't want to win anymore?

WRAITH

12

THE FIRE IS DYING. Frigid air creeps down the chimney of Dovan's home, turning the flames to desperate sparks and blackening coals and gasping twirls of smoke. I could stoke it. The poker is just to my right, but—*what would be the point?* No one's in the room except me. The rest have all gone upstairs to what can't be more than a half-dozen rooms shared among thirty people. *You counted?* I shouldn't have, but it was hard not to number all the faces Dovan's pitiful acting brightened with—

Laughter.

My fingers trace my lips. It was easy to believe they were the gatekeepers of only one kind of sound. I tried to content myself with singing deadly songs, weighing down my lips with lonely grief. What else could escape a mouth cursed to bring nothing but sorrow every time it opens? But tonight, I know different.

I can laugh.

For a single moment, I laughed. And not the polite kind reserved for proper dinners or parties. No, this was—*real.* Loud and childish. An eruption of joy that doesn't care what anyone thinks or about what happens after. *I was free.* There was no song, no monster waiting to kill another victim. Just me, and Dovan, and his adoptive family. As if nothing could be so normal, so right, then our laughing together.

What I witnessed, what I experienced in this room was the warmest, most wholesome thing I've ever known, and yet I sit here, letting the fire die, letting the gentle heat of their lingering joy fade from my skin. *It still wasn't enough to stop the curse.* Our laughter may have delayed my purpose, but long before their humor waned, mine was cut off. *I sang.* More notes adding to Dovan's death song, counting down like a musical clock. But when this one strikes the final hour, it won't chime and spin on. This clock always runs out.

The shadows deepen as frosty air stings my eyes, drawing tears as easily as Red Death's dagger draws blood. *What will they do?* The grandpas and grannies, the fathers and mothers, the children and siblings and cousins? What will they do when Dovan's dead? Will their home survive without its heart?

Death is so common that *yes* should come easy, but some deaths can't be survived. Not completely. I've seen what happens. Families and friendships shattered because someone was taken from them. *Like ripping the roots from under a great tree.* Without the support that holds it up and nourishes it, the tree falls. The tree dies. I fear it will be no different for the people of this home.

And it will be my fault.

Familiar warmth creeps over my back, warning me I'm no longer alone. Dovan takes the poker and does what I should have done. He stokes the fire and adds another log. It sparks, sputtering for a few seconds before eager tongues of flame lick up the wood in hunger, but whatever heat the renewed blaze offers—*I can't feel it.* Until Dovan, the only temperature I've known is numbness. The firelight shines off my skin, exposing how much I've weakened. I wipe the icy tears sliding down my cheeks away, hoping he didn't notice. *Please, just this once, don't see the real me.*

He pulls a wobbly chair closer and sits down, but not straight-backed like a soldier. He slouches worse than an old man. Darkness hangs in shabby crescents under his eyes, the cost of a long day spent serving others. His song tickles my throat, but I swallow against the cursed melody, hoping for a moment longer before I'm forced to sing.

Dovan props an elbow on the arm of his chair, fingers holding the weight of his head as he studies me. I suppress the shock this time. His irises are still a deep but vibrant shade of pine. A gift of color I will never deserve.

The familiar wrinkle between his eyebrows appears, a sign of the concern he should have no energy left to foster. "Why were you crying?"

Always so direct. I fix my gaze on the fire. All hope I had of hiding my pain from him fades like the shadows the flames chase away. *There could never be any shadows between us.* He's too perceptive, too sharp-eyed for that, but I don't have to answer his question. He holds no power over me. His words are not a command. They're a request. More tears bud along my eyelids as I fight to hold my crumbling walls together.

I pick at the torn strips of my skirt, keeping my face angled away from him. "Do you ever ask easy questions?"

He shifts in his chair as if uncomfortable and reaches behind him, pulling out a leather journal and tossing it onto the hearth between us. I resist the urge to pick it up and flip through Sanaa's drawings to find the sketch she made of Dovan and I in the lower market.

"Easy is a waste of my time," he says once he's comfortable. "I don't want to waste my time with you."

I face him, searching for a reason. For a way to explain his interest in my side of our story. *No one else ever cared why I cried.*

The uplifted corner of his mouth lightens the seriousness of what he wants, of how ready he is to choose me as the mission of his final hours.

"You don't know what you're asking of me," I say. *Only that I bare my entire soul.* An easy proposition for someone with nothing to hide, but my survival is based on hiding, of locking my secrets so deep inside I trick myself into thinking they're no longer there, waiting to become my ruin.

I'm ruined already.

"I want to know." He leans forward, left hand hanging off his knee within reach of my own. Inviting me to entrust more of myself with him. "I want to know everything."

Dovan pulls me in with the gentleness of his words, with the caring of his eyes, but it's not enough. *He only has tonight.* I have thousands of nights ahead of me. I could spend the few hours he has left telling him about a banshee's cursed life, or I could shift his focus to someone he actually can help. I know which of those would be a waste.

I grab the journal and offer it to him. "Sanaa needs you more than I do."

He sighs, his hand curling away from me as he sinks back into his chair.

"Are you going to return it to her?"

"I haven't decided yet."

Decided. Just the sound of the word chills my skin. The fire in the hearth wanes, the air cools, and Dovan misses it. How wrong he is to decide the future of another human being without even giving Sanaa a say.

My lips thin around the words as my voice rises, "What's to decide? Those are *her* drawings. Her art. They belong to her."

"I understand that—"

"Do you?" I'm on my feet, looking down on him. "Because I do. I know what it's like to have a part of your soul bound by someone else's choice. I know how it feels—" my voice cracks and I force myself onward, "—it's like your soul has been torn from your chest, like you're being trampled, but no one hears your scream because you can't even get it out. The truth of how much they've hurt you. They have all the power and you—" I glance down at my shaking hands, at the silver scars etched into my skin because I am cursed and always will be, "—you don't."

Dovan doesn't blink, doesn't say anything. He just sits there, stone-faced and quiet like a man gaging the severity of a storm from a distance.

"If I could die, I'd rather be dead than live one more day imprisoned by the very thing that once made me free." My hand rises to my throat. "My voice."

His eyes grow wet as his lips press harder together.

"Don't think Sanaa will feel any different, or that she'll get over it in time because she won't. There isn't enough time to undo —" I wince as the curse forces out the first few notes of his song.

What I wanted to tell him is no longer possible. My voice can only do one thing, sing or speak. The curse is so much stronger, but I strain against it, making myself hoarse until I choke the melody off by biting my cheek so hard I draw blood. Pain stabs me in the chest as Red Death's magic retaliates. I collapse onto the hearth.

You've only delayed the inevitable. I will sing. I always sing.

My hair falls around my face in a shield as my tears splatter Sanaa's journal. I shake my head, trembling and vulnerable, but I tuck a few loose curls behind my ear so I can gage Dovan's reaction. "Please, don't make your decision become her curse."

The anger I expected to clench his jaw and fist his hands, the offense he should take as I suggest his protection is harmful to Sanaa, never shows in his face. He's spent too much of his life as a guider, cultivating a stoic front in order to survive the difficult parts of his job. Unshed tears remain his sole weakness. They shine brightly like a string of clues along his eyelids even as he blinks them away, and they lead me to the wound in his chest. To the heart where he hides his secrets.

We sit in silence for a while, Dovan's eyes glued to the fire, mine to the journal holding the dreams of a young girl in his care. Neither of us are willing to open up yet. The cold air retreats toward me as his warmth begins to burn, revealing that he is anything but calm behind his soldier's mask.

His chin dips, and he straightens his guider's tunic over his thighs. "I wasn't." His jaw clenches. "I know how important it is for her to draw."

"And yet you'd take that from her."

His gaze narrows, hurt creasing his brow.

"It is not your right to decide this for her."

"You misunderstand me. I agree with you," he says. "I don't want to cause her more pain, but it is my duty to protect her."

"From what?"

He nods at the journal. "Look inside."

I've wanted to do nothing else since the moment I saw her drawing, but even with Dovan's encouragement, it's wrong to open something so private. Art is a craft of the soul no matter what form it takes. Whatever waits within the journal's worn leather covers, I'll find more than the souls of her subjects. Sanaa's soul is here as well, sprinkled over every page. Such an intimate exposure shouldn't be taken behind her back but accepted from her own hands. I glance at Dovan, but he gives nothing away. He's made her journal, her art, the answer to my question.

Why? I recall the young man who came after Sanaa in the lower market. The fear behind her Gran's harsh words matches the look settling over Dovan's face. *He doesn't know what to do.* Except to take the severest act of all and forbid Sanaa from ever drawing again. *What kind of art could be so dangerous?*

Keeping my touch light, I open the journal. The first image freezes my heart solid.

I stop breathing, mesmerized by an unnatural wonder. Or maybe *horror* would be a better word. A man and woman, dark as the night sky, stand tall and regal with flowing robes and faces that—*change*. I gasp. Everything about the drawing is *wrong*. The depth, the fluidity of the lights and shadows is so close to real life, and the eyes. The eyes express all things and nothing at once. A confusing, overwhelming rush of emotional cues and intuitive knowledge screaming in my face with the force of a thousand voices.

I slam the journal shut, my heaving breaths squeezing out a few mournful notes of Dovan's song.

"It's difficult at first," his voice grounds me and calms my whirling mind. "When you look again, you'll understand it."

I'm about to object, to swear I'll never open the journal again, when my fingers slide around the cover's edge and lift it from the strange drawings. The art *wants* to be seen. I prepare myself to be overwhelmed, but this time, it *is* different. The image doesn't throw everything at me all at once. The pictures progress slowly, a narrative of emotions and information ebbing like a sea tide of pencil strokes. *They're telling a story.* The whole life of the couple, from meeting, to marriage, to their first child, to their—death. *Wolves.* I look away from the gore, but their child holds my gaze. *Sanaa.*

I glance up at Dovan to make sure.

"My father and his men were too late for Sanaa's parents but not for her."

"And he brought her here?"

A twinge of pain twists Dovan's mouth. "As he did with me, yes."

A sudden urge begs me to ask him about his own story. How he came to be here, who his blood family was and if he's ever thought of leaving Riffen to find out if any of them survived. My mouth opens. Dovan fixes his stare on the fire, shutting me out. Whatever his past, this house, this city is his home, and he has no desire to leave. I tear my gaze from him before the rising shame of who I am and why I'm here forces me under.

I tilt the journal, hoping the drawing responds to my wish to see the man who took Dovan and Sanaa as his own children, but the figures no longer shift and reform. The art is normal now. The portrait flat, but still realistic. *Its story is finished.* Leaving behind a final image. A guider carrying a toddling girl from the massacre of her parents. But his back is turned, capturing Sanaa's face over the man's shoulder. My heart throbs a painful beat. *So much sorrow and anguish.* Two things I understand better than most.

I sniff, swiping a tear from my cheek as I turn the page. Another drawing, another story, the same old tale of joy shredded by grief. I flip faster, hoping to detach myself from the varying degrees of pain I see in their faces. A single word chants through my soul. *Starving, starving, starving.* Every figure, whether man, woman, boy or girl, withers before my eyes. The lines deepen, the shadows blackening with the frustration of the artist. No matter how the drawings begin, they all end the same way.

Ghostly gray and dying a slow, inescapable death.

Sanaa's art has captured the bleak truth of who these people are and what will become of them. Smudges showcase the desire breaking her heart. *She can't make it better.* Many artists find ways to bend reality. Painting a fanciful gleam over their subjects to give them their deepest wish. Sanaa's art is tied to what is true. Her drawings offer no comfort, no inspiration, no—

Hope.

I set the journal on my knees, leaving it open to a portrait of a young woman. *She's so thin.* All the joy and life hollowed out from her eyes. A name is scratched into the corner. *Emalyne.* This was the sketch the angry young man had asked for to save his sweetheart. To remind her of how beautiful she still is. Sanaa captured the beauty of her soul, but that was the beginning.

The ending is who Emalyne has become.

My soul twists, agonizing over such a horrifying gift. To see all the good, all the bad, but have no control over where the drawing goes still or what future it sets in stone. I'm glad her Gran made sure the young man received a fake. *This would've killed him.*

I close the journal and grapple with my thoughts. *Why would Sanaa ever want to draw again?* I wouldn't. Melody vibrates my throat, a wicked reminder of how deeply I understand. A curse may have enslaved my voice to a cruel purpose, but my voice was once free. *She can't stop.* Sanaa has to draw because drawing is woven through her soul. Just as I have to sing.

When I finally look up, Dovan is watching me. His expression has softened a little, still shaded by regret, but he's not resigned to restricting her art. *He hopes for another way.*

I find myself repeating Sanaa's own words. "Her art isn't evil." Calling her art evil or good is too simple, too black and white of a label for what she can do, but there's another word that fits. *Dangerous.*

Dovan lets out a slow breath, focusing on the fire's sparks as they dance up the chimney. "No, it's not evil. It's honest." His gaze returns to mine, ripe with things left unsaid between us. "Sometimes there's nothing more painful or terrifying than the truth."

"But we still have to speak it."

A hint of a smile appears in the corner of his mouth before vanishing. "I wish Sanaa could. Her truth must stay a secret."

"You won't stop her from drawing?"

"No."

I place my hand on top of his. The jarring sting of his hot skin prolongs the pause before I speak, giving him time to rotate his wrist so our palms touch and his fingers wrap around my hand. I swallow, nervous over the complete confidence of his grip as if his hand has always belonged here, holding mine. "Thank you."

"For what?"

"For not taking Sanaa's art from her."

He leans forward and a wave of warmth coils around me. "Like how someone took your songs from you?"

I stiffen. His hold tightens, as if he fears I will pull away and hide behind my icy walls.

"I'm sorry you didn't have anyone to fight on your side."

I ease my hand back, slowly, to prolong the touch. When my fingers are free, dozens of whisper-thin cracks of light brown run along my palm. They beg me to hope in him. To risk my heart, believing this game won't end the same way as the others. *Red Death shows no mercy.* There is no end for Dovan that does not include Red Death's dagger embedded in his chest.

I shudder and roll my empty hand into a fist to prevent Dovan from filling it with his own. "It doesn't matter if I was alone or not. The results would have been the same."

The way he looks at me heats my chilled skin. His steady gaze holds a promise. A belief that things would have been different if we had met before today, before Red Death stole my life. *But we didn't meet.* As my curse pushes us toward Dovan's end, our hopes are left behind in the choking dust of *too late.* The ice coating my heart cracks but doesn't thaw. Wishing he could have been there for me won't change the fact that he wasn't.

He's trying to be kind. Kindness is no great hero. It doesn't break curses or win wars. Kindness is the embrace waiting for you when the fight is over. Once everything has been lost. A consolation with no power to change a single thing.

Kindness is a dream.

The dream of a little girl who sang whatever she liked.

Her songs never brought death.

I wish she had met Dovan. I wish she was the girl with him

now. They could have had a future. They could've dreamed of a world where a kind touch has more power than a wicked blade. Where monsters fear the goodness in people instead of exploiting it as a weakness.

But such a world doesn't exist.

As the bitter magic of my curse slices against my heart in warning, I wake up, bowing my head in defeat as I obey. I sing. Five notes become ten, twenty, thirty, before I taste the salty moisture sliding into the corners of my mouth.

"You're crying again."

I study the fire, watching the flames dwindle as winter sinks down the chimney to suffocate its burning light, but there's another source of heat. Dovan's close. He's reaching, and I hold my breath as his fingers wipe my tears. Just the brush of his warmth against my chilled skin steams my tears away. I lean into his touch until the side of my face fits in his palm.

My heart sings a dangerous song of its own. *Meant to be. Meant to be.* This man who deserves to live and the banshee whose presence means he won't. What a tragic pair we make.

Dovan's thumb rubs along my cheekbone, drawing my gaze to his. "This is not your fault."

No matter how much I want to believe him, we wouldn't be here without my voice. *I wish I'd been born mute.* Then the banshee curse never would have worked on me.

"All the death you've seen, it's easy to hold yourself responsible. I know."

"You're wrong." I'm shaking because I cannot bare another second of this. Not one more word spoken to lighten the burden of guilt crushing my soul. Not one more touch given to thaw the icy loneliness entombing my heart. *He thinks better of me than he should.*

I angle my head to the side to break free of his hold, but he moves with me. His fingers glide through my hair to curl along the back of my neck. I wait for his grip to turn painful, to force me to see he's won, but Dovan isn't Red Death. He doesn't care about winning or using his strength to control me. Dovan's touch is firm but gentle enough I could escape if I wished.

He looks me in the eye, serious and confident. "I am not wrong. Not about you."

If his intention was to stop me from crying, he has failed. The lines of his face blur from the flood of emotions seeking a desperate escape from my soul. My breath breaks through my lips in small heaves as I scramble to find a suitable answer. The curse commandeers my voice before I can speak. Two more notes lengthen his song, bringing us closer to his death. I shut my mouth, gritting my teeth, but the melody resonates through my nose.

There's no containing it.

"It's okay. I don't fear your song." His thumb rubs prickling heat along the skin behind my ear. "I don't fear you."

He tugs gently at my neck, bringing our foreheads to rest against each other, and then he—*sings*. Dovan sings *with* me. Matching the speed of my own notes, the rich tenor of his masculine voice melding with my airy alto. A perfect duet.

Make him stop. I should, but I don't because for once, I'm not alone. So I close my eyes and focus on the blending of our voices, letting him share the weight of my sorrow before we're forced to remember who we are. A banshee, and the victim her song is meant to warn. *I never understood that part of the old stories.* If my songs are warnings, then my victims should have a chance at survival, shouldn't they?

"Dovan!"

We break apart, startled by his Gran. He stands as she crutches forward. Salt and herbs flavor the air and I spot the bowl in her hand. A bowl which she shoves into Dovan's chest.

"Gran, don't—"

"I got worried ye weren't eatin' and I see now I be right." Her empty hand flies toward me. I jolt to my feet, but with the fireplace behind me, there's very little room for me to maneuver. As her fingers flap against my arm, she gasps, livid horror sharpening her glare.

Dovan grips her right shoulder. She whacks at his boots with her crutch, forcing him to jerk back, and then continues her search.

Unlike him, her skin is tepid where it touches my neck. I twist against the fire-heated stones of the hearth, but there's nowhere for me to go as she explores further. Her fingers climb up my jaw and slide around my chin. They press against my lips, bending my nose and poking my eye, and I flinch backward. All while her gaze puzzles over the conflicting information being gathered. She can't see me, but she can feel me, leading her to the inevitable conclusion.

One word breaking like a storm across her face.

"Banshee!"

WRAITH

13

HER PALM SMACKS my cheek so hard my ears ring. I sway on my feet, bumping against the hearth, and nearly put a hand in the fire while searching for a solid grip to regain my balance. My cheekbone throbs and my skin stings and my eyes water as the echo of her furious grief punches into my soul. But hitting me once is not enough for her. Twice more she strikes me, smacking the right edge of my jaw first and then the left.

The cutting bite of jeweled metal scrapes the hollow of my cheek. I follow the flash of silver as her hand's momentum carries it over my shoulder. *A wedding band.* All I see in the humble blue stone is more grief. More loss. Drawing two words like poison from the never healing wound in my heart.

I'm sorry.

All I want to do is apologize. Fall to my knees and beg for her forgiveness. *Nothing I say will help her.* My voice will rob the old woman of her grandson. I could resist, I could throw my arms up to protect myself, but I'll still be the monster in her eyes.

She pulls her hand back again, teeth baring in a threat. "Ye'll not be takin' his soul."

"That's enough!" Dovan grabs her arm and slides between us. His widened gaze and raised eyebrows reveal his shock, as if what she did was wrong or even unusual.

When he glances my way, I quickly focus on the floorboards, noting the spots where the dark stain has rubbed off. Bands of warm air drift around my shoulders in a question he hasn't asked but I still feel. *Are you hurt?* The fact he wants to be sure I am all right first before dealing with his angry grandmother makes me shiver. The cold press of shame weighs me down. I curl inward, cracking apart from the inside.

This—the throbbing bone-ache on both sides of my face—*this is how I'm used to being treated.*

His Gran wrestles free from his grasp, leaning off balance before she plants her crutch and steadies herself. Her knobby finger stabs in my direction. "Ye would protect a monster?"

"She's not like that, Gran." Dovan sets the bowl of soup she shoved at him before attacking me down on the hearth. He lifts his hands, palms out, a calming gesture that might work on a child, but not on a fiery old woman who's realized she's going to lose him. "It's not her fault."

"'Course it be her fault. That's what banshees do." Her sizzling glare just misses my face, but I flinch anyway. "Worse than sirens they be." She spits, but it sails past me and hisses against the hearthstones. "She be seducin' ye with her song. Made ye believe dyin' be worth hearin' her." She grips Dovan's arm. "Yer life be worth more than a song."

She's right. His life is worth *every* song, and even then, music alone wouldn't be enough.

Would she care that the same desperate anger burns in my soul? I'd pay any price to find a way out of this where Dovan doesn't wind up dead.

He clenches his jaw and looks down at the old woman whose son adopted him. The silence grows heavy with tension as he refuses to answer her challenge or explain why he doesn't view me as a threat.

I could scream at him. *For once in your life be like everyone else!* My heart rips in two as a cascade of thoughts move from my mind to my eyes, tumbling as tears down my cheeks. *Tell her I'm not worth it. Tell her you will do everything to survive me. Tell her I will fail. That my song*—guilt thickens my airways, forcing me to gasp, and then I'm singing.

I'm proving her right.

I am a banshee and banshees always bring death.

Dovan's fingers find mine, a solid witness of his good heart, but he stays focused on his Gran. The back of my hand prickles as his thumb rubs heated circles over my skin. I choke on a sob. *Why does he have to make me feel*—seen. Understood. Maybe even desired. I grit my teeth and blink hard, trying to accept my truth instead of his.

All that waits for us is death. There is no happy ending to our tale.

"Dovan," Gran frowns at the way his hand hangs empty in the air, as if she knows we're touching, and edges closer. "What ye feel...it be monsters and magic...she be nothin' but a wraith preyin' on yer good soul."

His chin twitches higher.

"Yer death be a game to her. Nothin' more."

My free hand curls into a fist. It's a game all right, but it isn't mine any more than it's possible for me to win. For *us* to win.

"She didn't choose to be a banshee." Dovan's voice has thinned, the brittle tone of a man who's accepted his fate.

"That be no claim of innocence," His Gran snaps back.

"She doesn't want me to die."

"She told ye that, did she?" His Gran huffs and shakes her

head, pointing her angry glare where she thinks I am. "Then she be a liar and a monster."

"She's never lied to me. Not once."

Gran spins toward him. "Ye'll trust her over me? What be wrong with ye, boy?"

Dovan's gaze settles on me, gentle, but without doubt. "She's not a monster, Gran. She's been forced to sing so others die." He refocuses on her, "But she hasn't let it crush all the goodness out of her soul."

"Oh, I see. So she be a good soul? Then what have I ta worry for?" Gran whacks him with her crutch. "She'll be yer death, ye foolish bear-cub. And still ye defend her."

"Till my last breath."

His admission fills the space between the slow beats of my heart. They settle there, growing roots but never blooming into hope. The curse alerts my ears to the next note of his song. I hum the melody from the beginning, dreading the end where Red Death appears with a flash of crimson and metal.

This note isn't the last. Red Death hasn't come to kill him. Not yet. But Dovan's song tickles my throat, wanting to be finished, wanting to be sung in full, and if I stay here with him, the rest of the notes will come. I withdraw my hand from his and prepare to leave.

"Why?" Gran's voice has turned pleading. "What has that banshee done ta deserve yer protectin'?"

Nothing. The old woman and I, we understand my role. Dovan tries to make more of me, but I block out their voices as I slip past them. He touches my arm, his fingers sliding down to my wrist where he holds fast. A wordless request that adds a beat of life to the slow pulse in my veins.

Stay with me.

My chin trembles as a new rip tears through my heart. He's asking me to be stronger than I am. To face the end with him. But

I—*I can't stay.* Because staying this time means finishing his song. *I'm not ready.* A tear slides down my cheek, the scream of sorrow and rage I wish I could unleash resonating within its salty bubble. Yet another cry that goes unheard.

I can't watch him die.

This was a mistake. Letting him mean something. Letting him become more than Red Death's next victim. Frigid air wraps around me and repels Dovan's warmth as I walk away.

"Where ye be goin'?"

The old woman's question activates a forgotten instinct and I pause in the doorway. *She's not talking to you.* She's speaking to her grandson, who is— *No.* He's scooped up the bowl and is already halfway across the room.

He's following me.

"Dovan." Her crutch knocks on the wood floor as she steps after him. "Where ye goin'? I haven't finished speakin' with ye."

He lifts the bowl so she can see it over his shoulder. "I'm going to feed our newest guest."

"That soup be meant for ye."

Dovan sighs, slowing to a stop in front of me before looking back at her. "I've no more need for food, Gran."

"Ye must keep yer strength up."

"Why?" He faces her. "I'm not fighting this."

She goes pale, lips parting around another objection.

"I don't expect you to understand why, and I can't explain." He shrinks the gap between them, grips her arms, and kisses her head. "I need you to trust me. I'm doing what I have to."

Did he just imply he has to die? Seeing a banshee means you're *going* to die, not that you have to.

"Thank you," his voice drops to a whisper as tension twitches along his jawline. "For becoming my home."

Gran clings to his arm, holding him there with her as she fights against the emotions that would steal her voice and cost her their last moment. "I trust ye, my stout bear-cub. But trust a banshee?"

His shoulders droop.

"She'd never tell ye there's a way ta save ye."

What? I grip the door frame as my legs wobble.

Dovan's posture stiffens, and he leans back as if he doesn't want to know. But he can't stop himself from asking, "What do you mean?"

"A banshee's curse be a trade. A soul for a soul."

He's shaking his head, dismissing the idea before she finishes speaking.

"Stab her heart through and through, and ye'll live."

I watch as her solution shatters Dovan's confidence. He's unsteady on his feet as he retreats from her touch but finds no escape. Just me. Standing in his way. He goes so still he blends into the gray walls and the green fades from his irises, leaving them dark and colorless.

I grieve the loss of color, but the new spark of hope in my heart grows into a flame, burning through the doubts and the questions of how his Gran could know something I don't. Something no story has ever mentioned. An end to my terrible fate.

A soul for a soul means I can die in the victim's place.

It means the banshee curse can be broken.

It means Dovan can be saved.

If she's right.

I set my palm over the prophetic wound in his chest, but this time I don't blink the tears away. I want him to see. Ten years of grief, ten years of failure, ten years of never having a choice, but now, I might have one. I reach for his empty hand and guide his stiff fingers to his sword hilt, but the emotion wrecking him locks my breath in my throat.

Horror.

The idea of killing me horrifies him. *When did my life begin to matter more than his?*

A bead of moisture, the first tear I've ever seen him allow to fall, slips down his cheek as he shakes his head and presses his mouth into a firm line. All physical cues that tell me *no*. He should jump at the chance to stay alive, to survive me and my cursed song. *Why won't he trade my life for his?*

If Dovan had treated me like the monster I am—*this would be easy*. But he's never seen me through the label of my curse. I've never been a *banshee* to him.

"No." He jerks his hand free, blinking once to clear his vision as he faces his Gran. "I have searched the records. I have read every story. There is no way to break the banshee curse."

Even though he's talking to his grandmother, his words poke at me, coaxing out my curiosity. *Why would a guider research banshees?*

"It be the truth." His Gran crutches a step closer. "Ye can save yerself."

Dovan takes a deep breath and a change comes over him. His spine straightens as he clears the emotions from his eyes with a hard blink. The gentle man who finds horror in my death disappears behind the soldier who'd kill anyone if it meant salvation for his people.

Then why isn't he? He wouldn't risk much to find out if his Gran is right. I'll either die and set him free, or I'll survive and we'll face the same ending we were before. The greater part of the risk would be mine.

I place a shaking hand on his arm, gasping over the heat of his skin. Even with clothing between my fingers and his bicep, the contact burns. "Dovan, please."

He pulls away, but not before whispering, "You don't understand what's at stake."

Stunned, I stare at him as he wraps his grandmother in his

arms and holds her tight. *He's saying goodbye.* When he should be thanking her.

He kisses her cheek. "I have lived my whole life serving others. I will not die serving myself."

Why does he have to be such a hero?

His Gran presses her lined lips together and blinks hard as she fights off a choked sob. Dovan's shoulders twitch in anguish at the strangled, gasping sound, and he leaves before he loses control over his own composure. She's left alone with me, the banshee her grandson protects.

Grief weighs down her boney frame as she scans the room for where I might be standing. "If ye be the good soul he claims." Her head hangs low, chin trembling as she rubs her eyes, and I glimpse the pain of a woman who cannot protect the boy she raised into a man. "Save him. Save me boy..."

I will accept her mission, but as I leave her to cry alone, my heart is sinking, pushed under by a new fear.

Dovan believes he has to die.

I brace myself against the wall as a shiver ripples down my arms. *He wasn't lying.* All the times he said his death isn't my fault. That he *chose* this. Shouldering the blame for his own death while hinting at some hidden reason. A reason I don't understand as one thing becomes clear.

For the first time, the victim I sing to is a willing player in Red Death's game.

DOVAN

14

A GUIDER STANDS his ground until he breaks. The breaking point differs for everyone, but we all face that moment, tipping over a knife's edge between fear and courage, hope and despair, selfishness and sacrifice. I thought I'd faced mine. I thought my iron will unshakable. *I thought I could do this.*

One final sacrifice.

I've seen hardened guiders survive a pack of wolves only to be broken by the tears in a child's eyes because they returned when the child's father or mother didn't. Broke the will to endure right out of them. They couldn't face another day of this struggle, of what we guiders must always do.

The people we protect come first.

And here I stand at the top of the stairs, bowl of soup in hand, with a banshee's soft steps behind me and the strangled cries of the proudest woman I know filling the silence. I've never heard my Gran cry. She taught me how to be strong, but now, that strength is too heavy. My shield slowly collapsing and becoming a tomb. *Falling apart is like turning to stone.* Where every breath adds another weight to your already burdened soul, crushing you, while deep down inside you there's a voice uttering one word, over and over.

Stop.

But a guider cannot neglect his duty. People die if we give in to the desire to go numb, to close our ears to the never-ending calls for help, to let the fire in our hearts burn out and become ash. We cannot stop. *I cannot stop.* But I can't go on. The enemy is inside my chest, beating away. With every *pound—pound—pound,* my heart spreads something I'd never considered as a poison.

Hope.

I heard her laugh.

Joy, bright as sunlight, shining from a face many before me had fled when she started to sing. To them, she was the creature from the old tales, a death pronouncing wraith. I've killed plenty of monsters, both beasts and men, but the girl who laughed with my family tonight is no monster. *She looked like...* Flickers of memory finish what I won't put into words. She's been haunting me for longer than she knows.

Frigid air brushes my back as her footsteps fall silent. *She's close.* The cold she brings with her breaks the stiffness from my body. *Remember what's at stake.* I straighten my spine, spilling out a hot breath that fogs through her chill, and I step forward, past my breaking point. The fractures are still there. Flashes of our past, sparks of hope for what can never be, and a secret I guard for us both. *Remember who you are.*

I am a guider. The son of a guider.

I have never wanted to be anything else, anything more.

Not even for her?

The question slides between my ribs like a blade but doesn't pierce my heart. It settles there, a sharp invitation ever whispering. *Change your mind.* I grit my teeth as I force my focus outward. To a safer place than the storm waiting to break inside me.

The lanterns hooked into the pale walls push back the night shadows. I scan the rooms for the old man who joined my household tonight. My banshee keeps pace without stepping into my sightline. The old man has planted himself in the center of the third room. The other pallet beds and their occupants have retreated against the walls as he scratches the sores on his cheek.

With a grunted *for you,* I push the bowl of soup into his hands and leave before he can speak. *Enough delays.* Enough lingering with doubts. I have hours left, and I won't waste them. My shoulder brushes against my banshee's, eliciting a tiny sigh of steam, but I avoid her questioning eyes. They will hold the final blow, not some killer's knife, once she understands why my life must end.

I head toward the room to the left of the stairs. Snores cover the sound of my booted steps as I approach the small chest against the far wall with my pallet. There's no lock and the hinges creak as I lift the lid. The hall lanterns offer enough light to bring out the burgundy shade of a guider's tunic and the glint of a metal hilt. I remove the dagger first and then the tunic. They belonged to my adopted father. The guider who took me in and taught me to be a good man. The white bear on his tunic has four stripes where mine has none, signifying the highest rank among guiders. My fingers trace the jagged stitches at the feet of the standing bear. They close the blood-stained rips from the wolves that killed him. No other piece of fabric has felt so heavy in my hands.

He gave everything. *A soul for a soul.*

My Gran's voice knifes through my thoughts. *"A banshee's curse be a trade."* I am no stranger to that kind of sacrifice. A twinge of guilt twists her sharp words deeper. *My father made that trade.* So will I. But not in the way my Gran hopes.

I fold the tunic over my arm and almost close the chest when a strip of light shines on the last possession I prize. Inky swirls and ripped paper lying in the dust of forgetfulness. A cry rises from my soul, tempting me, begging me to look from the remains of the song that saved me to the young woman who wrote it. *I never forgot.* But she did. I shut the chest as the melody reaches out from my bleaker memories. They'll only get in the way. A dark twinge of humor stings my eyes at the irony.

A song brought me back to life, and a song will bring me to my death.

Both sung by the same person.

I just wanted one day. One day with her before I surrender to my purpose. *She's*—words fail me, and in their place writhes a pit of stewing emotions.

Neither of us are who we were. We've both been broken. Scarred. Shown the cruel side of life more than once. But where I have healed as much as I can, she remains stuck. Caught in a cycle she didn't begin and doesn't know how to escape. *I wish I could guide her.* That admission is a mistake, rousing a horde of other wishes from the shadows of my heart. The worst lands like a boulder on my back.

I wish there was another choice.

Like my father, I have a job to do, and so I stand.

She's leaning against the doorjamb, humming, her face blacked out by the light behind her, and I make my choice. The one that brings me to her but won't let me stay. The one that keeps us strangers, even though our hearts recognize that's a lie. Ignoring the whisper of ice and fire every time we're close, hissing as we part, speaking to our dangerous truths. So much potential. So much lost because of a curse.

Her icy fingers catch my hand as I pass, and I nearly drop the dagger. "Dovan, please. My life doesn't matter."

I go as rigid as the weapon in my fist. An ache settles into my bones over how much the banshee curse has stolen from her. Not only her identity, but her value. Her purpose. Her power.

"You're needed here." Her grip tightens, a subtle break of emotion in her voice. "No one needs me."

Being a guider has taught me how to be still in chaos, how to endure through exhaustion and heartache, and how to face the monsters, but nothing in my training prepared me for this. For my Gran crying downstairs, for a banshee—*no, stop calling her that!*

I duck my head, focusing on our touching skin. Hers is paler than mine, and yet two shades of skin have never looked so right next to each other. Maybe it's the lack of sleep or the restlessness inside me, but I'm tired of this charade. *She is...* My thoughts derail after those words because of the story lurking just beyond. A story that didn't begin in the snow when she sang the first note of my death song. A tale I have kept to myself. I twist to the right and let myself see her, the girl who saved me.

I skim over her torn dark green dress that drapes her womanly form and focus on the face that once gave me hope when I'd had none. Thick, loose curls of ebony hair close around her like a shield, and before I can stop myself, I switch the dagger to my other hand. My thumb is on her cheekbone, swiping a coil of hair behind her right ear, and there my rebellious hand stays. Her lips press together as she leans against the doorframe to create more space between us. A signal of discomfort I usually honor, but not this time. Not when she believes no one needs her.

I do.

In the lantern light, her hazel irises glow a gentle gold. A dimmed but still dangerous liquid fire that speaks of a soul not yet tamed. She's buried her true strength so deep she's forgotten what she is capable of, and I wish it was my duty to remind her. But it's not, no matter how much my heart begs.

My father once told me a guider's sole mission is to protect and nurture hope for our people. I can't do that for her because what she hopes for will damn our whole world.

I have to save everyone who's left, and the cost will be *us*. Whatever she and I are, or were, or might be if the future was kind, this is our sacrifice. *She'll agree with me.* Because our hearts are the same. The people we protect come first.

Knowing that doesn't smother even a fraction of what I feel. *You can't tell her.* That I wish things could be different. That I wish I could surrender to nothing and no one else but her. Take her in my arms and admit the secret that would heal her but break me.

I love you.

Our lives have never been simple enough to fit inside those three words.

If I didn't already bear so many scars, I'd give in to the cry of *this isn't fair.* I don't know why she and I were chosen for this role. That question is an abyss. I yank myself from its edge. I will not fall. Too many lives depend on me staying strong. But even though I must silence what burns to be spoken, I can show her a sliver of how much I care.

I break our stare, leaning down. She inhales sharply but doesn't tense as I kiss her forehead before resting my head against hers. This small affection will never be enough, but it's the only answer I can give her. I linger for a moment, breathing in her crisp chill, my eyes closed as I remember who she was.

She always arrived with a smile, as if the inn was a happier home than her own. Her black hair was braided with silk ribbons and jewels. They'd go missing by the time she left, snuck into the pockets of the other orphans or into Ioana's cloak to keep us clothed and fed. She hated her name or any title we used to address her. *"Call me Enna."* The part of her name that was still soft, that didn't jar the tongue or make one think of wrecked things.

Enna sang us songs.

As I pull back from the wraith she's become, I still see the real her. Buried deep, but not lost. Not completely. I'd die to set her free from the banshee curse without a second thought, but I can't give her what she wants. I can't let her trade her life for mine.

Her death might save me, but it would damn everyone else.

We carry more than can be seen. A shared secret I'll reveal soon. After I entrust what my father left behind to another boy who wants to grow up to be a guider.

I brush my thumb along Enna's cheek, savoring the difference in our temperatures before I let go. Before I turn away. A thousand things I want to say jam in my throat, but as I shove them down, one slips out. A whisper thin chord strung between our souls.

"You've always mattered to me."

I don't know if she heard me. I don't know if she'll ever remember, but she sang to me fourteen years ago when I couldn't break free of the nightmares. A wordless melody brought us together and tore us apart and grew into the song she sings tonight.

Our story will be the last melody I hear.

Darkness is not my home. It's my stage.

If there's one thing I am good at, apart from murder, it's never being overlooked. *Why else would I wear crimson?* A color made to stand out. Well, there are several reasons, including how pretty fresh blood looks against my pale skin. Blood is always so *vibrant* right after death, the fire of my victims' souls still burning through the gushing flood. They ran. I chased them down. Hunter and prey, killer and victim, victor and loser.

Tonight, I'm not hunting.

My performance has stalled.

I'm one more shadow in the dark, hugging the roof of my victim's home. My boots sink into a fresh cushion of snow as the sky broods black as oil above me. With the storm driven east by the wind, the stars wince their pathetic light over Riffen, and the night holds its breath, confused, since I never retreat.

I don't wait around to kill my victims. I don't stand still long enough for the consequences of my bloody games to forge their whispers into knives, stabbing holes in the persona I wear like a cape. Not when there are other things I could be doing. Riffen won't tear itself apart without my help, after all. *So many lives to ruin.* But I didn't choose more mayhem. I chose the roof, the place where I could breathe without being constantly reminded of—

Desperation explodes through my limbs, and I pound my thigh with my left fist. Once, for each word of my true identity.

I. Am. Red. Death.

I. *Am.* Red. Death.

But my old ally—pain—turns sour, churning my stomach as I sink onto the parapet lining the roof. Face to face with my crumbling lie.

I am Red Death, but I am also more.

I don't care. The past has no power without shame.

I have no regrets, but I'm betrayed by my own body as the bowl of soup in my right hand jerks sideways. Frost kisses the edge of the briny liquid and crowns a lone potato chunk large enough to stick out above the broth. New tremors travel from my hands, up my arms, sliding down my core to my legs. There's a metallic ring to my shaking, like the rattle of cold, unfeeling metal strapped to bruised flesh. *My first real taste of pain.*

The blistering heat pounding through my veins adds another symptom to the repressed life lurking under my skin. My heart is beating too hard. *Like I've been running.* When I've been sitting in the same spot for a solid minute, staring into a bowl of blasted soup.

The horror. A salty, watered-down vegetable nightmare.

I *hate* soup.

Especially when it comes from my next victim. The guider sacrificed his last meal for my sake. *He's in for a surprise.* Wasting his kindness on his murderer. *I'll have to save this face.* The visage of an old, helpless man. Showing it to him, right before I drive my dagger through his heart, will almost make up for what he did. My half-formed sneer freezes to my face.

He made Wraith laugh.

He helped her remember what life was like before I cursed her.

A chill climbs my legs. Numbness follows, biting into my flesh and clashing with savage heat at my side. The curved blade belted there centers my world, chases the cold away, and returns feeling to my legs, but the threat remains in my mind. A single word driven like an iron stake through flesh and bone to pierce my very soul.

Before.

The word falls like a stone into an empty chasm. Silent, and then rattling as it strikes bottom. *If* it strikes bottom. I wait for it to reach... something. Anything. But the word keeps falling. Made meaningless by a past it cannot call to memory.

I have no before.

I *need* no before.

I have everything I want: limitless power belted to my hip, bloody fun games where I get to stab beating hearts and punish the girl who runs away. *You lost focus.* An alarming slip that keeps happening. I sigh out a stream of breathy vapor and glare at the trapdoor that let me onto the roof. *Damn guider.*

I should have seen it before, the way he overpowers my red field of vision with his evergreen soul, the way he brings Wraith to life. *He's no mere man.* There's a power inside him. Far from equal to my own, but strong enough to weaken the curse, to make me wonder who I was. I slump forward as fire carves down my chest, and I trace the area over my heart. Moonlight as soft as pink pearls shines against my wet fingertips. Blood. *This is becoming a habit.* Thinking of him, of how he is different—*It makes me bleed.*

A warning I'd be a fool to ignore. The dagger at my hip buzzes in agreement. My next victim is more than just prey. *He's my oppo-*

nent. If I played fair, this game could have a new winner. *Nobody beats me.*

No one.

I lean out over the alley, savoring the jagged fall of rusty shadows between this house and the next. *I know just what to do.* Before I kill the guider, I'll find a higher rooftop and push him over the edge. See how well he flies. My, how Wraith will scream.

"Old age doesn't suit you."

Speak of the banshee. Wraith approaches with determined steps, but what's worse is the way the shadows trail along at her feet like whimpering dogs begging for the right to curl around their mistress. *They used to be her home.* Now she shows no intention of ever seeking their sheltering cold again.

When was the last time she sought me out? I search our history, barely caging my wicked grin at the replay of my victories, but I find nothing. Wraith stays as far from me as possible, both during our game and after, leaving me to force our delightful little interactions. *My second favorite part.* Next to the actual killing. But this... A rigid fear slithers down my spine and coats my bones as I stiffen. *This isn't the banshee I know.*

The moonlight splits down her face, one side a light golden brown, the other pale, frosty gray, and her eyes—*damn that guider* —are two different shades. The color of newborn fire and the shimmering ebony of a night sky. My grip tightens on the freezing bowl of soup. A soft *crack* shudders through the pottery, but my slip in control is small. I don't think Wraith will understand.

How close we are to a very different future.

At least her dress is immune to that guider's charms. Still black, still torn, still a hopeless reminder of my curse. I force my hands and my body to relax, stretching my lips into a knowing sneer as Wraith slows to a stop in front of me. She looks up, marking the position of the moon over our heads.

Midnight.

Winter's Teeth.

More curses ride the swell of rage from my soul to the tip of my tongue, but I grind them into silence with my teeth, forcing myself to reveal nothing. Especially not the fact that I missed our important killing date. *Well, this is bleedin' fantastic.* Distracted by Wraith's laugh, by what I locked away so long ago, I forgot to stab the guider at midnight.

Did I just *fail?*

I shove the ridiculous idea away. Even if I'm a little late, I always keep my promises and make good on my threats. *She won't win.* I focus on the tether of magic between us. The curse hums between our souls, pulsing with our mismatched heartbeats, ready for my command to finish this game.

Make her sing. Comes the order through my dagger. A twinge of annoyance drives the split in my mind deeper as I try to bury what I've always overlooked.

Wraith isn't the only one being told what to do.

You wanted this curse. For me to be Red Death and Wraith the banshee. I buried the explanation under a word I hate. *Before.* And I won't let it tempt me to destroy our game.

"I know it's you." She breaks the silence first. Her voice sounds so weak without a melody. Thin and scratchy, reminding me of a dying rasp. *Who am I to disappoint her?* Time to be the real me.

I draw my dagger and drag it over my old man disguise, starting at my legs and working upward. The pinkish cloth wrapped around my boney body thickens, sucking up the bloody red bleeding from the dagger's tip. *Finally. A color fit for a monster.* I press the flat of the blade to my sore-covered face and let out a sigh of relief as my skin heals, the aches of old age lessen, and my youthful vigor returns. Lean muscles fill out my frame, but my face remains hollow, a throne of sharp angles and vicious lines. Curls of hair rustle against my temples as they soften into ordered waves parted over my right eye. Each lock transforms from yellowed white to jewel-toned rubies, pale scarlets, and smoky mahoganies.

I stand because I will not look up to Wraith a second longer, my lips tugging higher into a twisted smirk. "Is this the part where you beg for his life?"

Her thin eyebrows sink into a glower as she nods at the bowl I'm holding. "You don't need that. You should give it back."

"And help a starving human survive another day? I don't think so." I toss the bowl over the roof. The crackling splash as it hits the ground and shatters isn't as satisfying as I'd expected. How can destroying pottery measure against destroying lives?

Her hands curl into fists. "Why are you so cruel?"

"Because it's fun."

"There must be a reason."

"For what?" I step closer to her. "You think something terrible happened and made me like this?" The weakness of a *yes* moistens her gaze, and it takes all my control not to throw her off the roof for being so *innocent*. My teeth clench around my words as I point my dagger at my heart. "This is who I am. Stop making excuses for me to ease your own conscience."

Wraith frowns at my weapon, expression filling with a foolish idea. *Oh, so she thinks the dagger is the cause?* That somewhere in my past I had the terrible misfortune of picking it up. An accident that turned me into a heartless murderer. *She is such a child.*

Killers like me don't happen by accident.

We choose what we want. Society frowns on our bloodthirsty hobby, but then, their souls are too straight to get the appeal. Through my game, I control death. A wicked thrill burrows into my skin from my dagger's warm hilt. Our desires unite until we burn with untapped violence. *We are owed a soul.*

I snatch her arm from her side and stab her forearm.

Her shocked gasp and violent flinch feed my victorious sneer. With the dagger's tip caught between her bones, the blade offers me the cruel leverage of pain. I use it, angling the hilt so she has to inch closer to keep from screaming.

"I want to hear you beg for his life." I twist the dagger and her face pinches in agony. "Go on. Convince me. Tell me what makes Dovan worth saving?"

Wraith firms her chin, daring to meet my gaze. My sneer falters at the fire in her mismatched eyes. "Maybe you should tell me why *I* should live."

Her words fracture the wall I built between who we were and who we are, and through the fresh cracks, I see...everything. Too many things. A whirlwind of chaos, of choices made and consequences earned, and she's standing at the center. So convinced she's right. But she was wrong. *It wasn't my mistake.* But hers, that set us on this path. And she's about to make another.

Stop her.

Be the monster she fears.

The monster she won't cross.

I rip my dagger from her arm, spilling a few drops of curse-blackened blood on the snow at our feet. She cries out at first but then bites off her scream. Tiny crystals of ice sparkle through her heaving breaths as she applies pressure to the wound, a pointless gesture. We both know she doesn't bleed. Her blood is too thick, too cold.

She matches my steps as I retreat. "You try so hard to prove you don't care about anyone, but there is someone, isn't there?"

I won't give her the answer. She won't get that kind of victory from me.

"My life matters to you."

I need to recover the control of this conversation and so I squeeze the dagger's hilt, pulling on the hunger and the malice burning through the blade. "The game wouldn't be any fun without an opponent."

"I don't see how when I always lose."

"You are rather boring, but I enjoy watching each loss hurt you."

As expected, there's no shock fracturing her expression, only a sinking of her shoulders. "Why don't you just kill me?"

I sniff, glancing out over the city with its dull red lights sparking through the darkness like bleeding fireflies. "I'm used to you."

"So you *can* kill me."

"Easily."

"Prove it."

The dagger grows so hot over her suggestion it scalds my hand but killing her would be a mistake. A blood-red pulse sweeps out from her body in inviting waves, guiding my predator's gaze to her chest and the organ I love most. I forgot how good the beat of her heart sounded. The gentle, but far from steady rhythm.

Her heart cost me everything.

As I shake the thought from my head, I cut through her distraction and expose her real motive. *Clever.* Making me defensive with a few well-aimed questions while she gathers courage to ask the one that matters.

I sheathe my cooling blade, but there's no resurrecting my sneer. *She knows.* Either someone dropped the right hint, or she finally figured it out.

There is a way to save the guider.

A trade, really. One I'm not interested in making.

"You don't want me dead?" Her voice holds a note of doubt. The fact she is unsure of what I want revives my wicked sense of fun.

"If you died, I couldn't hurt you anymore." I lean closer. "I'd miss the sound of your screams, the salty scent of your tears, and the—"

I snap my mouth shut as my mind loses its hold on which

Wraith I'm staring at. *The song of your laugh.* It's what I couldn't say. A memory that must stay buried even as who she was and who she is tangle together, laughing and weeping. Both are mine to protect and to harm.

"You're the one who's crying." Her words are sharper than any knife, slicing through the fog of our irreconcilable lives and drawing my attention to the moisture limping down my cheek. I restrain the urge to wipe the tear away. Such an action would make me look weak when I must remain strong. Our *before* won't win. It can't win.

Fingers tremble as they brush against mine, a pitiful attempt at contact before she decides to go all the way and *hold* my hand. "You must be tired of it."

I glare at our touching flesh. The sight turns my stomach, heating my blood with a fury I've taken out on countless innocents. "Tired of what?" I jerk my hand free before I lose control and stab her again. "Our little games?"

"Yes."

Half of a laugh gusts through my throat. "Unlike you, my darling banshee, I never tire of having fun."

She blinks, barely hiding her surprise by pressing her lips together. *Why is she shocked that I find our arrangement fun?*

With a shake of her head, her gaze narrows as she studies me, searching for the man behind the monster. Unease twitches through my shoulders as my heartbeat spikes, ticking like a clock that's counting down.

"Don't you ever wonder who we were?" she asks.

I don't have to. Not really. The truth is buried at the bottom of my soul. I turn my back on her and hurry across the roof, where I leap to the edge and gauge the distance between houses for my jump.

"Do you even know how many people you've killed?"

Another foolish question, but this time I'll answer. "I don't care about numbers." A number implies the count will stop at some point. *I don't want it to stop.*

"Three-hundred and sixty-nine."

I smile, cocking my head to the side so I can see her. "Does that include the guider?"

The glare she aims at me answers a defiant *no.*

Well then, unlucky number three-hundred and seventy he shall be.

"Tell me why. Why do you kill?" She reaches for her throat. "Why do I sing?"

My boots thud on the roof as I step off the parapet and match her advance until we meet in the middle. Her dark hair and my bloody cape flying in the wind. "Why does it matter?"

"Because Dovan doesn't have to die. Does he?"

Now we're getting to the reason for this little chat. *About damn time.* My fingers twitch closer to my weapon as I shrug. "Someone always has to die."

The wind stops dead. As her hair falls around her face and spills over her shoulders, she shimmers like sunlight on the first frost of winter. There's a melody in my head, a sound of joy, of two voices who don't laugh alone. It's almost like—like—

A memory?

Numbness spreads through my legs until they no longer feel like they're a part of my body. I reach for my dagger as my mind buckles under a flood of unknowable emotions. She's broken the dam I've trapped them behind. *Silence her. Before she ruins every-thing.* I slash at her, my blade tearing a line across her left cheek.

She stumbles back, fingers pressed against the cut, her eyes hollow and aching as if she's forgotten how wicked I am.

I leer over her, taller, stronger, and holding all the power. "Question me again and his death will be slow and brutal."

"Then this is about revenge." Her hand falls from her face. "What did I do to you? To make you hate me so much?"

"What did *you* do?" My voice lowers into a rumbling threat

best suited for enemies. *That's who we are.* I won the right to force her to play my game. I touch her sternum with my dagger, earning a delightful shudder from her. "You betray—"

GONG. The tower bell marks the first hour and I flinch.

The pain. It splits flesh, grates against bone, and tears hungrily into my heart. My grip on the dagger loosens, and the curved blade slips free and falls. Wraith sucks at the air, gasping, and we double over at the same time, each of us with one hand pressed against our chests. *No. It's not supposed to happen this way.*

An icy dread freezes the familiar pain where its razor edge has lodged in my heart. Whatever doubt I might have conjured to calm my mind, I have only to look a few feet across the snow-crowned roof. Wraith mirrors my pained posture, my panicked breathing, my unfocused gaze. This time—*she feels it.*

The threat I alone understand.

Blood stains our fingertips as we rub our chests, but her blood remains black, restoring a sliver of hope. It's not too late. I can still save—

"Tell me what is going on." Her eyes are wide and dark with fear. For once, I'm not to blame.

I reclaim my weapon from the snow, force myself upright, roll my shoulders and crack my neck. "Where would be the fun in that?"

I abandon her to the pain we share and step onto the parapet. My crimson cape fills with frigid air as I leave her with my flashiest sneer. "Don't forget to sing."

I open my arms and fall, flipping once to land with a jarring thud in the alley. As I stand, tortured melody rings through the air. She's singing the first note as the curse commands, but even as my dagger warms in pleasure, regret smothers my enjoyment.

I remember what her voice sounded like when her songs were free.

THE BOY

THE GIRL CREPT up behind him like the first frost of fall, careful to make no more sound than the soft sweep of her skirt on the marble floor. *For good reason.* Monsters were prone to violence when startled, a truth they'd both learned from their father.

The boy had left a bloody trail of bare, sticky footprints behind him. Murder had become justice in his bloodstained hands tonight, and he'd wielded it with rods of iron. The same rods were now discarded on the floor. A cage built for his betraying legs, except—*they don't betray me anymore.* The boy had broken the braces apart and used them to crush bone and tear muscle and stab another murderer's manhood.

Damn well deserved it. The boy sneered, holding his hands over the washbasin, but he hesitated. He'd killed before, but never like this. Those murders were for boredom mostly, a flare of wet red to spice up his suffocating life. This kill was—*everything.*

Washing the evidence from his skin would be another crime.

"Thank you." His sister's soft voice was thick with unspoken questions, but she never asked them.

Never asked him how he was standing unaided, how he'd slaughtered a high northern warrior as large as a bear, how he'd walked all the way back to his room, navigating several stairways from the dungeon cells.

She left him then, sniffling, but he heard the shift in her grief. A similar but heavy resolve they both shared. An ending, to the brutal loss of their mother. Their father had wanted to make a public example of her killer, but the boy knew two things. His mother's killer belonged to him alone. No one else had the right to end that bastard.

The second, his sister would never betray his secret.

WRAITH

16

"SOMEONE ALWAYS HAS TO DIE."

In the ten years I've served Red Death, he has never made a mistake. *Until tonight.* He said *someone* when he should have used Dovan's name. I glance up at the sky. The moon falls toward the west, drifting from the rule of night into the early morning hours, and I bite Dovan's song off in the middle.

Red Death missed his own deadline.

I wince from an echo of the pain that made my chest bleed. Dark blood still stains my fingertips, but tugging the bodice of my ruined dress away from my skin reveals nothing. No wound. Not even a scratch. *Red Death felt it too.* Doubling over at the same time I did, but he showed no surprise over his bleeding chest.

He knows.

Whatever is happening to me, to him, to *us*, he knows why.

I shiver, my stomach twisting over being tied to that monster in any way other than the curse. *Something has changed.* I sense the shift of fate in the slightly faster beat of my heart, in the warming tingle of my skin, and in the way the song I am bound to sing hangs back. The last notes are waiting, ready and eager, but I'm able to push them down.

This game has higher stakes than Dovan's life. *I wish I knew what they were.*

I rub my aching sternum and shake my head, closing my eyes to shut out the world as I focus on remembering every detail of Red Death's expression.

His sneer was wrong. Buried under the hatred he harbors for me and his twisted sense of violent fun, I saw—*fear.* A dark terror flashed across his face when he watched my fingers leave my chest, blackened with my blood. *He looked...* My thoughts derail, pointing me to an impossible word. One that's branded into my soul, not *his.*

He looked defeated.

But Red Death never loses. Our game can't change, or at least that's what I've believed until Dovan's Gran implied my curse is a trade. *A soul for a soul.* Her shocking revelation forced me to seek the monster who controls my fate only to find him rattled. Instead of answering my question, or facing the source of his fear, or demanding I finish Dovan's song—*he ran away.*

Red Death ran away.

Frustration shudders down my arms and legs. I kick at the snow, scattering clumps in every direction as I yell, but the sound I make has changed. The dying echo of my voice stripped bare and freed from melody. For the first time in a decade, my voice is my own. I cry out again and again. For me, for *my* pain, and my miserable life.

I grab fistfuls of snow but never throw them as ripples of emotion blur my sight. A new ache pounds behind my ribs, spreading needles of warmth through my limbs. The rhythm is strong, familiar, and yet strange. I press my palm to my chest, daring to hope even as doubt whispers *this isn't real.* But the missing beats the curse stole from me jolt my heart and it wakes up, thumping faster and harder. *It's beating like I'm—*

Normal.

I smile, and then I'm falling backward. My hope and my restored heartbeat shattered by the stabbing chest pain I don't understand.

The pain I share with a murderer.

The snow cushions my fall with a *crunch* that sprouts an echo. It grows louder and louder as I blink up at the moonlit sky. *Footsteps.* Rushing toward me. Followed by a stinging change in temperature as the snow beneath me melts.

"What happened?" Dovan kneels beside me, and I hide the injured side of my face behind my hair. "I heard your screams."

There was a time when such an admission would have meant everything, but the grateful shock of being heard has twisted into a reminder of all I'm about to lose. I roll to a seated position, holding my right forearm close to my body to conceal the other wound Red Death gave me. *The last thing I need is for Dovan to be protective.* How will he ever accept I have to die in his place if he's still trying to save me? Red Death never confirmed what Dovan's Gran had said, but his odd behavior lends strength to her argument.

A soul for a soul.

I can't be saved, but I hope Dovan can.

I pull away from him as he tries to help me to my feet and stand on my own power. His outstretched hand falls in disappointment as his heat cools, retreating, but I don't let myself miss it. Instead, I walk toward the parapet and focus on the view.

Moonlight softens the harsh lines of the wood and stone houses rising around us, draping like a silver skin along the rooftops and smoking chimneys. There's little movement and almost no sound, nothing to separate Riffen from a dead city. An omen of what is to come if winter never ends.

"My blood mother would wake me on nights like this," Dovan's voice fills the stillness as he joins me, and I hold back my surprise. *He's never shared about his blood family before.* I take his hand, hoping my touch might coax him to continue.

Heat radiates from his skin into mine as his grip tightens. "She'd help me climb the sand dune that hid our caravan."

He's from Abrykar. The desert country to the south, which makes sense with his skin being darker than most people in Riffen. *But he speaks like us.* A fact that weighs down my heart with understanding. *He must have been very young when he came here.* Young enough to lose the cadence of his nation's speech.

"We'd watch the sky until the moon started falling west, like it is now." A sad smile overtakes his face. "'The wishing hour' she called it."

"How old were you?" I ask, overtaken by curiosity. "Did you make any wishes?"

"Too young," he sighs. "Far too young to realize how precious such small moments are." I lean my shoulder against his arm at the subtle hint of grief leaking through his words. "But yes. I made a wish."

"Just one?"

The corner of his mouth twitches. "I wished for a sword."

I almost laugh. "Of course you did."

Silence falls between us as our conversation runs into the wall of my curse. He doesn't ask me if I had any traditions with my mother, and I'm grateful, because I don't remember anything about my parents or my childhood.

Dovan glances at me. I angle my head left to hide my cut cheek, but I glimpse the seriousness wrinkling his expression. Unease chafes my skin as I wait for him to ask the question I dread. A question that spills from his lips, wrapped in equal parts caution and hope.

"What would you wish for?"

He might as well have jabbed a shovel into my chest, prying away the protective armor of my bones to get at my heart. I squeeze my eyes shut to block the tears before they reveal even banshees resort to wishing when life hurts.

Sometimes all I have are wishes.

The need to take the cruel facts of how things are and reshape them into what they should be. *Daydreams.* Fragile sparks of false hope. The cost of tending them is too high for a banshee. Even as Dovan invites me to share in a precious tradition his mother gave him, I'm forced to remember how different we are. *He's free.* Free to dream and wish for things without a curse stripping away what makes wishes powerful.

Possibilities.

Banshees only know the possibility of a song that ends in death.

The weight of unshed tears and repressed grief tips my chin downward. When I open my eyes, I see our hands. We're still holding on to each other. I resist the urge to cry, to face him and tell him everything. He hasn't seen the mark Red Death's blade left on my skin. A reminder of our true roles. *This is still a game.*

I have to play, but I don't have to lie.

Straightening my weary posture, I focus on the stars as Dovan watches me. "I'd wish for you to live." I force a deep breath into my lungs. "I'd wish for you to go on serving your people. To find someone and make a life together and be happy and die—" my voice betrays me with a crack, "—only when you are old and have lived a full life."

He reaches across my body to turn me toward him, but I resist and put a few steps between us. Our hands pull apart, leaving my fingers exposed. Winter's chill fills the space over my empty palm.

"I'm sorry." He takes a half-step closer, his shoulders rounded in a clear sign of regret. "I shouldn't have asked you—"

"I wish we had never met." My words hit him like a physical

blow, bending him forward, softening his mouth, and widening his eyes, but I don't voice the reason behind my wish. *Because then you'd be safe.* Without me, his life would go on, no longer threatened by a murderer's cruel game.

Dovan blinks and clenches his jaw but doesn't look away. "Meeting you will never be one of my regrets."

I swallow the desire to once again ask him why he's different, but that would just waste more time. *I have to convince him.* To save his life and end my curse, I will make the trade.

My soul for his.

The prophetic wound in Dovan's chest widens, dripping a new crimson streak down his white bear. I grimace as pain slices my heart in a mirror warning, but I gather what little strength I have left and speak what no banshee has ever spoken.

"You don't have to die tonight."

Tension hardens his muscles and twitches along his jawline until a sad twist softens his mouth. "I wondered if you'd taken my Gran's words to heart."

"It's not just her words."

His eyebrows pull down in concern. "You weren't up here alone, were you?"

There's no easy way to do this, to admit I sought his future murderer, so I let my body speak for me. I take a step to the right and show him my whole face.

Dovan's gaze narrows on the cut on my left cheek and stays there as his shortened breaths swirl like bands of steam between us. "Who did this to you?"

It's not a question, not the way he says it. It's a promise. Once I name my abuser, Dovan will take swift action to ensure they never hurt me again. *You can't tell him.* He'll fall deeper into the trap of keeping me safe.

Protecting me will get him killed. I want him to live.

He touches my cheek, his thumb tracing the skin under the

wound and sending an icy shiver down my neck and shoulders. "Don't shut me out. Not on this."

I grip his wrist and take a breath to memorize the feel of his skin on mine. His gentle wave of warmth crackling through each of my frozen layers. *It won't last.* I push his hand away, but I can't let him go. Our hands fall, a link of flesh and bone tying us together by the power of hope when our destiny is to be torn apart.

I clear my vision with a hard blink, forcing my soul to swallow the seeds of grief again. Tears will only provoke his protective instincts further. "What happened to me doesn't matter." Dovan sucks in a breath as he prepares to object, but I cut him off. "I'm cursed, Dovan. *Cursed.* Do you understand that?"

He faces the city to avoid my gaze.

"Do you?"

His chin falls as he glances my way. "I don't believe in curses."

A hysterical laugh bursts from my throat. "Aren't you the lucky one to have the luxury of belief."

"I meant..." He sighs, rubbing his temples as if to sooth an ache. "Curses suggest there are no more choices left to those under their power. They make us truly hopeless, and I won't believe that. Not for one moment." As he drops his hand and reveals his face, sadness wets his eyes. "We always have a choice. No matter our circumstances."

I touch his arm and hope he means what he says. "Then let me choose."

My words hang between us like a bridge, but Dovan remains where he is. The wrinkle between his eyebrows digging in deeper as his concern edges toward guilt.

Within seconds, I can't see him clearly anymore. There are so many tears. New and old emotions threading themselves into knots around my voice, combining with the notes I cannot sing. They escape in a melodic groan as I grit my teeth, and my forehead falls into nothing. Or at least it should be nothing. But as a gentle rush of warm air embraces me, there's the tickle of wolf-fur and coarse cloth against my uncut cheek, the scent of leather, and the muscled-bone of Dovan's shoulder to support me.

"I'm not blind," he whispers, voice thick and rough. "I see how much this hurts you." The heat of his hands stings my shoulders as he pushes me back. He leans forward until we are eye to eye. "I know what this choice means. If my Gran is right, you could be freed, your banshee curse ended and my life saved, but..."

I shiver because I know what comes next.

"Whether you sing or don't, my fate won't change."

I jerk free of his hold.

Dovan's empty hands hang in the air for a moment before falling to his sides, left one resting on his sword as his posture straightens. "I have to die."

"Why?" A bitter taste coats my tongue, ripe with envy and anger. "You have everything, Dovan! People who love you. People who *need* you. An entire city that knows your name and respects you. Why would you throw that away? When all saving you will cost is me?"

His voice cracks in a laugh that's more exhausted than he is. "You still don't understand."

"Then explain it to me!"

My desperate outburst shatters his stoic mask. The weight of sorrow behind his eyes slams into me. All the deaths he's witnessed, all the bodies he's buried, all the parentless children and widowed couples he's tried to comfort, the number ticks up. Higher and higher. *He's never lost count.* The memory of each loss burns like unquenchable torches within his soul. Dozens, maybe hundreds of torches. My lips twist downward, mirroring his vast grief. *I can't fault him for this.* For wanting to die as he has lived.

For them.

He doesn't seek death as a selfish escape but as an answer, a solution to a problem I can't see. "Why are you so convinced you have to die?"

He nods toward the city. "Because my death will save them."

Whether triggered by my sinking hopes or Dovan's unexpected reply, the pain is back, and it's getting worse, cleaving my heart in two as the air is punched from my lungs. I gasp. Then the notes come. The curse strums my vocal chords, creating the final melodic phrase that will end this game.

His arms wrap around me as I hiccup the word *no* between the beginning notes of his death song. He pulls me closer, right into the wound in his chest. The salty copper scent of agony sears my lungs until I cannot breathe.

The song—his song—*it's finished.*

Red Death is close. So close to being victorious again.

I cannot sing.

If I sing, Dovan dies. Right here, right now.

I place my palms on either side of the prophetic wound. The curse calls to its master, and I feed the energy swelling through my muscles with every dark moment, every tear, every time I begged for freedom. *I'm done begging.* I shut my eyes and focus on one word. The most important word I will ever say in my life.

No.

That word becomes a decree of defiance.

The song builds in my chest, tears through my throat, and scrapes past my lips in a wail befitting a banshee. The force of the cry I unleash is worse than the scream of a raging blizzard. Dovan stumbles back, arms shielding him from the tiny bits of ice whipped into the air from my scream.

As my lungs empty, my cry weakens to a gurgle, and then a cough, and then I once again prove Dovan wrong. *I have no choice.* With a single inhale, I give the curse what it needs to finish him.

Silence spreads like a tentative layer of frost between us.

Silence, *unbroken.* I breathe in and out, but there's no melody, no notes forcing their way free.

I'm not singing.

I'm. *Not.* Singing.

I finger my sternum, waiting for the pain, for the curse to exert its control over me. *His song is finished.* I know all the notes, but I am silent, musically becalmed all the way down to my soul.

All I did—*I said no.*

A word I've whimpered, and wept, and pleaded a million times before, and it never worked before tonight.

Cautious warmth nips at my skin as halting footsteps crunch closer. Dovan stops in front of me and holds out his hands. I search his face, reading a conflicting battle between pride and regret in his pine-green gaze, but nothing can dampen my spirits.

"I'm not singing." A giggle bubbles out, and I duck my head, dizzy from the strange emotion pressing in from all sides. *Is this what happy feels like?* A giddy, buzzing, hot and cold rush of elation and hope, as if I am filled with sunlight and butterflies and the homey comfort of baked sweet rolls.

My mouth waters, but the lump in my throat makes swallowing difficult. *You're not free.* Everywhere I look, mopey grays, bleak whites, and heavy blacks color the world. If I were free, my sight would be restored. Dovan's eyes remain the only colorful break in my grayscale vision. *This isn't over.*

"Please," I place my hands in his and draw strength from his firm squeeze. "Let me save you."

He steps back, his palms sliding from mine, and I blink against a fresh assault of tears. Color blooms along our skin and our clothes where we still touch. My creamy, golden brown against his darker skin. My torn green sleeves against the rich brown of his bracers. I curl my fingers and lock our hands together. For so long, I've lived without fear because I had nothing to hold on to, but my hands aren't empty now.

I'm terrified of what I will lose if I let go.

"Do you trust me?" Dovan's question spears through my heart. It's the first cackle of fate turning against us.

"I...I..." My voice trembles, the edge of each tone dipping into a familiar melody. His song's still waiting to be sung. It won't wait forever.

"Because I trust you." His right hand tugs free of mine and cups my face, lifting my head. "I *trust* you. When you understand what I'm doing, you won't want me to make a different choice."

I search his eyes, hoping to find a fighter preparing for battle behind their evergreen shield, but the soul I see is a giver, a man who's ready to sacrifice himself. His conviction guts me. My bones go soft, and as I fall forward, Dovan pulls me against his chest. Once again, I'm in his arms, but his embrace remains loose, timid, as if having me this close is dangerous.

"Trust me enough to show you. That's all I ask."

How can I deny a request that trembles through his tightened throat?

I restrict my answer to a nod because the only words I have to speak are traitors to his cause. *Don't ask me to watch you die.*

WRAITH

17

THE PALACE of Riffen rises like a shining crown at the heart of the city's highest circle, all sharp corners and ornamental columns and pointed arches. Winged monsters roar threats from the higher balustrades framing the giant-sized front doors, icicles bearding their open jaws and fringing their serpentine bodies. The childish corner of my heart wonders if the gargoyles were merely trapped by winter and will wake with the next thawing. *If spring ever returns.* A dull stab of pain cuts into my chest as my vision blurs and I stumble.

Dovan's hand steadies me, sending waves of heat to clash against the frosty chill of my skin. "What's wrong?"

I shake my head instead of speaking. The notes of his song sting my throat, so close to escaping, but I swallow them down. *I am in control now.*

I will never sing his song.

It doesn't matter what Dovan wants to show me. *He must live.* He will live.

I return my focus to the palace. Rows of arched windows puncture the pale stone walls on each level, and the lightless rooms behind their panes turn them into black voids streaked in moonlight. Like mirrors, they reflect every movement of the guards patrolling the dead, snow-dressed gardens that once softened the palace's sharp structure with lush vegetation. The skeletal arms of rose bushes used to hold out their vibrant buds to visiting guests, but now they stab at the air, winter's chilled breath tripling the length of their thorns.

There's no welcome waiting here.

Only a warning, as the torches near the front doors spark and hiss in a fiery laugh, deepening my chill because the palace feels empty. Hollow. Starved of the multitudes of guests it once hosted before winter. The palace's tiered floors and domed towers slant over us, sharpening the contours of its moon-kissed bones. A skeletal facade hiding untold numbers of shady secrets. *I'd settle for one.* Like why Dovan brought me here to convince me he should die.

His determined stride eats up the ground as we approach the wrought iron gate separating the palace from the city. The metal curls and weaves into a tangle of thorns and flowers wrapped around a standing bear. I prepare to stop, but Dovan forges ahead. The guards never demand he provide his name or give a reason for his presence. Before we have to slow our pace, the bear splits in half with a jangling screech as the gates open. *Why would they let Dovan in?*

There are rumors about how the guiders forced the old king and his palace guard to surrender control of Riffen. Most say the guider council held the king hostage for days before he agreed, but nobody knows the truth. *But these gates.* They're not to be crossed by anyone. Especially not a guider with no rank.

The old king allows the guiders to rule the city, but his palace remains his kingdom. Unless invited here by the king himself, no guider would dare set foot on the polished cobblestones leading to the palace's doors. Never mind entering through them.

Dovan must have an open invitation. That thought gives the chill coursing down my spine teeth. I flinch as the gate rattles closed, locking us in, and as the tallest guard hoists a torch, I squint. My gaze falls to her tunic, to what's stitched across her torso.

A white tree stump with a curved blade standing where its trunk should be.

The symbol of the king knocks the breath from my lungs. An unexplainable fear grips me as I glance away from the female guard, but they all wear the same tunic. The same image. Their uniform, their sign of service to the man who abandoned his people. A shard of icy fear stabs my heart. I grip Dovan's arm and lean closer, seeking refuge in his shadow.

Motivated by whatever look Dovan gave them, the guards move aside. They snap straight as we pass and tap their right fists on their chests, saluting him as a guider would. Their gesture of respect adds to the wrongness of this exchange. *I never thought Dovan would be on friendly terms with the palace guard.* Not when they'd sit back and watch the city burn, safe within the palace grounds. As I pull away from Dovan, I spot a dark smudge on his sleeve.

Blood. My curse-blackened blood.

I pretend to examine our surroundings, sneaking a glance at my forearm. The one Red Death stabbed. I miss a step, my heart tripping with me, but no amount of reassuring myself it's a trick of the light can erase the new truth dragging down my soul.

The wound hasn't healed.

Isn't healing.

The cut is still open and oozing cursed blood. Before I can stop myself, I reach for my face. The slice in my cheek is in the same condition.

I'm not healing.

"What is it?" Dovan asks, and I snap my hand to my side.

"Nothing," I manage between the swelling horror as melodies that don't belong to Dovan's song slip through my curse.

Songs that have no victims.

I shudder, rubbing my chilled arms in a weak attempt to focus, but a new tick starts in my chest. And it's not counting down to Dovan's death.

The cobblestones under our feet transform into a frosted gravel drive near the palace doors. A pair of pearl-toned columns thicker than two men support the upper balcony and frame the entry. Black lacquered wood shimmers under a suspended lantern large enough to house a bonfire within its glass and iron cage. Another tree etched in silver foil spreads its limbs across the door, but the knocker is odd. Shaped like a dagger, it will stab the tree when pulled back. A variation on the old king's symbol.

The door guards each take a curling iron handle and push inward. Light blazes snow white through the growing crack, and the creaking sound of wood disappears under the warbling chatter of hundreds of voices.

I glance at Dovan and find a playful glint in his eyes, but he waits until the doors close with a soft thud behind us. He leans in close to whisper, "I told you this morning we would dance."

That's when I hear the music. Familiar melodies written for the changing of the seasons invites us deeper. I pause in the center of the receiving room, surrounded by polished marble tiles, diverging hallways, snapping torches, and another pair of grand doors where the music is coming from. The toes of my boots catch in the thick fur of an ice bear rug. Dark splotches stain the white fur. My legs bend, bringing me closer to the largest spot.

Ink stains? I almost touch them but yank my hand away at the last second. "He'll be so angry."

Dovan's warmth bathes my face as he kneels in front of me.

His worry wrinkle pinches between his eyebrows. "Who'll be angry?"

"I don't know," I say, wincing as I'm distracted by another voice.

"Why were you even writing here? It's drafty and a good place to get yourself trampled." The boy's voice throbs through my mind as I spin my head left, and then right, searching for him. *He isn't here.* Whoever *he* is.

Dovan's hand grips mine, focusing my attention on where our skin touches, but the clash between our different temperatures fades in importance. I dig my fingers into the bear's stained fur, the mark made by a clumsy girl and a broken bottle of ink.

"This is where she wrote her letters." *Is that supposed to make sense to Dovan?* It doesn't even make sense to me.

A connection pulses between me and the stain, a strange sense of knowing, beating through the rug and into my fingers. All those long days and worried nights, she was here. I face the front doors just as she did, but the explanation I'm waiting for doesn't walk in the way her greatest love would.

He always came home.

But she wasn't always here.

A tether of melody tugs at my soul. I scan the corridor to my right, expecting to see *someone,* but the shadowed hall is vacant. It's narrower and darker than the others, as if to discourage people from using it. An icy breeze sweeps through my hair, and the notes grow louder.

She's singing somewhere in the dark.

Find her.

I'm on my feet and running toward her song.

Find her.

A desperate, hopeful, but terrified need to hurry pounds through my veins.

Find her. Find her. Find her.

I slide around a corner, my boots squeaking on the marble floor as I break through the shadows into a patch of dingy moonlight streaming through a glass ceiling. The hallway ends with no answers. Only a closed door greets me.

I run my fingers over the measure lines and notes carved into the wood panels. *It's her song.* The woman's voice fills the air, rattling the doorknob. As I reach for it, I notice there's no light escaping through the crack under the door. The pitch-black line of shadow grips my chest in a cold vise.

Find her before it's too late.

My stomach twists, my hands tremble, my lungs heave as a knowing fear takes root. *When have I ever been in time to save a life?*

Dovan's heat traps me from behind and icy unknowns press in from the front. I lunge for the knob, turning and jiggling the dingy brass handle, but it won't open. *Locked.* From the inside. I bang on the wood with my fists. Ash rains into my eyes and I choke, coughing through the taste of charred dreams, but I'm not giving up. Not this time. I throw my shoulder against the hard wood. Pain lances through my muscles, scoring my bones, but I don't care.

I don't care what happens to me.

I have to... I have to... I have to... Warm hands grip my shoulders and rescue me from the broken loop of my thoughts.

"No." I struggle to break free of Dovan's hold. "Let me go!"

He turns me around so we are facing each other. I can't bring myself to look at him. I blink through a sea of emotions with no foundation, no reason for existing.

"What's in there?" His tone is as gentle as his touch, offering me comfort, but I don't know what my injury is. I don't know why I hurt or how I'll ever get better.

Nothing can make this better.

I go still, torn between my own thoughts. They brought me here, and now they urge me to flee. I stare at the ash smudging my fingertips. *What happy discovery ever began with the remains of fire?*

I search for the answer within myself but find nothing.

Dovan's warm breath brings a rush of cold to my face. *He must think I'm losing my mind.* If he does, he keeps those thoughts to himself. Metal screeches as he draws his sword. I stiffen. The last time he used it he killed two people.

He nudges me to the side and wedges the sword's tip into the crevice between the doorknob and the doorjamb. With a sharp thrust, the lock surrenders with a click, and the door swings inward with a groan of hinges left too long unused.

Dovan sheathes his sword as he motions to the opening. "You lead. I'll follow."

I take his hand in mine. Just knowing some part of me isn't empty, when so much of my past might as well be a vast cavern, eases my trembling. He gives me a slight smile and an encouraging nod.

I face the door. Silence blankets the hall as I push it open, and the hinges' agonized creak replaces the sound I followed. The woman has stopped singing. A quick glance tells me why.

The room is empty.

She was never here.

No one's been here for a very long time by the looks of things. To my right, a large window stretches from floor to ceiling. The dirty panes taint the moonlight shining through, casting a grim pall over the dark destruction that answers to only one force. *Fire.* The hunger of rabid flames scorched the wooden wall panels, ate jagged chunks out of the curtains, and turned the chairs and sofas into skeletons, all their soft parts burned away.

Uncertain, I step inside the room and then quickly withdraw, leaving a perfect footprint in a layer of fine ash and dust. I sniff, but the smoky scent is so faint. The room is bitterly cold. Whatever started the fire, it happened long ago. The hairs along my forearms spring upward as dread nibbles up my arms. Fear's twisted cousin reaches my heart in seconds and sinks its teeth in. Deeply. But the pain I'm experiencing doesn't belong to the curse. This is different. This is knowing things without remembering them. What waits for me in this room is—

Death.

"Do you want to go in?" Dovan asks.

There's a line before my feet. The oppressive weight of an invisible warning shoving my shoulders down. *Don't cross me.* But this threat is weak, and my heart is beating faster. A pounding *whoosh-whoosh-whoosh* of blood warming in my veins. And then I see it.

The heart of the room. Where legs of sleek wood lie shattered. Where a case made to amplify melody fractured into dead coals. Where black and white keys litter the floor, the rusty wires of the instrument's voice curled beside them by intense heat.

A harpsichord.

I rush toward it, kicking up a cloud of shadowed ash, but I don't get far. Searing pain stabs up through my back, piercing my heart, and my legs crumple under me.

I fall. The ghost of a scream I haven't unleashed echoing off the walls.

My body jolts when my knees hit the marble tiles. The room tilts side to side as bands of ash and moonlight waltz around my head. Dovan's anxious questions pelt my ears, but I'm still falling, my mind caught in a maze of measure lines and warring notes.

Sheet music covers the floor.

The pages are burned, or torn in pieces, or crushed into balls, but I know—*every*—note. The sharper, slanted ones were his, while the flowing, curling ones were mine.

These are our songs.

Ours.

Because I wasn't always alone. *I had someone.* Someone I could count on. Someone who would fix things. Someone who wanted to give me the future we both knew I couldn't have if our situation didn't change.

Red spots drip onto our songs like a rain of death. My heart spasms inside my chest, the slow, steady rhythm warping into an erratic beat, but the only sound I hear is laughter. Two young voices so full of life. Two children having fun in this very room.

Together.

As if nothing in the whole world could ever tear them apart. My body convulses again and again, drowning the sheet music in a flood of red.

All I taste is blood.

All I see is blood.

And I think—*this is where I die.*

FOUR YEARS BEFORE WINTER

"You should keep it," the boy had said. But the girl would rather hold his limp hand. The torn edges of her defiant letter, the black smears of ink on the white fur rug, the throbbing, hand-shaped sting in her right cheek, none of it mattered because the boy was bleeding.

He'd stepped in the way. He'd paid for her foolishness. He always did.

The monster who owned her future cast his shadow over them. "You will write a proper letter and accept the north prince's proposal."

She cowered, nodding and biting deep into her lower lip. Their father didn't need to clarify what *or else* she would face if she disobeyed again. He'd left it explained in blood across the boy's bruising skin. *Obey or he suffers.*

The girl let go of the boy's hand and set about her task. She snatched a blank sheet of paper, the ink that hadn't spilled, and her quill, but the words *I happily accept* dug into her throat as if wrapped in barbed wire. One glance more at the boy's busted lip and swollen eye and she forced the words onto the paper.

It didn't matter that she was only fifteen, it didn't matter that the north prince hung the dried hearts of his enemy's children from his belt. It just. Didn't. Matter. She'd marry a monster to keep the boy safe. She'd have four years before she'd have to keep her promise. Four years was plenty of time for the north prince to meet an untimely fate. *If fate were kind.*

"You should keep it." The boy had murmured before passing out, a bloody finger pushing the last line of her first letter toward her. *"It proves you can say no."*

Saying no just made things worse.

RED DEATH

18

I crash into the wall, gasping for air as I claw at the slick marble of the palace, but there are no cracks, no veins, nothing for me to hold on to.

I can't feel my legs.

But I *won't* fall. Not here. Not when she needs me. *Wraith.* Foolish, soft-hearted Wraith. The curse won't be cheated, and our game won't end in a forfeit. *She should have sung the guider's song.* Her refusal tips everything over the edge of death's cliff.

My heart lurches against my ribs, and I miss my next breath as cursed magic throbs through my blood. I touch my chest and hope, but my fingers are dry. I've stopped bleeding. *Don't you dare.* I grip my dagger to ensure my partner receives that threat. *Don't. You. Dare.* The blade's benign warmth insults me, a sign of forgetfulness I'd expect in humans. Not—*it.*

Fine. Time to remind my partner I'm not just a pretty face.

I close my eyes and focus on listening. *There.* Underneath the ribs, and muscles, and the humming essence of our linked souls, there's a rhythm that's more than sound. The tether in our blood. Death tried to cut it once before, and then I showed up. *No one takes what is mine.* My lips twitch in triumph, but the dread of being left alone ruins my past victories.

"Hold on." That promise feeds my strength from a reserve that doesn't belong to the dagger. I take a step, and then another, keeping my left hand against the wall for support.

I'm coming.

I sneer at the sentiment, but it is my truth. Day or night, curse or no curse—*I'll always come for her.* Because she was right about me. There is one life that matters, that means more than any other.

Hers.

The dagger sends a hot pulse up my side, and the black void of my vision strobes with crimson flashes. A weakening heartbeat of partial sight that allows me to see my way down the dark hall. Regrets pile up in my throat, threatening to choke me as I stumble into a stiff-legged run so feeble the smallest height difference in the floor tiles will bring me down.

I shouldn't have left her alone.

I shouldn't have waited.

I shouldn't have.

I shouldn't.

I've never been good at knowing when to stop. Extremes have always been my form of language. *This is not my fault.* No, the guider's to blame. He doesn't act like a victim, the way he encourages her to hope for what will be her undoing instead of treating her as a banshee. *He's going to suffer.* As soon as I find them.

The open door at the end of the hall sends a tremor through my legs, and I slow to a limping walk. Chills dance giddy marches along my skin, matching two pairs of feet that ran to the harpsichord in *that* room.

It's *the* room.

Where our anchor shattered.

Where everything went wrong.

Where our lives forever changed.

Curses foul my lips as I risk a little more speed. The guider's bending over Wraith, calling to her, but there's no response besides a wet gurgle. These dying rasps are usually one of my favorite sounds. They should taste of victory instead of souring against my tongue. A stab of icy terror guts the thrill of our game because Wraith isn't supposed to be the victim. She's my—

I can't name our connection. It's the loose string in my web of lies. If I pull it, if it crosses my lips—*we'll unravel.* The curse will enact a terrible price, and everything I have done will be for nothing.

The guider is too focused on Wraith to hear my uneven steps, but something warns him as I bring my leg back. He turns, eyes widening for a fraction of a second before he moves. *Too late.* My boot drives hard into his gut. His soft grunt of expelled breath as he falls does little to temper my rage, and I kick him again before he can recover.

He started this. Putting Wraith in danger.

I'm going to finish it.

I yank the guider up by his hair. He bites down on a groan and claws at my grip, his boots squeaking against the stone, but I wrench his neck backward, slamming my knuckles into his jaw. He flops onto the floor, his body twitching as he tries to shake the dizziness away and get up. I savor every time he stumbles.

When he's almost standing, I kick at the side of his knee when a crippling pain rips into my chest, making me miss. *Cheater.* I throw the insult at my dagger as I sway on my feet. The guider's knuckles speed toward my chin. I dodge left, swinging my fist in a sloppy hook. The curse punishes me with another jab of pain and my fist barely grazes his jaw.

Instinct takes over as our fight becomes a blur of moves and countermoves. I'm still faster, still stronger, and unlike him, I hold nothing back. Injury isn't a problem for me, not as long as the magic in my veins burns, repairing the damage. Crimson speckles our clothes and the floor, but none of it belongs to him. I don't even get the satisfaction of cracking his bones or splitting his skin.

The curse *protects* him. From me.

My swings slow as the dagger drains my strength, and I try not to focus on why. On the choking gasps behind me or the frosty chill spreading through the room. The guider remains agile on his feet, holding his guard tight, blocking my punches and deflecting my kicks. His eyes are sharp and focused while my vision blurs and my muscles ache. My heart labors in my chest as I wheeze. I gasp, as if I am drowning. *But I'm not.* She *is.* I groan through the rage such a fear ignites, attacking him in blind fury, but every hit does more harm to me than him. The curse guards our game, ensuring the rules remain unbroken.

I can't kill him.

Not without a banshee's song.

Black sparks explode through my crimson vision as the guider's fist connects with my left temple. He's knocked me off my feet with one blow. A normal human would be unconscious, but me, *well*, I'm a great pretender.

I hold still as the guider grabs my tunic and pulls me up. *Novice mistake.* My dagger slides free, and I bring the hardened end of the hilt to his skull. His eyes roll back in his head as he goes limp. I jerk his falling body hard to the right to avoid being his cushion. See how he likes kissing the floor, all his weight ramming his face into the marble tiles. *Thud.*

I win.

I crawl toward Wraith and my sneer vanishes. *No, no, no.* She's bleeding. Bright ribbons of red flowing down from the cut on her cheek, from the corners of her mouth, and from her chest. *Too much blood.* It pools along her right side in a ruby puddle, but on her left side, it's black and foul. *She's—*

Dying.

Because Dovan woke the part of her I had to kill.

Who she was. Who we were. That was the price.

I cup her cheek and blood oozes through my fingers. It's hotter than it should be, like a fever burns in her veins. Her eyelids twitch open, pupils failing to narrow and focus on my face.

"Sing." I stick to our roles, but my command has the opposite effect as she bleeds even faster. Wraith has won what I've always feared. The right to choose the outcome of our game.

I squeeze her shoulder hard. "You need to sing." It's a weak hope, relying on a deal that's breaking before my eyes, but the curse saved her once. It could save her now. "Sing the guider's song, Wraith."

Her lips form her last act of defiance. "No." Then she coughs, her back arching as a mixture of black and red blood streams from her mouth.

"Sing, dammit!"

"No." Her eyelids close and she's—she's smiling. Like this is the best ending she could hope for. Me, begging her to survive, to do what is necessary and trade a life for hers.

All the heat in my body turns to ice as I hold her.

As I watch. Her. Die.

Again.

"No." I shake myself free of defeat. I beat death once before. I can do it again.

I snatch the dagger from where it gleams in the pool of her blood. My legs are stiff and slow to respond as I crawl to the guider. I roll him over, earning a semi-conscious groan, and then I raise the weapon over his chest.

There it stays. Safely in the air, hovering several feet above his heart. I jerk and heave and swear, but the dagger has its own rules. It won't break them. Not when the blade's lust for a soul is being met.

"Damn you." I fling the dagger away, but the blade doesn't need to be near her to feed. Wraith denied my partner the guider's soul and so it will take hers.

There's nothing I can do to stop it.

I drag myself to her side. "I'm still here." A feeble promise, but I've never broken this one. "I'll stay with you." The softening of my razor-edged voice draws her fading notice, her eyelids slitting open. *Does she see me?* Does she spot the vengeance licking like newborn flames at my grief? A fire I'll unleash upon this city once she's gone.

Another secret tumbles free as I rub a sleeve against my wet cheek, my shoulders twitching from the threat of losing control, but I hold on. I will hold on until she lets go. *All this time.* She thought she was my captive, but her life has been my chain. One I wore with pride. But as her failing breaths spread new fractures through the soul-forged links, once they break—

I'll be free.

And all I'll have left will be rage. Rage and the hunger for bloodshed no amount of killing will ever satisfy. Though I'll certainly try throwing a city's worth of bodies at it until Riffen's streets transform into a colorful but cautionary tale of what happens when I don't get what I want. *Sounds like my kind of fun.* Of a hollow sort.

Admit it. My own thoughts taunt me. *Wraith is your something more.* That extra reason a person lives for, kills for, even dies... I shake my head. Some bargains are too strong. Our choices—mine and hers—have already decided our fate.

I smooth her hair away from her cheek, but there's no recognition in her pale gaze. She doesn't know me. She doesn't even know herself. I'll never hear my real name from her lips again, but nothing's stopping me from speaking hers.

"Wrenna." My throat thickens as I whisper her name against her forehead with an accompanying *sorry* and a flinch of a kiss. Affection was always her thing. *She was the hugger.* I was—I am—a killer. I broke things, and she tried to restore them by wrapping them in her arms and squeezing tight.

There's a scuffle of movement behind me, but I've no desire to fight. All of my fighting was for her.

She was my cause.

The guider's hand bruises my shoulder as he yanks me around to face him. His irises are glowing, a fierce and vibrant green. *Definitely not normal.*

"Get out of my way." His forceful shove sends me to the ground, and I barely move my legs to safety before he drops to his knees beside her. *Rude.*

"What are you doing?" The question is out before I can stop it.

"What you can't." The guider's sharp tone cuts off my mocking reply. "Don't interrupt me."

Curiosity overtakes my annoyance, so I sit in silence and just watch. Him. Do. Nothing. All while Wraith's breaths grow irregular, the gaps between them widening. My fingers tap off a slowing rhythm against my knee. The ultimate fear of my subconscious leaks out through the beat, and I flinch, struggling to stay above the realizations hitting me in waves.

Her heartbeats are running out. Her soul is losing its shine.

Her expression relaxes into vacant peace, and I can't take it.

I seize the guider's arm, jerking him out of his stupor. "She's dying! What are you waiting for?"

He throws off my hand, glaring. "There are other lives to consider."

I really wish I could stab him right now. Bitterness and panic forge my resolve into a plan as I eye the weapon I tossed away. *I could start a fight.* Twist the guider over the dagger and hope he gets cut deep enough to kill him. The action would distract me at least, from what I'm losing. *The best part of myself.*

The guider breathes in and reaches toward Wraith's head. Hesitation weakens his movements with a tremor of uncertainty. *Does he doubt she's worth saving?* I make a mental note to carve all the reasons she should live into his skin.

She's kind.

She's gentle.

She's... just *good.*

Everything I'm not and never wanted to be.

The guider's breath hitches in his throat when his palms settle against the sides of her face, sparking my protective anger. "You better not be thinking anything dishonorable."

He doesn't respond. *Boring.* Except his hands are... *Interesting.* The same irritating green glow that made him stand out in my red field of vision is concentrated between his skin and hers. The air bristles, a clash of hot and cold—*no, it's more than that.* It's a fight for dominance between two forms of ancient power.

The curse and—a *season.*

A bark of a laugh thrusts through the stern line of my lips, as the true missing piece presents itself. *Winter's Teeth.* The guider's annoying green shade, his resilient spirit, his ability to affect Wraith. To wake her up and weaken the curse's hold on us when no other force could even scratch the power of our bargain. *It makes perfect sense.* This guider, this man of the people, has torn a gaping hole in our game.

"You're the bleedin' Ember of Spring."

He doesn't deny it. *He is rather busy.* Doing what I couldn't do.

I sit back, left elbow propped on my knee so my fingers press against my mouth. After a decade of winter, few remember the full truth of season magic anymore. Each season gives its ember a choice. *All that power.* Waiting and eager at their fingertips. They can either release the season and send the magic out into the world or keep it for their own use, though the latter comes with a price.

All or nothing. Season magic only blooms once.

Why would he do this? Of the four seasons, spring and winter are the strongest. Winter is a withering of life. Spring is a revival of life. *Is it enough?* To save her? To channel the full power of spring into Wraith's body, to change her soul season from death to life? Only an Ember of Spring would stand a chance.

I lean forward and stop blinking as the reversal begins. It starts with her blood. The pools shrink as her blood flows backwards, returning to her veins, her heart. The cut on her cheek closes and becomes a scar. The color of her skin brightens, throwing off the pallor of death and the restricting gray of the curse. A creamy gold, like pale winter sunlight. Her chest heaves with a full breath.

The guider tears his hands from her face. He's breathing hard, shoulders heaving up and down, but he's *leaving*. Scrambling to his feet and walking in a crooked line to the door where he grips the frame to steady himself. *You'd think he'd want to stick around to be thanked properly.* I squint, but his color, that *shove a pine-needle in your eye* shade of vibrant green, has faded a little. It's darker. *Weaker.*

What a fool. To give up his power for a girl. Even if that girl is my sister.

That's the difference between him and I. He gives of himself to save people. I take what I want through manipulative control or outright savagery. My solution to the problem of not being enough has always been to steal more power. Until I am the most dangerous, the most feared, the monster that never loses. *I saved Wraith before he knew she existed.*

The dagger catches my eye, glinting silver as the soft moonlight falling through the window brushes the curved edge. A distant chime repeats twice. We're an hour closer to the darkest part of the night. A spark of hunger kindles in my soul, tugging at my strings as the curse strokes the vile edges of my heart. *Does it really expect me to coo like a pet bird in a cage?* My hands curl into fists as I clench my jaw, resisting the order that's tempting my pulse to spike.

I'm no one's pet.

And I'm done being caged.

I leave the dagger to cool alone and brood over its mistake as I send a single thought down our bond. *You could have listened.* To my need to save her. Instead, my partner's soul-lust cast aside twenty years of friendship between us. I don't forgive. And I never forget.

I focus on my sister, the girl who became a banshee. *There were worse options.* I doubt she'll see it that way if she ever remembers who we are. The weight of responsibility on my shoulders draws winter's chill into my chest. I still have secrets to keep.

I don't want her to remember. Because I failed.

I couldn't save who we were, so I made a choice. *At least I kept my sense of fun.* Poking sleeping bears comes to mind.

My sneer is already growing as I wobble to my feet. It's harder to stand without relying on the dagger's power. I sway, my arms swinging to counteract my balance, but the movement is too jerky. I teeter too far forward and fall. Stone smacks my palms and knees. I grind my teeth to bite the head off the pain firing along my nerves.

Worn boots appear before me as the guider extends his hand, offering me a way up. *When did sheep start helping wolves?* I almost laugh. "Are you so predictably heroic by default or by choice, *Sir* Guider?"

"I'm no hero."

My villain's grin widens at his dejected tone. "You do a marvelous impression of one." I take his hand and he pulls me up.

My legs sting, half-numb from sitting on the floor, but they hold this time.

"Then you've missed what's staring you in the face."

I give him a quick once over. His rounded features lack the sharp bone structure to be truly distinctive. *Well, we can't all be handsome devils.* "You are rather disappointing to look at up close. Best to keep your distance for the sake of the ladies."

He grips my tunic, jerking me forward. "This isn't over."

My grin tightens, baring my teeth in a grimacing smile, but I take his bait, glancing down at my sister. *She's*—gone gray. Her veins blackened by cursed blood. The healing he gave her is already fading.

It won't last.

A flare of heat floods my muscles with power, making my legs strong. I ignore the warning my partner is trying to get back on my, well— Not good side. I don't have one. But I won't waste the offer as our fury unites against a common target. The man wearing a white bear on his chest.

He stopped too soon.

I jab my elbow into Dovan's stomach to upset his balance and then take him by the neck. My fingers dig into his throat as I pin him against the wall. His head tilts higher to ease the pressure, but he doesn't defend himself. "Why did you stop?"

"I had to."

Which sounds too much like *I had no choice.* Regret weighs down the guider's eyelids, but apologies are wasted on me. I pull the guider away from the wall and slam him against it. "You could've healed her! You could have restored her to a normal life!"

A chance I never got. *All I had was a decision between two bad choices.* I let him go, breathing hard as I limp backward. "You're right. You're not a hero."

"I've given her time." He rubs his throat, voice scratchy.

"For what?"

"To accept what must happen."

"And what is that?"

The guider dares to pick up my dagger. I'm repulsed by the sight of my blade in his hands, but whatever holding so much power feels like to him, he offers the weapon to me without a second thought. I snatch it from him and a sigh of relief escapes.

The dagger's poisonous heat pulses up my arm. A comforting sense of coming home, of belonging, passes between me and my partner as my fingers coil around the hilt. Whatever disagreements we may have, we are right together. *A deal is a deal.* The thread is still there, the curse restored to normal by the guider's futile use of spring's power.

"I have to die."

The iron conviction behind Dovan's words raises my eyebrows and sets him so far apart from all my other victims. "You are a strange one."

"Why?" The guider's pointed stare drills into my head. "Because I hold the lives of others higher than my own?"

"Better you than me." My sneer slips dangerously close to a genuine smile, but I won't admit to liking this guider. *Maybe after I kill him.* Yes, I'll give him a eulogy guaranteed to explode people's guts. *Killer joy.* Now that is my style.

"If you are serious about convincing her to watch you die, then I'd take her far from this room." I scratch my neck. "Too many...memories. They'll trigger her death."

The sorrow filling Dovan's gaze as he looks at Wraith is gagging. "She deserves a choice."

I grab his tunic and yank his attention back to me. "We can't let her choose. She won't survive it."

He nods, agreeing with me, his *murderer*. "There's a painting beyond the ballroom."

"The season painting?" A twinge of unease loosens my grip on his tunic.

"You know it?"

Better than he does, but I'm not going to reveal that.

He steps around me, and I follow until we both stand over Wraith. "She doesn't know what she is."

For once, I have no urge to belittle his concern for her. *Explains why he mentioned the painting though.*

He moves to pick her up, but I draw my dagger and stick the curved point against his chest. There's nothing left in my heart but cold-burning rage. "If she doesn't sing your song soon, she'll die. If she dies, I'll kill you, and then I'll kill your Gran and your precious orphans, and then I'll kill everyone else. *Understand?*"

Dovan grits his teeth, eyes flashing with a protective rage I know all too well, but he dips his head in a silent *yes.*

"Then we have a deal. I won't kill anyone," my villain sneer returns, "except you. But you'd better be right about your special powers of persuasion."

"She isn't selfish like you. If you understood that, you wouldn't doubt her."

He might as well have called me out for a duel. *I understand her.* Better than he ever will. But I bite my tongue, maintaining the tense silence as he scoops her limp form into his arms. *I know how to make her laugh. I know how to make her cry. I know what makes her soul sparkle and what makes her heart break. I know what she fears and what she hates and what she finds boring. I know she's stronger than both of us.*

And I know—my heart constricts with the words—*she loves you.* An unforeseen consequence. I never considered her falling in love as a potential problem. *She never trusted anyone with her heart before Dovan.* Not even me.

I fume in silence, staring daggers at the guider's back as he leaves *with* her.

The girl I kill for.

The sister I forgot so I could save her.

A secret this room broke wide open. The dagger's power comes with consequences, and it's time to make my own plans. *Our deal be damned.*

I won't risk her life on the word of my next victim.

I swipe my dagger at the stone wall as I hurry down the hall toward the main entrance. Sparks fly in livid red bursts of anger as fresh confidence drives me forward. *Isn't it lucky that guider brought her here?* The very place our game began.

The inner set of doors off the receiving hall are open, revealing a ballroom stuffed with innocents. I sniff, savoring the hot air salted with their pumping blood. My murderous nature may be bound to one victim at a time, but making people bleed, making them scream, making them beg for death while cruelly withholding it—

Well. What can I say? I have *many* violent skills.

WRAITH

19

DEATH DOESN'T SOUND like I thought it would. I had expected a solemn, peaceful quiet stretching on forever because the struggle is over. There will be no more songs to sing, no more victims to watch die, no more blood staining my hands.

No more curse.

Instead, I hear music. Flutes trilling in excitement, violins sweeping the air into a tide of sorrow and then joy, and drums beating a repetitive threat, a command to dance to its rhythm. The violas and cellos dip lower, as if mourning the loss of their freedom, and my heart sinks with them. *My music instructor hated that about me.* I never could keep perfect time.

Whatever tempo the composers chose, their notes whispered to me at a different pace. I sped up what was meant to be slow and slowed down what was meant to be fast. Sometimes I even added my own notes. My teacher would pull on his untamed beard, reduced to muttering Abrykarran curses under his breath as he flapped around the room like a fretful rooster.

"Play it the way it's written!"

But music was the one thing in my life that gave me a choice. It didn't need to be anything other than what I was feeling, or thinking, or struggling to understand.

I know this piece.

They're playing the Gallant Waltz. A song I never needed to change. Everything about the melody was already perfect, a mix of hope and fear, light and darkness, as if I had written it myself, but it was Alec's creation.

Alec.

A sharp pain slices my chest as I suck in a breath. *It's just the name of a stuffy, old composer.* He's long dead, forgotten by everyone but me. I preferred the composers that weren't well known or loved. That way, if I needed to augment their songs, I could do so without my teacher lecturing me the rest of the day. The pain eases, replaced by a numbing prickle as I exhale.

I'm not dead.

But I was dying. Bleeding out over sheet music left behind in a room some tortured soul set on fire. The music survived. *Music always does.* Nothing can truly end a song because melody is born of the soul. It leaps from person to person, living a hundred, a thousand lifetimes, and even beyond that, someone will still remember the notes, the message of a fellow human being saying:

Don't let go.

Don't give in.

Don't forget who you are.

Moisture swells against my eyelids, threatening to force them open because I—*I forgot everything.* Someone made a choice. I don't know if it was mine, but a single decision caused the curse, stripping me of my memories and leaving me with nothing but guilt and sorrow. *I didn't even get to keep my music.* Still, I'm not without melody. The notes of Dovan's song wake with me, locking the brutal conditions of my banshee life into place. *I was almost free.*

Pain drills into my temple, scattering images through my mind so fast I can only grasp one. *Red Death's magic didn't save me.*

Dovan did.

I ignore all the other memories of that moment aside and focus on him. On his hands as he held my face, on the pine-green light shining through his skin and absorbing into mine. The color of a force as powerful as my curse. Maybe even more powerful than death.

No. It can't be.

He's not.

He wouldn't.

The answer is there, wrapped up in his sweet evergreen scent.

Gusting mouthfuls of air rush in and out of my heaving lungs as I jolt upright. Everything spins. The glitter of glass walls and stone pillars lit by wall torches stings my eyes, a chaotic assault of silver-tipped shadows and creeping darkness pointing me toward one constant.

The man I met because the curse chose him to die.

Dovan shares a padded bench with me along the curtained part of a curving glass wall. As he leans toward the sound of music, he braces his arms on his thighs, but his cloak is missing again. A quick brush of fur at my neck as I shift my position reveals why. He's tucked the worn fabric around me, but the chill scraping over my skin refuses to thaw.

The air is cooler than it should be.

The last few times we were this close, Dovan's warmth surrounded me, banishing winter's chill, but now, his warmth doesn't reach past my knees. A single tear catches the torchlight in a wink of sorrow before falling down his cheek, and I spot the bruise above his jaw. *He fought with Red Death.* While I was dying. But the bruise is too pale, the skin showing no sign of swelling like it's in the final stage of healing. More proof for the fear spreading vicious roots through my mind. *No one heals that fast.*

No one *normal.*

"Tell me it isn't true. Tell me you're not—" I stop myself before I expose his secret, before there's no going back.

Dovan sniffs hard, lifts his head, and looks me in the eye.

I wish he'd shoved his sword through my chest because this is a thousand times worse. *His eyes.* Their once vibrant green has darkened, the physical sign of the price he paid for my survival. I gasp and then I heave, but there's nothing in me my body can expel. Pain won't be cast out of its hosting soul, and neither will shame.

His hand settles against the middle of my spine, rubbing warmth into my chilled skin. "You're safe."

I have never felt more unsafe in my life.

It hurts. Being this close to him but never any closer to the future I wish we could have. I freeze, captured by the thought that came alive with so little effort. I didn't have to dig for it, or force it out, or try to untangle it from a web of other distracting feelings. This desire for more bloomed in a quiet corner of my heart, over-looked and hidden, a place where some part of him will always belong. *But there will be no future.* Not for us.

He had no right. To risk so much to save a banshee.

He would have lived. Now he will die.

I spring to my feet. My heart pounds faster, every muscle primed and ready to run. The first step is hard. A gasp of grief breaks through my lips because I'm tearing in two, a piece of me remaining with him, but I can't stand here.

I can't face this.

I don't want the future we *can* have.

I'm halfway across the circular room when he speaks. "Don't run."

Each word jabs at my legs and I trip, but running away is the only power I have left.

"Stay with me."

I fall, my palms stinging and my knees throbbing from the jarring slap of polished marble. As I force myself up, I leave a sprinkling of tears behind on the stone. *I'm almost there.* To the stairs descending into the ballroom. *And then what?* Will Red Death suddenly decide I've been punished enough? The answer weighs on my shoulders, heavier than this entire palace of stone and glass.

I'm the girl who runs away but never escapes.

The truth shreds my heart, grief ripping into my chest until my lungs fail and black shadows crowd my vision. My balance shifts, and my shoulder strikes the braided archway above the steps. The pain is sharp, piercing muscle and bone, but it can't compare to the ruin of my soul.

I distract myself by noting our surroundings. We're in a rotunda made of glass with a domed roof stained with patterns of snowflakes and flowers. A thick curtain drapes the back curve of the rotunda where the bench rests. I glance away before I see Dovan.

The stone arch supporting me gapes open over two dozen steps leading down into a ballroom. My mouth opens in awe. *The* ballroom. Every girlish conversation about dancing I've overheard in my cursed state ended with sighed wishes for an invitation to a palace ball. *"You wouldn't even feel the effect of dancing all night in such splendor."*

Marble floors, polished to glassy perfection, spread through the rectangle room like a still sea of shining pearl, silver, and onyx. Columns of standing bears six men high support vaulted ceilings of stained glass. Tapestries boasting the symbols of every clan, whether beast or weapon, hang along the sides, adding a wild and daring touch of softness. Chandeliers built like entire galaxies of twinkling stars dangle from thick chains, ready to drop a crystalline star for a guest to wish upon for fairer fortunes.

Trestle tables line the walls with meager delicacies, most made from potatoes. Guiders patrol along their lengths, giving warning glares to anyone who dares to fill their plates too full. The musicians cluster in the corner to my right, and my throat tightens over the desire to join them, to sing their melodies. But my voice is enslaved to a curse.

I said no to it once. There's no guarantee I can resist the command again. Not after what Dovan did. He saved my life, yes, but he also kept the curse alive. *He must have had a reason.* I rip my attention from him before the curse forces a note through my lips.

At the bottom of the first tier of steps below me sits a simple throne. *Empty.*

The pale stone seat waits like a hungry dark hole, eating away at the wonder and dimming the shine of the ballroom. *It shouldn't be empty.* The old king should be with his people. *All of them.* Not just the few hundred brought here by invitation. I fix my attention on the crowd, to those the old king considers worthy of his palace.

They're all so young. And terrible at dancing. They step on their partners' feet, they hold each other either too tightly or too loosely, and they spin into the other couples, bumping and falling and *laughing.* Despite their failures, they seem happy to be here.

Happy to be alive.

To them, it doesn't matter if they look silly, or if their patched clothes make them appear as dusty moths flittering around in the queen's royal closet. They revel in who they are. *They act like this is their last chance.* To be young and hopeful instead of facing the horrifying facts of their reality. Their world is starving to death, and yet here they are, their faces shining, their feet light, their shoulders unburdened. *I envy them.* Banshees don't get to forget our fate.

Dovan's heat ghosts along my skin, which means he's close. I focus on anything but him. The marble walls, the clan banners, the music, the dancers. Luckily, there's a boy below who's happy to maintain the distraction.

He stops in the middle of the dance and gives his partner a rushed kiss. The edges of my vision succumb to teary fog. *I've seen people kiss before.* But I didn't realize what it meant.

A kiss is a seal of hope for the future. *Their* future. The boy towers over the young lady wearing a simple scarf where gorgeous piles of curls should crown her head. The musicians soften their melodies, and the other dancers slow. Everyone watches as the boy waits in terrified anticipation for her response.

I resist the urge to glance behind me and find the source of the gentle heat stinging against my back. *What would I have done?* If Dovan had kissed me like that? Without warning, without any form of request?

But he isn't spontaneous. He's methodical and focused on putting others first. *And he wouldn't risk hurting me.* His respectful consideration of my fears about touch, about falling too deep, should lift my heart, but it slips further into the cold well of my soul, closing itself off in ice. *We'll never be like them.*

The girl's face lights up with a smile and she nearly topples the boy as she springs a sudden return kiss upon him. I lower my gaze because we have nothing in common. *She's free.* I'm cursed, and I will stay cursed if Dovan changes my mind.

If I let him die.

Dying in his place is my sole chance at freedom.

Applause and cheers break out through the crowd as the young couple blushes and grins. The musicians strike the next note, and I double over, pain jabbing my chest. They've moved on, speeding through the waltz's melody, but I'm stuck. The first note they played also begins Dovan's song. His melody grips my voice, demanding to be freed.

Sing. Sing. Sing.

My legs weaken as I grind my teeth. Dovan's arm wraps around my waist, holding me upright, and the heat of his season breaks my focus with a gasp. The note slips free. A pitiful, defeated wail. I bite my cheek hard, refusing to sing, but the curse is patient. It will wait for my body to grow weak and then force me to do what I've done hundreds of times before.

Sing.

I clench my fists and endure until the demand passes. The prickling in my lungs eases, and my breathing becomes normal. Strength returns to my legs while the remaining notes fade, filling my mouth with the coppery tang of the curse's confidence. I'm allowed to delay Dovan's death for now. But not forever.

The young dancers below share a laugh in the pause between songs, and I taste the bitter salt of envy sliding down my face. "How can they find joy when their future is in pieces?"

"They're making the most of what they have," Dovan's voice brushes my ear as he speaks, and I remember how close we are. My back against his chest, his arm curled under my ribs, his head over my right shoulder. His warmth pushes against my chilled skin, searching for cracks, seeking a way into my frozen soul. I stiffen and he loosens his hold.

Chilly air rushes through my hair as he breathes in, but I'm not ready for what he says next. "No matter how broken we are, joy never leaves us. We simply stop looking for it."

I slump forward as the curse adds its painful threat to his thoughtless words. My heart loses three whole beats from their joint stabbing. I push his arm away and face him. "Are you suggesting I should be happy about your death? Should I dance on your grave? Should I throw flowers over your bones? Should I—"

The second note of his song interrupts and I groan, locking my teeth around the rest. Violent shudders wrack my body as I tip forward. Dovan grabs my arms, triggering a flinch of cold from my core. New tears form and fall faster than I can clear my vision, a cascade of regrets and long-dead hopes. All while he stands at the center, a man who won't run away. Not even to save himself. Not even to save me.

He lifts my chin so our eyes meet. "I can't undo what's been done." His other hand slides higher, both resting on the slope of my shoulders as he cradles my head. "But the future is ours to shape."

Does he realize how different he is? With Dovan, the future is a promise instead of a threat. My own ribbon of life to tie to anyone or anything I choose. I lean into his touch.

He brushes my cheekbone as his tone turns achingly gentle. "Will you sing for me?"

The cracks running through my heart tear wider. *I thought he saw me as more than a means to his end.* There was a moment, as I bled over the sheet music, where I thought I could be more. Because I *was* more. A girl who wrote songs and sang them when *she* wanted. Her voice never summoned death, but mine always will.

My fist curls against my chest, pressing against the ache savaging my soul. *Make it stop.* But the shattered scream of my heart is too primal, too lost within the emptiness inside me, and goes unheard. "You should have let me die."

"I couldn't."

A caustic mix of humor and heartache escapes my trembling lips in a laugh that shrivels the air with a sparkle of ice dust. "Of course not. You want to use me. Like everyone else."

Dovan's warmth cools, abandoning us both to the sting of winter's never-ending assault. His palms tilt my head up, but I stare at his shoulder. "Look at me."

My heart cracks with every beat as new doubts fracture the trust we've built. *He's no better than Red Death.* The curse made me a tool. *Why shouldn't Dovan take advantage of what I am?*

"Please, look at me."

Hearing him beg forces me to meet his gaze only to find his eyes hollowed out. *It's gone.* All his confidence, all his strength, all his hope has been wrung from his soul. His walls have shattered, broken by two emotions at war.

Guilt. And love.

They're both so strong I can taste them. The acrid salt of *this is all my fault* and the tender sweetness of *no price is too high.* Behind them, pulses the source of his heat, a season that's ready to bloom. The spring he carries inside him extends gentle fingers of warmth in a plea that matches Dovan's own voice. *They want this.*

For Dovan to die.

But embers don't need to die to change the season. Nothing about this makes sense. Except the part where he risked his ability to bring winter to an end just to save my life.

Season magic is an all-or-nothing bargain. It can't be used in pieces.

Unease churns my stomach as I trace the wound on the underside of my arm, but the torn skin remains closed. A scar, a temporary pause in a game only one thing will satisfy. *A soul for a soul.* Dovan's watching me, the wrinkle between his brows deeper than ever, but his irises are more vibrant than a normal green. He's still spring's ember, even though my healing should have drained all its power, which means whatever he did isn't permanent.

"You didn't save my life, did you?"

His lips part before he presses them into a hard line, chin dipping down. "I wanted you to have a choice."

"But I've already made my choice." I bring my forearms up and push out, breaking his hold on my face.

He retreats. One step becoming two, and then three, because I am not letting this go. Not even as his expression hardens, his jaw clenching.

I stand taller as I match his backward momentum. "I choose to save you. I choose to die free."

"Some deaths are more costly than others." He's stopped with his back against the curtain, looking right at me as if I am supposed to understand. I don't.

"No one depends on me, Dovan. My death won't cost a thing."

He shakes his head, whispering a curse as he rubs his temples and rocks on his feet. *I've seen this before.* When Dovan fights against himself, his mind and his heart go to war. *All I want is the truth.*

I take his hand, hoping my touch will be enough, but his continued silence forces me to speak. "You said once you didn't want to waste your time with me. Did you mean it?"

Dovan answers with a sharp nod.

"Then no more half-truths."

He studies our linked hands, his shoulders rounding as his chest expands with a full breath. "When I woke this morning, I didn't know if you would find me and sing my song." He meets my gaze, the shadows under his eyes deepening. "I didn't know your banshee life would be bound to my fate."

He's nudging me toward the suspicion my near death has already confirmed. *If I don't sing, I die.* But hiding behind the obvious is a nugget of truth he's buried. I yank my hand free, my lungs failing to find enough air.

"You were expecting me." I gape at him, daring him to deny it. "You couldn't have known a banshee would come."

"I wasn't waiting for a banshee." Dovan grimaces as if in pain, his head tipping down. "I was waiting for *you.*"

"That's not possible."

"You'd be right if any of this was normal." He pauses, his tone deepening as he lowers his voice. "But we're not. You and I—we aren't normal."

My mouth opens, but nothing comes out. A jarring implication strikes the kindling of a long dead hope, fanning new life into my forgotten past.

The depth that has always lurked behind every weighted glance, in every *knowing* look, and in every touch. The way he carefully chooses his words, keeping his shield up so I wouldn't recognize he knows too much to be just another victim in Red Death's bloody game. *No, it can't... he can't...* But what if he does? What if he remembers what the curse stole from me?

The life I left behind.

I swallow and my voice drops to a whisper, "Did you know me...*before*?"

By the soft flinch of Dovan's lips, and his sudden glance away from me, and the twitch of tension in his shoulders, I have my answer.

"You *knew* me."

WRAITH

20

My slow pulse thunders in my ears, replaying those three words with every beat. Before I can ask him how, before I can reclaim who I was, Dovan shakes his head.

"It's more complicated than that."

His quiet dismissal hits me like a slap to the face. I jolt backward, trying to make sense of this colder Dovan standing before me. He cages his heart in iron and locks his secrets behind a jawline of stone. Secrets *we* share. Knowledge I have longed for, and yet he keeps it from me.

"Don't I deserve the truth?" My voice sounds as hollow as I feel. Maybe it's my paper-thin tone, or the hurt in my watering eyes, or the way my body is sagging in defeat, but Dovan's soldier mask fractures in a wince of pain. He sways forward as the lines of duty, the threads binding him together, snap, and then the man who never stops fighting, who never gives in—falls.

I reach for him on instinct, but he's slipped past my grasp, saved by the padded bench. The wood creaks while the curtain behind him shivers in an echo of the tremors threatening to shake him apart. He covers his face with his hands, hiding the tears and the emotions curling him inward until he looks like the grieving little boy he carried to the inn. The change is so drastic I don't know what to do or how to help him.

I kneel before him, the cold marble biting at my knees as I wait for him to do what he's never done before. Open his heart.

Dovan drags his fingers down, revealing the depth of his brokenness. His lips are pale and pressed thin. Strands of dark hair stick to his hollowed cheeks while a choking mix of sorrow and guilt redden his green eyes. This is the guider I've doomed and the lost boy I've never met. The orphan who's spent most of his youth trying to hold his world together.

"What do you want to know?" The way his lips twitch around each word whispers of an anxious dread, as if the question is made of jagged glass, but nothing can stop the swell of hope building in my chest. Behind the tangled mess of what he's feeling, I glimpse what I've been waiting ten years to discover.

My past.

And he offers all of it to me. Without a hint of darkness or ambition that would shape his answer to benefit him, to further his cause and bind me to his decision. Everything Dovan is—his keen, calculating mind, his stubborn but soft heart, his usually straight spine—has gone still. He's letting this moment hinge upon what I choose.

Was I happy?

There were moments in the past ten years where I played with a dangerous idea. *My life before had to have been better.* A life where I had a family who loved and cared for me. Where I had a place in this city. Where I was free to do what made me smile. But the game twisted as the cost of my songs stacked more and more bodies on top of my soul. A poisonous fear seeped in. A belief that wrongness is always attracted by wrongness. And the hope that I had been happy before my curse died, leaving me with only one question.

I hang my head because I don't want to see the answer I expect write itself across Dovan's face. Rough fabric scratches my skin as I grip the torn strips of my skirt so my hands won't be empty. The tip of my tongue forms the words, but I can't push them past the wall of my teeth. Most knowledge comes with a price. *Am I ready to pay?*

A bitter taste fills my mouth as I slump on my knees. I've known so much pain in my life. The thought of enduring a little more shouldn't break me, but I am breaking. Dovan is breaking. His control shattered because like me, he wants more. More than one day. More than one song. More than desperate choices.

Maybe he was right. To protect me by withholding my past. To protect us both by keeping us grounded in the present we can't escape.

I am a banshee. That won't change, no matter what I learn from Dovan. *We have so little time left.* A shiver travels through my body as I wrap my arms around myself.

I have to know. Just one thing, and then we'll lock the rest away.

"Tell me," I start, my breath catching on the fear of what comes next. "Did I deserve my curse?"

The music rising into the rotunda from the ballroom pauses as a song ends, and the silence snaps along my skin. It feels like punishment. Like confirmation. *How could you think you deserved anything good?* Shame blackens my vision, and I hide my face behind my hands until Dovan pulls them away, stripping my shield and baring my soul.

No, he says. *Never,* he says. But the part of me he's trying to reach is buried so deep. Too deep to be rescued by a mere touch or a handful of well-meaning words. *Don't listen.* My arms curl tighter around my stomach, my fingers itching to trace the scars left behind by the victims of my songs. They're the proof of what I deserve.

Pain.

Damage.

Despair.

These things are mine to reap. But even as that thought lands like a blow, a stubborn corner of my soul rebels with its own challenge. *Weren't you taught that's what you deserve?* Taught by the cruelty of a monster who uses me. Taught by people who were scared and angry, who couldn't see past the word they branded to my skin. *Banshee.*

Dovan's palms press hard against my cheekbones, drawing my blurry gaze to his chin. "You listen to me." Iron-backed strength has returned to his voice as fresh tears drip from his clenched jaw. "You never deserved this." Each word is a hammer swinging for the wall of shame around my heart. "You could *never* deserve this."

I look Dovan in the eye and I'm frozen by his righteous fury, a fierce and yet wonderful anger. Because it recognizes every broken piece of my life, every vein of poison that spread from what happened to me, every bit of damage I've been forced to own because someone else made a wrong choice, and yet Dovan doesn't recoil. He stays.

He sees me.

The banshee who just wants to save one victim. The girl who just wants to help others. Who I was and who I am made whole in his sight.

"There is not one part of you I find unworthy of love."

Shock opens my mouth and I suck down a gasp. I wait for the *but* to come. For a tremor of uncertainty in his touch, for a ripple of regret in his eyes, for a shadow of disgust to darken his expression. But his declaration stands alone. Free of conditions or disqualifiers. I lean back, needing more space than the few inches between us, but he won't let go.

"You deserve to be loved." A twitch of pain shapes his mouth into a frown. "I'm sorry all I can offer you is right here. Right now. You deserve to be loved tomorrow, and the next day, and the next..." His voice trails off and he sniffs hard before releasing my face. "But I can't watch anymore people die."

He's returning our focus to the problem of my curse and his spring and the winter that never ends. My soul joins with his, screaming for an end to this cycle of death, and I do the only thing I can. I fill his empty hands with mine.

The taught line of his jaw relaxes as he stares at our joined fingers. "Not even you." His gaze sharpens in a knowing look as I prepare to deflect his tender admission. "Before you say that your life doesn't matter, or isn't important, I need you to understand. I was lost once." He squeezes my hands. "Your song saved me."

My muscles tense, a defensive response meant to soften the weight of his words, but they roll through me in waves. Years of longing to be more than a banshee, to have the power to heal instead of condemn, well against my eyelids, unleashing several large tears.

The barbed wire of my truth coils around me. "My songs don't save people."

"They used to." Gratitude burns in Dovan's gaze, but his answer leaves me to fill in the rest.

Before I was cursed, before I became a banshee—my songs helped people. Relief thaws another layer of ice from my heart. *Then I wasn't always a monster.*

"There's something else I need to explain." Dovan stands, a signal of change. Not only for our conversation, but for our understanding of each other. He pulls me up to stand with him. "My death doesn't depend on your song."

A twinge of pain pinches my chest. Dovan's melody tickles my voice, but I swallow against the notes, pushing them back down.

"You don't even have to be there." His palm brushes my cheek with a sting of spring heat as he lifts my head. "There's a guider I trust who knows I carry spring. She'll be waiting for me at dawn."

"To kill you?"

"Yes."

The tightness in my chest eases, but he still hasn't answered the main question. "Why?"

A flicker of indecision flashes across his face, but he holds my stare, dropping his hand to his side. "You don't remember what's special about tonight, do you?"

Distinguishing one night from another as a banshee is almost impossible after a decade. All the screams, all the deaths, they blur together.

"It's Spring Eve."

Spring. Eve. A date that has become a cruel joke after ten years of winter.

When he brought me into the city this morning, the guiders were decorating the lower market for what used to be the most important night in Riffen. The night of the season change. There would be feasting and dancing as spring was reborn. It's why there's a ball proceeding below us.

I glare at Dovan, gesturing toward his chest. "You're the Ember of Spring. You don't need a banshee's song to change the season. You don't even need to die."

"But this winter isn't normal."

All of my defensive responses sputter out like dying flames as a well-timed chill slides up my spine. *Abnormal* is a word that now ties me and winter together. Neither of us fading with time or being allowed to rest, to find our ending. *What if he's right?* What if something is wrong with the first season? Something that has changed the rules of season magic?

I reach out as my legs bow under the weight of such an idea, my palm finding the glass wall of the rotunda for support. Frost spreads along the panes as winter fights to get in, and I jerk away from the biting sting in my fingertips, from the unstable notion that winter is coming for me. A gust of wind hurls snowflakes at the glass, and with each soft *tink-tink* of their crashing scrape, a single word snaps against my skipping heart.

Mine. Mine. Mine.

I retreat further, shaking the strange thoughts off, but pieces of knowledge once lost within my mind find their place, forming a picture. *Why would an ember need to die?* The answer floods my veins with the acid of fear and I start to burn. A cold burn of exposure. *The Season Wars.* Where the warring kings and queens of the four kingdoms made the embers into weapons by using Red Death's favorite tactic.

Murder.

I shiver as I hug myself. Killing an ember creates a vengeful season, its power unrivaled and almost—*unending.* Until the next ember was killed. The bloody act forced the newer season to overcome the old instead of letting the natural process of surrender unfold gently.

As I face Dovan, the chaos of my thoughts order themselves into an arrow, pointing in a direction that deepens the pit in my stomach. "The last Ember of Winter was murdered."

He reaches under the throat of his tunic and pulls out a leather pouch. With a snap, the tether breaks and he tugs the drawstring loose. "Hold out your hand."

I'm tempted to refuse, to choose denial over facing whatever truth he's about to reveal, but I untuck my arm from my waist and offer him my palm. The curse jabs my sternum. I wince, my reaction raising Dovan's eyebrows in the center to form his worry-wrinkle, but he tips the pouch over my hand.

"This is why I have to die."

A flower drops into my palm, the dried petals tickling my skin, and the moldy tang of decay fills my nose. "What does a dead flower have to do with—"

As Dovan cradles my hand, heat blazes against my skin. A wave of cold air races down my arm, and where the opposing temperatures meet, there's a hiss and swirl of steam. His intense stare shines with the vibrant green of spring as he focuses on the flower. I do the same and my mouth opens. *Winter's Teeth.*

The flower's petals brighten from moldy black to brilliant white, uncurling around a sunshine-golden center. My heart squeezes out an extra beat over this surprising gift of color, but the flower's not done transforming. The damaged or missing petals regrow, the stem and leaves thrumming with a fragile but new evergreen life. A sugary scent fills the air with the fragrance of a season our world hasn't known in a decade. *Spring.* The bringer of flowers and fulfiller of long-deferred hopes. Tears bead along my eyelids as joy lifts my lips into a trembling smile.

"I forgot—" I start, but I'm overwhelmed by a surge of wonder. "I forgot what flowers were like."

"It's a sugar daisy," Dovan says. "My mother's favorite. I picked it the year before winter came." A shadow dims the season-magic brightening his irises. "She died a year later." His breath streams out in vapor, robbing me of the chance to offer any comfort.

A strange prickling sensation blankets my exposed skin. *The temperature's dropping.* Dovan flinches, his hand twitching beneath mine. I blink over and over, but what I'm seeing only gets worse.

The flower is dying.

The flower is—

Dovan snatches his hand back as a rustling, scratching sound sends a shiver down my spine. Frost sparkles into being, consuming the flower and curling the petals, and then comes ice. Layers and layers of ice weighing down my palm.

The flower freezes solid.

"What's happening?"

Dovan's eyes fill with an emotion I never expected to see. Pity. "You are."

"What? This isn't—this isn't me. I can't—" A soft moan of horror escapes my lips. There are cracks in my skin, but they aren't bleeding curse darkened blood. They're overflowing with ice. The same ice entombing the flower.

No.

The frozen flower falls from my hand, and as it shatters, a scream lashes out from the ballroom. But nobody could be hurting as much as I am because I'm— *No. This must be a mistake.* Even as I grasp for anything, for another answer that won't make me responsible for so much devastation, I feel it.

The delighted chill in the air, the happy sigh of millions of snowflakes covering the ground, the crackle of untapped power surrounding my heart in a frigid embrace. *At last*, the magic whispers. *She knows.* A terrible, wonderful truth that never should have been forgotten.

I am the chosen of a season.

The most powerful season of them all.

I am the Ember of Winter.

THE BOY

TWO YEARS BEFORE WINTER

NO THREAT THE boy had ever faced was worse than the chill creeping into the air. Most people feared the first season, but he'd never been afraid of winter. Until he felt—no, he *heard* the chill. The sound of magic and melody becoming one. *Winter wouldn't.* But why shouldn't it want his sister's soul? Winter was the most melancholy of the seasons. The music slipping through the doorway into the hall where he'd paused mid-stride dripped with an aching sorrow.

The song was one of theirs, written for their triumph over their wicked father.

He threw off his limp, not caring if anyone saw him. There were worse things than destroying his crippled prince persona and inviting questions about how his legs had healed. They hadn't. He'd simply found a way around the problem. Yet for the boy, problems loved to multiply.

The proof he dreaded, that had forced him to betray his secret, glittered around her as he rushed into the room. Tiny bits of ice caught the torchlight like scattered diamonds. The keys her fingers touched, the harpsichord's frame, her emerald sleeves and unbound raven hair, even the air sparkled with frost. Winter's new ember looked up at him with hope because she knew he would understand, and he did.

Their father had stripped away her choices and left her powerless, but their world was at war because of the magic now bonded to her soul. Season hunters kidnapped, traded, and killed embers for the four kingdoms. Embers were now weapons. Weapons who never survived. *Not like they had a choice.*

"I finished our song," she said, oblivious to the dire fate locking like dungeon bars around them.

The boy swore and slammed the harpsichord's lid closed over the keys. He didn't care if she moved fast enough or if he broke her fingers. In his mind, physical pain was always preferable to death. *She will heal.*

The girl's face reddened and puckered as she tucked her hands close to her chest. Winter's power made her hazel glare burn cold, but the boy gripped her jaw hard before she could call him all the terrible names he deserved.

"Never let them see what you are. It'll be one more reason to kill you."

He hated that he sounded like their father, hated the fear and betrayal smothering the rare spark of fire in her sad eyes, hated the sting of the ice particles seeking refuge in his skin as the room warmed.

But he would not watch her die.

He would not. Lose. Her.

WRAITH

21

Chaos erupts from the ballroom. I'm the only one who doesn't look, who isn't searching for the source of what's gone wrong. *I already know.* The clock *tic-ticking* down in my pain savaged chest, the brush of winter against my skin, the notes trying to claw their way free—*too late* has finally come.

The music cuts-off with a flare of discordant noise. Shock sweeps through the room like an invisible fog, a pause of silent horror before desperation takes hold. A silence that swaggers, that's made of eager strings waiting to be pulled by a master performer.

He's here.

With a fresh scream, the moment unfreezes. Trestle-tables thud against the floor as people scramble for safety, bronze goblets clattering as glass bowls break. The tang of iron and the salt of panic laces each breath. Boots stamping and squealing against stone becomes the new pulse, a rhythm pounding faster and faster as more screams ricochet off marble walls. The evening's delights of dance and food transforming into a game for survival, and no one plays that game as well as the monster who never loses.

Red Death has come for the soul he is owed.

Dovan's already gone. He hesitated long enough to squeeze my shoulder in an offer of sympathy before he hurried down the stairs. He left me standing over the shattered flower and the bits of ice *I* created. I keep staring at them, knowing what they mean, knowing what I am, but there's no bridge forming between the two sides of myself.

How can I be both?

A banshee and an ember?

I beg my eyelids to close, my body to run, my soul to shut out the truth coiling around me like a snake made of iron. It's going to break me in a way I haven't been broken before. *All this time.* I walked the snowdrifts surrounding the city. I watched the wolves prey on refugees, the guiders risking their lives, and the people starving day by day, losing hope because of—

"No," I whimper, blinking back tears, but my denial dies on teeth of ice biting into my heart. This winter that never ends—

It's my fault.

The weight of every life crushed by my season piles on top of all the victims I've sung to their deaths.

I'm a worse monster than I ever knew.

Frost sprouts in crystalline vines at my feet. I jerk backward and nearly tumble down the stairs, but everywhere I step, winter escapes. *It's already winter.* The first season has ruled for ten long years. There should be no season magic left in my soul. *How can winter be in two places?* Out there, covering everything in sight in a white blanket of death, and here, inside me. I rub my chest. Prickles of cold respond until my skin sparkles with a thin sheen of ice.

I scratch at my arms, desperate to be normal. To be anything but this. Another scream sends me running into chaos. But I'm not like Dovan. He was racing toward something.

I'm running away.

Frost crackles to life every time my boots strike stone, leaving a pattern of frosty footprints behind me. Young men and women run in random directions, knocking each other over while others fall without cause, blood slashing their faces. The guiders and palace guards shout orders. No one listens. Dovan's with them, putting himself between a stampede of wild-eyed youths and a girl who's on the ground.

My foot slips out from under me when I reach the ballroom floor. As I hit the marble hard, I bite into my cheek while my bruised joints send out flares of icy pain. I almost don't look, expecting more frost, but my boot made a smear mark.

Frost doesn't smear.

Frost isn't a violent ruby shade.

I scramble back and bump into a pair of legs. A glance over my shoulder reveals the prone body of a boy. I roll him over, no longer caring if my invisible touch freaks him out. *Please be alive.* His hair lifts from his cheek with his breath. *He's breathing. He's alive.* But his hair is damp. My hand trembles as I pull a few strands aside. I gasp in horror, half-covering my mouth as the sight locks my muscles in place.

Jagged, bleeding cuts crisscross his face. The work of a particular villain's knife. *They'll leave horrible scars.* Scars that didn't need to exist. The tips of my fingers sting as the shock fades into disgust before freezing into rage. A fury so cold it becomes physical, but the form it takes isn't soft like frost. This is frigid iron. This is solid anguish. This is ten years of being powerless paling before a power more ancient than my curse.

Ice rises from where my palms press against the floor.

Sharp and deadly spikes to rival Red Death's curved blade. *More proof I'm a monster.*

I push myself to my feet, hands shaking into fists at my sides, but I don't know how to speak to winter or how to shape its power. *Breathe. Just breathe.* I force my mouth to open and suck down a breath while focusing on anything that isn't white. There are other boys and girls lying in unconscious blobs of gray throughout the ballroom, their faces carved up by a monster who doesn't even deserve a name. The guiders have regained a sense of order. They hurry small groups toward the pillars, working their way closer to the main doors, but the screams aren't stopping. More victims wrench in pain as blood spills down their cut skin.

They can't see him. Not in his true form.

Red Death wears a smirk christened by drops of innocent blood, his crimson irises flashing with pure delight. He darts between people, slashing his dagger here and there, feeding on their panic as he herds them away from the doors. His cape dances around his lean frame, a stain upon the very air, but my fingers uncurl with a desire to rip the cape from him. Maybe then he'd be visible, giving them a chance to fight back. *He'd only become more wicked.* Taking pleasure in the added variable of being seen.

He's unstoppable.

Is he? Whispers a voice inside my head that isn't human, and I shiver. Before I realize what's happening, a crackling surge of cold magic tears through my veins, and the ice spikes grown from my anger fly past me. Winter rising to Red Death's unspoken challenge.

"No!" I lunge after the ice, but winter is their master, not me.

The spikes aim for Red Death without a care for anyone in the way. My heart shrivels in shame as they slice a few arms, one going right through a palace guard's shoulder.

Stop it! Winter ignores me as the spikes find their target.

Red Death spins on his heel to meet them, throwing a hand out. I stumble forward, grabbing at my chest. There's no explaining the feel of his fingers sliding through bone and muscle to curl around my heart when he's a dozen feet away. He squeezes, closing his fist, and my vision turns black. The single point of pain fractures like broken glass into several pieces, all of them slicing deeper. A gust of wind whips against the palace, shaking the chandeliers, but winter's spikes remain hovering an arm's length from his body.

A stalemate? Between the monster I serve and the most powerful season.

Red Death sneers and relaxes his fingers. As the pressure releases a little, I gasp, trembling, but I refuse to look away as my life hangs from his loosened fist.

Finish it, I mouth.

The crimson glow of his eyes dulls as his sneer falters, giving winter time to surround my heart in layers of protective cold, but only one person controls my fate.

Until the man Red Death never should have chosen as his next victim intervenes. Dovan drives his right fist into Red Death's jaw. The invisible hand lets go as Red Death stumbles back. My heart resumes its slow rhythm and I straighten. Winter's ice spikes vaporize when they cross Dovan's wall of heat, and the first season recoils from his spring. I can't stop myself from wondering if Dovan feels like death to winter. *He is the source of its ending.*

Red Death dabs at the corner of his mouth, grinning over the trickle of blood he finds. "Oh, I knew I liked you."

"Behind me!" Dovan's voice breaks through all the noise as he urges people to move. "Get behind me! Now!"

They all run at once, but Red Death's twisted grin deepens. He waves his dagger in a slow arc. Pain rips across my chest like I'm being carved open, and I fall to my knees as winter magic is ripped from my soul. With a violent crack, ice erupts from the marble floors, rising in thick sheets and sealing everyone except

Dovan inside their walls. They beat their fists on the ice, shouting, but they're trapped.

Red Death's newest toys.

My stomach upends, bile stinging my throat at the idea. The season magic inside me quivers and retreats deeper as if afraid of —*him*. But the part of winter that escaped me and doomed the world with its fury isn't frightened. Icicles form along the ceiling while spikes sprout from the floor. One shooting toward Red Death's back. He spins, snatching the spike from the air, and as he crushes it in his fist, all of the icicles and the other spikes disintegrate. Winter *bowing* to his control.

How?

How can he manipulate a season he doesn't carry?

"You bastard." Dovan shoves him several feet. "We had a deal."

What? Shock punches the air from my lungs as my focus whips from season magic to Dovan.

Red Death laughs, a shriveling, arrogant sound. "Why should I keep the deals I make when breaking them is *so* much fun?"

Dovan nods toward the ice-prison. "Hurting them wasn't necessary."

"It was though," Red Death flips his dagger, drips of blood falling from the curved tip. "I was getting bored waiting for you to get to the bleedin' point."

"I only needed a little more time and she—" Dovan stops talking when he catches me staring, but the damage is done.

"You made a deal with that monster?" Dovan doesn't avoid my gaze, but the hurt in my voice weighs down his shoulders, curling them inward. His stoic soldier's mask wavers and a single feeling leaks out. A fear of loss, of losing something he deems irreplaceable, and shock parts my lips as I realize that something is me.

You were dying. His eyes say.

We stare at each other, caught in an emotion we won't dare name.

"Well, well, hellooo Wraith." Red Death's cape sways as he faces me and bows. He sidles close to me, and I flinch from the weight of his arm against my shoulders. "How is my favorite banshee?"

I elbow him hard in the ribs. Apart from a slight stiffening, he shows no sign of pain.

"That wasn't very nice," he whispers to me, tightening his grip until it becomes possessive before he focuses on Dovan. "What's it to be, guider? Shall I tell her? Or are you finally man enough to say it?"

I wait for Dovan to explain, to make sense of why he'd ever work with the killer who cursed me. He sets his jaw, the muscles clenching. A thin line of tears along his eyelids remains the only softness left in his expression as he glares at Red Death.

"Nothing? Really? In that case, which face should I carve up next?" Red Death points to a young woman who's passed out on the floor. "She's rather pretty."

Dovan moves between the girl and the monster draped around my shoulders, his right hand gripping his sword in a clear threat.

I twist, a shiver sweeping down from Red Death's touch as I look into the face of a killer. Ruby curls, far too soft for a monster like him, brush the sharp line of his cheekbone and highlight the dimple in his cheek. This close, his sneer isn't frightening. There's more mischief in it than I ever noticed. "Why are you doing this?"

"To win the game."

"Then punish me." I beg as I survey the cost of defying him. A heavy price found in the unconscious young men and women surrounding us, their faces cut and bleeding, while those trapped behind ice continue to cry out. Shame pours into my soul until my heart is swollen, laboring for every slow beat. "Punish me. They've done nothing wrong. They're innocent."

Red Death's fingers dig into my shoulder. "Do you think I care about innocence or guilt?" He scoffs, a strangled laugh that sounds more weary than triumphant. "They're leverage. Leverage against you, Wraith. If carving up their faces doesn't make you sing, I'll take all the skin. Leave their faces nothing but naked meat. Would you like to see that?"

He'd do it too. I wrap my arms around my knotted stomach.

Dovan draws his sword, sending a metallic shriek through the air. "Come near them again and I will cut your hands off."

Red Death winks at him. "You, Sir Guider, appreciate my kind of fun."

My whole body sags. *Please don't fight.* I'm so tired of the fighting, of the killing, of the game. Tired of the scars multiplying across my skin and my soul. Tired of wrecking more lives than just mine. *If Dovan is hurt.* If anyone else suffers because of me—

"Well, look who's feeling stabby now."

I follow Red Death's slanted gaze and find a new batch of frost growing at our feet. It's thicker this time, with thorny instead of feathered fronds aiming for Red Death's shins. *Is winter...defending me?* A thrum of frosty magic resonates behind my ribs. A whispering *yes* sweeps down my arms and transforms my fingernails into ice-tipped claws. Of course, winter would understand only one kind of fighting. The kind that leaves a trail of blood.

I don't want to hurt anyone. The icy points melt from my fingernails with a quiver as the season hears me and relents.

"Winter's power is wasted on you." Red Death moves behind me, gripping my shoulders as his breath warms my ear. He points me toward Dovan. "Do you want to know why this idiot wants me to kill him?"

"Let her go," Dovan takes a halting step forward. I search his face for a clue to what he hasn't told me, but Dovan's stony expression is impenetrable. Red Death positions his dagger above my collar bone, grinning the whole time as Dovan inches closer, his voice deepening with the power of a guider's command, "I said, let her go."

Hot metal stings the skin of my neck as Red Death strokes my throat with his blade. "You had your chance, *guider*." I try not to tremble as the curved tip comes to rest under the corner of my jaw. "It's my turn."

Dovan's pine-green gaze locks with mine. "I can't change the season. I've tried, but it never lasts more than a moment. You saw the truth with the flower."

The sugar daisy he restored to life only for my winter to kill again.

"You are horrible at explaining things." Red Death spins me toward him. His irises are darker, no longer a violent crimson as they settle on me. "It's *you*. You are why he must die."

"Me?" My whisper echoes through me, cracking and breaking, all while an icy power builds inside my chest.

Me.

I slip from Red Death's grip. He lets me go because we both know there's no running from this. I back into Dovan, but his touch brings no comfort. His warmth drags me down into a deeper horror, a brittle shame circling my heart like a strand of barbed wire. The tighter the shame pulls, the more it rips me apart.

I am not winter.

But winter is bound to my soul, and I. Am. Cursed.

The frost mixes with blood at my feet. Dripping, dripping, blood. Red against white, truth against lies, and yet, I don't understand.

"You have to sing," Red Death swipes his fingers along my left cheek, and then holds them up between us. They're covered in blood. My *crimson* blood. "Or all of this will be for nothing."

I freeze. *Is he suggesting every person he's killed died for a reason?*

Before I can ask, another male voice echoes through the ballroom as hasty footsteps invade our tense standoff.

"What happened here?" The hardened tone of the stranger's demand, the arrogance, the bristling authority, as if none would dare question him—*I know that voice.* My shiver ripples up my limbs as each word the man speaks cuts through the wall the curse erected in my mind. I whimper in pain and grip my head as images, as *memories*, burst free. Memories of him, of me, of others, and then I hear laughter.

Two children lost in a joyous romp as their ghosts race by me.

The boy has red hair curling around his ears. *Just like…*

I lose them as Red Death moves. The mirage of softness, the flicker of his concern for me, vanishes. His bright red eyes flash with a hatred so fierce winter recoils deeper inside me.

"*You.*" Red Death spits the word out like a weapon. He pulls up his hood, his face disappearing into shadow, and pushes me into Dovan's chest.

A plea rises from the empty places in my mind. *Stop him.*

Dovan rushes after Red Death. Then I see the older man who belongs to the voice I knew before my curse.

Flanked by palace guards and wearing the crown of thorns and flowers, the king of Riffen strides into view. His short black and gray hair hugs his scalp, but his tall and narrow build mirrors the killer I serve. The old king's sharp glare sweeps the room for an explanation, landing on the ice wall last.

He can't see Red Death. Or the dagger standing between him and his final heartbeat. Red Death's cape whips behind him as he picks up speed. An anguished roar escaping his throat. *What did the old king do?* To earn Red Death's hatred?

I sway on my feet, reaching out for the comfort of an arm, a shoulder, anything to help me regain my balance, but I'm alone.

There's nothing to hold on to as the king's baritone orders bleed into older threats.

"You will do as I command, or I will break you."

It was me.

He threatened me.

A strange tingling sense of familiarity lures the answer from the past. *Someone was going to kill him.* Repay the old king for all the times I'd been hurt.

Who are you? Cries my oldest question, but my identity isn't the focus. The sides of my face sting, wet by salty grief. Dread grips my heart, crushing out additional beats until my pulse pounds as though I'm in a race.

Because I am.

I'm running after that blood-red cape, after the boy who took its madness onto his shoulders. Red Death's true name tears through my lips, sharper and more bloodstained than his cursed dagger.

"Alec! No!"

The bell tower rings out three times, sinking us all into the darkest depths of night. My heart stops. Pain caves in my chest, and I fall into the tortured memories that were locked away for ten years. The key to who I am is his name. It was always his name.

Alec. The boy who wrote the Gallant Waltz.

Alec. The boy who loved getting blood on his hands.

Alec. The boy who was on my side until I wasn't on his.

I always believed there was a seed of good in him, needing to be nurtured, and I tried. But that was my mistake. I have paid for it with hundreds of songs, watching him kill, watching him destroy as he punished me for a betrayal I will never regret.

Alec *is* my curse.

RED DEATH

22

I SKID to a panting stop an arms-length from the old king. With his guards gone to inspect the ice wall I created, he waits alone beside a pillar carved in the shape of a standing bear. An easy and almost too convenient target as fate smiles on me. The dagger burns my palm, and the breeze caused by my haste rustles his fur-lined cape, daring my father to look. To see me.

The boy he threw away.

He'd never admit to that. *No, he prefers a coward's denial.* Pretending I meant nothing to him after a streak of clumsiness uncovered a shocking truth. The crown prince was losing the ability to walk. With our ruthless neighbors to the north, no king or queen has held the throne of Riffen without being feared, and fear thrives best on violence. *How did the old man put it?*

"Sitting in a chair won't intimidate the north prince into submission."

He expected me to be dead by the time my legs completely failed. Killed by a court rival or a northern assassin. *Always a disappointment.* That's me. Well, not only me. But I could bear his disdain. *I damn well did better than that.* Using his rejection to build my own kingdom, I lurked in shadows. I became a nameless terror. I made myself a monster worthy of his ridiculous standards, and after a few years, his opinion ceased to matter in my game. *All that mattered*—a sharp pain cuts into my chest, driven deep by two words.

"Alec! No!"

My hand freezes in the air, poised to perform the act of murder. Glittering chandelier light winks off my curved blade as Wraith's voice echoes through our past, making a plea I've heard over and over. *Alec, no.* I grit my teeth, resisting.

I will not be weak.

Succumbing to Wraith's soft heart is a mistake I won't make again. The fury running through my veins sinks into dangerous territory, burning cold, licking up power from two magical sources instead of one. A dull warning pinches between my shoulders, but I am owed this kill.

It was always his face. Every person I have murdered became *him.* Their features transforming into his frigid brown eyes, his crooked nose, his arrogant jaw and heavy brows.

The monster responsible for my sister's curse. And I don't mean the one I gave her.

The king of Riffen, my equal in height and savagery, turns his head. The history we share overpowers the magic that usually makes me invisible. We see each other. Cruel father and wicked son, reunited at last. The corner of his mouth twitches, a sneer begging to be born as his glare taunts me, but this moment does not come without a cost.

Death whispers in my ear, tuning my hearing to Wraith's labored breathing.

A soul for a soul.

My hand falls. *That damn phrase ruins everything.* Reminding me of the most important line between past and present in my life. My legs wobble, a prick of numbness stinging up my shins. *The deal. Protect the deal.* I tighten my grip on my dagger, using the blade's magic to strengthen my legs.

I should have killed him. Because he hurt Wrenna. Because he knew she was a vulnerable choice for the throne and did nothing to protect her. Because he tried to tear us apart.

The flat of a sword presses against my chest as the man I'm supposed to murder ruins our wonderful family reunion. *Damn guider.* Dovan's always butting in, but the smug look on my father's face pushes the guider from my mind.

I slice my palm, and when my skin is slick, I strike. Slapping the bastard who broke my sister, who drove us into the arms of a curse in order to survive.

The old king staggers back, nostrils flaring in rage, but Dovan's sword never swings for my throat. Instead, he lowers his blade. *Interesting.* He's not protecting his king like a dutiful guider.

"No love for my old man either, then?"

Dovan's clenched jaw and sharp look precede his wordless answer. He sheaths his sword. *Well, he's full of surprises.* I tip my chin down in a nod of respect he has earned.

My father's glare sears my cheek, reclaiming my attention with a threat. *This isn't over.*

Now it's my turn to enjoy the moment. I bare my teeth in a savage grin because I left my own ultimatum across his face. A bloody handprint marking him for all to see. A promise written in blood.

I will kill you.

Calling in the debt he owes me and my sister, but he's not the only one in debt.

The first warning of my debt coming due stabs me in the chest.

I lurch forward, hacking. My blood mixes with the splatters on the marble floor from the faces I slashed. I straighten my spine, willing my quivering legs to pretend they're braced by steel rods.

I turn my back on the king of Riffen.

In a normal setting, he'd have to fight me to the death to erase such a blatant slight. *My favorite tradition.* But I shove the longing down, sheathing my dagger and lengthening my stride until I'm running.

Wraith is unconscious when I reach her, blood dripping from the cut on her cheek. I brush my knuckles under the wound I caused, torn between shame and pride. *She remembered my name.*

Alec.

It's been ten years since I've heard the name our mother gave me. *Our game is changing.* Wraith and I are no longer strangers. The bargain I made is breaking, and I can't let that happen. I won't surrender to her gentle nature or to the memories of who we were.

She's hated you.

Doesn't everyone?

I am an acquired taste, and that's if I don't stab you in the heart. Losing her good opinion, losing her trust, never mattered. *Because she lived.* She was safe until *him.* To her, I'm the monster while Dovan's the hero. When it has been *me,* all these years, doing what needed to be done. *I protected her.* The only way I knew how. Bloodshed.

"She will always betray you." The sudden tension in my muscles is a familiar reflex. It's *my* voice, in *my* head, but I'm not speaking. My partner is.

The tricky part of being *a* Red Death is that there's more than one power-hungry voice in my head.

"You repulse her." My partner mocks me. If things were as they should be, I wouldn't notice. I'd sneer in triumph and bathe my soul in my sister's disgust. Red Death feels no longing other than a savage hunger to kill.

But Alec does.

The wound in the guider's chest calls to me, his strong heart-beat making my skin tingle in anticipation of the kill, but I tear my gaze from him. Not that looking away helps. More blood spills down Wraith's cheek as I resist, the curse punishing her for my rebellion. *Damn guider.* Everything that has gone wrong in this game is Dovan's fault.

The strength of his spring weakened the curse, allowing Wrenna to remember and giving her a chance to remake the choice I had already made for us. There's no fixing it, which means it's time for a new deal. *Risky.* My deception barely worked the first time. Now my partner is stronger and possesses a crucial fact I concealed.

My sister has what it wants most. The first season. *I do like a challenge.*

Sharp, finger-sized spikes of ice sprout around Wraith as I reach for her, the season defending its ember. "Don't throw a bliz-zard fit. I'm on her side." I bend closer to the tallest spike. "You know I'm the only one who can save her."

Winter kisses my skin with frost, an unspoken oath between two powerful souls who love her more than anything. The spikes melt away, and the cut on my hand stings as I gather my sister into my arms. *Now for the real trick.* Lifting her from the ground.

I'd never suggest she's...heavy, but she is far from small. After staggering a few steps, legs wobbling worse than a newborn colt's, I find my balance. *She has the largest heart of anyone I've ever known.* That is a heavy burden to carry. Worth it, when it's your job to keep her heart beating. A task I'd destroy the world to fulfill.

The old king's voice rises to a shout. The guider I'm still going to kill just stands there and takes the abuse. A coil of begrudging respect entwines with the shredded chord of my honor, but neither can resurrect my soul from the damage I've done. *Dovan doesn't deserve this.* He doesn't deserve to die either, but the curse chose him.

The guider can't help Wraith. No human ever could. Not even an ember. *We need the source.* Lucky for us, I am on speaking terms with the source of all seasons. *We're still playing my partner's game.* And the only way to win is to kill Dovan. Trade his life for the one I cannot lose. *I hope his soul is still tempting enough.*

At sight of the two dozen steps ahead of me, I rethink my life choices. *Why are people so fascinated with multi-leveled buildings?* We could get along just fine in single floor houses. Each step is a gamble, its own game of chance, but I've never played a game I haven't won.

"That's because you always cheat." My sister's voice chimes in from the past. She said that every time I reminded her of my undefeated status, but how does one cheat at stairs?

I avoided them growing up. Too easy to fall and become vulnerable. Vulnerability in my father's court carried the same exciting stench as fresh carrion to vultures. Crack under the pressure within these walls and your broken body would be found the next morning in a darkened hall. *You should know.* I left plenty of my own human wreckage in deserted halls.

Up we go then. Hefting Wraith a little higher so her head rests on my shoulder, I start the climb. *Bend, lift, down.* My legs follow orders like two soldiers at their first battle, shaking and nervous but snapping into action at my command. The dagger remains cool at my side, waiting but far from calm. The buzzing in my head warns me of what's coming. *Rage.* The very emotion that made us the perfect team simmers into a boiling threat.

Pay. Up.

I will pay whatever price my partner asks, but I won't risk using the dagger's magic while holding the Ember of Winter. The blade's hunger is shifting, whipping between the guider's soul and hers. It wants them both.

Until we strike a new deal, I'm on my own, but being alone has never been my weakness. I was alone when I changed the minds of my court rivals from the disdainful *what good is a cripple,* to the confused and marveling *but he's a cripple.* I earned an entire court's terrified respect.

One savage choice at a time.

Savage is what I need to be if my sister is going to survive. So I keep my eyes straight as I pass the throne, shoving down the indignity the plain stone chair represents. *I was to be king.* But reclaiming my birthright was a two-person plan. *Together in life. Together in death.* Our simple pact, repeated over and over throughout the years. *Except for that night.* A twinge of chest pain causes my breath to hitch. I glance down and find my sister's face has gone deathly pale as another trickle of blood flows down her cheek.

The throne be damned.

Her life for my throne was a trade I would never make. I bloodied any mouth who even suggested such an idea. *"She's weak."* The courtiers said. Far worse things were said about me because walking was my challenge.

But I learned how to turn my weakness into my greatest strength. They forgot about their crippled prince while I studied them and discovered their secrets. They underestimated me. Plenty bled for it. *And the old man thought sitting in a chair couldn't inspire fear.*

I conquer the final step and enter the rotunda of glass. The moon spears through the panes with ghostly light as I head straight for the ruby curtain draped over my other secret. Bending forward, I let Wraith slide onto the bench, and then I rip the curtain away. The fabric falls, rippling like a bloody sea, scattering flecks of dust and moonlight and the hopeful wishes absorbed from a set of twins into its thick velvet over many years.

"You won't believe what I found."

I'd been looking for an answer, for a fate-changing secret lost to time. We'd told the legend of the Dagger of Souls to each other late into the night on this very floor, our eyes filled with winking starlight and budding darkness. The answer was above us the whole time. I take a wobbling half-step backward to study the work.

The season painting.

The Ember of Spring defeating the Ember of Winter without shedding a drop of blood. I sniff, my sneer twitching the corner of my mouth. I found it boring. She found it terribly romantic. How our ancestors changed the season with a dance. At least both embers were armed with knives, even if their hands were more preoccupied with holding each other. My lip curls in distaste.

In the lower right corner of the gilded frame, hidden behind a tangle of icicles and flowers, there's a thorn. It was my fascination with knives that helped me notice this thorn had a hilt and a slight, unnatural curve. *The dagger.* A perfect match to the weapon I wear. So I did what all curious children do. I pushed on it.

Our first taste of *real* magic.

Real magic doesn't put on a show. It happens in the space between the blink of an eye.

I lean forward and press the carved dagger. There's a soft click, like a sigh of relief, a whiff of iron and sawdust and soured earth, and then we're spinning with the painting from the palace's rotunda into another. But this one is three times larger, and fear, not wonder, inspired the design. There's no pretty patterns of flowers or vibrant stains of color adorning the glass ceiling. The panes are as wide as my palm and the metal frame thickened from narrow bars into beams, creating a heavy dome of foggy glass and salted iron.

A cage. Built around the oldest secret in the world.

The painting and the bench remain in the same place, anchored by a spell to the palace rotunda. I run my hand over the frame and pause when I find the pulse woven between two places. *There you are.* Magic stronger than my partner protects our way home, bound to a single rule. *Only humans may pass.* I might have just found my winning snare, but the rustling, woody creak behind me rakes a shiver down my spine, a warning I'd be a fool to discount.

This isn't just a game. It never was for me or my partner. I firm my lips into a line and clench my jaw. *Time to play the most important round.*

My sister hasn't moved from where I set her on the bench, unlike the marble that used to be under my feet. I hiss the moment I touch her. Tiny particles of ice coat Wraith's skin and sting my hands as her temperature falls. Strange. I thought winter would rejoice over coming home.

"Bring her." My partner expands my vocal range, diving lower and lower until the unnatural bass-tones rattle the glass against the beams of the rotunda. I lift my sister and face the bones of a ruined myth. I'm standing on rough wood, splintered and weeping bloody sap.

The entire floor is the stump of an ancient tree.

I've been here before, but the shocking size of it still needles a twinge of awe from me. The rotunda rises into a dirty dome fifty feet high at the center, while the whole structure spans twice that length. The palace, even the upper level of the city, must have been unknowingly built around the stump. Pale roots rise from the edges of the splintered trunk and writhe against the curving glass and iron beamed walls in a search for a way out. I swallow and force myself into my partner's domain.

There are so many rings, some as wide as my shoulders, that the tree's true age remains uncountable. Whatever name the tree was once called has been lost, but there's no disguising what it is. Even sixty feet away from the hollow center of the stump, I see it. The division between four living seasons.

Crimson fall.

Golden summer.

Emerald spring.

Ice-blue winter.

The first two sections of rings belong to fall and summer. All the sparks of their season magic flicker from within the wood like trapped fire-bugs. A winking pulse of crimson and gold light. The two inner sections stay dark because spring and winter are still free, existing solely outside this prison. And I've brought one of them here. *Let's hope this isn't a mistake.*

I grip Wraith tighter as we journey to the heart of the tree. The roots scratching *tap-tap* grow frantic, creating odd patterns of moonlight on the trunk as they thin and then crowd around each other. Our presence has distracted them from their desperate search for an escape, and as they leave the glass walls to track our magic-enhanced scent, the roots reveal yet another secret.

Paintings.

I've never counted them, but they hang like trophies along the entire circle of the rotunda. A display of my partner's impressive skill at ensnaring troubled souls. I don't bother looking at the faces captured within the gilded frames nearest me. All the paintings are the same. Two people in each. One in red who kills and one in gray who sings.

I'm not the first Red Death to walk the streets of Riffen.

Wraith is not the first banshee to sing to its people.

The tree likes to recast its curse. I might be the only human who knows why, but then, we are near the end of this tale of song and death and season. *I'm counting on that.* It's my last bit of leverage.

The crisp autumn pocket of air around the outer quarter of rings gives way to bristling summer heat near the halfway mark. My sweaty palms weaken my grip on Wraith, and I shift her position in my arms while trying not to trip over the uneven texture of the stump. Summer fades to a numb temperature somewhere between too hot and too cold that reminds me of empty stomachs and hollow souls. I wrench my thoughts from the fact my sister carries the answer to the hunger lacing the air.

Wraith's shudder vibrates through my arms and pain pierces my heart. I stumble but stay upright even though my legs have gone numb. I'm walking from memory. A killer who makes his own fate forced to rely on nothing but hope. *It's a good joke.* If we survive this, I'll let myself laugh.

Several roots snake across the trunk and jab their finger like points at my feet, trying to trip me, as a familiar stain comes into view. The black mark on the splintered wood beneath my boots spikes my pulse. *This is as far as we go.* I juggle Wraith's limp weight as I kneel. I place her on her side and check for signs of the curse's treachery. Her cut cheek is still bleeding, but her chest isn't, and her—*damn.*

It's so much worse.

When I pull my hand from her back, it's covered in blood. The same blood that left the stain on the stump. That's where I fell when I brought her here ten years ago. When she was—

Dying.

Stabbed by an assassin I knew was coming for her.

This isn't the time for guilt. I push all the emotions down, locking them away to keep my mind sharp. The crackling grows louder as more roots slither toward us. We're surrounded before I draw my dagger. I stab the first one that nears the wound in her back.

The root recoils as I level my glare at several others. "You don't touch her."

A pulse of the tree's power rattles the rotunda in response to my drawn line, but the roots stay out of my reach. *"You have betrayed me."*

I grimace, hating how the tree uses my voice. I stand and

almost fall. The numbness is getting worse, rising past my knees. Soon, the paralysis will set in. I'll be no good to her if this comes to a fight. *Better move things along then.* Taking a deep breath, I begin what will be a tricky dance.

"I betray everyone," I point at my sister, "except her."

"You knew her soul belonged to me."

"No, it belongs with her."

"WINTER IS MINE."

I spread my feet apart for balance as the entire trunk ripples like a wave. Glass crinkles above me but doesn't shatter. I press a palm to my ear against the vicious ringing. "No sense making me deaf. I've come to renegotiate our deal."

"Deals require trust. You have broken all trust."

The crimson cape I wear peels from my skin, flitting through the air, hood up and shoulders rounded as if covering another body. There isn't one, but the tree likes to pretend. Without the cape's direct magical link to my partner, my legs crumple under me, and this time I fall.

The rough wood of the stump makes a terrible cushion. I'm scraped raw, and my right sleeve tears, but I'm not broken. *Damn it!* I punch the tree, splinters stabbing my skin. For a moment, I stare at the tiny pinpricks of blood. The scent of iron wrapped in notes of copper and salt grounds me. Tears well against my eyelids as I try to shake off the strangeness of seeing my legs but having no physical connection to them.

I can't stand.

I can't walk.

I can't feel my legs.

The secret of my childhood exposed once more. The healers called it a wasting disease, but none of them could explain the cause. I was six years old when I noticed I was different. My legs were stiff, and my feet dragged the ground, catching on everything. A fall caused my first broken nose. Not that I'd ever admit that to anyone.

The crippled prince.

That's what they called me. *Their biggest mistake.* They thought I was broken and assumed I could never be a threat.

I was always a threat.

I learned to walk with iron rods strapped to my legs even though they tore the skin and left me in constant pain between the spells of numbness. I bested the fiercest in the court from a chair. I can damn well outsmart a chopped down tree. So I do what I've always done. I try again.

"Thanks to an assassin, she gave you the vengeful winter you wanted." I push up on my elbows and drag my legs to the side so I can sit, leaning on my right hand for balance. "Through her, you're starving an entire world."

"Perhaps."

"The real threat is your inability to control spring."

The hood of the cape twists, revealing nothing but darkness. *Knew that'd get its attention.* "What you need, what we both need, is for that guider to die. Then the only one who can bring the world back to life will be you."

The cape floats closer, pooling behind Wraith as it sinks so we are on the same eye-level. *If the spirit of an ancient tree had eyes.*

"Humans do not harm what they love."

I swallow a derisive snort. "Maybe not, but we can be convinced to sacrifice what we love. If the reason is good enough." I lean forward as if I'm about to share a tantalizing secret. "My sister is nothing like us. She hasn't realized why yet, but she will watch the guider die."

"How can you be so certain?"

I glance at Wraith. A prick of guilt dares my heart to change course, but our paths are set. "She knows the truth of what she is now. This winter may not have been her choice, but it is her fault.

That knowledge will drive her to act." I brush her cheek. "She'll do anything so the people she's harmed can have a future again." I face the hood. The crimson fabric hovers inches from me, but I will not retreat. "If I gave her the dagger, she'd probably kill him herself."

"I am unconvinced."

"She always puts the needs of others before her own." Another prick of guilt, but this one slices deeper, edged with envy. "To save them, she'll let Dovan die."

"You offer me nothing I would not already take." The cape moves as if an arm is reaching out toward my sister. She shivers as an invisible hand swipes across her hair. *"From his soul to hers, I shall feast."*

I control the urge to lash out, to claw at the cape and rip it to shreds. *You can't kill a spirit.* Not without a body. Luckily, I have one of those to offer. I keep my face relaxed as I bait my own trap. "You told me there were five of you once. Five spirits in one tree. One for each season and one to bring unity."

"And then your kind cut us down and forced us to shatter into a thousand souls."

"Embers."

The hood hisses and the roots crackling against the rotunda's walls thicken and block out the moonlight. The crimson light of fall and the gold of summer's rings slash through the darkness to the beat of my stolen voice. *"They were our pieces. Fragmented and lost. A power too great to be entrusted to such greedy mortals."*

This is the riskiest part. I deny the urge to suck in a deep breath, locking down the twitch in my fingers, or anything else that might tip off the season tree to my real plan. "For ten years, I have helped you gather many of those pieces, killing anyone with the tiniest spark within their souls. Because of me, you have reclaimed all of summer and fall, and soon I will bring you spring. But winter belongs to my sister."

"All seasons are mine. Winter is mine. Her soul. Is. MINE."

"I'll trade you something better." I lift the dagger and open my hand so the blade is between us. An invitation a spirit can never accept. "A way to break the enchantment of this room."

The cape jolts forward and I restrain my sneer. *Hooked like a gutted fish.* "It must be so boring to be trapped here. Never feeling the sun, never breathing the sky, never tasting the rich earth."

The trunk shudders with a desperate groan of desire as the roots sink down the glass walls, letting the moonlight blanket us in soft silver light. All this time, the season tree has been in my head, and yet it never considered I could be inside its mind as well, tasting its deepest desires. There's one flavor I know better than any other. The acidic tang of unfulfilled revenge.

"What you propose is not possible. My prison opens for humans alone."

I flip the dagger, sneering. "And certain pointy objects."

"You promise what you cannot deliver."

This is the moment. I savor every second, letting the tree's anticipation, its conflicting hope and despair, build to a humming pulse. When the glass windows rattle in their iron frames, I know it's time. My voice dips lower as I tempt the tree. "If the fragments of a season can inhabit a human soul, why can't you?"

The cape shrinks back, the crimson fabric fluttering from emotion more than the movement of air, but the roots have gone still, the rotunda silent. I have the tree's full attention.

"If you want your freedom, if you want to taste the blood of the humans whose ancestors trapped you here, then I'm your best chance." I jab the dagger into the darkness between the sides of the cape where the heart would be if it were human. "Wouldn't you like to be the killer for once? Instead of receiving the magic in their souls through my dagger, you could take them yourself."

The cape reaches for me with empty sleeves, and the warmth of its pleasure courses through my blood. *"You would carry me?"*

Carry is a rather optimistic word. Possession would be more accurate, but I'm not going to correct the tree. I need it to believe my offer is genuine. "I'd give myself to you. For a price."

"Name your price."

What I want has never changed. "My sister lives."

Another hiss as the hood shifts its focus between my sister and I.

"Spare her life, and you can have me."

"My fullness will destroy you."

"I'm a survivor." That might be my best quality, apart from the blade skills and charming personality. "Do we have a deal or not?"

If the darkness within the hood could smile, it would don a toothy grin as wide as a dinner plate. *"Agreed."*

The cape flows toward me, brushing my shoulders with a hint of what I'm about to face. Layer upon layer of hatred and loss stretching across hundreds of years. A tapestry of throbbing reds and whites fiercer than any sunrise snarled around a midnight core that's laughing at me. At how ignorant I am to make such a futile deal. The season tree's hunger for revenge bleeds into my mind, weaving us together until it is my plan. Almost. But not quite.

I know how to hold on. A skill I learned from my sister until —*she gave up*. On the brother who broke her heart. *But I never gave up on her.*

I use the dagger to push the cape back. "Not before I say goodbye."

A grumble shakes the trunk. *"You have until the fifth hour."*

Relief frees my heart of ice, but my expression remains cold as the cape flutters away.

Now the real game begins.

I check Wraith's back. The wound that should have killed her has stopped bleeding. The cut on her cheek is once more a scar. I glance at my injured palm to find the wound healed as well, all signs of good faith between me and the season tree. It's restored the curse. For one reason.

It thinks I've lost.

A half-smile twists my mouth. *I never lose.*

 The Girl

THUNDER BELONGED TO more things than clouds. Things like the rapid *thump-thump* of the girl's heart as she slammed the door closed, or the strike of the boy's fisted hands on the wooden barrier between them. When the old ones told stories, thunder announced the villain's arrival, but this time, the girl had locked one away. *He gave me no choice.*

"Don't do this!" The boy threw himself against the door, earning a sharp crunch as his ragged breaths roughened his smooth voice. "Damn it, Wrenna! I told you I'd handle everything."

But she was tired of her life being handled by someone cruel. Her fingers shook as she turned the key and locked him in his room, the metallic *click* sounding so final.

"No!" The boy's palms slapped the door. "You can't *do* this."

His kick sent a torn shred of sheet music sliding under the door. As she stared at their latest melodies captured in ink, her soul fractured, and the jagged pieces provoked a new hemorrhage of tears. *This will be our last song.*

Sorrow seized her throat, choking her as memories of all they'd lost, all they'd survived, blinded her. She pressed her back to the marble wall and clamped her hand over her mouth, hoping to silence the one thing that summoned his wicked nature.

The sound of her pain.

The boy grew quiet, and she pictured him pressing his forehead to the door. *So close.* He was so close to her. Her twin, who'd stood beside her even when their entire court wanted him to kill her.

"Sister, please."

Hot lines of tears ran down her face, but she firmed her trembling fingers into fists. *I'm not the one tearing us apart.* Her father and the boy had done that together. To them, murder solved everything, but violence still left scars, even if she was the only one who felt them. *Haven't enough people been hurt?* Her answer to that question would always be different from theirs.

"Listen to me," the boy's softened tone revived her desire to trust him, to fall into the comfort of their familiar but twisted roles. "I know you're scared." She sucked back a sob, her hand reaching for the key in a twitch of weakness. "But you don't need to be. You don't have to marry. Let me out and the north prince will be dead before the wedding trumpets fall silent."

A threat for a threat, a cut for a cut, a kill for a kill—that was Alec's way.

It isn't mine. She filled her lungs, elongating her spine until she stood tall. Gilded torchlight splashed against the marble walls and pointed the way out. *This is how our story ends.* Their family had been breaking apart for thirteen of her nineteen years. She had been the piece holding them together, but tonight, she had decided to say *no more.*

"Goodbye, Alec," she said, taking her first step away from him, away from the shattered remains of their family.

He struck the door so hard a splintered piece broke off, flying past her. "Winter's Teeth! How naive are you?"

The girl froze, waiting for what she knew best. Rough hands grabbing her arms, shaking her fragile will into pieces so she would succumb. Bow her head and accept the life she wished for would never be hers. But the bruising reminder of being powerless never came.

She glanced over her shoulder. The door was missing a chunk large enough for the boy's arm to slide through and turn the key. *He'll be free in seconds.* As if he heard her pulse spike, his head tipped down, his irises flashing the strange crimson she'd learned to fear.

"Go on then." He spat the words at her. "Run. Run like you always do." He leaned forward, splinters scratching his cheek and drawing beads of blood. "But don't expect me to save you. Don't expect me to care when the real villains find you."

Dread prickled her skin. Physical threats were a normal part of her day, but nothing prepared her for the wicked smile taking control of his mouth. The night shadows creating long hollows under his sharp cheekbones. "Running away has consequences, sister. What fun it will be to collect."

Her emerald skirt twisted around her legs as she ran, but she never looked back. Never saw the single tear gliding down the boy's face. Never dared to believe he'd let her go, because the boy who'd kill Riffen's biggest threat to save her, the boy who'd murder the king to free her, that boy would never understand.

Sometimes locking the doors behind you was the only way to survive.

WRAITH

23

"Wake up! You hear me? You can't die! Wake. Up!"

The slap comes without warning. A bone-jarring hit to my cheekbone that joins forces with the pain stabbing my chest. I flinch upward, gasping for air, before collapsing against the hard and prickly ground. Panic takes control and I flail. Rapid muscle contractions shake my numb limbs from the fingers of death but fail to restore my full heartbeat.

The slow, limping pulse drums against my ribs and claims me for a monster's use. But the monster who's here, the monster who's preparing to hit me, he's—different. The rage burning so cold in his brown gaze rises from fear. A desperate terror pales his face and leaks from his eyes, turning a killer back into a boy.

A boy who doesn't want to be alone.

He strikes me again, teeth bared in violent sorrow. *He's so young.* Too young to be this shattered. This twisted. All his pieces fracture around me through a dozen memories, each one darker than the last and drowning in innocent blood. An oily slick of dread coats my soul as the hands that love to kill curl under my cooling body, and then Riffen's crippled prince lifts me from the ground.

He runs with me in his arms, never tripping. Not even once. *I never asked him how.* How he could walk when the numbness in his legs had progressed into paralysis. How he managed to violently remove those in his way. *I didn't want to know.* But I saw the change in his irises, their soft brown growing sharper and flashing crimson. Even his red hair took on an unnatural jewel-toned shade.

"I will save you." He repeats those breathless words over and over as if they possess the power to overrule death.

As my breathing slows, hot moisture beads against my eyelids but never rolls down my skin. *My eyes are closed.* Sealed shut by a crust of dried tears. My cheek no longer aches because there's no bruise forming from a recent hit. I'm not jostled about because I'm not being carried. *It was a memory.* A beginning to who we became, but I'm yanked from the ending by a male voice. The same voice that controls my curse.

The copper tang of blood coats my tongue as I swallow, and *winter* shivers inside me. Afraid of something worse than my death.

I remember who I was.

I remember the ballroom, the innocents Red Death harmed because I wouldn't sing. I remember the old king's voice—*our* father's *voice*—breaking down the wall between who I was and who I am, and then I screamed.

Alec, no!

As my past cry fades, my other senses come alive. I'm surrounded by a rustling crackle, like creaking wood or branches tapping glass. The air is heavy and smells of sawdust and iron. A steady, silver glow of light paints my eyelids while whatever I'm lying on scratches my back and thighs. Power, beyond anything

I've felt before, rumbles through the spiky ground, raising the hairs on my arms, but the music has changed. A variety of instruments stripped down to a single voice.

I turn toward the singer and crack open my heavy eyelids. The blurred shape of a young man resting on his stomach, his upper body braced by his forearms, triggers another shudder. Hair too vibrant a red conceals everything but the side of his jaw and the corner of his mouth. *Red Death.* Except, he's more than that title now. He's—

Alec.

My brother.

My twin.

My *family.*

Alec's long fingers drift across the splintered floor, creating notes only he can see, and fresh loss slices into my heart. *We used to write songs together.*

I shut my eyes, blocking out the casual way he lies next to me on his elbows. He changes the melody into a call with no answer, a duet I am meant to complete, and his assumption sends a crawling itch up my arms. *Does he expect me to jump back into our old roles?* For ten years, he's been nothing but cruel, forcing me to take part in his violence while perverting the music we once shared. A chasm of mistrust stands between us, and I won't cross it. I won't join *him.*

"I can feel you judging me through your eyelids, *sister.*"

Sister.

My entire soul revolts against that title. I roll away from him, pushing onto my hands and knees as my stomach rejects who we really are. I heave, spots cascading like dead sparks through my vision.

I'm the sister of a monster.

"Which version of me sickens you the most?"

I sit on my heels and lock my teeth around my tongue. *Don't play his game.* He'll count any answer I give as a personal win. I scan our surroundings instead.

Where are we? There's no marble, no standing bear pillars, and no music playing, so we're not in the ballroom. *Maybe not even in the palace.* Silver light falls in a diagonal shaft that shines on me and Alec alone. Everything else is black, a darkness that creaks, that pushes and pulls at my hair as if breathing. I follow the moonlight to its source and spot the faintest wink of glass curving against thick bars of metal. *Another rotunda?*

The humming starts again, drawing my gaze down, and the monster who's killed hundreds of people flashes a dimpled smile up at me. Alec's crimson cape is missing, revealing a ruby tunic with fancy embroidery. Black trousers cover his thin legs, his grungy boots caked in what I assume is blood. Layer after layer of blood. My stomach clenches at his lack of discomfort. *Has he never cleaned them?* As if walking around with the evidence of over three hundred kills on his feet holds no weight. *Red Death has no conscience.* But I thought—*no.* I wanted my brother to be different.

Alec scratches his head. The torn sleeves of his tunic reveal a bright white shirt underneath, but its feigned purity is as spoiled as his boots by his stabby trade. Dull red stains speckle and streak the fabric. Even without his signature cape, he looks like Red Death. The embroidery points to his royal identity, but nothing else reminds me of the boy I knew. The boy with eyes so deep a brown they appeared gentle. Appearances with him were always deceiving. I know better than anyone how savage those soft brown eyes become when you got in his way.

I grab my head as more memories come. They crash into each other and break into fragments, leaving me with an incomplete picture, but I *hear* us. I *see* us. *All this time, I thought our sole connection was a curse.* I never imagined the monster who uses me could be anything other than a stranger. *That's not even the worst part.*

The worst part is I was never free.

Every hope I had for a happier life before the curse shatters, and the pieces of my foolish dream slips through my hands. My brother wasn't the only monster controlling my life. *Our father—* I dig my fingernails into my palms, desperate for any distraction from the memories of sharp words and hands bruising my skin and the slaps that came whenever I disappointed him.

Another pattern surfaces through the shreds of my family history. *Alec.* Standing in the way, promising retribution, and giving me a warped but needed type of shelter. *His shadow.* I could hide there, unnoticed, because his games left the court scrambling as our father focused on maintaining his dominance.

The pit in my stomach deepens, and I grasp at the edge. *I don't want to fall.* I don't want to share their blood or their name— Ryvelt. As a banshee, the curse kept me separate from them. *Maybe that was a blessing.* To not remember. To be spared from the wreckage of the family that shaped me. *Knowing who I was was supposed to make things easier.*

Alec's fingers brush my thigh. "Stop fighting it, Wrenna."

Wrenna.

I ignore him and the ruin of who we are because this is a gift. *My name.* The sound of each syllable fills my soul like a new song, tickling my throat with anticipation. I whisper it, I breathe it in, I bask in the soft glow of its truth.

My name is Wrenna.

Not Wraith. Not banshee. Not girl.

Wrenna.

A surge of joy bursts through my lips, but the unexpected laugh is too loud and clatters through the silence, dislodging more memories. So many desperate moments. The darkest one claws at my soul, ripping it to shreds. Alec sneering through a broken door, and me—preparing to run.

"Running away has consequences, sister. What fun it will be to collect."

Those were the last words Alec said to me before everything changed. They were cruel and wicked, but they also hinted at what was coming. *Oh.* Pain splinters through my chest as my heart lurches an extra beat. Each shaky breath I force down my tight throat stings, but I can't lift my head above the rising horror.

Alec knew.

I shouldn't be surprised. My brother prided himself on always being two steps ahead of everyone else. What I thought he'd meant as a threat, or even worse, a promise—*he was making a joke.* Laughing at the futility of my escape because he knew I'd never make it out of the palace alive.

The cool blood in my veins turns frigid, scratching at my insides like chips of ice. "You knew what was going to happen."

Alec stops humming. "Ah, yes. Because predicting the future is one of my severely underappreciated qualities." His lips twist into a smirk, his tone becoming playful. "If only the stabbier parts of my personality weren't so distracting."

Ten years ago, I would have laughed at his dry humor, but I let the silence between us grow, forcing him to meet my accusing glare. The boy, the monster, and the game-player—all three unite in his pinched expression, asking me a silent *what's wrong now?*

Pressure builds against my ribs, making each breath painful. *He still thinks he's right.* Right to murder, right to curse me, right to force me to play this game that leaves my heart shattered in pieces, my soul twisted in knots, and my body ill.

I fist my hands, holding onto the betrayal scraping like needles along my skin. "How could you?" Simple words, and yet they possess an edge sharper than his dagger. "How could you do this to me? How could you do this to us?"

Alec's head dips down, his expression obscured by crimson curls.

"You owe me an answer, *Alec.*"

He snorts like this is funny and pushes himself up, twisting his upper body so he can recline on his elbow and hip. The moonlight falling diagonally through the glass dome glints off his sharp cheekbones. His skin is wet, eyelids red and puffy, but I refuse to believe the tears are real. When monsters cry, it's always a trap.

"You think I wanted this?" The muscles along his jaw bunch together as he levels his own barbed glare at me. "If my goal was to become Red Death, why did I wait so long? Hmm?" He lifts his curved dagger into the open. "I've held the key to the banshee curse since I was nine."

I squint, studying him, but how can I trust the exhaustion sagging his shoulders? Or the tightness around his mouth, signaling pain? *He cursed me.* My own brother cursed me. "Why should I believe you?"

He heaves a heavy sigh, the dagger falling as his fingers grip the hilt.

"You'd do anything for more power." He'd even sacrifice me.

"Well, when you put it that way, the answer is obviously yes," Alec's tone sharpens as if he's annoyed. He leans forward, a thread-thin line of crimson circling his brown irises. "I have killed, I have lied, and I have betrayed for more power, and I'd do it all again. But I didn't..." He groans through his teeth, and then, without any warning, he stabs the stump.

The whole room flinches like a wounded animal under his blade, and I stare at the boy who was my brother. The boy who became *more* than human. *This is still a game.* It has to be. Alec doesn't know any other way to exist.

"I didn't..." He fingers his forehead, rubbing in slow circles. The gesture makes him appear vulnerable. Yet another trick. "No one makes this deal if there's another way."

"What do you mean—"

A violent shudder rips through the floor.

We're flung apart. I claw at the stump until my grip holds, saving me from being tossed onto my face. Five distant gongs echo through the darkness, and the glass rattles like a shaking drawer of silver. Frost skitters down my arms as winter churns inside my soul, screaming its own warning while a new pulse fills the air.

A metallic *clang, clang, clang*, counting down to something. Alec goes pale. He swallows hard and grips his dagger, knuckles turning white as he tries to stand, only to fall. Curses slip through his clenched teeth. I reach for him but yank my hand back as the circle of moonlight expands, revealing a pattern to the rough floor.

Rings. Some narrow, some wide, but their irregular curves are familiar.

This isn't a floor. We're sitting on a massive tree stump.

Winter drags a chill down my spine that's far colder than the ones brought on by my deepest fears, begging me to run, to leave this place. *I ran last time.* But the instinct is hard to ignore as I gather my legs under me and untwist my torn skirt. My muscles tense as I make myself ready. The moonlight spreads further with another jolt and an ear-splitting *crack*. I throw up my arm to shield myself, but the broken glass I expect never falls.

A single thought steals the air from my lungs. *This place isn't normal.*

Rotunda, or dome, regular glass couldn't endure such violent force. I take a hesitant breath, searching the black wall of air circling us, but while I see nothing, my skin prickles from a rhythmic *thrum, thrum, thrum*. The power I first felt when I woke is getting stronger, rising in wave after stinging wave. *Magic.* Old magic, left alone to fester. I turn my questioning gaze on my brother, my ears ringing from the abrupt return to silence.

"You should have run that morning," he says, his tone bitter.

He's blaming me. But the implication that we wouldn't be here if I had run before the north prince arrived, before Alec promised to kill him, before everything went wrong, clashes with the hard resignation in his eyes.

We both know I was going to die that day.

The first casualty in a new war with the north.

Wood snaps and creaks, and whatever was blocking the moonlight moves. Silver light shines through branches of shadow, illuminating a stain on the stump to my left. A tremor starts in my right hand and travels toward my chest. My pulse spikes into a disjointed rhythm as serpentine shapes made of wood emerge from the dark. *Are those...roots?* They slither and writhe and hiss, surrounding us, but I hardly pay them any attention because that mark demands my focus.

It looks like blood.

No. I'm shaking my head, trying to correct the defeated bend in my spine, but the gift of more light has never felt so heavy. A glowing blanket of solemn silver weighs me down as my shoulders curl inward. Pressing me lower. Forcing me closer. Until a thick, coppery scent fills my nose and coats my tongue.

This is where Wrenna died.

This is where Wraith was born.

This is where Alec traded our souls.

Pain stabs upward through my back and drives into my heart. I arch away from the sharpened point of agony, but my lungs seize. I can't draw a full breath. I can't blink my vision clear as two different rooms flicker in and out of focus. The giant dome of this rotunda, and the wood paneling and marble floors of our music room. Two places linked through my memories by an assassin's blade. Alec is screaming, but his words are just noise, buried under the slow pulse in my ears.

Moonlight knives through the shrinking dark, slender blades cutting the shadows into pieces. *This isn't... This isn't real.* The assassin isn't behind me. I'm not being stabbed. *This is an echo.* A memory grasping at the present for a chance to live again. I inhale, my right fist against my sternum where the tip of a blade should be protruding. But there's no blood seeping through my clothes, no wound rending my flesh, no weapon lodged inside my body because I—

I survived. For one reason.

Alec knew where I'd be.

My mouth dries out as horror ricochets from my heart to my soul. *He wouldn't.* All those years of being hated by the court, of being told I was all that stood between my brother and the throne he deserved by ruthless deed alone. Tears slip over my eyelids, drip, drip, dripping down as my mind reels. *Alec never listened to them.* He promised to protect me.

What if he lied?

What if he's always been lying?

I lurch backward and stumble to my feet.

Alec's hand shoots out and grips my ankle. "Sister, please," his voice is strained, but he won't even look at me. "I can't chase you if you run."

"I don't care." Only one person has the right to ask me to stay and Dovan isn't here.

I jerk my foot free and run, lifting my skirt to prevent the torn strips from snagging on the rough texture of the trunk. The moonlight thins as the branching structure above me thickens, but I keep running, half-blind and without direction. Every other step a root darts in front of me. I jump over as many as I can, but there are hundreds of roots. Creaking, twitching, and snapping their pointed ends at my legs.

"Wrenna, stop!"

The panic in my brother's voice distracts me as the roots mass themselves into a writhing hedge. I stumble and pivot on my heel, barely avoiding a collision, but my momentum carries me too close. My loose curls snag on the grasping roots. I bite down on a cry as I tear my hair free. The hedge curves, pushing me back toward Alec as I race against its faster growth.

Is he controlling it?

Several roots lash at me. I dodge the first, but the second connects with my right arm. Hissing through my teeth, I touch the welt. A mix of black and red blood stains my hand as the trunk jerks upward and then drops, knocking me off my feet.

I fall.

Splintered wood scrapes my arms as I roll into the hedge, but instead of the crack of wood against my weight, I hear a solid thump and a rattle of glass. My right elbow, skull, and back throb in protest as I rebound forward, giving me enough room to realize my mistake.

It wasn't a hedge. Behind the tangle of roots, iron beams and murky glass panes curve upward into the weakened moonlight. I scramble backward on my hands. *The wall.* But there's something else hidden underneath the writhing wood. A rectangular shape, a gleam of crimson and sooty black and palest silver.

"You still think this is a game," Alec says, his voice sounding so small. I glance over my shoulder. His forehead shines with sweat as he drags himself closer. "This was never a game. This is about one thing. Survival."

The roots branch away from the wall. Some slither along the trunk, others twist through the air, and still more descend from the ceiling as they target me. Panic wraps a belt around my chest and pulls tight as what they kept hidden is revealed.

A painting.

"Wrenna, don't! Don't look at it!"

But the ornate frame guards an impossible sight.

The painting's immune. To the grayscale vision of my curse. The reds bleed, the blacks devour, the golds shine, and the silvers shiver, pulsing with their own tainted light.

Rough wood scratches my skin as the roots coil around my

legs and arms to bind me here, but I'm already frozen, taken captive by the tortured image of two lost souls. A young man in red with countless skulls at his feet and a young woman in black with musical notes woven through her ragged gown.

They stand side by side, looking away from each other, but his face—Alec's face—is hollow, his eyes sharp and wicked. Her eyes brim with dark tears and her cheek is scarred like mine. I trace the cut Red Death gave me, unable to tear my gaze from the portrait.

Our portrait.

How is this possible? Alec and I haven't been painted together since we were ten. And yet there we are, as we are *now*, the mouth of a familiar curse swallowing us whole. *Is that how the curse tracks us?* Some part of our souls captured in paint?

The colors spiral as if the painting itself is alive and primed to tell a story. *Like Sanaa's drawings.* The portrait sucks me into the past, pummeling my heart with every memory. I'm in pieces with the first few images of two children so close they slept in the same room.

"Why do my nightmares run from you?" I'd asked, as he tucked me into bed.

His boyish, cheeky grin warped into the sneer that would become the calling card of a killer. *"Because I'm worse."*

It shouldn't have brought me comfort, but the promise behind those words did. *I was safe with him once.*

The painting's story speeds up, blurring nineteen years of uncursed life. *My life.* Alec's life. Until the moment we became monsters.

The killer and his banshee.

My heart spasms, sharpening each breath I gulp down. *This is the answer.* The *how* and the *when* behind my curse. Fresh shock comes when the painting reveals a third person. A servant girl in a dark blue dress. *Why was she there?* Distraught and pale, the girl hurries to my prone form, her hands patting my face as she tries to wake me.

Alec creeps behind her as a root traces the scar on my cheek. He grips her shoulder, his curved dagger already in his hand. I choke on a scream, but the past cannot be changed. Confused, the girl faces my brother, and the painting focuses on her. On the way her mouth opens in a silent cry, on the flash of metal reflecting in her wide pupils, on the twitch of her shoulders and the spasm of her chest.

Alec moves so fast. His dagger pierces her heart in a single blink, breaking her bones, rending the organ in two, and stealing the soul from her body. She crumples beside my limp form on the trunk. *His first kill as*— I avert my gaze because I don't want to see anymore. I don't want to listen to the terrible whisper of truth pulsing through my veins. A root circles my throat and squeezes, forcing me to keep watching.

Draped in crimson and hands bloody, my brother kneels beside my body. He sinks his dagger into my chest, the movement slow and careful, before pulling it out with equal tenderness. Nothing happens until he turns the blade on himself. Stabbing his own heart. Holding it there, as shakes ravage his torso.

Pitching forward, he grits his teeth as he jerks the dagger free. The metal glints an unspoiled silver, clean of all blood. The wound in his chest disappears, and when he lifts his head and opens his eyes, they glow an unnatural shade of crimson.

Red Death.

He extends his wicked blade over me. I watch myself rise at his unspoken command and become his tool. My black gaze empties of the life I had lived. My mouth opens in a banshee wail as words appear on our once again still portrait.

Three hearts. Three souls. Three lives.
Bound by song, by blade, by blood.
One to sing, one to kill, and one to die.

The song that can never be unsung.

My stomach churns as I begin to understand what kind of game Alec's been playing. *All the people he's killed.*

The curse's pain cuts into my chest. The burning, piercing friction of a metal blade entering my heart—*it's been a threat this whole time.* The cost of the bargain my brother made when he bound our souls to the soul of his victim.

All the lives he's destroyed. All the souls he's taken. All of it was for me.

He murders for me.

They die or I do.

MOMENTS BEFORE WINTER

HONESTY HAD KILLED his plan to save her. A mere wooden door was no obstacle to the boy but overcoming the wound the girl had carved into his heart was another matter. *She should have trusted me.* Their kingdom ran on violence. Murder was the sole language the courtiers and other rivals respected. *She would have been safe.* And all for the price of two more lives.

Instead, she'd betrayed him, locking him in his room and running away like the coward she was. *She deserves her fate.* But fate knew how to sink its hooks deep, and the boy had no desire to rip them out. He could curse her in frustration and entertain the idea of a future without the weight of her life on his shoulders, but he never stopped counting. The beats of their twin-bonded hearts, the pat of her fading steps, the ache squeezing his chest, this melody they shared could never end.

He had left one thing out when he'd revealed his plan. The north prince would never buy a throne through a bride when he could infiltrate their home and take it himself. It's how the boy knew where to look. He'd become a creature of the night, stalking and creeping and killing whenever it pleased him. The assassin the north prince had brought with him was no different, although she wore gloves while she shadowed the girl, as if afraid to be touched by blood. A fact that fed the boy's confidence.

Murder wasn't a clean business, nor for those obsessed with cleanliness. The assassin would fall to his dagger just as all the other threats had.

Then his sister had said a word she'd only ever used once before.

She'd said *no*.

No, when his plan was perfect. Now she'd soon be dead, her body stuck on the assassin's favored knife like a scarecrow on a pole. *I tried to warn her.*

Running away had consequences.

The dagger was out and in his hand, fueling the rage building into fiery chaos within his soul. He didn't bother reaching through the broken part of the door to turn the key. The boy was finished waiting, finished with letting his sister plead for a non-violent solution. He stepped back, drawing on the weapon's power, and kicked the door open. The *slam* reverberated down the hallway and in its echo, he heard the pulse of the girl's heart.

Already failing.

The boy ran toward her, the cold promise of vengeance following in his wake.

She could call him a monster, see nothing but cruelty in his choices, and even betray him, but he'd never abandon his sister. Whatever it took, he would find a way.

He would save her.

WRAITH

24

METAL FLASHES BESIDE ME, followed by a *crack*. The roots hiss and recoil as Alec spins his dagger, slashing left and right in a blur of movement. He tosses the splintered pieces of my rooted restraints away before collapsing on his elbows with a satisfied smirk. Fresh blood streaks his hands and torn sleeves. I sit up, palms pressing into the trunk. *He came for me.* Whatever warmth such a sight might have once brought me, all I feel is cold.

Three-hundred and sixty-nine lives taken.

Three-hundred and sixty-nine souls traded for mine.

The sheer number, the sickening truth of what I've cost so many families—*I can't.* There are no words sharp enough to express such horror, no emotions deep enough to contain the flood of misery pouring into my soul. Chills rip along my exposed skin as I exhale particles of ice, and the monochrome grays of my vision brighten into an icy blue.

For ten years, I thought Red Death killed for his own twisted sense of fun, but each death lengthened my life for a few days, a few weeks. *He was buying me time.*

My fingers coil into fists against my bent knees, winter gifting each knuckle an tiny spike of ice. A door within my heart unlocks, and I open myself to the fury of the first season. Winter's wrath rages through me until my veins are humming with the same power that summons blizzards and wields ice storms and drops the temperature so low living creatures freeze solid.

The room grows darker, the air frigid and moist. Alec's breath cloud streams into my sightline. His mouth opens when he spots my armored knuckles, and then he smiles. *Pleased.* Thrilled by my stabby use of magic.

"Better," Alec says, and I'm pulled into a memory.

I was thirteen and standing in the stable courtyard. A palace guard ripped a covered basket from my arms, throwing it to the ground so the proof of my disobedience could roll free. My father arrived in seconds as if he already knew what I'd done. *He smashed all of them.* The potatoes I'd snuck from the kitchens would have fed three hungry families. Now they circle my feet in mashed blobs, ruined by his boots.

How could you.

I wanted to scream those words into my father's face, but his hand was already moving, connecting with my right cheek and jolting my body to the side. We'd played this game so many times before that he didn't stay to savor his victory. He just ordered the palace guard to make sure I cleaned up *my* mess and left.

It was my silence, my lack of tears, that made my father turn back. I clenched my fists as I reached for a different emotion. Anger, instead of sorrow. And in my father's softening expression, I saw the briefest flicker of hope. Hope that I could be hardened, warped into a monster worthy of the crown.

Better, he'd said. Better—because there was rage in my eyes. Because I wasn't shrinking into my body or falling into a sobbing mess at his feet. The very reaction that had earned a different word from him. *Pathetic.*

An oily shame pools in my stomach. I shake off the memory and swallow past the nausea. The roots go still as frost sprouts from my skin. Icy thorns spreading an accusation as bitter as blood on my tongue as I meet my twin's expectant gaze. "You're just like him."

Alec's smile vanishes, his lips tightening into a straight line. His breaths grow short as he leans forward. "*Don't you dare* liken me to him."

"Why not? Our father would be proud of you."

"That bastard wanted you dead. He sold you to a prince who planned to murder you and make a crown from your bones." Alec's voice rises, his teeth baring in frustration. "I wanted to save you. I *did* save you, but none of that matters because you don't approve of my methods."

"You didn't give me a choice!" Tears roll hot down my cheeks as I match his exasperation, slapping at my chest. "Look at me Alec! Can't you see what your choice has done to me?" His gaze trails from the scar on my cheek, to the rips in my dress, to the silver scars on my arms before returning to my face.

"You're alive," he says, his tone fragile around the edges of each word. His expression betrays none of the sorrow or understanding I hoped for.

I sit up straighter, digging for whatever confidence I can find. "I don't want anyone else dying for me. This game *has* to end."

"Don't be boring." He flicks an errant tendril of frost from his sleeve like my words mean nothing, like the season I carry poses no threat, but the muscles around his mouth remain tight. "What do you want me to say? That I regret killing them? That I was wrong to cheat death for you?"

"I want my life back."

"No, you don't," he sneers, tapping his chest. "Without me,

your life is worth about twenty seconds of agony while you drown in your own blood. Winter's Teeth!" He jolts forward, teeth flashing in the light as the veins in his neck bulge. "YOU. WERE. DY-ING."

Each syllable slams into my heart. The fractures run so deep they reach my soul, and all the unspoken things hanging between those three words slip through the cracks. I hear again the melody that binds our souls. A twin song never sung.

I couldn't stop the bleeding.

I couldn't keep you breathing.

I couldn't lose you.

I couldn't. Let. Go.

The icy spikes melt from my knuckles as I wipe my tears. "You were wrong, Alec."

Alec's quick smirk reveals a dimple. "When has knowing what I do is wrong ever stopped me?" He reaches his arm behind him, his fingers stiff and slightly curled. The dimple disappears with a shudder of unease, and fear squeezes an extra beat from my heart as a flash of crimson slips through the dark. *His cape.*

Red Death's cape.

"Alec, please." I hate that I'm begging, but nothing else has worked. "Don't do this." I grab the arm he uses to support his weight. "Don't make me responsible for Dovan's death. I…" There's a catch in my throat, a hitch that stabs all the way to my soul. Three simple words almost escaped. A declaration of affection a banshee has no business in speaking. I shove them down, locking them away. Yet my near slip was enough.

A rare display of sympathy softens my brother's expression and rounds his shoulders, his raised hand sinking. I put aside how he figured out what I feel for Dovan and cover the hand of Alec's weight bearing arm with mine.

"Let me save him."

"Guiders die every day." He snaps, the words so cold and

sharp they ring false. Longing and anger battle through Alec's brown eyes as if he secretly wishes I never had to share the cost of his choice, but my brother never surrenders. "There's nothing I won't do for you."

His upheld hand twitches closed, his body tensing, and crimson cloth speeds toward him through the dark. The stump beneath us rumbles. The roots creak, scraping against each other. Our painting thumps hard against metal and glass. Even the shadows move, closing in as Red Death's cape brushes his extended hand, slithers up his arm, and folds around his body. Alec's face disappears into the darkness of the hood. He flinches, once. A sharp spasm of lost breath and quaking bone. Then his hooded head tilts up, revealing his ruby irises, each glowing with a hunger so wicked it whips shivers across my skin.

Red Death.

I bite my cheek as my eyes burn. *He chose this.* He's choosing the curse. Even knowing how I feel, knowing I don't want this anymore, my brother betrays me, and that truth cuts me deeper than his dagger ever could.

He'll never give me a choice.

His rough fingers brush my clenched jaw. "Don't be sad. We've plenty of fun ahead of us still."

"*Fun?*" The bark of my voice makes his wicked slash of a smile grow wider.

Fun. The word echoes in my head, a loop made of screaming victims and broken songs and blood splashing on snow. Red Death's twisted laugh chasing me through each bitter memory. *There's no escape.* There never has been.

Deep in my soul, I break. The tension in my muscles hardens into purpose as I watch him stand. This monster I share blood with rises on legs that no longer buckle, no longer tremble as he savors my hurts and hungers for more. More killing. More power and control.

"Did you really think I was finished with you?" He pats my cheek and I look away to hide my fury. "I've been patient long enough."

I hold my spine straight, my shoulders squared, as the chill seeping through me grows into something solid in my hands. The wild, untamable rage of winter sharpens every break in my heart into a weapon summoned by a single word. *Fun.*

He points his dagger at my heart. "It's time we finished our game."

The curse's threat extends from his blade and stabs into my chest, but I don't fight its demand. I embrace the next note of Dovan's song, inhaling until my lungs feel ready to burst, and then I unleash myself. My *whole* self.

The daughter of the old king.

The sister of the crippled prince.

The ember of the first season.

The banshee who is *done* playing along.

I spring upward and launch myself at Red Death, my arms swinging, my hands filled with winter's weapons. His gaze widens in shock as moonlight gilds the ice blades I wield in brutal silver. They're just as sharp and curved as his own vile dagger. A rush of frigid pleasure courses through my veins as I slash his face. He throws himself back as a crimson line opens in his skin.

Now we'll both have matching scars.

I press my advantage, forcing him to retreat as he dodges my next swing until his back thuds against the rotunda's wall. Our portrait jerks beside us and a flare of guilt cuts through the surging chill of winter.

This isn't who you are.

I gnash my teeth, screaming a second note as I ignore the trembling of my limbs. The softer part of me weakens while the part that enabled me to survive fights back. I was born into a family of monsters. I was raised by one and protected by another. They took my innocence and left me in pieces.

This is who they made me.

I drive a blade through his cloak and pin him to the thickest root on the wall. He snarls, a hiss of teeth and vengeance. My own magic pulses, rising to meet his threat and making us what we have never been.

Equals.

"You don't scare me anymore." I snap my second blade forward and throw ten years of repressed fury, ten years of gnawing despair and aching guilt into a thrust for his chest.

My arm jolts as Red Death's dagger catches my blade, sliding up its curve to cut into my thumb. I've no energy left to scream from the pain firing like hot, liquid metal along my nerves. All I can do is stand and hold my ground.

"Rage looks good on you, *sister.*" The approval lacing his voice sends a shockwave down my arms to my chest.

I'm shaking. Blinking through wave after emotional wave as my song gutters and—*I can't do this.* The thought hits my shoulders like bags of stones. My injured grip slides on my blade as my strength fails, and I pull back.

His blood—my *brother's* blood—drips from the icy tip of my blade in sparkling ruby beads. The weapon I felt so proud of creating induces a flood of shame. As I stumble backward, I throw the ice blade away and cover my mouth, smothering the choked sob rattling against my ribs.

"Pity," Alec sniffs. "You were finally acting like a Ryvelt."

My gaze snaps to his face, snagging on the wound I caused. The edges are already fusing together, and the same healing power closes the deep cut between my thumb and forefinger. But the curse's magic can't bind the tear in my soul.

I hurt him.

I *cut* him.

I tried to kill him.

My stomach roils and I lurch to the side, dry heaving.

Fabric tears as he frees himself, and he clicks his tongue as he surveys my shaking body. "This is why you'll always lose." He pulls my hair from my face like he's never stopped taking care of me. "You think losing control is a mistake. You think hurting people is unnecessary."

I slap his hand away as I straighten. "Don't touch me."

Alec's hand hangs in the air for a second before curling into a fist as his chin tips down, his crimson irises glowing through the hood's shadows. "Even your precious guider knows some bones must be broken." He advances and I retreat. The roots leave the wall and gather behind him like his own personal army. "Some lives have to end."

"Dovan's nothing like you." I lock my trembling knees, willing my body to overcome the instinct to run.

"No?" Alec's left eyebrow rises, a smirk tugging at his lips. "During his last day, that guider has killed two people when I haven't even killed one yet."

"He had his reasons."

"And I don't?"

I open my mouth to answer when I notice the beads of sweat forming along Alec's hairline and dripping down to his jaw. The hand holding his dagger is shaking, his knuckles turning white. *Something's... off.* There's a swagger to Red Death. An easy confidence so slick it embellishes his every movement. But this, as the crimson shrinks from his brown irises, as the roots mirror the rippling tension in his own body and go still—*he's fighting.* Against what?

Alec's head twitches to the right.

Our portrait hangs behind his shoulder. We're close enough to the wall for our painted features to be clear, except our faces are different. *That's not me.* Both figures are male and neither one is my brother.

Alec lets out a clenched groan as I find dozens of other paintings circling the entire rotunda. *The roots were hiding them.* A tremor of power jolts the trunk beneath my feet as I move closer, but I don't recognize the two men captured in the same shades of red, black, silver, and gold.

Their faces are similar enough to mean they're brothers. One wears red, the other gray rags. My mouth falls open. *Another Red Death?* And *his* banshee. I gasp as the colors swirl, telling a familiar story of violence and betrayal. Of a sibling bond so deep death couldn't break it because of what one was willing to do. Followed by the curse and then—*wait.*

Why is the banshee holding the dagger?

The banshee raises the blade over the other Red Death. *Is he—*

A rush of air warns me as my Red Death moves. He wrenches the painting from the wall, and I leap to the side to avoid being crushed. The roots echo his fury, shoving all the other paintings from the walls, creating the sound of a failing heartbeat.

Thump, thump, thump...thump.

Thump. Thump... Thump.

Thump.

"No more games." Alec pulls the cape's hood down, his left eye the soft brown of my brother, his right the wicked crimson of Red Death. "No more threats. You want to run away again? Return to your precious guider?" He points over my shoulder at a painting that doesn't fit in this room. Two season embers dancing within its gilded frame. "Then run."

Confusion tempers the twitch in my legs, but I remember that painting. It hangs in the smaller rotunda above the palace ballroom. When we were children, Alec touched the hidden dagger and brought us here. *Why is he showing me the way out?*

"You want a choice? Then here—" he tosses his dagger so the hilt lands near my boots. "—take it."

My gaze flicks between him and his dagger. "Is this a trick?"

"Pick it up and find out."

My fingers rise as my knees bend, but then I spot the blood on my skin. *Alec's blood.* A twinge of shame helps me resist, and I lower my hand. "I'm not a killer."

"Always the coward," he sneers, voice rough, but he doesn't reclaim his weapon. He steps forward, head cocked to the right. "I used to wonder why you never gave in to the rage in our blood." Another step. The vapor cloud of his breath brushes my face. I stiffen my spine to rein in the urge to flee. "There's a truth our father taught us." He traces the scar on my cheek. "A truth you've been trying to outrun."

I jerk away from his touch, desperate to escape, but Alec is faster. He grabs me. His iron-hard grip digs into my arm, holding me here as my heart snaps into a pounding rhythm and flushes my limbs with winter's cold.

"Some people shape the future. Others just get swept out in the tide."

A spark of the fire he's trying to fan into flames takes hold of my tongue. "Neither of us has ever seen the sea."

The gleam of victory dances in his eyes. This sparring of words is a game he'll win, but he drags our pointless battle out, watching me squirm. "People are only as powerless as they choose to be."

I gasp, my insides wrenching away from the invisible blade he's shoved between my ribs.

"You let our father break you."

I whimper. Hammers of fire and ice-tipped needles abuse my skin, ghosts of past trauma, until I'm left standing without armor. All my deepest fears exposed. His voice replaces the one in my head, whispering—*you brought this upon yourself.*

Because I wouldn't repay their violence with violence.

"You let him decide your future." Alec's arm circles my back in an unwelcome embrace. "Do you want to know why?"

"When has what I wanted ever mattered?" If my bitter honesty has any effect on him, he hides it behind his smug Red Death mask.

"Love."

My heart trips as my stomach roils, sickened by such an idea. "What would you know of love? The only thing you love is yourself."

"We both know that's a lie." He lifts a tear from my cheek. "Love has always been our weakness."

My shoulders curl inward as tiny cracks of doubt work their way into my mind. *What if he's right?* At least part of his claim is true. *I've always loved my family.* It's why my father could break me so deeply. But what he did, what Alec did—*isn't love.*

Love doesn't leave bruises on your skin or tear open wounds in your soul. Love doesn't make little girls cower or marry them to monsters. Love doesn't butcher innocents for fun, and then pass it off as heroic, as saving a life. *That's*— Fear. Rage. Greed. The kind of insanity that drove my brother to enact our curse. That drove me to cut him.

Winter answers my distress by freezing the splintered wood beneath my boots. Like my brother, the first season favors violence.

I just want this to stop. Without anyone else getting hurt.

Winter's magic pulses with my heart, its power building and building, ready for my command, but I'm not afraid. I reach for the side of winter that endures, that doesn't cut but stands as a wall. A silent, protective guardian calling to my soul. *We are the same.*

A calming scrape of frost glides over my skin as I place my palms against Alec's chest. "No matter what you do to me, I will never be like you." I shove him back. Ice erupts through my palms in twin spouts of fast-flowing white, throwing Alec against the wall.

He hangs there, stuck and surprised, but I'm not finished.

"I am done being your tool."

I lift my hands to the sides, directing the ice to pin my brother's arms and legs. The stump quakes, and the roots come alive, snapping toward me. I sweep my arm over them and they freeze solid. They stand like glistening snakes, twisted and looped between me and Alec. The rush of using winter's power bends me forward, and I brace my hands on my thighs.

I did it. I stopped my monster.

A rasping laugh stabs holes in my relief.

"You say you will never be like me, but if you leave now, if you save your guider," Alec twitches his shoulders, testing the strength of the ice covering his arms, "you'll become a monster far worse than I could ever be."

With that taunt, my brother strips me of my victory. I feel my spine sagging, my shoulders wanting to curl and protect my vulnerable heart, but I force myself to resist. Replacing the instinct to cower with an emotion that's more detached. *Look at him.* With his body pinned against the wall, he's not the victor here. *Don't play his game.*

My whole life has been controlled. First by my father, and then by Alec. *They knew how to manipulate me.* How to twist their orders into something noble. *For the good of the kingdom,* they said. They only cared about what was best for them. Using me as a stepping stone to the future they wanted.

I'm tired of being trampled.

I study my brother, my gaze lingering on those crimson-brown eyes that dare me to fight, at those sharp yet elegant cheekbones, at the teasing lips wrenched to the side in superior confidence. The boy who once chased my monsters away is gone, and the young man who's left—*I don't need him anymore.* Even if I did, I don't think I'd want him anywhere near me. Not after all he's done.

Words form in my mind, sinking toward my tongue, and for once, the truth is my weapon. "No one could be worse than you."

I turn my back on him.

Silence follows heavy on my heels as I pick my way through the frozen roots, the moonlight making them shine like crystals. I'm a quarter of the way to the season painting when my brother laughs, a bitter scraping of breath against his voice.

"My dear sister, I'm staring at such a person. Right. Now."

I trip over a root.

"I may be a murderer of hundreds," he says, "but you, you're the end of the whole damn world."

He's lying. He's playing games with your head. Just leave him. But my feet stay still, my body stiff, my lungs full of a breath I'm afraid to let out.

"The seasons are like echoes." His tone softens as he continues, grunting as he struggles against my ice. "They carry the strongest emotions of their embers. It's why they made such fantastic weapons in the war. Feed an ember enough pain, enough betrayal and fear, and you're guaranteed a genuine world killer."

I'm trembling, fighting against an idea that will destroy me.

"I didn't know how the curse would affect winter." The hint of annoyance in his voice twists dangerously close to regret. "It split the season in two. This ten-year-old, world-killing winter isn't even fully born yet. Do you know what it's waiting for?"

I swallow hard as the answer nails itself to my soul. *My death.*

"The problem with winter is that it didn't get to avenge you."

My knees buckle as all the air in my lungs wheezes through my clenched teeth in a strained wail. *I wanted to fix things.* To heal things, to make things better. Instead—*I make everything worse.*

I shake my head, my arms curling around my waist in a desperate attempt to protect myself from reality, but I am the Ember of Winter. The ember who was murdered and then cursed. The ember who unleashed ten years of ice and snow and bitter cold upon my world. *Winter was just reacting.*

At the time of my stabbing, winter was still normal. Its vengeance fresh. Its power limited by the laws of the seasons, until the banshee curse made the first season a prisoner. Freezing winter's rage, letting it build and build without full release for ten years.

"Hate me all you want, sister, but if you die, we all die with you."

I fist my hands to find some small semblance of control, but inside, I'm falling apart. Shattered by a horrible fact. A consequence I shouldn't have to pay, and yet I will. Because I'm the only thing holding winter back from finishing its world-ending revenge. *This isn't fair.* The thought rings hollow as all the hope I'd gained crumbles. *I was... I was going to save Dovan.* I was going to end this game and break the cycle.

I had a choice. My first real choice in ten years.

"There's only one way this ends," Alec's tone has gone soft, but his slight acknowledgement of how much I'm hurting pours salt into my gaping wounds. "You know what needs to happen."

My brother's right, and I—I *hate* admitting that. I hate that Alec's wrong actions will force me to bow. To break. To accept the limits of the damage *he* caused. *I don't want to be his tool.* I don't want to be the end of Dovan.

How will I survive this?

My lungs shudder as I gasp through a terrible realization. *Alec doesn't have to do anything.* He doesn't need to make any more threats. He doesn't even need the curse to force my obedience. My soul will scream, my heart will shatter, and I will remain a banshee, but I will surrender to this choice. I have to. Because I'm not normal. Because the world is dying. Because curses like mine never break.

"There's only one way this ends."

If Dovan dies, everyone will live.

If I die, winter will destroy everyone who's left.

RED DEATH

25

Good people always have doubts.

Those pricking questions dredged up by a conscience that isn't yet ruined. Their doubts whisper and cry and plead, painting colorful pictures of consequences and lines crossed and damage. *So much damage.* It's a game of helpful threats meant to save you. *When have I ever been interested in saving myself?* As I struggle against Wraith's ice, my arms and legs still pinned, I've never been more grateful to be a monster.

A good person would have gone for help when they found her bleeding out, trusting her fate to the inadequate skills of others. They would have accepted her death because normal people can't beat death. But I was nineteen, several brutal kills already behind me, and I'd been using the dagger's magic for a decade. Making wicked bargains was my specialty. So I didn't go for help. I didn't put her life in someone else's hands and wait like an idiot for the inevitable.

No, I killed for her.

And not once did I *ever* doubt.

What we'd become didn't scare me. She has tried to rattle me with her pain, forcing me to see her scars and weigh the cost of my choice, but all I hear is her heart. Still beating. Steady and strong and protected by the deal I made. Even though I'm frozen to the rotunda's glass wall with a vengeful spirit seeping through my cloak to possess me, I know this game is over.

I've won. Because I told my sister the truth.

Good people think all we villains do is spin traps made of falsehoods. *Idiots.* Lies are a villain's cheapest trick. They're flimsy, like shadows, and only work while your victim is afraid of the dark. To be a victorious monster requires a strategy based not on lies, but terrible truths. The kind that don't just break hearts. These revelations shatter souls. I've used them as weapons against all my victims and my city, but—never her.

That damn guider should have told her everything. Instead of leaving the key to breaking her, to getting what I want, in my bloodstained hands.

I never could resist a killing stroke.

There's no cry of *what have you done* within my soul. No twinge of guilt. Only the bitter sting of anger because I could've prevented this. *If I had reached the assassin first.* I see the weight of that failure in the slumping of Wraith's posture, in the hitching breath she exhales, and in the tears slipping down her scarred cheek. It's the shame I will own.

A cloying, sticky film of meddlesome emotions coats my tongue. Winning has never tasted so sour. Ten years of playing this game with my sister, breaking her one victim at a time, and until now, I've enjoyed every moment.

A shudder works toward my chest, trying to shake something, anything from my stone-cold heart, but these feeble quakes of emotion were Alec's weakness. Not mine. *Alec is dead.* I killed him the same night Wrenna died. Still, the tremors spread, growing worse.

She begged you to make a different choice.

If it were possible to save her without the curse, I would.

A sharp pain slices into my chest in a familiar threat. Dawn is coming and we owe my partner a soul. My sneer doesn't come easy, but I force my lips wide as I craft the perfect speech to get her moving.

"Winter may be yours to command, but the first season has a soft spot for me."

That gets her attention, her mouth falling open in horror. I flex my fingers, and a small piece of her ice absorbs into my skin. The chill sinks deep, scratching at my bones with vicious nails. *Does winter want to play?* The season sends dozens of ice needles into my body. It's a pointless act of desperation, like my sister's triumph. In the past hour, they've forgotten that pain is my food. Bloodshed, my drink. And death, my tool.

"Did you really think I could be trapped so easily?" I ask, grinning like a wolf.

She staggers back, head shaking, skin pale as I reveal her victory was a simple illusion, yet one more terrible truth for me to wield.

I dip my chin as my entire field of vision flashes red. "Enjoy your little reunion with your guider. Find a room, for blood's sake, and give that man a proper goodbye." I jolt forward and the ice around my shoulders cracks. "I'll be coming to kill him soon."

WRAITH

26

For the first time in my life, I don't run.

I step forward, again and again, dragging myself through invisible claws of fear and shame toward the season painting. My skirt catches on the frozen roots, my hands tremble, my vision blurs with wave after wave of sorrow, but I keep moving. *There's nowhere else to go.* Nothing else for me to be but a banshee.

I don't want this.

A smothered cry escapes my lips, but I clench my jaw, blocking the feeble objection from growing into a dangerous storm. *You can't beat this. You can't beat Red Death.* Two simple truths I have carried like stones piled upon my heart. I was weaker then. A wraith, with no past and no future. Until Dovan showed me what my life could be.

Rebellious emotions rise with their own chorus from my soul, but I bite my tongue. *What you want isn't important.* There's a cost to everything. Each choice causes a ripple that touches other lives, sometimes many lives, or in my case, every life. *I always wanted to care for my people.* To serve them. To offer them kindness and understanding instead of cruelty and threats. *I didn't think it would look like this.*

Choosing to stay cursed.

Choosing to sing a good man to his death.

Of all the kinds of pain I have endured as Wrenna and as Wraith, nothing compares to this. I'm in agony, my soul skinned raw by how close I came to being freed, to finally saving one victim. *There has to be another way.* My heart beats in my chest like an executioner's drum, pounding the truth of what I must become through my veins.

With a shaking hand, I grab the decorative frame of the painting. The hidden carving of a dagger gleams at me, and I don't give myself a moment to think, to feel, or to face what waits on the other side. I push the dagger and shut my eyes.

The soft click carries the prickle of magic, the tang of iron, and the scent of paint. Everything spins. I'm jerked sideways as the rotation comes to a sudden stop and squint against the harsher light. The dark metal and dirty glass and frozen roots of the larger rotunda have transformed into a much smaller space bathed in silver moonlight and flickering torches. But the world is still gray. Many shades of gray framed by marble floors and glass walls and the lean figure of a man that makes my breath catch.

Dovan.

The shock widening his pupils quickly narrows in fear. Moonlight flashes off the axe he's swinging at the painting behind me. My mind goes blank as I brace myself. He jerks the weapon to the side, trying to save me from the worst of the hit, but my winter rises to meet the threat. A wall of white appears between my shoulder and the axe. The head glances off the ice and falls with a heavy clink to the marble floor. I exhale and sag forward, releasing the tension from my body.

Dovan swears as he snaps his empty hands to his sides. His

lips remain parted, his shoulders tight, but his gaze darts from me to the ice between us, to the axe at our feet. *He's horrified.* Of how close he came to hurting me. *I would have survived.* I would have healed because of my curse. Seeing Dovan feel the full weight of almost wounding me, watching it pain him, scare him, even shame him a little, breaks the last flimsy layer of my control.

The ice crumbles as I launch myself at him. My momentum forces Dovan to step back to maintain his balance. I'm on my toes, arms around his neck, my cheek against his stubbled jaw. His pulse beats against my skin as his breath heats my ear. He remains rigid at first, arms hanging at his sides as if he doesn't believe this is real, but then he moves. Holding me, breathing with me, surrounding me in his gentle, spring warmth.

My voice is thick as I say, "Thank you."

"For what?" Dovan tilts his head to look at me, but I rest my cheek on his shoulder and stare at his chin.

It takes me a moment to find an answer that fits everything I'm feeling. "No one else in my life cares if I get hurt."

Dovan stiffens as spring reacts to his emotions and heats the air. Little wisps of steam curl off his chest near my cold face. *He's angry.* With the sting of fresh tears, I realize he's the first man to disapprove of how I've been treated.

"I'm sorry." Dovan kisses the top of my head. His gentle affection draws a tentative smile from me. "I'm sorry you have known so much pain."

I could stay within the strong circle of his arms forever, but he grips my shoulders and holds me away from him.

"I lost track of you and that red bastard, and then you were gone." He scans my body, searching for fresh wounds. "I tracked a black and red blood trail to the painting."

My blood trail.

"Where have you been? It's been hours."

I glance to the rotunda's west wall and mark the moon's position, hanging just above the city's rooftops. Dawn is close. *What do I tell him?* What can I tell him? In my father's court, information was a weapon. A tool to break you or turn others against you. *Dovan isn't like that.* But trusting someone with your whole self, trusting them to be different than the monsters you've known, is hard. Worse than that, it feels like a mistake.

Dovan rubs my shoulders as he lowers his head so we're at the same eye level. "Enna, talk to me."

Enna. A shiver runs down my arms as threads of sorrow and joy knot around my throat. *That was my mother's name for me.* I don't know when Dovan learned my nickname, or how our past connects, but I only asked to be called Enna in one place. The Mermaiden. *Was that where we met?* The memories of my time helping the orphans there are still too fuzzy, but as I curl into Dovan's chest, the weight on my shoulders grows lighter because I don't have to carry this burden alone.

"I remember," I say, my voice low and soft. "I remember everything." And so I tell him about my life before the curse. How I ran instead of marrying the cruel north prince, only to be stabbed by an assassin. How my brother used the banshee curse to save me, and how I nearly killed him with ice-knives.

When I finish, Dovan holds me close, rubbing my back, chin pressing against my temple. His silence is a balm. A soothing peace that absorbs into my soul and makes my chest seize. *I'm going to cry.* Because I have known so many types of silence. The lonely silence of ignorance, the cold slap of silent apathy, and the bruising silence of intentional harm. But this, this is the comfortable silence of understanding. From a man who has been shattered and is exhausted but still finds the strength to rise, to embrace joy even in the bleakest of situations.

The stubble along his jaw scratches at my forehead as he nods toward the painting of the season embers. "I tried to find a way through."

The echo of my own pain rings through his words. *Sometimes trying is not enough.*

The evidence of that fact surrounds our feet. Two shattered axes lie next to the one he was swinging when I appeared. The bench we once sat on is broken into splintered pieces, the velvet curtain cut and torn, and even a few glass wall panels are cracked. Their damage tells me the story of Dovan's deep concern, of the frustration of not being able to do anything to help someone you care for. But like me, the painting is protected by powerful magic. *There's nothing he could have done.*

I shift my position so I can see him.

Dovan's heart lies open in his eyes, in the tension between his eyebrows and his jawline, and in his slightly nervous smile. His display of affection becomes a duet, stitching a bridge of melody between our souls, but this song doesn't need our voices to be heard. It plays through the arms we have wrapped around each other, through the grip that declares we will not let go.

Dovan brushes a tear from my scarred cheek, the heat of his hand stinging my skin. "I would have come for you."

With those words, a small fracture in my heart heals. *He would have helped me.* Not like Alec would, where threats and violence and murder overruled my voice. No, Dovan would have been my shield, my defender, my friend. Whatever I needed from him, even if it was to simply stand at my side, he would have stepped into that role.

His melody tugs at my voice, notes full of honest strength and familiar sorrow, but the curse doesn't punish me for swallowing his song down, because it knows.

My choice is made.

I place my hand over the one Dovan rests against my cheek, but the added pressure causes him to wince as a familiar copper scent taints the air. I pull his hand down, exposing his palm.

"It's nothing." He shrugs as I count half-a-dozen cuts crisscrossing his skin. They've stopped bleeding, but one is deep enough it needs to be bandaged. "I'm fine."

How many times has he hidden behind that phrase? Using them to minimize his own pain so the wounds of others stay the focus.

I tear a strip from my skirt. "Everyone deserves to be cared for, Dovan. You taught me that."

He opens his mouth and then closes it, letting me wrap his hand in silence. I tie the extra length and tuck the fabric in so the strip doesn't hang loose. When I glance up at him, I expect him to ask the obvious question of how a princess learned to bandage cuts, but he remains silent. The wrinkle between his eyebrows has deepened, telling me he already knows. I take a shuddering breath and fix my gaze anywhere else, but there's no shutting out the truth.

Experience taught me. Because my father's palm often came too fast and too hard and I fell on objects that were the opposite of soft, leading to cuts and bruises.

"Enna, I'm—"

"Don't." I pull away. "Don't apologize. Not for him. Not when you've done nothing wrong."

Dovan's head tilts back, surprised by the razor edge of my tone, but I don't want to waste time discussing my miserable family. *We have better things to do.*

"What happened here while I was gone?" I slide past him and pause at the top of the stairs overlooking the ballroom.

"Nothing worth repeating."

The gritty defeat in his voice makes me glance at him, but there are no clues in his stony expression as he stares down into the ballroom.

Half of the candles lighting the chandeliers have gone out, casting long, twisted shadows across the standing bear pillars and the clan tapestries hanging on the walls and tainting the air with scratchy hints of smoke. Evidence of the chaos Red Death caused litter the ebony and pearl marble floor. Broken glasses, precious spilled food, and discarded scraps of clothing revive my memory. The temperature plunges.

I mark the patches of frost from my boots and the splatters of blood where my brother slashed people's faces to teach me the same old lesson we learned from our father. *Innocents suffer when I disobey.*

Dovan joins me in surveying the damage. "None of this was your fault."

"You're right." I push my shoulders back and stand tall, but they sag a few heartbeats later, undermining my outward show of strength. "I still brought the monster here."

Before he can respond, I blink away the tears and descend the stairs.

Apprehension builds in my stomach as we reach the ballroom floor. Dozens of shattered axes, broken swords, and splintered spears surround the ice wall that blocks the way out. I spot just as many torches lying in their own ashes, leaving scorch marks on the marble, but there's no visible harm done to the ice.

Dovan touches my arm, stopping us both a few feet away as if it isn't safe to get any closer.

I clench my fingers to hide their shaking. "Where is everyone?"

The muscles along his jawline twitch as if he has plenty to say, but all he says is, "They left."

"But the people who were dancing," I point at the glistening wall, "they're still trapped."

He nods, exhaling a long breath that steams against my chill.

"How could they leave them?"

"King's order's," Dovan's tone deepens, his teeth gritted around the words.

I shouldn't be surprised. The old king has as much talent for abandoning people in trouble as he does with cruelty. A sour knot of bitterness lodges in my throat because he's my father. My blood. And he'd kill anyone who defied him.

I search Dovan's tunic for signs of a fight, but only the prophetic wound bleeds down his chest. "They let you stay?"

Dovan's half-grin appears as he flexes his hands. "I might have broken the nose of the palace guard who tried to make me leave." He steps closer, his mouth forming a stern line, and he points at the ice wall. "I wasn't going to abandon them." His chin tips down as his tone softens. "I wasn't going to leave you behind."

Cold rushes to my face as I'm struck by his words and the fierce emotion behind them. That emotion has a name and an equal in my own heart. *Naming it won't make things any easier.* I study the ruined weapons scattered around us instead.

I picture him standing alone, defying a king's orders and searching for *me*. Exhausting his body and wrecking his hands as he tried again and again. "Was all of this you?"

"Most of it." His answer is so simple, so free of pride or demands for a reward.

I find myself staring at this man I've known for a single day.

I've seen him stop a mob with nothing but words. I've watched him kill and then spare a life. I followed him as he carried an orphan to safety. I laughed as he acted out the ridiculous story of a child. I cried as he sang his song with me and wanted to scream when he revealed my winter magic.

I once thought Dovan's refusal to fight for his life meant he was giving up, a sign of succumbing to despair and fear, but I was wrong. The only despair he harbors comes from the fear of failing his people. It's why he keeps trying.

He never gives up.

Dovan's been fighting for so long, persevering through hunger and danger, surrounded by death and by sorrow, losing family and friends, but he didn't harden his heart. He didn't walk away.

He didn't lose hope. He's a man of many broken pieces who refuses to crumble, standing between Riffen and a future of endless grief. *There's no place he'd rather be.* None of his scars took something from him.

They gave him more reasons to serve.

I finger the scar on my cheek. *Could mine do the same?*

Pain shouldn't be a requirement for finding purpose or for helping people, but pain can be a bridge that unites your journey with another's, that reminds the broken of a simple truth. *We are more than our wounds.* More than the scars we bear. More than the cages and the shackles others have used against us. And there is more to life than pain.

What if winter is more, too?

Standing before this wall made from winter's power, I feel it in my bones. The all-consuming rage that dooms my world ripples outward in icy waves, twisting and snarling and reminding me of one person. *Alec.* This ice was born of my brother's malice, and I have never been able to beat him.

Winter's sole enemy stands beside me. "Did you try using spring?"

"I tried everything," Dovan replies, rubbing the back of his neck. "Apart from firing a cannon at it, which would just get people killed, there's nothing I can do." He kicks a spear. The metal head scrapes against the ice before spinning away.

I slide my fingers through his. He returns my grip but doesn't face me, and my heart aches over how difficult it is for him to admit failure. *He can't bear seeing anyone in pain.* It's why he tries so hard to find a solution.

"I don't have the power to bring it down." He inhales as he pieces his armor back together, straightening his spine and squaring his shoulders. "But you do."

"It's too angry." My mouth goes dry. I rub my arms, chilled by the memory of when winter became my weapon and I almost stabbed Alec. "You don't understand what could happen."

"Then tell me."

"Winter wants to kill. Winter has judged everyone for what the assassin did to me." I shake my head, my chin trembling. "I'm not. I'm not strong enough to... I... If I lose control... I could kill them."

"Then you don't know who you are." He cups my face and my tears hiss against his warmer skin. "I do."

"Dovan," a tiny huff of a laugh escapes my lips, "we've only spent one day together."

His half-grin reappears. "That's more than enough time for me to know you're the bravest woman I've ever met."

"You've said that before," I deflect, but it's half-hearted. I'm standing on a precipice between who I was and who I could be, and I'm ready to fall forward.

"I don't think you've heard me yet." He rubs another tear from my cheek. "When I look at you, I see...such jagged pain. The kind that turns people bitter and cruel. But not you." He inches closer, emotion deepening his voice. "You still look for the good in people. You still see beauty in our world. You have a gentle heart, a strong heart that loves so deeply. Even after the curse and all the deaths you've seen and all the ways you've been hurt. You would give anything, sacrifice anything, if it meant saving just one soul from experiencing the pain you have."

He presses his lips to my forehead, and I'm trembling from the gift of seeing myself through his eyes. "That's who you are, Wrenna. And I love every broken piece of you."

The gasp that opens my throat feels like a first breath, like coming up for air after drowning for so long. My whole being is singing as a new song is written on my bones. The pride and the love he's confessed shines through his expression, and for once, heat spreads across my face. Not cold.

"Red Death, the curse, winter," he continues, "they should be terrified of you. You're stronger than them. You always have been."

As his declaration breaks through my fears, the old doubts that have fed on my wounds lose some of their power. The ice wall radiates with fury and threats, but I face them, stepping within winter's reach. I lift my hands, palms out, and close my eyes. The gentle brush of heat against my spine tells me Dovan has moved closer, ready to intervene if this goes badly. And I—

I love him.

My father believed love was a weakness. A flaw your enemies would exploit. It's why I built walls between me and everyone else, why I denied how much I feel to spare myself pain, but now I wonder if Dovan's right. If love is my strength.

I lean forward and place my palms on the ice wall. The freezing cold bites into my hands, a warning and an invitation, and as I pity the season that's been cursed with me, I direct my thoughts to those trapped behind the ice. I think of the boy and girl who shared a kiss in the middle of a dance. I focus on their innocence, on their hope for a future together that not even winter could dim. That's the power of love. I channel that power from my heart, down my arms, and through my hands into the ice, paired to a single thought.

They deserve to live.

And through the hum of magic vibrating my bones and speeding up my heartbeat, I hear a drop of water fall to the stone, and that sound changes everything.

RED DEATH

27

I AM SO DAMN HOT.

On scales of attractiveness, I burn hotter than most, but I'm not talking about my killer cheekbones, although they are sharp enough to take lonely hearts as trophies. This is deeper than appearances and far more dangerous. There's a fire in my veins, an infection that's just beginning as the ancient spirit I made a deal with spreads through my body. So far, the tree's sticking to my right side.

Confidence buzzes through my skull, but the emotion isn't mine. *Someone's feeling cocky.* Despite the lifetime of proof in my memories that no one's ever been able to make me disappear. Plenty have tried. The corner of my mouth pinches into a sneer as I play the tree a bloody show through our linked consciousness. Broken bodies and pleading faces wrecked with fear. *Such good times.* My past victories do the trick as my partner's confidence sours. The season tree will not be my ending. After all, I still have a city to burn and a guider to kill.

Goodbyes like most emotions are best kept short and punchy.

She's had long enough. I roll my shoulders, popping my neck as I shift my weight forward. The ice holding me against the cursed rotunda's wall crackles. Clumps of white fall away as I draw some of winter's magic into my soul. I sigh in relief, but the delightful chill barely lasts a few heartbeats before my blood returns to a maddening simmer. Beads of sweat glide down the hollows of my cheeks, giving my tongue the taste of salt and something else.

Sawdust.

It's fine. Just one small side effect of being possessed by an ancient tree spirit. My laugh quickly turns into a hiss as pain lances through my right forearm. I pull my torn sleeve up and find another problem. *They really are multiplying tonight.* My enlarged veins push against my skin, their once-smooth path corrupted into a twisted claw that looks like a root system.

Well, damn.

The spirit of the season tree is acting like an actual tree, my flesh becoming its soil. *We're in for a fun night, aren't we?*

I retrieve my dagger, snatching the curved blade from among the frozen roots. The ancient weapon has always had a soft spot for me. Holding the hilt soothes the fever and the tickle of madness scratching at my mind. But the root veins in my right arm don't change. The damage most likely permanent. *As long as I don't start sprouting leaves.*

The quick crunch of ice crusted wood matches my fast pulse as I stride toward the season painting and our exit. Patchy moonlight illuminates the way, but the stillness is so heavy, so complete, my breathing becomes loud, labored. Yet another physical sign shouting *stop* at me, but as I slow before the painting—*We're past warnings now.* Only consequences are left.

She survives. I stake everything on that promise and push the hidden dagger in the frame.

Iron coats my tongue as the painting begins to shake. I grab the frame, the decorative ridges digging into my palms, and clamp my teeth down on a scream. We're turning, but the movement is so slow. Too slow. Fingers of oppressive magic dig into my soul, searching for the bargained threads binding the season tree to me. My right arm, ribs, and right eye throb with panic. The roots in my veins slice through my forearm and blood splatters the painting.

A strangled roar scrapes my throat raw as pain shatters the walls between my mind and the tree's. I draw my dagger and stab the heart of the painting. Slashing in all directions, I cut the enchantment that made this rotunda a prison in pieces, and as the strength of its attack weakens, I launch us into the void of a dying portal. We're spinning and spinning. Colors and light flashing as I throw my hand out and strike stone.

I spit blood as I stagger into the ballroom's small rotunda and land hard on my knees. The impact jars my bones as I sag under the weight of a spirit who's harboring a grudge more than a thousand years old. *It's so heavy.* The emotions too potent for my scrambling mind to understand as I succumb. I slip under the tree's raging surface, I lose the sense of my own self, the feel of my lungs pulling in air, the beat of my heart, the colors and shapes of my physical world.

Who I am and why I'm here fades away until the bite of metal slicing into my flesh yanks my consciousness to the surface. The dagger is pinned between my left hand and the marble, my thumb pushing against the sharp edge. The tiny but growing pool of blood sends a ripple of pain up my arm to my chest, connecting my drifting mind to my soul once more, and I shudder.

I was drowning.

I was disappearing and I didn't even know it.

A rare doubt splits my heart. *What if you're wrong?*

I grind my teeth, resisting as I shield myself with familiar walls built of pride and stubbornness, but my soul is flailing. Lost in the season tree's massive wake.

What if I picked a game I can't win?

Never. I snarl. The sound is desperate, like a wolf with its leg caught in a trap where there's only one way out. Pain scratches through every vein in my body, and I cough out a dark chuckle. *Losing a leg won't save me.* As useless as my legs can be, I am rather fond of them. They make me quite tall. No, escaping my trap will require a far steeper price because the tree has taken what I offered—me. Which means I had better be damn right about my ability to hold on.

Freedom. The tree's thought rumbles through my mind, tempting me with a taste of wicked joy. A delicacy I have sampled every time I stabbed my victims in the heart. Hunger ignites my chest, roaring, demanding, and needing more.

More blood.

More violence.

More power.

No. I *am* power.

My arms are shaking even though both palms are planted on the marble floor. I'm falling. Sinking deeper and deeper into myself as my partner throws back my head and sucks at the air.

The tree's first breath.

And maybe my last.

Oh stop being so fatalistic. I knew what our bargain would mean. Possession implies surrendering control. The twitch of my lips might as well be my little secret. A mocking grin I'm unable to form since the tree controls most of my face. *Surrender has never been my style.*

My fingers flex against the stone as I force my gaze down to my right forearm where the truth of the deal I made remains visible. The roots that ripped through my flesh are retreating, sliding back into my veins as the curse heals the damage, but I hold on to that image. The duality of it.

There have always been two sides to my nature. The brother

who loved Wraith and the monster who protected her. My left hand curls around my dagger as I slide the weapon into the sheath at my hip, and it responds to my claiming touch with a pulse of power. *Still mine alone to wield.* More than that, the dagger is my anchor in the coming storm. I tighten my grip until the hilt digs into my skin.

The season tree distracts me as it uses my senses. Together, we sent the salty tang of fear and hear dozens of heartbeats. Some are steady, some are fast, and a few are weak, ready for the end. Delight spikes through my chest as we stand and look into the ballroom. Past the stairs and the throne that sits empty, a mockery of my birthright. Past the standing bear pillars and the bloodstained marble floor. *There.* A dazzling wall of white stands where I left it.

The innocents waiting within the ice wall were my leverage against Wraith. Now they're nothing but pulses of red, targets sharpening the focus of our hunger, and together, we grin, breathing in winter's deadly chill. *They shall suffer our retribution.* But first we deal with the two threats standing in our way.

The banshee winter loves and the guider with spring in his soul.

WRAITH

28

FOR A HEARTBEAT, winter listens and the ice wall melts. Tiny streams of water dribble between my spread fingers and down my hands as winter lets go. *Thank you.* But as the air whirls around me, bringing a scent that doesn't belong here, my body tenses and gratitude gives way to stomach-churning concern. *Sawdust and iron.* The sharp but earthy combination reminds me of the other rotunda where I left my brother.

Alec said he'd give me time. He's never broken a promise yet, so I force another breath in and put aside the horrible things I learned from him in that cursed place. The calming drip, drip, drip of water shifts higher into the crinkling pitch of crawling frost, and a thousand dull needles of ice stab into my palms.

I jolt backward, trying to pull away, but the trickling droplets have solidified, freezing my skin to the ice wall. *Let them go.* I push that thought into the ice, but the first season can't hear me. All that exists between us is a roaring abyss. A blizzard made of entwined souls and emotions and—*nightmares.* Any confidence I had splinters like glass.

Stop this. The images continue to flash through my mind. Scenes of chaos and horror where everyone in Riffen is screaming. People run but there's no shelter from winter's fury. Level by level, the city fills with statues. Men, women, and children, all frozen solid as they tried to shield loved ones until the silence is so complete only one word can describe it.

Death.

Winter has shown me our future.

I blink away tears, my arms shaking as I fall to my knees. Every breath I take quakes through my chest. *How could you want this?*

The season who shielded me from Dovan's axe, who armed me against my brother, who tried to avenge my death, answers by widening the wall. The white base shoves me back a full stride while muffled voices heightened by panic bleed through my failing concentration.

Help!

Save us!

Please!

The bitter sting of failure closes around my soul with barbs of hot iron, but Dovan squeezes my sagging shoulder, a silent witness of one fact. *He still believes in me.* Even though I am broken and frightened and without a plan, he believes I can save them.

I flatten my palms against the ice and tell the first season what will happen. *You will melt.* Because the guider standing behind me is willing to die, because I am willing to stay a banshee, and because there's one emotion more powerful than rage.

Our love will melt you.

That's what I show winter. A world reborn from my song and Dovan's sacrifice.

Winter looks at the future I have promised my people and breaks. A loud crack jars my hands as a fissure rips through the ice wall, spider-webbing outward in all directions. Frightened cries fill the air as the wall sways. Dovan yanks me out of the way as a giant chunk of ice lands where I was kneeling. My chest grows tight as I suck in a breath.

I could have been crushed.

A tangled flood of emotions whip between winter's curse-torn halves, but I don't understand them. More screams erupt as the stone floor trembles from the impact of another section of ice. A thread of winter's wrath lashes out at me, and every piece of the breaking wall tips inward.

"No!" I throw my hands out, desperate to keep the boulder-sized pieces from killing the innocents who came to dance at the Spring Eve ball. A surge of cold races down my arms as the half of winter I carry within my soul responds. White explodes every-where. Dovan shields my body with his, but I have to know if I failed. I scramble free of his hold and blink away the fog to an impossible sight.

Snowflakes.

Harmless snowflakes fall by the hundreds where the deadly chunks of ice once were. The people who were trapped catch the snow, confusion and shock coaxing survivor's laughter from their lips. And I smile as the palace guards and guiders quickly assess their injuries and lead them from the ballroom.

I saved them.

I served life instead of death.

A bubbly joy fills my heart and runs over as my throat goes tight and my vision blurs. I want to shout and leap and dance, and as I face Dovan, as his normally serious gaze shines with the same desire to celebrate this victory after all we have both lost, I know what I want.

I want him.

Even though my life is a broken mess, even though I doubt I could ever deserve him, even though our story ends in heartbreak, my ice-guarded heart is ready for more. *He's worth the risk.* Because he's still here. The curse hasn't won yet, and we have the right to share the happiness love brings despite all our wounds and responsibilities.

Two more steps and we are together. We fit like the separate melodies of a duet, a song I wish I could sing, but I steer my thoughts from the hollow ache of that desire. Dovan's hands settle on my waist as if they have always belonged there, but mine go higher, driven by a girlish dream that shattered long ago. A dream to love and be loved. To find my equal, my friend, my partner in all things. I cup Dovan's face and guide his mouth down to mine.

I *kiss* him.

The shocking heat of his lips sends a shudder through me as the fire of spring and the ice of winter meet upon our skin. I am breathless and burning with life, my whole being focused on holding the kiss for as long as I can, but Dovan doesn't respond the way I expected. Our eyes are open, allowing me to see the surprise lifting his eyebrows. *I've shocked him.* A nervous flutter unsettles my stomach. I start sinking on my heels, my lips pulling from his, when he tugs me against him.

The awkward bump of our bodies almost ends our kiss, but his arms circle my waist, tightening until there's no space between us. His hand travels up my spine to my neck, spreading waves of heat across my icy skin. Some reach so deeply my winter-trapped soul feels its first touch of spring, but I'm not afraid. I've never felt so safe, so completely whole.

Dovan leans into our kiss, and the change in pressure alters the slow rhythm of my heart. My pulse is pounding as my eyelids flutter closed. All I can think about is him. The strength of his arms, the tender brush of his mouth, the soft hissing steam our different temperatures create. We're no longer the embers of opposing seasons, no longer a cursed banshee and Red Death's next victim.

We're just a boy and a girl lost in a moment.

I wish it could go on, a kiss that never ends.

But we are not alone.

Loud, slow clapping breaks us apart. Dovan pushes me behind him. My frosty handprint sparkles across his flushed cheek, proof that winter and spring don't have to be enemies, but my ripple of amusement dies when I see *him*.

The boy who became Red Death.

The prince of Riffen, finally seated on our father's throne.

With a final slap of his palms, my brother leans forward, a jagged sneer stretching his mouth wide. He pushes off the throne, crimson cape swishing behind him, and saunters down the steps. Power radiates from him in a chaotic pulse that makes my skin crawl. His right hand touches his chest as his expression twists into a mockery of rapture. "I have never witnessed a more moving scene. Truly." He begins his slow clap again. "Bravo, Wraith. Bravo, Dovan."

Red Death stops clapping when he stands two strides from us. "I am glad the cursed little ember has found her power."

Cursed little ember? Alec's staring at me like I'm the answer to his hunger, and I recoil. The familiar scent of sawdust and iron sends needles of alarm down my spine as winter's split power unites into a desperate command.

Run.

Spring must have sent a similar warning because Dovan draws his sword, the metallic ring opening a pit in my stomach.

Red Death clicks his tongue as if correcting a foolish child, but his crimson gaze remains fixed on me. "Is winter betraying me, little ember? Is it flooding your veins with terror? Do you hear winter's song for you?" He snorts a laugh, his head tipping to the left at an unnatural angle. "It must be strange as a banshee to have someone sing you a death song."

"You don't come near her," Dovan points his sword at Red Death's heart. "I'm the one you want."

A wicked dare sparks in Red Death's gaze as he steps into Dovan's sword, not caring as the blade cuts him. "Oooh," his voice comes out deeper and rougher, the syllables dragging out, and as he breathes in, his eyes roll back into his head. "Oooooh, you cannot fathom how deeply I want you. Myyyyy spring."

Dovan stiffens, his near constant flow of spring heat guttering. Winter gives me my second pair of ice blades.

"Pity," Red Death's mouth twists in disgust as he focuses on the fact I am armed. "I so wanted to chase you down and rip the beating heart from your chest with my bare hands." An odd laugh punches through his serious threat and softens the savage line of his lips into childlike amusement. He lifts his palms and wiggles his fingers. "I have hands now."

Dovan leans toward me to whisper a question that's racing through my mind. *What's wrong with him?*

"And this voice," the monster coughs, rubbing his throat. "The tone is quite cheeky."

As winter retreats deeper into my soul, the ice blades melt, sliding within my grip. "You're not my brother."

"No?" Red Death stalks closer, the swing of his hips both arrogant and bored at the same time.

Dovan tries to intercept Red Death first, but I step into the monster's stride, forcing him to an awkward halt. "Alec would never kill me."

Red Death's cold fingers drag along my cheekbone, tracing the scar. "Your brother certainly enjoys making you bleed."

I hold myself still while every part of me is screaming to run, to fight, to do anything except stand here.

"But I suppose you are right." Red Death leans closer, and I smell sawdust on his breath. "Can you hear him screaming?" He runs a finger along his left temple. "Chanting his foolish promise of *'she survives'* over and over." A flare of brown circles his left iris. "It's all very pathetic and pointless. If he wanted to save you, he shouldn't have let me out of my cage."

I open my mouth to respond when he moves. Red Death punches Dovan so hard in the gut Dovan flies backward and slides on the marble tiles, and then Red Death grabs my neck. He lifts me high, like I weigh no more than the crimson cape hanging from his shoulders. I kick at his stomach and dig my fingers into his wrist while trying to choke out something, anything, that could reach my brother inside the monster, but I can't get enough air.

I can't die. My soul is still owned by the banshee curse, but there's no familiar pain stabbing into my heart as both a threat and a promise.

The crushing grip lessens on my throat as Red Death jerks my body, and I suck at the air. "Scream, little ember," his tone drops into a sickening croon. "Scream, so your brother can hear you as I take your soul."

"You...can't..."

"I am freed from my bonds." His nostrils flare and his fingers dig into my throat. "There are none who can stop me."

The bones in my neck pop and sparks fracture my darkening vision with bursts of light. My lungs spasm as my heart struggles to break free of its curse slowed rhythm. *I can't die. I can't die.* But the song I'm supposed to sing, the song that holds our bargain together and keeps me alive, is gone.

Then I feel the fire. A blazing inferno of heat envelops me moments before Dovan appears. The vibrant green magic of spring flickers around his body like living flames as he lunges, driving his sword under Red Death's ribs.

The scrape of metal on bone turns my stomach, but as Red

Death chokes on a gasp, the force of the thrust bends him forward. He stumbles back, releasing me, and I fall into Dovan's arms. I'm coughing hard, my throat bruised and raw as Dovan carries me toward the nearest standing bear pillar. Using the carved marble as a shield, he eases me onto my feet. He brushes my hair from my face and swipes tears from my stinging skin.

"Just breathe," he commands in his guider tone, the one that is all duty.

I sag against the pillar and inhale a stilted breath, only to set off another coughing fit. Dovan's fingers cup the side of my neck, and spring's magic flows into me, easing the panic and the scratchy burn in my throat until my breathing returns to normal.

I place my hand against the one he holds to my neck, a thin tendril of steam hissing by my ear. "You were on fire."

"I was," he offers me a weak half smile, and my pulse gains an extra beat.

There's a playful glint in his gaze. Even as a banshee who has been robbed of real relationships for a decade, I recognize the unspoken cue. An ache strikes my heart like a hammer, sending out a call, a deep, ringing bell of desire the rebellious part of me hopes he will answer. *This is where a regular couple would flirt.* But he is the last hope our people have of survival and I am a banshee. A banshee who shouldn't have fallen in love, and yet, I did.

We did.

Dovan glances to my right, exhaustion softening his stern guider mask as he keeps watch, and I realize—*our moment has passed.* We don't have time to be a normal couple. Our world is dying, and my brother just tried to kill me.

I draw my soaring heart down into its cage of bones and swallow. "You shouldn't have risked so much of spring's magic to save me."

Dovan's gaze snaps to mine.

I force myself to continue, "We don't understand how the

banshee curse affects our seasons, but our world can't afford a weakened spring."

"I couldn't watch you die." The desperation cracking through his voice steals the air from my lungs.

Dangerous ground. We are on dangerous ground as possibilities shift under our feet and our future teeters between duty and desire. Dovan takes hold of my face and pulls me against him as if he needs to feel the chill of my breath and the solidness of my body to banish his fear.

"I couldn't," he repeats, but his admission is equal parts oath and plea.

Once more, I glimpse the crushing burden he carries, the weight of all the lives he's seen cut short, and yet it is mine—*my death would be the final stone*. The one that breaks him, that puts him on his knees with no fight left.

No one has ever placed such value on my life.

I kiss his wrist, sniffing back tears of gratitude while grasping for a way to lighten his burden. "I've survived worse."

Dovan's thumb traces the scar on my cheek, but it's one of many. All of them marking my skin with the truth of what I've endured. He clenches his jaw, angry over how I've been abused as Wrenna and as Wraith, I bring his hands down, cradling his hot palms between my colder ones. "You don't have to worry about me. As a banshee, I can't die."

"Then where was your song?" Dovan's question guts my confidence as the memory of Red Death crushing my throat replays in my mind. "Where was your song when your brother broke the rules of his own game?"

An unspoken question steams between us as our seasons clash. *What do we do now?* Because if I don't have the power of my song, our plan to save the world will fail.

It's on the tip of my tongue to promise we'll find a way together, as if our hearts have been pledged to the other, but they haven't. Our love is as fragile as the first flower of spring, blooming in defiance of the last snows of winter, and we face a new threat neither of us understands. Silence becomes my answer. Dovan sighs, shifting his focus to the right where Red Death's muttering fills the air.

"My last day should have been simple," Dovan remarks quietly. "Serve my people. Find you. Release spring." When he looks at me, the magic glowing through his pine-green gaze intensifies. "But I fear the game has changed."

I don't know how to answer that without testing the magic that binds my soul. Focusing on my limping heartbeat, I call on the banshee curse. *A soul for a soul.* Just the whisper of those words should summon a sharp chest pain or the taste of blood. Nothing happens. The curse remains distant and my song silenced, all while the prophetic wound mocks me from Dovan's chest. *He's still the victim.* But how do we keep the curse's bargain in place when Red Death no longer cares about keeping me alive?

A low chuckle chafes the air with the promise of violence, jarring me and Dovan from our hiding place. We do the only thing we can. We stand together between Red Death and the city we hope to save.

My brother's left hand keeps twitching open and closed, jerking toward the dagger sheathed at his side, but he hasn't removed Dovan's sword from his body. Red Death gestures at it with his right hand. "Clearly, I've seen the best you can do."

He spits blood to the side, smooths his red curls, and stands to his full height. "Sad little humans. So tightly bound to your mortal bodies." He stretches his arms out, eyelids closed as his voice becomes so deep it resonates in my chest. "It is time you humans learned your place."

Pulses of magic speed away from him in staccato beats. Dovan and I both flinch as the invisible waves rush past us, stinging our skin and rattling the chandeliers. Underneath the heavy hum of their power, I hear a chant of voices. Many voices. Male and female and genderless, all stolen by an oath. A promise of murder and salvation. The curse's signature pain throbs to life, sharing their desire.

Ven-geance. Ven-geance. Ven-geance.

Tears run down my face as a tremor almost sends me to my knees. The glass ceiling panes clatter against their iron frames, small cracks inch along the pillars, and the marble floor trembles under our unsteady boots as the waves echo back on themselves, clashing and escalating until the entire ballroom is shaking. Nothing feels solid anymore. Not even the stone we stand upon. All while Red Death remains unphased, his face set in a mask of concentration.

I grab Dovan's hand as the snowflakes I created from the ice wall rise from the floor. Their silvery edges spinning and casting reflections of light everywhere. The tang of iron and singed wood grows so thick it becomes choking. A clan banner rips free and falls to the floor seconds before the throne my brother has always coveted crumbles like it was made of sand.

"Alec, stop!" I cry, my face soaked in tears. But the version of Red Death who meets my gaze shares nothing with my brother. He jolts forward as something tears from his back, and as if that was the point of his display of power, the ballroom falls still and silent. My snowflakes glide to the floor, but the stark change squeezes my stomach up into my ribs.

I clutch Dovan's hand tighter, head shaking in denial as I wobble on my feet. But the long, twisted shape coming from my brother's back, that muddy brown color showing between the dripping blood, cages my heart in a new prison of fear.

It can't be.

But I was there. I stood upon a splintered stump in the larger rotunda where Alec cursed us. A stump that rumbled with the same power coming from Red Death. *All those roots.* Hundreds and hundreds of desperate roots were trapped there, searching for a way out, and now one of them has escaped inside my brother. *How?*

The root arches over his shoulder, sliding toward his abdomen. Dread buzzes in the pit of my lungs like a nest of spring wasps my questions keep kicking, but the nightmare has only begun. I watch, frozen, as the root coils around the sword, yanks the blade from my brother's body, and then breaks it in half.

"Winter's Teeth." Dovan's swear is lost in the clang of his broken sword hitting the stone floor as the wound in my brother's torso closes. Omens of how outmatched we are.

My head is spinning, my body twitching as the chipping scratch of uneasy ice in my veins whispers of winter's desperate panic. Even Dovan's heat has changed, going from soothing waves to a harsh, scratchy sting.

It can't be. But we were told the stories of the spirit who ruled our world's climate as children.

It's real. The season tree is real.

And it has possessed my brother.

WRAITH

29

"ALEC, WHAT HAVE YOU DONE?" My voice is no louder than a whisper, but the monster wearing my brother's face huffs in amusement.

"Predictable." With a twitch of his shoulders, the root shrinks into Alec's back with no visible sign of pain. "There was but one price I would accept for saving your life again, and your brother was happy to pay it."

But he won't be the only one paying. That was always the problem with my brother's plans. He never cared about the damage his choices caused. *I do.* Stepping away from Dovan, I allow myself a single breath to clear the choking taste of sawdust from my throat. "Whatever deal Alec made with you, I won't honor it."

"Such a feisty little ember now that you've tasted real love." Red Death's mocking tone drags icy claws up my arms. "Your wants mean nothing in my game."

"I'm not your tool." Those words come out through my

clenched teeth, every syllable sharp as a knife and digging into my chest. Dovan's hand squeezes mine, giving me strength because we need answers. We need to know what the season tree has planned. "Only Red Death can use me. You're not Red Death."

"No, I'm so much worse." He flashes a wicked grin at me before glancing down. His crimson cape flutters around his calves as he stoops to swipe a handful of snow from the ballroom floor. "The soul of magic has always been a bargain, and you, my dear," he examines the snow in his palm, "are my favorite kind to make."

"What do you mean?"

"Your guider's sudden frown suggests he knows exactly what I mean." He selects a pinch of snow and lets the rest fall with a wet *plop* while my mind reels from his words. Dovan is indeed frowning, his body gone taut like a bowstring, but Red Death isn't finished. "The answer you're looking for is still bleeding down your guider's chest."

I glance at the prophetic wound that marks Dovan as the next victim, and I shiver as the final piece fits into place. How many times did I hear my brother say he'd made a deal, and yet I never wondered what that meant. *Who* it meant. *But now, I know.*

The season tree is the master of the banshee curse.

A jagged pain pierces my heart as a chill races down my arms, but winter's warning comes too late. Red Death has transformed the snow into a slender spike longer than my foot. He thrusts his palm forward, and I forget to breathe as that spike flies toward us. I latch onto Dovan's arm just as the spike drives into his chest.

Dovan gasps and sways on his feet, fingers rising to touch the ice protruding from his ribs. The vibrant green of his eyes flicker before they roll upward and his knees collapse.

My wailing *no* that's half choked sob, half enraged cry echoes in the ballroom as I fall with him, grabbing his shoulders before we hit the marble floor. He blinks at me, forcing his mouth to shape his final order as a guider.

"Not...your...fault..."

A dozen emotions reach their clawed hands for my throat, each one capable of strangling the hope from my soul, but I blink hard and rock forward. Every inch of my thin frame trembles as I shake him, begging him over and over to please—*stay with me.*

Dovan goes still.

The very air I breathe turns toxic. I'm suffocating, lungs seizing with panic. *No. He isn't...he can't be...* But the courage to finish those thoughts has fled from my heart.

I run my hands over Dovan's face, his neck, his chest, searching for signs of life. I slap his cheek, demanding he look at me. He doesn't respond. The awkward weight of his limp torso forces me to lower him to the floor. I press a fist to my lips to lock a wail of acceptance behind my teeth.

This is all wrong. Red Death's victims are supposed to die on a blade of wicked steel, not stolen ice. I grasp that thread and hold tight, because the rules of my curse have become my last hope. *I didn't sing for him.* I didn't finish his song. *He can't die like this.*

I caress his cheek, and steam curls into the air. *He's burning.* His temperature rising instead of cooling as emerald light surrounds the slender ice spike. Spring's magic protects its ember, and as Dovan takes a shallow breath, a desperate laugh bursts free. *He's alive.*

Boots crunching snow against marble temper my relief. I push my emotions down as Red Death grips my chin so all he'll see is devastation paired to the salt of my tears. *Let him think he's won.* While my fingers, hidden in the torn folds of my skirt, spread in a call for aid from the first season. A frigid crackle responds, pulsing through my veins until winter's magic pounds with my heart.

"Eyes on me, little ember," Red Death croons as he yanks my head up. "Plenty of time yet to see what plans I have for that guider."

I control the twitch of fear over what he means and keep

tugging at the tether between me and winter until I detect a soft rustle. Behind Red Death, the snowflakes are drawing together into white mounds. I send winter an image of what form they should take.

"But first," Red Death pulls on my chin, making me stand as pain pinches my neck, "let's finish what we started, shall we?"

Red Death seizes my wrist with his right hand, his sharp nails digging into the skin over my pulse. Black blood pools in the cuts, but he doesn't let me go. He lets me bleed. One slow drip at a time.

I wrench my body away from him with all the force I can muster, but his grip tightens, his fingernails splitting the last layer of skin to pierce muscle. My arm jolts with a spasm as my voice catches on a wince of pain, and his twisted smile deepens.

Red Death tugs me closer so our bodies are nearly touching, hoisting my captive arm between us. "Have these scars taught you nothing?"

My cursed blood oozes over the silver lines marring my skin. I stop struggling, sagging forward, as a lifetime of regrets and broken dreams weigh on my soul. *I'm so tired.* Tired of the grief, and the horror, and the misery of my curse.

"You can't win, *Wraith.*"

He's right. I've proven him right for ten years, but the banshee who received those scars didn't know she had a fierce season slumbering in her soul. *I am not powerless.* Winter chills my skin as I hold his red glare.

The temperature drops around us, his breath clouding before me, and I fist my captive hand in front of him. "I will never give you winter."

His nostrils flare, pupils widening in arrogant amusement before he leans in to whisper, "I don't need you to do anything." He rotates my wrist the wrong way, pinching nerves and straining the joint. I bite down on a scream as my thighs weaken and my eyes water.

Snowflakes rise from the floor as winter's rage surges through me. The first season reforms the flakes into an army of deadly spikes, but instead of releasing me to defend himself, he twists my wrist further. I can't stop my body's natural reaction to my bones breaking.

I cry out, and winter answers.

The spikes whip through the loose coils of my hair as they race for Red Death. Just when I think this will all be over, that winter will end him, he snaps his palms up and the spikes stop, frozen in midair. They hover around him like a ring of crystalline teeth.

I cradle my broken wrist. Sudden pain carves into my chest, ripping and tearing a piece of my soul from me. Tears mingle with trickles of icy sweat as I double over. The chandeliers, the standing bear pillars and clan banners, all of them tilt as my sense of gravity shifts, and I fall. My body jolts as my knees hit the stone floor. I'm forced to look up at the crimson monster who's playing with winter's magic, making the spikes perform a twirling dance.

"You should be more careful, little ember," Red Death says, his fingers flexing as he draws the spikes together into one as thick as his arm. The entire act should be impossible. He sighs, annoyed by my confusion. "Everything has a weakness. Winter gave its power to protect you, and now that sliver of power belongs to me."

I don't want to believe him, but there's a tear in my soul, a tiny fracture where a piece of winter's magic has gone missing.

"Pretty, isn't it?" He tosses the large spike into the air, and the smack of the ice against his palm strikes my soul like a stinging lash. "This piece of winter is not enough to kill the world, but it is what I need to kill this traitorous city."

Before I can react to his words, Red Death casts the spike to the floor. I lunge for it only to be thrown backward by a fierce autumn wind. My skin squeaks against the marble as I glide across the floor. The pointed corner of a pillar jams into my back, stopping me, and the spike shatters into hundreds of pieces.

Red Death prowls along the glistening particles as they flatten and join into a dangerous slick. He lifts his arms, and the ice rises like the swell of a wave. As he whispers new commands, winter shrinks deeper into my soul even as the stolen spark of its power throbs, building into a crackling rush.

Stop him, urges the part of winter I carry, while the half the curse separated from me savors the rage he's pouring into the ice. I twist into a seated position, reaching for the season that chose me, but the pull of his tainted vengeance is stronger.

Red Death stamps his boot. Ice races across the floors, climbs the pillars and the walls, and frosts the glass ceiling. Nothing is safe from its reach. Not even Dovan. Horror wrenches my stomach as the ice flows over his unconscious form, covering him.

"No!" I scramble to my feet. As I start to leap forward, icy pain slices up my stationary ankles. I swing my arms backward to keep from falling and look down. A thick layer of ice coats my boots, freezing my feet to the stone.

Running to Dovan is no longer possible.

The chandelier above me goes dark. Icicles tainted with smoke stab downward from the snuffed-out candles. A few grow too heavy and break off, shattering on the ballroom floor, but they're not the worst threat. The ice-wave Red death unleashed hasn't stopped. It sweeps through the decorative arch of the main doors and keeps going, turning down each of the palace's halls. A startled cry echoes through the entry. I tense, muscles desperate to react, but I am trapped as winter turns against me.

"Please," I face the monster, wincing as more screams cut short. "Don't do this. They're innocent."

"Innocent?" The anger rasping through Red Death's voice raises the hairs on my arms. "I have languished in a prison born from their ancestors' betrayal until all hope of freedom crumbled into dust and despair became my nourishment." His pointed chin tips down, ringing his eyes in shadow as he comes to stand before me.

"I have waited untold centuries to have my vengeance. Forced to survive on the scraps of magic harvested by the Red Deaths I slaved to my will through a curse." His fingers curl into claws as his glare turns mocking. "And yet, for all my captors' cunning, for all the Red Deaths and banshees before you, none of them could stand in my way, not even your wicked brother. What chance does someone as broken as you have against me?"

None, whispers the old Wraith, the girl who cowered and ran away. But while the season tree gave its speech through my brother's mouth, the jagged throbbing in my injured wrist dulled, fading into a stinging itch. I rotate the joint without pain and curb my smile.

The banshee curse has been used to control me for a decade, but after everything I've learned tonight, I see the banshee curse for what it truly is. This cycle of music and murder is a looped chain linking me and Alec together. *He didn't just bind me.* He bound himself, which means—

I don't wear these chains alone.

"You're right," I answer the season tree, earning a slight upward twitch of his eyebrows. "I am broken. So broken I doubt I'll ever heal, but do you know what isn't broken?" I raise my right arm. "My wrist."

He laughs, his left hand drawing his dagger. "There's only one way this ends."

Alec said the same thing. The season tree's making the same mistake I did, thinking he's unbeatable. *Our bargain is still in place.* And bargains work both ways.

The rich brown ringing Red Death's left iris expands as the left corner of Alec's mouth twitches open to whisper a word between clenched teeth, "Sssssssing."

Red Death's pupils narrow at my brother's treachery. His right hand flies to my throat to cut off my ability to breathe, but not even an ancient spirit can escape the magic that binds us all together. As the curse's warning jabs my heart, I surrender to its demand.

I accept the deal Alec made to save me.

I close my eyes and return to yesterday morning when Dovan found me. To when I first felt the heat of his touch, saw the prophetic wound claim him for death, and heard the note that would begin our fall into sorrow but also, love. That deep, melancholy note resonates through my chest, my throat, and my nose until my whole body vibrates with its power.

I sing, because a banshee's song cannot be stopped.

A rush of air proceeds a snarled cry. Warm liquid splatters my cheek. I flinch backward, the ice around my boots cracking as I stumble free, and the taste of copper cuts off my song. Wiping my face in a panic only smears the blood across my skin.

"What have you done?" The raw, wretched sound of Red Death's voice snaps my focus to him. He's panting hard, his left hand pushing the dagger deeper into his right forearm.

It's such a weird sight, to see him stab himself, that when the curse squeezes my heart in a hungry threat, I ignore it. I follow Red Death's staggering form until he collapses against the steps that lead to the smaller rotunda.

With one hand, I summon the ice he created, reversing its spread through the palace and drawing it back to me. Soon, Dovan is free as the ballroom glitters in the moonlight once more. I put aside the desire to run to him. The ice the season tree intended to freeze my city rallies behind me like a wave of frigid justice.

"What have you done?" Red Death asks again, but his left eye is solid brown and crinkled at the corner in a triumphant grin that doesn't reach his mouth. *I see you Alec.* Still fighting to save me no matter the cost.

I stare into his glowing red eye and pronounce the sentence we both share. "You made a deal that can't be broken."

Red Death's right hand lunges for me only for the left to slide the dagger up to his elbow, unleashing a scream of wild pain. He snarls as his blood pools along the stairs. "You can't defeat me."

"I don't have to. You've traded a prison for a curse." I bring my ice closer, and the cold makes him shiver. "There's only one life you're allowed to take tonight," a prick of sorrow wounds my heart, my gaze turning to Dovan's unconscious form before I continue, "but his life doesn't belong to you until I've sung his song."

As Red Death's face reddens in rage, I close my hand into a fist, and the ice wave crashes over his writhing body, freezing him into a solid cocoon. I brace my palms on the ice and slow my breathing as I glance up the stairs to the season painting. The top of the gilded frame is visible from this angle, and the shiny metal resurrects my hope.

I know what to do. I know how to save Dovan and everyone else.

Was this Alec's plan all along? I study his twisted expression, the right side caught in an enraged yell while the left frames an arrogant laugh. Whatever he intended—*he's not in control.* I am.

My heart stutters a panicked beat, an echo of my twin's pain as I push away from Alec and leave him behind. I fist my hands and keep walking toward Dovan. The ice won't kill my brother, not with the curse still in place, but it will give me time.

Time for one last goodbye.

RED DEATH

30

The lancing lung pain, the chaotic flood of memories, the desperate fall into unconsciousness. It won't be long before the fun begins, and I start the first round of the *I'm so glad I can't really die* cycle. My body will revive and succumb to the same problem over and over—no air. All thanks to the curse.

Most people would call this ice coffin Wraith trapped me in an act of poetic justice, but for me, being forced to be still is the worst kind of torture. Survival is all about moving. *Be quick, be brutal, be feared* was my father's advice on keeping hold of your power, given to me when I was eight. *Such a delightful childhood.*

The first spasm strikes, seizing my chest and wrapping my lungs with hot, iron bands, but with the ice draped over me like a rock-hard blanket, there's little room for my body to express its panic over a lack of air. The pounding in my head matches the beat in my root-infested veins as a swallowed scream sears my throat.

Desperate for relief, I sink into the void of my chest. *Let the season tree enjoy the symptoms.* I have work to do. Like figuring a way out of this that doesn't kill us all. But instead of focusing on the problem, I'm distracted by the cold stinging my skin.

Getting myself trapped in ice is becoming a habit.

An annoying and yet timely habit, since we were a heartbeat away from murdering my sister. Again. Revulsion wrenches my gut at the remembered feel of her thin neck in my hand, of her muscles and tendons, arteries and airways collapsing and straining under *my* grip.

I almost killed her.

Arguments can be made about how I wasn't in control, but those objections die as soon as they form, melting in the boiling acid pit of my stomach. *I made a deal.* And the consequences didn't matter because I've always been strong enough to master them. *Until tonight.*

After so many years of being feared, of playing the victorious monster and manipulating magic through the dagger, the chance of losing never occurred to me. And when the moment came, when it mattered most—

I wasn't enough.

I couldn't make my hand let go. I couldn't. Save. Her.

My throat thickens with the sour taste of failure as the two words I've been avoiding lock like chains around my soul. *I lost.* Or I would have if that irritating guider hadn't intervened, bright green flames and all. *At least he put on a good show.* All I could do was scream and promise death to the tree by every means possible.

A violent twitch smashes my face against the ice, but the pain splintering across my nose is dull, muted to a fading throb, confirming that the distance between my body and my consciousness is increasing. My soul is being lowered into a grave, and there will be no rising from it if I can't solve the riddle of why I failed.

Mistakes aren't death sentences. Well, this one almost was, but I shake off the flashing images of Wraith's choking face and bury the sounds of her gasps. *Fear is your knife. Cruelty your hammer. And ruthlessness your armor.* Yet another one of my father's sayings saves me from the clutches of regret.

Stinging heat pulses from the weapon in my left hand. It was a desperate move, stabbing the arm the tree controls, but it worked, weakening my partner so I could tell my sister to sing. Then the char of wood coated my tongue as the tree writhed through my veins. The roots recoiled from the hot metal as if fearing for their survival. *Interesting.*

A soft crack sharpens my mind as the ice shell coating me trembles. My chest expands, and as I inhale, the air whistles through the fracture. *I suppose this means our loop of suffocating to death is broken.* Any gratitude I feel for escaping the physical trauma of running out of air dims under the surge of glee coming from the tree. *Such a proud block of wood.* I sample a few of its thoughts and find them predictable. More oaths of vengeance and proclamations of triumph and woe, so much woe promised to the little ember who dares stand against us.

No, *not* us.

I yank my consciousness from the tree's, secretly wishing for a wince of disgust to separate me from the monster I gave my body to, but the simple fact is—*we are alike.*

Needing a distraction, I use my left eye as a window. The ice is crystal clear, and since I'm reclining against the steps, the angle of my gaze allows me to watch as Wraith helps Dovan stand. Annoyance flares through me with a spark of grudging respect. *That guider is almost as hard to kill as I am.* And they're...embracing again. *Wonderful.* As if there isn't a clock ticking down to our deaths. My left eye rolls, focusing on anything other than those two tragic lovebirds, but my sarcasm gives way to exhaustion.

What a bleedin' mess.

This game should have been simple. I bet on my strength, like I always do. My record of three hundred plus kills speaks for itself, but the ruthless killing skills that made me unbeatable also made me a good match for the season tree. The tree and I both want to see this city destroyed, although my plan would be far more entertaining than a quick freeze. *Fire is chaos.* I wanted Riffen to die of chaos. But gambling on my strength, on my cruelty and killer's prowess didn't guarantee my victory. It fed the tree's strength.

I'm not the hero. I don't make selfless choices or protect the vulnerable or see value in ordinary lives. No, I see targets. I see prey. Different games that fate might have me play to a familiar bloody conclusion. I am equipped to fight one enemy.

Goodness. In all its boring virtue.

My sister fared better, stopping the season tree by accepting her role as a banshee, but even she needed help. *Lucky for her I'm so good at sneaking around.* I pushed through the smugness of the tree's arrogance and hissed the command for her to sing before the tree caught on, and the curse obeyed because *I* am Red Death. No matter how far down the tree shoves my consciousness—*the curse answers to me first.*

My lips twitch, giving birth to my sneer, but the slip in the tree's control returns its focus to me. Pure, iron-tainted rage pumps through my chest as the roots claw toward my left shoulder. My body shudders from the skin-tearing sensation of their movement. Even my own mind turns against me as the tree noses around, searching for the memory threads keeping me here.

Keeping me alive.

It won't find them because they aren't anchored to my soul. *They're bound to hers.* To who Wraith and I once were. A secret twin bond that frustrates the ancient spirit into making a bitter threat.

I. Will. Crush. You.

How many times have I said those words to my victims? To Wrenna?

How many times have I been the one with all the power?

I was the killer. I *am* the killer.

I was the victor. I *am...*

Nothing.

Is this what dying feels like? Becoming a prisoner in your own body? Helpless and exposed to the cruelest fate? My heart refuses to soften as I lock onto the sound of my sister talking with Dovan. *Is this what it's like to be her?*

Knowing the horror of what's coming but being powerless to stop it.

Her voice pierces me with a single word—*painting*. My heart stumbles, a spike of fear betraying us both to the tree because I know what she's planning. *She means to imprison the season tree.* By taking me through the painting's portal and into the rotunda seeped in spells meant to keep the ancient spirit contained.

The grin baring my teeth guts me as the tree revels in what will be an epic failure, all because of me. *She doesn't know.* I wrecked the portal. There is no way back, no chance of trapping the monster I freed.

There's only one way this ends. The season tree mocks me with my own words, opening the door between us to reveal the full terror of its plan.

Winter's Teeth. The swear comes easy as the game I thought the tree was playing collapses and rips my confidence in being an excellent problem solver into shreds.

The memory of when she brought the ice wall down replays in my mind. There was a moment the season tree weighed carefully, pouring over every tic of time passing. Half of winter is consumed by vengeance and ripe for harvest, but as the first season shifted the breaking ice, intending to crush the innocents I trapped, my sister said *no.*

She wouldn't do it.

She saved them and doomed herself. Even worse, she doomed us.

The tree doesn't want her.

The panic flashing through my soul reaches my physical body. My breathing becomes jagged as the tree meets my tangled emotions with the scratchy sawdust flavor of its triumph.

I warned her. That love was our weakness.

My sister's feelings for Dovan have spoiled winter for the tree, turning part of the season soft. The tree knows she will never join it, never let winter rage, never become half the monster I am. *And a monster is what it needs.* Killing Dovan will devastate her, stripping the softness from her season. Then the tree will take her soul, absorbing a grieving, vengeful winter season into a vessel built for lashing out in destructive ways.

Me.

Damn. For once, the curse is meant for me. I'm falling deeper into the black, sinking into a pit I'll never escape if I don't find something, anything, to anchor my soul, but I have no plan. I have no power. And for the first time in my life, I don't know.

I don't know how to win.

WRAITH

31

Moonlight skims the ballroom's glass ceiling, leaving the torches and the pale sections of marble floor to reflect their muddy glow and fight off the final black gasp of night. Dovan would find courage in the flickering torchlight, but all I see is a fire that's dying. A hope that could only live a single day. *Our time has run out*. And instead of keeping Dovan close, keeping him with me, I sent him away.

You did the right thing.

A cough rattles my chest as the curse stabs my heart and I taste blood. I heave a breath that feels like I'm inhaling splinters of glass and bark an exhausted laugh. *For ten years, my body has been dying.* Saved by the souls Alec traded for mine. Now, I'm at the end. When I finish dragging my frozen twin up these stairs to the painting that hides an ancient prison, there will be no more songs. No more deaths. No more sorrow or guilt.

If this works, I will be free and winter will end. The decision I've made still weighs on my shoulders. Leaving Dovan, climbing these steps, going through the portal alone—*This is my chance.* My one chance to save him because he's wrong.

He doesn't have to die.

Before we separated, he asked me a question. Three simple words that won't stop repeating through my head. *Are you sure?*

I told him yes, acting the part of a confident heroine, but it wasn't my answer that choked me with grief and forced me to embrace him to hide my face. No, it was a single word. *Goodbye.* The word that best suited what I was planning. I swallowed it down before all the other unspoken things longing to be released overwhelmed me.

I wanted... A tremor rattles through my shoulders, the first warning of the emotional storm building in my chest. *I wanted to thank him.* To share how one day with him has been full of more love than my entire lifetime.

But I stayed silent.

I couldn't let him see. As a guider, Dovan is too good at reading people. My trembling lips, graying skin, and watering eyes would have revealed my plan. A barb of guilt hooks into my heart, pulling me toward the consequences of my decision. *I didn't lie to him.*

I chose not to explain why I wouldn't be coming back.

A bead of sweat falls through the chill radiating from my shaking body and becomes a snowflake. I watch it fall, but the flake's beauty isn't enough to drown out the wail of my soul. A jagged howl of melody that is my story and Dovan's woven together. I blink hard and force myself onward, but all I can see is him. Standing there, so tired but still so strong, as he waited for me to answer.

Are you sure?

Absolutely not. Fissures of doubt run through my confidence as I rub my wet cheek against my shoulder. Sending Dovan to help those harmed by my stolen ice, all while the bitter resolve for what I was about to do solidified into an anvil in my stomach, was the hardest thing I've ever done. *We weren't meant to have a future.* The tears keep rolling down my cool cheeks, transforming into more and more snowflakes until my pain creates a mini snowstorm around my boots. I bite my lip to sharpen my focus.

He's worth this. The lonely trek up these stairs to my ending. *They're all worth this.*

Another step and the painting comes into full view. I look at the embers dancing across the canvas, and I remember the promise Dovan made when we stood before the gates of Riffen.

"I'll save you the last dance."

Dovan and I will never have that dance, but we shared so many other things.

The first touch that wouldn't leave a scar on my soul. The first embrace that was a pure gift with nothing demanded in return. The first kiss—warmth rushes my face over how perfect that kiss was, and I can't hold back my smile. But more than those precious moments of affection, Dovan gave me his wisdom. He gave me his time. He gave me truth. *Even when I wasn't ready to hear it.*

He helped me see who I am and who I could become.

He gave a banshee the rarest gift of all—the chance to intervene.

Winter needles my skin in alarm as a sharp *pop-pop* startles me. I glance at the ice coffin keeping Red Death trapped and find two new cracks fracturing the surface. The scent of sawdust and iron leaks into the air along with a pulse of vengeful power.

Move! I snap toward the small rotunda. My hands stretch behind me, clutching the link of magic tethering me to the ice, and as I grit my teeth, every muscle straining, I pull the season tree closer to its prison.

I pump my legs faster, groaning from exertion as sweat stings my eyes. Walls of curved glass and thin iron rods surround me as I reach the top. I whip my arms forward, and the ice coffin with my brother slides over the broken pieces of the bench and the discarded axes and *thunks* against the wall. I double over, panting as winter's magic nips at my skin, wanting to know what comes next, but that's a secret I won't share. Not until we're through the portal.

With a deep breath, I approach the corner of the painting where the key to its magic is hidden, but after examining every curling flower and thorn in the decorative frame and running my hands over them, my chest goes tight. I'm shaking my head, shrinking back as I fight the wave of horror rising to drown me.

The dagger—the key that opens the portal—is gone.

Desperation drives me to jab each thorn, hoping I've simply lost the ability to see through the magic guarding the portal. Cold, unmoving metal meets my fingers every time. Frost sprouts from my agitated touch as I slap my palms against the frame. My hope is drowning, my soul as wrecked as the painting above me. Strips of canvas hang in jagged pieces from the corners as if someone clawed their way out of the prison with curved blades.

No, not someone.

I know who did this.

One moment I'm broken, the chance to change my fate shattered right in front of me, and then I'm screaming. My burning throat becomes a channel of pure rage as I beat my brother's coffin, all while he sneers up at me, ever the smug villain.

My knees buckle as ice races across the stone floor and climbs the walls of the rotunda. I've never cursed anyone before, but the hateful words come, frigid and dangerous and crackling with the full wrath of the first season behind them.

"Damn you."

Over and over I pound those words into the ice, needing them to reach Alec, needing him to feel the utter hopelessness he's once again left for me to reap. I can't stop saying the curse, can't stop hitting the ice, not even as black blood oozes from the broken skin over my knuckles or as pain lances my bones. Frost coats my fists, snow clings to my hair, spikes sprout around my bent legs, but I'm nothing like him. Destruction and curses drain my energy instead of empowering me further, and my fury gives out with my body.

I fall forward, sobbing, because the one place that's strong enough to contain the season tree and winter's wrath is gone. *I could have let the curse take my soul.* Ending this cruel game without the risk of my season killing everyone else in a final act of vengeance. *It would have been over.* Dovan would have been free to bring spring and save the world without losing his life.

I could have saved Dovan.

Now I will watch him die.

WRAITH

32

T HE DRY PALMS of my hands scrape across my cheeks as I wipe the frozen trails of tears away. After the chaos of my anger, numbness has set in, smothering the piercing ache of my heart and giving me a moment of quiet to recover. I almost snort at the idea of recovering from any of this, but instead, I stare through the rotunda's western curve. The horizon has lightened from a midnight black to a smoky gray, lining the buildings in the path of the sun in brightening silver as the world spins from one day to the next.

Dawn is coming. And Dovan and I have a date with death.

The burning in my chest sharpens as the wound in my forearm that Alec gave me on Dovan's roof opens and begins to ooze. His melody writhes through me, demanding to be sung, but my mouth remains shut, my breaths shallow, and my mind still, fixed on one thing. *Dovan isn't here yet.* So I wait.

I kneel in silence, until the sound of boots tapping stone in a heavy but determined gait reaches my ears. Dovan has finished assessing the damage from the ice the season tree stole from me.

How many more people have I hurt? Dread squeezes my stomach as the answer draws closer with Dovan.

I unfold my legs and get up, needles pricking my feet as I pass my brother. He and his monstrous partner are still trapped, but the ice coffin is riddled with fractures. His glare glows crimson with a single promise.

Pain.

How could they make my suffering any worse than it already is?

With a shaky step, I stand under the braided arch of stone where the stairs lead down into the deserted ballroom. Dovan approaches through bands of charcoal shadow and weak torchlight. The patches of ice my rage created melt on contact with his boots, filling the silence with the hiss of steam, yet another reminder of our purpose.

His path ends with me.

I'm his ending.

That fact kicks me in the chest. I bend forward, my body bowed under the weight of this moment, but I fist my trembling hands, grasping for any good thought. *This is what Dovan wants.* If I'm honest, it's what I want too. For winter to end. For no one else to die of starvation or be eaten by wolves. No more families forced to take dangerous journeys to survive. No more widows. No more orphans.

No more hopeless futures.

Except for my own.

Dovan's pace slows as he reaches the stairs, but he begins the climb without breaking his stride, his legs falling into a smooth rhythm like this is just another mission, like death isn't waiting for him at the top. A weak flash of anger whips through me at his ability to always keep going. As if sensing my growing turmoil, his vibrant green gaze rises to my face, and the fresh grief burning there fractures the ice shielding my heart.

People have died, as I feared.

I gasp, the sound hitching around a spike of sorrow. My boot slides half-a-step backward. Frost claws along the marble beneath my feet, falling down the stairs to scrape Dovan's boots while ice thickens over the glass walls of the rotunda, casting us both into heavy silver shadows. The chill in the air creaks with fear, twisting disfigured snowflakes from my breath. I tell myself it's winter. Winter is afraid, not me. But the shiver wrecking my soul isn't born of season magic but something very human—the fear of too much.

Too much sorrow. Too much pain. Too much despair.

Hold on. But my fisted hands are empty.

I have endured being broken again and again. I have born the weight of hundreds of lives on my conscience. I have agreed to sing Dovan to his death because our world's survival depends on his sacrifice, but what if I can't do this anymore? Be responsible for so much death? *What if I'm not strong enough to let him die?* I've survived a decade of being cursed by running from the pain and letting winter numb my soul. *What do I hold on to now?*

A blast of winter's power lashes out of me as the first season mirrors my distress. Dovan steps through the wave of cold without being affected, unlike the ballroom. From the marble floors, to the standing bear pillars, to the tapestries that hang, frost covers everything. *It'd be beautiful if my ice hadn't already killed people tonight.* I recoil from that thought and focus on the man who has come to end winter.

The freezing air hisses against Dovan's spring warmth, shrouding him in a glinting ring of mist, but he doesn't slow down or show fear. His back is spear-straight, his shoulders holding their determined line. Though his eyes ripple with more emotions than can fit in a single word, his face radiates a peace so confident I start shaking, my body unable to contain the fracturing of my soul.

It has to be this way. I let those words pierce my chest, staking my stubborn heart to their truth. *At least I got to try.* Dovan is the first victim I could have saved. The flinch of gratitude for that chance, even though it can't happen, gives me strength as he halts two steps down from me. The extra space he's giving me sends a pang of sorrow through the hollow of my ribcage.

He should be careful. I'm not safe to be around. Banshees never are, but then, I'm also the ember of a season that wants to avenge me by freezing our whole world. I tighten my grip on winter and my rebelling heart, and the ice spikes shrink below my calves.

Dovan glances down to my left, noting my brother, still encased in cracking ice on the marble floor. When he spots the torn remains of the painting behind me, his jaw flexes, matching the tightness in his shoulders. "It didn't work then."

I shake my head and keep my breathing even despite the spike of defeat lodged in my chest. *He doesn't understand.* How close he came to losing me, to being the sole survivor in our tragic tale. *We weren't supposed to see each other again.* Yet here we are. The chains of my curse binding us together more tightly than ever before.

Dovan's worry wrinkle creases his brow as he focuses on my arm, the one with the cut that has reopened. I tuck it behind my skirt, but he already spotted the trickle of my blackened blood. That I'm bleeding again means my death cycle has restarted.

He sighs before he looks up at me. "I'm sorry."

I have never hated two words more than I hate those at this moment. I tear my gaze from his and focus on anything but the growing list of apologies present in his eyes. *What does it matter?* If he hurts with me, if he shatters with me, it won't change what has to happen.

"How many?" The words slip out as I shiver, but I resist the urge to curl my arms around my torso. "How many died from my ice?"

My question strips the softness from Dovan's expression until

I am once more staring into the face of a soldier. The subtle shift in his posture as he leans away, his shoulders dropping a fraction, tells me all I need to know.

"How many?" I ask again.

"It wasn't your ice." He's pointing out the obvious truth. Instead of sinking in, instead of bringing me comfort, it rolls off my captive soul like rain drops on feathers.

Would he evade shame so easily if his ember magic had killed people? I clamp my teeth down on a grimace because that comparison doesn't work. Loneliness gnaws at me as I'm reminded of how different we are. Dovan is spring. He is life reborn. His season was never a threat. Not like mine.

"How many?" I repeat, my shoulders drooping lower than his.

Dovan relents, realizing I won't be denied this answer. "Eighteen."

Eighteen. The number is higher than I expected and plunges deep like a spear, skewering my soul. I lock my knees as the invisible blow lands and keep my spine straight, but I can't stop imagining them. All eighteen people freezing to death.

Horrible images flash before me. Men and women becoming statues in various poses of panic, their bodies heavy but sparkling with winter's icy glass, and my steady breaths turn ragged, sharpening into a wheeze.

Was it slow? Was it fast?

My chin trembles as I muffle my gasp of horror. *Did it hurt?* Did they watch the ice climb their legs, knowing there was nothing they could do? *I heard them scream.* Wild, hopeless screams so similar to the ones I hear when I sing a final note.

"Wrenna." Dovan's spring heat brushes my arm, warning me of his coming touch, and I recoil.

I cover my ears, shaking my head as I fight the longing his voice brings to life. *Every time he says my name, I want more.* I want to be the Wrenna who could love him. The Wrenna who has a future. The Wrenna who isn't cursed. *But I'm not.*

The spikes rise higher, reaching my knees, and my breaths grow short. I grasp for the only emotion that has made the horrors of my life a little easier to swallow. *Shame.* Its heavy weight falls from my crown and covers me like a blanket of chains, wrapping tight and locking me in with the screams of Red Death's victims, the copper tang of their spilled blood, and the emptiness of their lifeless stares.

As a banshee—*I deserve to have my heart broken.*

I deserve to lose the man I love, to face a future of never-ending songs while bound to a twisted combination of Red Death, my brother, and the season tree. I deserve to lose and lose again because I have wrecked so many lives there is no hope of repaying their loss.

No.

The defiance behind that unspoken word roars through me, fisting my shaking hands in a cry of—*enough.* I've had enough of this shame, enough of being a target for the cruel men in my life, enough of bruising my own soul out of some desperate need for atonement.

A trail of black blood slides down my arm, crossing dozens of scars earned from my banshee song, and the crushing weight of the curse's invisible blade wedges between my ribs. A threat meant to drown out the fact that none of this—not the winter that raged at my death, not the twisting of my brother into a monster, not the price the curse demands—none of this was my fault.

My life was twisted against my will.

My heart was broken by those who should have cherished it. My body was marked by the hate and fear and disgust of others, but I ... Shame closes around my throat, but I finish the thought.

I don't know how to survive as a banshee without believing I deserve this.

I don't know how to survive without punishing myself for what someone else did, without seeing myself as responsible, as some broken, monstrous thing, or without pushing away the few who showed me kindness. Yet the truth breaks through wall after wall until none remain.

No one deserves this.

It hurts, but I keep going, snapping the thorns of the shame I never earned. *I don't deserve this.* Every song I sang, I was forced to sing. *I didn't kill those people.* I didn't rip them from their families. *I didn't even cause this wretched winter.* But I will see it end.

"Wrenna, look at me."

The command of Dovan's tone yanks me back to the present. Pain tightens the line of his mouth as frustration and surrender battle through his shifting muscles, but he stands his ground, a warrior who won't stop fighting.

"Their deaths were not your fault." He points at my brother. "This was Red Death and his madness. Not. You."

"I know." My admission is quiet but strong because—*I believe it.* I'm done carrying the shame that belongs to someone else.

The concern drawing a line between Dovan's eyebrows softens as a mixture of relief and pride fills his eyes, warming the chill from my skin. His chin dips down in a slight bow as he recognizes my victory. It's a look of respect I've seen shared between guiders who understand the cost of winning a fight, not just against external threats, but the internal ones.

I stand taller, a victor despite my curse, but the next battle is already here.

Dovan holds out his hand, an invitation I've always known was coming, and the old instinct to run, to avoid the pain of our future, twitches through my muscles.

"Are you ready?" he asks.

I nod at first, trying to be brave, but the melody tickling my throat whispers of a lonely fate, of a sacrifice we both must make if our world is to survive. My fingers roll into a fist even as my arm slides forward, inching closer to beginning our ending.

"Me either." The broken honesty in Dovan's voice and the growing puddles of grief lining his eyelids draw a gusted half-laugh, half-sob from me, but he doesn't withdraw his hand. And I don't run away.

It takes all my strength to uncurl my fingers and place my hand in his.

As the sting of his hot palm presses against mine, as I lead him into the smaller rotunda where the growing dawn light gives us a single shadow, I'm overwhelmed by the desire to speak three little words. Three words that mean everything. They're a beginning and an ending and Dovan deserves to hear them before I sing his song.

I guide his hands to my waist, while mine slide up his arms to rest on the slope of his shoulders. My gaze does a slow climb from Dovan's strong jaw, to his full but stern lips, to the hollows of his cheeks and the proud rise of his cheekbones and the slight waves of dark hair crowning his head. I memorize everything, imprinting his image on my soul, and when I finally look into his eyes, into the shining pine-green of their depths, my heart is ready to burst.

My lungs fill with a song that doesn't need music, just my voice. "I love you."

His eyebrows twitch upward as he blinks, but his surprise is softer than when I kissed him. *He's guessed what I feel.* But there's a tentative hunger to his gaze as he studies me, a yearning for more that my declaration of love barely touched. *How long has it been?* Since he slowed down long enough for someone to tell him why he is loved?

Dovan's fingers curl into my sides, drawing me closer.

I trace the line between his eyebrows that has imbedded concern into his skin. "I love how deeply you care for people." The heat of his breath flushes the cold from my face as I massage his shoulder. "I love how willing you are to carry the burdens of others so they can rest." I lower my hand further, stopping at his chest where the prophetic wound drips fresh red down the standing white bear stitched over his heart. "But I love your stubborn heart most of all. You never stop hoping for the best. Even for a banshee."

His lips curl up at the corners as he breathes in my winter chill.

"You've made me happy, Dovan."

Joy blooms across his face in a wide grin, crinkling his shining eyes and overcoming the pain we share and the loss we will suffer. For a moment, Dovan's armor falls. The serious guider who is driven by duty transforms into a carefree young man. He picks me up and spins us in circles.

We start laughing, my hair whirling around my face, but I savor this feeling instead of pushing it away. Not even the curse's painful jab can darken our joy. We steal these precious seconds from fate and live out a tiny piece of our dream to be together.

When our spin slows, and my body slides down his, every note of his song rattles within my ribs as if his melody is already breaking me apart. I swallow hard, defying the curse to finish what I started telling him. "Thank you."

"For what?" He brushes the long waves of my hair over my shoulders.

"For treating me with respect and kindness." I pull his right hand to my cheek, savoring the gentle swipe of his thumb. "For reminding me I am not powerless," my voice breaks and fresh tears fall, but I keep going. "For showing me what real love is."

A familiar anger for what I've endured sparks in his irises, and he clenches his jaw before surrendering to bone deep weariness.

He slumps forward, his forehead resting against mine. "My only regret is that I didn't get to show you sooner."

No one has ever loved me like him.

There were always conditions I had to meet. A narrow-minded, crooked, and severe kind of love. *But this.* Dovan's love is straightforward and open. Resolute, without being heavy. Gentle, without being weak. It's nothing like what I imagined as a little girl, before my father crushed my dreams of falling in love. This is bigger than giddy feelings and flushed skin and silly daydreams. There's nothing shallow or flimsy about the love Dovan and I share. *It's still a fall.* A leap from what I've known into something new.

He lifts his forehead from mine, and his fingers glide along my jaw, releasing tiny tendrils of steam. "It was my honor, Wrenna, to spend my last day with you."

The fragile smile I offer him in return is far from enough, but as I breathe his declaration in, his words bind the pieces of my broken heart together. *This is what you hold on to.* All the good things and the hard things he's shared with me, all the ways he's made me feel seen and worthy and powerful—this is the glue that will hold me together when he's gone.

Dovan's left arm circles my waist as his right hand cups the back of my neck. Mist sparkles around us, infused with ribbon sized rainbows as spring and winter merge. I gasp in wonder over the display of so many colors.

Red, the playful shade of joy-heated faces, flares into fiery orange and sun yellow before slipping into a pale, new leaf green that whispers promises of reborn life. Blue, indigo, and violet, a trio of colors mixing hope and sorrow, the past and the future, dance along the edges. They encircle us, a bond of more than magic and bone. Our connection is soul deep.

The curse ruins the moment and shoves a note through my lips, but I bite the rest of the melody off despite the pain. When the demand to sing eases, I ask, "Is there anyone else you need to say goodbye to?"

His head bends closer until the air I breathe heats into steam. "Just. You."

"Me?"

Dovan moves slowly at first, giving me every chance to pull away, but the moment our lips touch, whatever little doubts I once had about his feelings are singed all the way to their roots.

I've stretched my fingers over a fire, I've basked in the summer sun, but this—*heat*, seeping through my skin and lapping against my heart's icy wall, is an inferno. Spring burns on his lips, and he brings that fire to mine, sending a shockwave through my half-frozen soul. It's a taste of life, vibrant and wild and evergreen, awakening a hunger so deep I'm shaking for the fear of it. The fear of what will happen once our kiss is over, but I push that thought away, sliding my fingers into his wavy hair.

Winter and spring clash with our every touch, a promise of flowers and ice thorns, of life and death, and we pull each other even closer. His lips, his hands, his arms, they tell me *you're worthy* through a dozen different touches. Neither of us holds anything back because the only thing we have left to lose is time.

The pressure of his mouth against mine increases, guiding mine open, and Dovan breathes into me. All the warmth and hope of spring. It surges toward my frozen core and explodes in blazing sparks through the dark and the emptiness of ten years living as a wraith. In his arms, I'm no longer alone. No longer feared. No longer hated. No longer *lost*. I didn't just find him. He found me, and he fills my soul.

Then it's over.

My hands and arms wrapped around his neck and shoulders, his arms belted around my waist, our quickened breaths stirring the air with a glistening halo of mist and ice. We stare into each other's eyes, our tears falling on flushed half-smiles. My lungs pull in another breath, my lips contracting to form the next note. *Not yet.* I swallow, resisting the curse as Dovan straightens and my heels touch the ground.

"Promise me." Dovan presses his forehead against mine. "Promise me you won't run away from our people when I'm gone. Promise me you won't live in the shadows." He leans back to search my face. "Promise me you won't forget the truth of who you are."

"I will try." But my fingers clutch his tunic because I don't want to let him go.

"Trying is enough," he reminds me. "My home will always be yours. The children take turns telling ridiculous stories most nights. Promise me you'll go there and laugh with them when you need to remember there is still joy."

"With them," I nod, "and at the memory of your terrible acting."

"I was terrible," he admits. We share a weak laugh that doesn't last long enough.

In the quiet that follows, we study each other for a while, our souls speaking without words as he cradles my head and I grip his shoulders. I fight to be strong for him and for me, but there's no hiding from how deeply losing him, losing *us*, will hurt.

As if he senses my secret fear, he says, "This isn't forever."

"I know." Someday, somehow, when the world has recovered from winter, I will find a way to sing my last song, and then the curse will end and our souls will be free to find each other.

He kisses me again, quick and final, and my heart breaks as he lets me go. Our hands slide along our arms until only our fingers touch, and then he steps back, my skin itching with sorrow over the loss of his warmth. "It's time you sang for life instead of death."

This is the last gift Dovan offers me. The chance to undo a great wrong. A chance to save our world by singing for everyone who's starving and hopeless. My banshee song breaking free of the curse to bring new life far beyond his death. And I'm ready. As painful as watching him die will be, I am ready to sing.

I take a deep breath, fresh tears pooling along my eyelids, but before I begin, Dovan interrupts.

"I have a promise to keep first." He gives a dramatic bow and extends his right hand, eyes alight with mischief. "Dance with me?"

My stomach does a rebellious but giddy little flip as I accept. "You remembered."

"I never forgot." His left hand curls around my waist as his right raises my left hand into the air. "The last dance of Spring Eve was always meant for us."

As the embers of winter and spring, it would have been our duty to perform the final dance at the Spring Eve ball. We'd hold this pose as night gave way to dawn, waiting for the musicians to play, and then with an embrace and a twirl, we'd begin the season change. Winter would become spring through our dance of leading and following, of holding on and letting go. But the ball-room is quiet, the musicians long gone.

"There's no music." I point out.

Dovan's half-smile turns serious. "You are my music."

Streams of tears slink down my skin, filling my mouth with their salty taste. *I'm the last song he'll ever hear.* And our song begins, not with a command, but with a final request from the man I love. "Together?"

"Together."

I am his music. I am his song. And I sing every note for him.

RED DEATH

33

DEFEAT MAKES most people look inward.

First, because they are in shock and are desperate to understand how they lost. Second, because they are idiots who rather bury their empty skulls in a steaming pile of denial and pretend everything is fine. And third, because they believe the key to winning is in the past. An utterly useless strategy for a killer like me. I'm not interested in unravelling the web of my choices or searching for redemption or trying to understand where I went wrong. *Going wrong was the point.*

I just want my sister to survive, and so I stall.

I use our twin bond and steal enough magic from winter to keep the ice trapping me and the season tree from shattering. It's a futile tactic in the long run, but effective for now. *Come on, you bleedin' dolt. Think of something.* But my mind strays with the focus of my left eye to the black blood staining the cracked ice above me.

"Damn you."

The flinch that jars my body overrules the tree's control of my right side and makes me whole until the scraping of roots in my veins splits us back to our chosen sides. Desperate for a distraction, I welcome the pain of the tree's possession, but for once, there's a torment that's worse. A piercing ache that won't be denied its reckoning.

The memory replays like a nightmare.

I hear the sharp crunch of my sister's fists, the tortured break in her voice, and the shriveling sob as she collapsed in defeat. *She cursed me.* My soft hearted—*everyone deserves another chance*—sister, cursed me. Using her voice for a purpose I never would have thought possible. My lungs long for the taste of air that isn't laced with the bitterness of shame, but she's locked me in with my regrets. There's no escape, and like the wretch I am, my first instinct is to deny they exist.

I wreck people.

A skill I've mastered and love to use, yet as I stare at the blood she left smeared on my icy prison, a foreign emotion invades my soul. One that focuses on that damn guider. Not as a target, not as prey, but as a man to be envied. I envy his life-giving power. I envy his world, his upbringing that allowed him the luxury of weaker, more wholesome pursuits.

We had to survive. So I studied the art of fear and the techniques of killing until my hands were so bloodstained they could never be good for anything but brutality.

Wrecking people has always fed my pride. There's nothing quite like the thrill of being the sole victor in a battle of wills, but I —*I didn't mean for our game to go so far.* And as we near the end of the path I started us on, I fight against the savage guilt choking my throat.

I have destroyed her.

Not our father. Not the assassin sent to kill her. Not the ancient spirit I sold our souls to. No, it was me. *I didn't mean*—I let that thought go. What I meant doesn't matter. What I do now will mean everything, except the plan to save her hasn't magically appeared yet.

Perhaps the flaw in my plan was having no limits. No lines drawn between what was acceptable and what was not. *I'd do anything.* Rises the familiar cry from my soul. *Anything*—to end our father's reign so my sister would be free to do whatever she liked.

I wanted to give her everything she deserved.

Well, that and become the most feared king Riffen had ever known, but that's no longer an option. *A true shame.* What a bloody good time I would have had.

The curse's unsatisfied hunger jabs my chest so hard the season tree recoils, resenting its new shackles. *What? You don't like being bound to a song?* The acidic burn of vengeance in my right shoulder is the tree's sole response, but the pain doesn't reach past my bicep. *Interesting.* My whole arm should be on fire. *Unless...*I quickly test who's in control of my right hand. When my fingers twitch from *my* order, curiosity dares me to hope the tree is weakening.

I clamp down on the desire to wriggle, to shift into a position where I could glimpse the veins in my arm. *Don't be a fool.* Making such a move would proclaim my suspicion to the tree. It sees what I do. *What's changed?* The obvious answer is *nothing*, until another twitch sends a spike of fire-hot pain through my right elbow. *The dagger.* Its blade is buried in my forearm.

A single note rings through the air, seizing my chest and widening the ice fractures. *She picked the perfect time to start singing.* Right when I was on the verge of discovering something that could save us. A grimace snarls my mouth as my body struggles against the ice in answer to my banshee's summons.

I search for a glimpse of my sister and Dovan. They're dancing. The mirror image of the painting I destroyed. As they spin and sway and face his approaching death together, surprise lifts my soul. The broken girl who raged at me for ruining her last chance to save the man she loves is gone.

But I watched her fall apart. Convinced there would be no return for my sister from the final shattering I'd dealt her, and yet, here she is. That wounded girl—transformed into a woman who's known more cruelty than anyone should, and yet she's—strong. Her voice unwavering as she sings, her heart shining through her face, her steps certain and free of regret. And it hits me, the clanging reminder of a fact I've often denied.

She's stronger than me.

Strength that I can use.

The pieces of a plan begin to form as my left hand tightens on the hilt of Red Death's dagger. The blade's curved edge pulses with heat and with hunger, biting into the quivering muscles of my right elbow. Dread rattles through my right side, tainting my sharp inhale with a sour tang, and I suppress the urge to sneer because I know this flavor so well. My nostrils flare, predatory instincts picking up on a scent my victims share. Fear.

I drive the dagger deeper to confirm the season tree's terror, but the song of my banshee is an invitation I cannot resist. Just as nothing can stop her from singing, there is no force strong enough to prevent me from taking the life I am owed.

Dovan's life.

Crackling fills the air. The ice surrounding me is so weak a simple touch will send it crumbling, but as the magic of the curse's bargain compels me to rise, I listen to a different order. A call that doesn't come from my banshee or from me. A metallic ring that centers my focus on the blade I'm holding.

The Dagger of Souls remains imbedded in my right arm, throbbing with desire for a soul that's far too ancient to be human. Frantic scratching starts under the skin above my right elbow and retreats over my shoulder. With a clear high note, Wrenna's song brings clarity.

Winter's Teeth. I am an idiot.

I push against the ice with my forehead to gain a little extra room. As winter obliges, stretching the coffin, I prepare myself for pain. A practice that's as natural to me as breathing. I breathe in and exhale slowly to loosen my muscles and calm my mind, and then I jerk the dagger from my arm, hissing as I rake the tip all the way across my spasming chest to the center of who I am.

There are many types of hunger.

The hunger for food, for companionship, for power. But I've never experienced one so fierce, so strange, as the hunger coming from my weapon. *Is it strong enough?* To change the rules of our game? I push the needling doubt away because I'll soon find out.

Red Death's crimson cape peels from my skin as the dagger's wicked point cuts into my chest, carving a line as prophetic as the paintings that hung around the cursed rotunda. I mark myself, not caring about the consequences. I know what they are and who will pay them, and I don't care. I don't care who dies. I've only ever cared about who lives.

Wrenna's nearing the middle of the guider's song, her voice swelling with power, while a new war begins inside me. A writhing, roaring battle of wills as the tree realizes how far I'm willing to go. I meet the tree's fury with my own raging hurricane of vengeful threats and use the channel between our minds to deliver my final promise.

When I am through with you, you won't be fit for axe bait. I sever the connection before the tree can respond. A twisted chuckle escapes my throat. *I'm going to win.* Because if one thing is true of me—

I. Never. Lose.

My hand clenches around the dagger's hilt, and I draw

strength from the blade's heat. For so long, I have been Red Death. I have been the monster. It's time I played a different role. It's time I took off the bloody hood.

To save Wrenna, I will become Alec again.

And then, I will end this game.

WRAITH

34

Dancing with Dovan is effortless. We spin, we dip, and change directions, keeping to the front of the rotunda to avoid the broken pieces of the bench and my brother's cracking coffin of ice. As we glide from shrinking shadows into gleams of torchlight, I sing louder, clearer, Dovan's song filling the air until there's no hiding who we are and how we feel. *This is for love.*

For love, we surrender to the beat of our hearts and the tap of our boots and dance closer to our fate. The bitter certainty of his death and my survival weave together through the melody of his soul, through the hissing touch of our skin, and the rippling currents of winter cold and spring heat churning in eddies around us, forming a promise.

Together. We make this choice together.

Dovan spins me away from him. Our fingers are still touching, my torn skirt twirling around my legs, when the next note vanishes. My voice stumbles over the gap, failing to jump to the rest of his song. Dovan tugs at my hand to draw me back into the dance, but my feet, once so nimble, remain rooted to the marble floor.

Panting, I repeat the previous note, once, twice, three times, but the melody has been severed. I touch the place where my brother sank his dagger into my chest to seal the bargain for my life. *What's happening?* I nudge the thread of magic that binds me to the curse, expecting the season tree to demand I sing, but the curse twitches like a pulled muscle, whipping between me and Dovan like our tether's been cut.

"What's wrong?" Dovan asks, moving closer so our joined hands hang between us.

Frost crinkles over the rotunda's glass walls, and the torches sputter, giving the night one last laugh of darkness. But it's the sudden breaking of Dovan's song that raises the hairs on my arms. All the notes I've gathered through the day we've spent together shift up and down, ripping the melody from its natural key.

His song is changing.

I meet Dovan's concerned gaze seconds before a *crack* like the snap of a whip and the bark of thunder combined shakes the whole rotunda. I'm tossed forward a step and Dovan catches me, keeping us both from falling down the stairs.

My stomach clenches as the scent of salted iron and singed sawdust saturate the air. Every muscle in my body tenses as my heart thumps out several extra beats.

The monster I trapped, the brother I couldn't save—*he's almost free.*

Winter curls tighter around my soul, guarding me. As I exhale, our combined fear sends malformed snowflakes spiraling into Dovan's searing wall of spring heat.

Red Death is coming to claim his victim.

This is supposed to happen. I force a calming breath into my lungs, leaning in to the life-giving power radiating from Dovan. But as I hum through his song, picking up the melody before the phrase where it broke, heated metal stabs upward into my back. I gasp, choking as the blade slides deeper, and my knees buckle.

Dovan holds me up as I glance down, expecting to see the curved edge Red Death's dagger poking through my ribs, but there's nothing there. No weapon inside me, no wound bleeding, nothing but a familiar, sharp ache meant to remind me I'm enslaved to a curse. As quickly as it came, the invisible blade withdraws, leaving behind a gaping, internal chasm.

The curse lines up more notes in my throat as I breathe in, but I—*I don't understand.* The next note divides into two. One for Dovan, leading me toward his death and the birth of spring. But the second note doesn't belong to his song, and it points our future in another direction.

Dovan squeezes my shoulders, his voice brushing my face with warmth. I can't hear him. Even if I could make sense of what he's saying—*I couldn't tell him.* Not as the choice we've made is being rewritten.

There are *two* songs in my heart.

This is all wrong. A banshee sings for one victim at a time. That's the rules. *When did Alec ever live by the rules?* If this even is Alec. I shudder over the idea the season tree could be behind this change and listen closely to the fresh stream of notes playing in my soul.

They're bitter. Frightening in their passion and drowning in a melancholy so deep it smothers all hope. *I know these notes.* A broken boy pounded them into the air through a harpsichord's keys as he raged against the chains of our life. The melody's sorrow twists into a savage crescendo, becoming a cry of blood-stained victory over the heart. *His* heart. It's his past and our future. It's every hope and every failure, every fear and every truth.

It's Alec in a song.

For whatever reason, Alec is giving me the very thing that

could defeat him. His song. I might have been grateful for such a gift once, but I know my brother. *He never loses.* He will crush my heart with this new twist. *And I'll still be in pieces when he's done.*

The callouses of Dovan's palms scratch the sides of my face as he lifts my head. "Tell me what's wrong."

My heart melts at the gentleness of his tone, at how he cares far more about why I'm hurting than about losing his life. I meet his gaze and mark the concern wrinkling his brow, but before I can answer, my voice is summoned for another purpose.

Sing.

A command I've never been able to disobey. Not when it comes from Alec.

The notes slip out, but they jump between two different songs. The pitches clash, the rhythms compete, the disjointed melodies pushing my voice higher and higher into screeching noise.

Noise holds no power in this game.

Frustration radiates from my twin seconds before his ice coffin shatters, throwing me forward into Dovan's chest as glistening shards pelt us. I gag on the heavy stench of bloody iron and straighten just in time to see Dovan's eyes widen. He reaches for his weapon, but his sword is gone, lying in broken pieces on the ballroom floor.

Winter's power flares, chilling my skin, and Dovan spins us so his back faces the threat. That's when I feel it. The soft but insistent *tap-tap-tap* against the door of my heart. The rhythm builds, becoming a request sent through the bond I share with a monster.

Trust me.

Pain burns red-hot across my chest, and while my brother uses the curse to pull his song to my lips, Dovan looks down at me with a brave smile and whispers, "I have always loved you."

Goodbye—he's saying goodbye. Fear quickens my breathing while both songs tear my soul in different directions. The note I finally choose wrenches into a scream as a figure in crimson rams into Dovan, knocking us off our feet.

We fall.

Dovan tries to shove me toward the rotunda while I try to pull him closer, but neither of us is fast enough to prevent the beating we're about to take. We land on the seventh step. The impact crushes into my right hip and shoulder, while Dovan's left knee and ribs hit after me. Our momentum flings us apart, but he throws out his hand, barely missing my calf.

We bounce up and find a brief cushion of air before falling again. Dovan flails awkwardly, trying to right himself, but his attempt to save me trapped his arm behind him. And as the tenth step bites into my gut, stealing the air from my scream, Dovan's head strikes stone. His body goes limp, and my shriek is cut short as I smash into the ballroom floor.

Trembling, I push myself up on shaking arms only to cry out at the searing pain in my right forearm. But even if the bone is broken, my curse will heal it, so I endure the jagged pulse with gritted teeth, and drag my legs under me. My left thigh aches in protest, bruised by a step's pointed edge, but I'm able to sit up.

Dovan lies beyond my reach, his body twisted, but he's breathing. *He'll live.* But for how long? I bite my lip as the sorrow of that thought opens beneath my heart like a hungry chasm, ready to devour me.

"Wrenna!"

I flinch at the sound of Alec's voice. The marble floor ices over as anger pulses unchecked through my veins, but as I glare up at my twin, confusion wriggles between me and the fury winter is itching to unleash.

Alec's holding himself up at the edge of the rotunda, his left hand on the top step, the other on the step below. His legs are out of sight, his body on the floor, but I refuse to believe the image he's selling. The one that's meant to soften me up so he can mold me to his will. *As if dragging himself here with his hands erases the fact he's just as deadly off his feet as he is when standing.* Soon, this mask will fall. And he'll be grinning that devil's smile he loves to torment me with as he saunters down the steps.

I keep glaring until he breaks our stare. He does a quick sweep over my mostly uninjured body and sags in relief. His tunic gapes open along a new tear, revealing his curse mark, but instead of being a silver scar from the deal he struck a decade ago, I spot an angry, fresh wound. The notes of his song vibrate in the back of my throat. I push them down, and the curse punishes me with a wicked pain that thrusts through my chest.

Alec frowns at me. I expect him to order me to sing, when the snap of fabric snatches his focus. Red cloth flaps along Dovan's side as if trying to pull free of his dead weight. Recognition dries out my throat. *Red Death's cape.* My wide-eye gaze returns to my brother, noting the obvious fact I missed.

My brother is no longer wearing his cape.

But Alec never took it off. He was twelve when he appeared in our music room, draped in fabric so red it looked like he'd soaked the material in fresh blood. Whether he was attending court, performing whatever cruel act he felt sure would earn our father's notice, or even while sleeping in his own bed, the cape never left his shoulders. *What if the dagger isn't the source of Red Death's power?* What if it was always the cape?

A cape that can move on its own.

We were pushed. Thrown from the rotunda by the red clad figure who struck Dovan.

I'd assumed it was my brother, but the way he's relying on his arms instead of his legs offers an answer I don't want to consider. *It wasn't him.*

Red Death didn't push us.

A tremor starts in my hands and rattles up my arms, and layers of ice rush across my skin as winter prepares me for a fight.

The crimson fabric tears free of Dovan and rises, shoulders and hood filled out as if draped over an invisible body. I scoot backward, trying to be quiet, but my boots squeak against the marble. The hood angles down, zeroing in on me with an eyeless stare seeped in malice, and ice spikes sprout from the floor as winter bares its teeth.

Dovan figured it out. Right before we fell.

The cape is the season tree.

I look to my brother for confirmation, and Alec offers me a grim nod. *So that's how the tree took his body.* Using the cape to possess him, and yet he leaves me with that horrifying truth. Alone, and with no offer of aid as the hood turns, slowly, like a predator tracking prey. Winter fills my hands with large ice spikes as the shoulders of the cape follow that faceless hood and twist in my direction.

"I always have a plan, sister," Alec says from the top of the stairs, his tone devoid of any feeling. "Trust in that."

I blink. The cape charges me. A rush of frigid air throws my hair back as bloody strips of cloth weave around my arms, my shoulders and torso, tightening until I can't draw a full breath. Every instinct I have screams at me to run. I push against the floor as I pull my knees up and stand, but my legs are weak. Before I've gone more than ten steps, I trip and crash into a standing bear pillar.

My skin burns as the cape spreads, covering me in crimson folds until the ruined ballgown I'm wearing vanishes from sight. With a startled cry, I claw at the red fabric, but my ice sharpened nails break before doing any damage. All while the season tree claws at my skin, seeking entry.

"Alec, please. You're my brother," I plead, blinking back tears. Cloth as soft as velvet but as strong as iron covers my mouth, preventing me from saying anything else.

Panic seizes my muscles, tightening like a belt against my

lungs and throwing my mind into chaos. *Get it off get it off get it off.* I stumble as I spin, clawing at my arms, my chest, my stomach, and kick Dovan's broken sword. The sight of sharpened steel gives me hope. *Cut it off!* I lunge for the hilt and turn the blade on my left arm, slicing at the cape's sleeve, but no matter how hard I press down, the crimson material remains uncut.

Pressure builds against my right arm. Velvet fabric becomes coarse as the cape constricts and cuts off the blood flow to my hand. I ignore the throb of pain and keep sawing. Too many times before, I've given in to what a monster wants, but not this time.

I won't surrender.

"You know that this is hopeless," whispers a rasping voice that's like the rush of a thousand roots scraping together, and its words are everywhere. Resonating in the air, and the stone floor, and the fabric trying to claim me, but I refuse to listen.

I struggle, every movement a declaration of war. The cape cinches with a savage twist and breaks my right arm.

I scream.

Metal rings against stone as Dovan's broken blade falls to the floor, and my knees follow. I bite my cheek, reminding myself I've survived worse.

"Give yourself to me," the tree croons, the cape's crushing grip relaxing to allow the curse to snap my bones into place.

I swallow a second scream and focus on what hasn't changed —my heartbeat. I cling to its slow rhythm, widening my awareness until I hear the pulse of Alec's heart. A faster melody written over mine and bound to our blood, a connection that the tree cannot sever or silence. I call to his soul.

Help me.

He's on the sixth step, his expression hard but determined. This is the brother who told me there was nothing he wouldn't do to save me, and so I ask again. *Help me.*

Alec's chin angles down, darkness clinging to his eyes. "No."

A wail builds in my throat at his betrayal, as I'm once more offered to a monster by the men of my family, and Alec moves. He slides himself down another step and then stops. Stops, because we both know the truth.

Alec isn't coming for me.

He's coming for his power.

For this wicked thing attacking me.

The crimson hood swallows my head and my vision goes black. I fall forward with a groan, my left hand finding the floor and holding me upright. Shivers spread from my shoulders to my fingers, and my ice coated limbs creak with each shudder.

I'm so cold I can't breathe. I can't think. I can only sit here and survive.

Survive. I chant within myself as the season tree's power jabs my flesh with a thousand needle-points of pain. Beads of liquid drip from my skin as the ice between me and the cape begins to melt. Each drop that hits the stone ticks toward my doom.

I open my mouth to call Dovan's name, but the tree stuffs fabric between my lips, gagging me.

A vicious pain spears through my left hand like slender pieces of wood are being shoved up my veins. *Don't look.* But the season tree bends my body to its will and makes me focus on that same hand. The hope I've carried, of helping Dovan bring the world back to life, shrivels into a dried-out husk.

Veins, that were once thin black lines, are now burgundy, branching outward like a network of roots. My pulse doubles. The rapid *boom, boom, boom* of a drum calling soldiers out to war, but I'm the only one standing, my movements only half-feeling like my own. I blink once, twice, and my view of the world changes.

Gone, is the black and the gray and the white of my banshee vision. There's another color bleeding through, glowing with violent anticipation, and it brings a sneer to my twitching lips.

Everything I see is *red.*

WRAITH

35

ALL MY LIFE I've been afraid of what I am. Afraid of the voice that whispered only monsters come from monsters. But as the power my father and my brother would kill for crackles along my bones and pulses through my veins, it feels—good. Good to be so beyond their ability to control.

I was a frightened girl, once. Abused and broken. A coward who ran.

I was a banshee. Alone and enslaved. A tool to be used.

Now, I am neither. Now, I am more.

I imagine the shackles of my curse, the notes that defined my purpose and doomed Red Death's victims coiled like chains in my palms. When I fist my hands, all those songs shatter. Gone, crushed into dust because our game belongs to me.

The curse is mine to command.

No more songs in my throat, no more pains in my chest, no more fear of anything anymore. Nothing shall prevent me from getting what I at long last want.

I open my hands and my ears pop at the change in pressure as the temperature plunges. The ballroom's glass ceiling goes dark. All signs of the sky lightening in the west with dawn vanish as my storm is born. The clan banners rustle and the chandeliers sway, their glass jewels tinkling in the frigid wind I create. The giddy laugh that parts my mouth heightens my hunger for destruction. With a twitch of my fingers, snowflakes fly. Their sharpened tips dig into every surface. Stone, glass, metal, cloth and soon, flesh.

"Winter chose you well," the creaking voice of my partner whispers to my mind.

Cold magic constricts my heart, causing a missed beat, and brittle ice frosts my tongue. *Winter is afraid.* But the first season's focus has shifted inward from some external force to me. Its own ember. *Why?* The wind slaps my cheek with an icy gust. I sway on my feet, bracing myself against a standing bear pillar, and this time I hear a man's voice.

"Promise me you won't forget who you are." The air warms around me, but I don't remember who's speaking or why he affects the temperature.

Soft fabric squeezes my throat. I blink at the oddity of a snowstorm inside a ballroom and my body shudders, a violent spasm meant to throw something off. On instinct, I lift my arm. Not a single snowflake lands on my crimson sleeve and my mouth goes sour.

Wrong. This is wrong. I stare at the cloth hugging my wrists, unable to shake the overwhelming sense of wrongness. *But I've always worn red.* Haven't I?

No.

Yes.

Which is the truth?

"The truth is you were born to rule winter." My partner's power hums through my blood, pumping its influence into every cell

until the flicker of doubt drowns. *"How the mortals shall tremble before their queen of ice."*

Yes. That is what I want.

A pained cry alerts me to the fate of my first target.

The voice is deep enough to be male and draws my attention to the humans at the bottom of the steps. The boy with faded red curls who thought he could control me, and the guider who believed dying would save the world. *Enemies,* both of them. A fact that produces a vicious sneer as my sharp snowflakes slice into his back. Alec slams his fist into the guider's stomach, trying to wake him. As if we'd allow that.

I trip halfway through the first swaggering step toward them. *We?*

My mind spins, confusion gnawing at the shadows that have taken root among my memories. I toss my head and finish planting my foot. *Yes, we.* Because I'm not alone. *And we haven't finished with him yet.*

The guider's soul is ours to take. And take it, *we* shall.

Still, that doesn't mean other people can't enjoy the fun. With a wave of my hand, I feed my storm more power, expanding the clouds until they hug every ceiling of the palace. The first shouts of alarm play out like a symphony. *Oh, this is going to be such a good show.* I've known that I am deadly for a few hours, but I never considered how much fun it could be. To be the thing everyone in the room fears. Monstrous, wicked, and starving.

The orders being shouted outside the ballroom become desperate screams. I savor each screeching note of my master-piece, my hips swaying to the beat of chaos as I approach the boy who is looking at me. *Yes, he understands this dance.* He schools his sharp features into a blank canvas, but there's no hiding the emotion in his brown eyes.

Shame.

This boy, whose hands have killed hundreds, is ashamed.

Once again, my feet falter. Pain slices into my chest, bowing me forward as I gasp. My mouth is moving before I even realize I'm speaking. "*You*. Did this. To me."

Alec doesn't respond. He just stares at my left hand. *When did I raise it?* Or curl it into a threatening claw? My right hand grabs my other wrist, jerking my arm down. *Is my body fighting itself?*

"Of the two monsters here," the boy says, his tone sharp like a slap to the cheek, "you aren't one of them."

He's wrong. Because my storm is the doom of this city. Because I could freeze his blood into ten thousand icy splinters and shred his heart inside his chest. *Because I am worse.* That thought clangs through me, sounding hollow and foreign. Somehow, I know that phrase was never mine.

A strange laugh that doesn't match the pinch of sorrow between my ribs overpowers my voice. I'm sinking. I'm falling with nothing to catch me. *It has been far too long since I enjoyed myself.* The monster inside forces my eyelids closed, and when I open them, I'm not the girl without a future anymore.

I'm the girl with the only future.

"Torches!" Cry the humans scattered throughout the palace as my spikes spread, joining my snowflakes in the game. *Fools.* As if fire is any threat against what I am.

I am ancient. I am young.

I am fall. I am summer.

I am death. I. Am. Winter.

And soon, spring will submit to my rule. I am the unity. I hold together and I break apart. A world of my own making. Or unmaking. *Everything dies.* There will be no mercy for the humans who trapped me and stole my seasons.

Not even for the vessel who freed me. I tower over his weakened form. It's jarring, seeing him from the outside. He's all ruby curls and pinkish skin and calculating eyes. They're brown and wet, the color of fresh graves, but they remain true to his warrior soul. *His will is strong.* Death won't claim him until he decides to surrender.

"You," he speaks through bloodied teeth, "have made your last mistake."

Idle threats for one who has no power. I dig my ice-sharpened fingernails into his shoulder, relishing his wince of pain, before I hurl him off to the side. With him out of the way, I advance toward my true prey. The brilliant green of my missing season shines through the guider. Spring is keeping him alive but not safe. Not from me.

My former vessel chuckles. "My sister will be the death of you."

"Your sister is no more," the rasp of my voice speaking through hers is as rough as the scrape of splintered wood on glass, and it pleases me. To finally speak as myself instead of through them.

Alec's laugh deepens at my declaration, broken by a wet cough. My nostrils flair, filling my mouth with the iron-tang of his impending death. Still, he smiles. "Tell me, you weevil-blighted stump."

His use of dramatic insults won't keep me from my prize. I raise my left hand over the guider's chest.

"If my sister is truly gone, why do you still have Wrenna's eyes?"

My extended hand curls into a fist as my head twitches, wanting to focus on Alec instead of the guider, but I am ancient. There's no strategy I don't recognize, no plan I haven't foiled. Mastering his sister's body is no challenge, despite his attempt to distract me.

Infuriating child! I should snap his neck, but ice glides over my palm, creating a mirror I didn't summon. My eyes stare up at me, flickering with golden fire. They should be red. *Treachery.*

I scowl at the boy I once possessed, moving closer until I am standing above him, but I refuse to ask or waste time on what he knows. *It matters not.* He will lose this game.

"You think the curse worked because my sister is weak?" Alec pushes himself into a seated position, the bottom step bracing his backside. "It worked because she's stronger than us. We feed off her strength, like the parasites we are."

I strike his cheek with enough force to crack bones, but he survives the blow.

Stretching his jaw, the boy turns his head, slowly, until our gazes meet. That devilish sneer he favors so often appears as he waves his dagger in greeting. "Forget something?"

I've taken a step back before I can control the instinct to retreat. The desire to curse itches my tongue, but the mind I'm possessing only has knowledge of the tamer swears. None of which are foul enough for our current situation. The dagger's soul-trading magic flows unrestricted through him now that I have left his body. Another betrayal. *It shall be his last.*

I snarl, the heat of my summer scorching my new vessel's skin, but the boy won't taste fire. He deserves ice, like the rest of this treacherous world. "You cannot stand against me."

In answer, Alec spreads the tear in his tunic wide with his fingers, revealing an open wound. It drips blood instead of gushing.

The mark of the dagger's hunger.

The sign of the curse's chosen victim.

My hands clench, knuckles popping.

"What did you expect me to do?" His voice drops low, shaking with an emotion I don't understand.

I make a point of looking at his useless legs. "I stripped you of your ability to walk."

He snorts as if the wound those words once represented is of no consequence. "And you thought I'd take defeat lying down?"

He leans forward, gaze narrowing as I become his target. "I don't need my legs to finish our game."

I summon a dozen spikes from winter and aim them all at his heart. Each one fails, dropping to the floor as if striking an invisible wall. Notes tug my vocal chords. My hands tremble, light brown skin flashing gray as the banshee within me fights, trying to claw her way out.

"Look at me with murder in your eyes all you want," the boy sneers, "but that's all you can do. *Look.*"

I rake my fingernails down his face. Blood drips from his cheekbone to his chin, and my trembling worsens, pinched by a trivial emotion. *Horror.* But nothing horrifies the unity who has moved beyond human shackles of right and wrong. *I answer to no one.*

Ignoring my former vessel, I study my prey again. The Ember of Spring remains lost in his nightmares of death and grief. He doesn't awaken when I arrange my fingertips over the prophetic wound. The thrum of his steady heartbeat throbs through my fingers and my palm flattens. Unease at the sudden shift in my hand's position bobs through my throat.

Icy liquid splashes against the back of my hand. The droplets lack a name at first, but they sparkle and taste of salt and human frailty. *I will wipe them from this weak face.* My arm jolts backward, but my palm remains stuck to the guider's chest. *No.* I blink, but my vision keeps blurring as my new vessel cries.

She is fighting. Her tears form sheets of ice between me and my prey. Winter protecting spring. *Impossible.*

"You really are a dumb block of wood, aren't you?"

The satisfaction in Alec's tone fuels my desperation. I claw at the ice, but it spreads from the guider's torso to the floor, rising into a wall and pushing me back from the Ember of Spring.

"There isn't a monster in this world so powerful it can overcome love."

Enraged, I spin toward my betrayer, ready to rip the heart from Alec's chest, but the banshee's wall is already there, blocking me.

He raps his knuckles on the ice before flattening his hand, waiting, and as if he tugged on that cursed twin bond they share, the banshee places her palm over his. Tears line his lower eyelids as he grins, arrogant as ever. "Love is my sister's true power."

My vessel starts shaking. "I will have my vengeance."

"Not with her body you won't."

Her soul's cry rips through my web of roots, a sound so pure my magic can't oppress it. Frost crackles between her skin and my cape. I, becomes we, becomes just *her*.

The banshee tears through me, throws back her head, and screams. As her scream rises into a fearsome shriek, I send a wave of power toward my storm, casting it beyond her reach and into the city before she severs my hold with her truth.

I am not ancient. I am young.

I am the princess who was lost, the banshee who was found, the ember whose winter froze the world, and I will not forget.

Glass shatters. Hearts miss their next beats. Colors vacillate between monochrome and shades of blood as I stand here and watch the ceiling fall. I'm too tired to move, my mind and body reeling from the oppressive weight of the season tree.

The boy I once knew latches onto my right arm and yanks me down. Red curls tickle my face as Alec rolls over me, becoming my shield.

"Hold on to me." His cheek presses against my temple. "I'm going to save you."

My brother's one truth.

He has defied kings and fate and an ancient spirit. All to keep me alive. Yet as we lie here, exposed under a curtain of glass falling like jagged stars, their twirling pieces catching the pale glint of oncoming dawn in the east, I know Alec will be the one who bleeds.

It's my turn to save him.

I reach behind him, fingertips stretching toward our doom, and winter meets glass. Ice swallows every tumbling shard and transforms their deadly edges into rounded shapes. Alec flinches as a few strike him, but most crash harmlessly into the floor.

A spasm arches my back, but my brother holds me down. "Stay with me."

He spoke that order once when I was dying, but I'm not fading. I'm waking up, my senses amplified until nothing escapes me. I hear the pulse of every heart in the palace—dozens of them. Each one unique, but they're all beating so fast. The air is thick with the salty tang of their fear as an impossible winter storm shakes the palace with a clap of thunder.

Why don't they run? Everyone should run because I am not free.

The tree's promise of vengeance sears my frosted skin through a cape soaked in the blood of thousands. So many lives have been taken by this curse. *This has to end.* Not just winter, but the banshee curse.

"Wrenna?"

I don't know what's worse. The genuine pride in my brother's tone or the uncertainty making it crack. *He's never uncertain.* But then, I've never been more powerful than him in any of our games.

No. *My* game.

I shut my eyes and gasp. His heartbeat drives my senses nuts. All that hot, iron rich blood coating his soul like a delicious invitation. Frigid air stings my palm, hardening into a familiar, pointed shape.

No! I wrench myself away from him, flinging the half-formed ice-blade across the ballroom, and collide with the wall guarding

Dovan. The hunger becomes a hundred times worse as my pulse races. *Kill him. Kill him. Kill him.* A command I fear I cannot resist.

"You're strong enough to fight it." Alec brushes my arm. A tentative gesture full of requests when he used to tell me what to do.

I pull myself from them both. I crawl away, each movement worse than walking on a bed of red-hot nails. Agony rips through my muscles as my vision flashes from black to gray to red, but I force myself to my feet. *Run. Run as far from them as possible.* But the hunger is so strong, I double over.

"Fight!" Alec's palm slaps the stone floor. "Fight Wrenna, because I need you to win. I can't—" my brother's voice breaks and my heart wrenches over what it means for him to allow his fear to show. "I can't do this alone."

I look back at Alec, avoiding the sight of Dovan lying unconscious. "You forget, brother. I always lose."

RED DEATH

36

I am still alive, and so is that meddlesome guider along with everyone else, but why waste energy on relief? The plan is in motion. *No rest until it's over.* I snort at that word—rest—because it's a fitting description for how this is going to end. *I could use a good, long rest.*

The next part of the plan requires Dovan. Well, Dovan's legs, since mine stopped working after I lost my cape. *What a delightful conversation that will be.* If I had any coin, I'd bet the stinging scratches on my cheek that they'll soon be joined by a black eye. Maybe two. Depending on how the guider reacts to what I've done.

I switch my weight to my left hand and brush my chest to check on how my changes are faring, but my fingers come away clean. As I feared, the wound that allowed Wrenna to hear my song and forced the season tree from me has nearly closed. *One of us has to die.* And soon. Before the curse chooses for us.

I focus on different spots around the ballroom. The bear pillars, the clan banners, the chandeliers, and the brooding storm waiting above for the season tree's next command. Starbursts of full color streak through my monochrome vision. The curse is gasping, reality leaking in, but time ticks on, relentless and uncaring about the difficulties I must overcome for my plan to work. *I've faced worse challenges.*

None come to mind.

A familiar sharp pain stabs through my heart. I lurch forward, hacking. Saliva mixed with blood splatters the black and white marble tiles and drips from the large pieces of broken glass littering the floor. *Well at least the curse has kept its stabby sense of ill-timing.* But the phantom blade the pain mimics is pulling out instead of pushing in, undoing our deal.

Dammit. I'd hoped I was strong enough to keep the full terms of the curse's bargain in place, but it no longer recognizes my authority. My partnership.

I'm the victim.

A victim who still has Red Death's dagger. *Careful.* I resist the desire to hold the burning hilt of the blade sheathed at my hip. There will only be one chance to recreate the curse's mark, and I have no intention of wasting that moment. *To work, then.*

With a resigned sigh, I begin dragging myself toward Dovan. *At least he's close.* I should reach him in about four hand-pulls, but like me, the ballroom has had better days. My path is littered with debris. Spikes of ice, piles of snow, and glass. So much glass.

She shattered the damn ceiling.

I shove the pride I feel over such a feat aside as I remember how she just stood there. Under those jagged pieces. Some were as long as my torso, but she didn't run. *It could have been the season tree.* Holding her body there, trapped under a rain of glassy death, because she was too much to handle. I can't shake the image. The shame I've denied access to my heart digs its dull point into my ribs.

Was it her choice? To stand there? To trap me behind ice so I couldn't reach her?

As usual, she underestimated both me and winter. Before my dagger could split the ice wall, the first season let me through so I could protect her, and then she saved me. After everything I have done, after all the ways I have broken her, she still saved me. *A waste of power.* Pointing me to yet another problem. *They really are multiplying today.*

There's a flaw in my plan.

I don't need Wrenna's protection or her selfless disregard for her own safety. *I need her to fight back.* I need her to buy me time. I need her to stop choosing the easier path. And though I'll never admit it out loud, there's a part of me, a younger version of Alec from our childhood, who desperately needs her to understand.

I did not surrender her to the season tree's attack without a reason. I couldn't break the rules with it possessing me, which meant leaving my sister vulnerable. Vulnerable, but not alone.

Even if the hurt in her eyes sang me a song of abandonment and betrayal—*I am guilty of neither.*

I punch the marble, focusing on the prick of glass stabbing at my knuckles. *She does not die today.* I don't care what I have to do to get Dovan to fall in line. I don't care what lies I have to tell him.

She does not. Die. Today.

The scraping of glass, the squeak of my boots, and the soft whisper of my clothes against stone fill the air as I drag myself through the final pull. Leaning on my left hand, I bend my numb legs to the side to help support my torso and scan the dripping wall of ice between me and my prey. I wince at the thoughtless slip, my mind falling into familiar patterns, but prey isn't the right word for Dovan anymore.

I'm not Red Death. For a little while longer, at least. After that, when I reclaim the cape that was meant to be mine and don the crimson hood—*we shall see.*

Unlike the other structures Wrenna's season has created, this ice wall would be shorter than me if I were standing and is no wider than my palm. *Flimsy.* And wet. I flick moisture from my fingers in distaste, but only a fool would smile at the ice's weakening condition or expect an easy victory. Despite the wall's obvious flaws, winter is never more dangerous than when it's melting.

I clear a section of the wall by swiping through the beads of water, but the other side is fogged over. A consequence of guarding the Ember of Spring. All I can make out of Dovan is a shadowed form lying on the floor. My lips tug upward in amusement. For a guider who prides himself on fighting for and protecting others, he keeps winding up unconscious. *Rather convenient.* Leaving me and Wrenna to do all the work while he sleeps.

Time to wake him up.

I ram my fist against the wall's slick surface and swallow a curse at the loud crack. The bones of my knuckles throb with pain as I shake my hand out, but the ice remains undamaged except for a web of micro fractures. Twice more I strike the wall. It sways with each hit but doesn't fall. Blood oozes hot between my knuckles as I draw my fist back. Dozens of spikes sprout from the ice wall like thrusted spears, warning me to stop.

Impaling my hand was not on today's agenda.

A scowl sharpens my features as the small cracks I've caused refreeze. "I don't have time for this," I mutter.

I almost reach for my dagger, but stabbing is not the answer to this problem.

Opening my fist so I'm less of a threat, I curl my palm against the spike pointing at my heart. An invisible blizzard slams into my mind. The first season is in chaos. A hurricane of threats and pleas crash into me in waves as if winter can't discern friend from foe.

The slow breath I take brings the bite of frost to my tongue. I focus on the command holding winter here and keeping the wall before me intact. "I'm not here to kill Dovan."

The spikes grow longer, pricking my arm, my shoulders, my chest, and my anger matches winter's fury with the searing indignation of a man running out of time.

I am tired of people not believing me.

With a flare of power from the dagger at my hip, I break the spike and toss it over my shoulder before gesturing to my legs. "If you haven't noticed, I'm not myself right now." I break a second spike. "It's Wrenna you should be worried about."

Frost crackles, spreading over my boots, but I brush the fragile fronds aside. The contact between the ice and my skin unleashes another swarm of threats against me and of promises made to her. Winter shows me my sister's last wish, a choice of words that makes me go rigid.

"Enough," my voice trembles, dipping low as I speak. "I don't care if my sister told you no one touches Dovan." I plant my palm on the floor and lean into the spikes, giving winter the opportunity to fulfill its oath, but the first season doesn't take it.

"I knew you liked me," I smirk, patting a spike like it's a dangerous pet.

The slightest brush of icy air slides along my cheek and down the half-healed marks made by my sister's fingernails. I feel winter's request even though it comes without words or voice. *Tell the truth.*

For once, I don't choose sarcasm or deflect with a list of unimportant truths. Like the fact I've never danced at a ball or how I hate soup in all its varying forms. My playful smirk falls into a look that's as grim as what is coming.

"I need him." My admission brings to mind the pinch and pull of the metal braces I once wore on my legs, the pain of which I've never forgotten. I clear my throat, eager to get through with this baring of my soul as fast as possible. "Loathe as I am to admit it, Dovan's the closest pair of working legs. I'd find someone else if they wouldn't go out of their minds as their dead prince suddenly appears and orders them around." *It would be entertaining though.* Freaking out a member of my father's palace guard.

"Plus," I babble on, wincing as the curse's ill-timed stab of warning spears into my chest. "Think of how tedious it would be to explain everything. Madness, that would be. But more than that," I swallow down the taste of blood, fixing the ice wall with my fiercest glare, "Wrenna will need Dovan. So shove your frosty tantrum at someone who's actually afraid of you and get out. Of. My. Way."

With a crackling rush, the spikes recede and the wall shrinks until there's nothing left as winter reabsorbs its power. *One challenge down.* Three more to go.

I pull myself to the guider's side, anchoring my position by adjusting my bent legs and bracing with my right hand, and then I slam my left fist into Dovan's gut. The guider lurches upright, coughing and sputtering. It takes him four blinks to focus on me and find his voice.

"*You.*"

I sigh. Being greeted with such dark fury gives me chills. "Welcome back to the nightmare," I wink.

Dovan stiffens, right shoulder angling away from me, and I make the unfortunate mistake of blinking. Burning knuckles plough into my left cheek. Pain, like the weighted hit of a branding iron, flares across my cheekbone, and my vision flickers black. *Here I thought the guider would lead with "where is she?" or a host of other accusations.*

Without the help of my legs, I'm powerless to counteract the force of his punch. Unforgiving stone breaks my fall. A dozen pricks of pain from shards of glass cut through my clothes, and if it weren't for the hand closing around my throat, I'd laugh. Still, I can't keep myself from grinning. *Violent greetings truly are the best.*

"Is this funny to you?" Dovan presses my skull against the marble floor as he hovers above me. "You *cursed* your own sister. You let an ancient spirit loose, knowing it would come for her because she carries winter within her soul."

Ah, so he knows about the season tree. Good. That will simplify everything.

"You used her, you selfish bastard." His fingers dig into my airway, forcing me to choke on a gasp as my vision goes fuzzy, but I resist the urge to claw at his wrist. "What was her crime? That she loved a miserable wretch like you?"

He bangs my head against the stone hard enough to make his point, but not cause any real damage. *Pity.*

"Who gave you the right to break her heart and turn her existence into a cruel game?" Roughness edges his tone as he adds. "You bound her voice. Caged her soul." His lips curl into a snarl that shows his teeth. "And just when she remembered who she was, when she found her strength and made her choice, you took that choice from her again."

His hold on my throat loosens as if he expects me to answer for what I've done. *Soft-hearted fool.* Even though he has spoken the truth, I am not obligated to do the same.

My lips cut a vicious line across my face, a distraction as I grip the hilt of my weapon. "I find I prefer your fists to your speeches, Sir Guider. After all, violence is the key to my secrets. Care to beat them out of me?"

Dovan's face contorts as if he's taken a bite of rancid meat, but he doesn't recoil or let me go, reminding me that his job is to protect people from monsters, killing them when necessary. *What fun we could have had.* If this game had followed the normal routine.

Spring's heat sizzles over my skin as Dovan leans closer. "If any more harm has come to her—"

I meet his threat with the point of my dagger against his chest.

His gaze narrows, the power of his spring magic brightening his irises into blazing rings of green fire. The movement of his fingers is jerky, as if releasing me is the last thing he wants, but he lets me go.

"If you are done speaking nonsense." I poke his sternum. The guider shifts onto his knee, allowing me the space to sit up, which isn't easy. My first attempt, where I grab the fabric of my black trousers and try to hoist myself up, fails.

Muttering a curse as glass sticks my back, I roll onto my side and push myself into a seated position. Dovan watches as I arrange my unresponsive legs to the side and the corner of his mouth dares to lift. The secret smile of a man who's discovered another's weakness.

I can't chase him.

Before I can say anything clever, Dovan is on his feet. He turns his back to search the ballroom for signs of my sister. The insult of it draws my nerves tight. There was a time when no one would dare show me their back. But those days are gone, and they're not the ones I'm worried about.

If I can't get the man who loves her to help me—*Today could be Wrenna's last day.*

Reclaiming Dovan's focus is going to cost me. Something personal. Something I don't want to share. The curse jabs my heart, and as I spit a spray of blood that's both red and black, I sense how close we are to losing.

Tell the truth. Winter's chill caresses the arm I'm using to hold myself upright, a whisper of encouragement from the only living thing that has always seen through me. Through all the lies and the violence and chaos. I told Wrenna there was nothing I wouldn't do for her, and if that means letting my mask of sarcasm and violence fall—*so be it.*

"You're right about me," I begin, and Dovan's posture tenses. "I have used my sister. I have betrayed her trust and failed to protect her. First from our father, then from the obligations of our cruel court, and now, from the season tree."

Dovan looks over his shoulder, but I need him to face me. I break the lock on the door separating me from my guilt and let it flood my cold heart.

"Do you think I feel nothing?" My elbows bend under the sudden weight crushing my soul, lowering my body until I snap them straight. "Do you think I don't know that I've left more scars on my sister's soul than our father ever left on her skin?"

Dovan turns around, and I blink angrily against a pathetic rush of tears. I smash my fist into the floor just to taste a pain that isn't so personal. Spittle flies from my trembling lips as I dig my grave even deeper. "I do not deserve her forgiveness."

I do not deserve her love. Whispers my heart, but that admission I keep to myself.

Dovan has moved closer, the line between his brows deepened into the emotion I hate most. Pity.

"I don't want her forgiveness," my voice sounds like a hollow husk, rasping and brittle, denying the very words I speak. I lean into the pain of how deeply Wrenna and I are broken, into the memories of our life before the curse and the ten years of screams and songs and loneliness. I lean into the burden of my failure and drag myself to the guider's feet. Rage quivers through my body. Rage at how wrong I am and yet how right. No matter what kind of colored lens Dovan uses to look at me and judge the choices I've made, one fact remains.

"All I want," I say, "All I have ever wanted, is for Wrenna to live."

The brief silence that follows as Dovan considers my words

itches against my skin. He eventually nods, a concession that resurrects my sneer.

"You know where she is then?" the guider quirks a brow, still suspicious of my motives.

"I do."

"And you have a plan?"

"My plan is simple," I lower my gaze to his boots before smirking up at him. "I need your legs."

He widens his stance, ready for a fight, and I almost laugh.

"Relax, I'm not going to cut them off. I need you to carry me to my sister."

He studies every corner of my expression for any hint of trickery. "Then what?"

"Then, I will break her curse." It's another lie, since the banshee curse can't be broken, but it's the only answer I have that guarantees his help.

Dovan considers my request for a moment longer before kneeling. He wraps a stiff arm around my upper torso and gathers my legs with the other. I grip his shoulder as he lifts me from the floor with a grunt, and he glares at me with the lethal calm of a soldier who knows how to handle dangerous things. "I still don't trust you."

This time I do laugh, a wicked chuckle that belonged to me long before I became Red Death. "Where would be the fun in that?"

WRAITH

37

I NEVER THOUGHT RUNNING AWAY WOULD BE hard.

Every hit of my boots on the cobblestone streets rattles up my bones until pain splinters through my legs, my sides, my chest. Even breathing turns to gasps of torture as I'm caught between the clawing grip of two opposing wills. One is mine. Begging me not to stop, pleading with me to fight harder than ever before, but I can't ignore how things have changed. Pulsing circles of red mark the chests of anyone I pass, and the corner of my mouth forms a predatory sneer.

Everyone I see is prey.

I stumble, catching myself on a wooden trough that would have watered horses before winter. Snow piles up against the sides of the trough while a layer of ice covers the bottom. My lips frame a silent cry at the sight of the young woman looking up at me.

The long waves of dark hair, the light brown skin, and the scar on my cheek are all the same, but I'm covered in red. Fabric that moves, coiling around my body in an embattled embrace that's half searching for a way in, half-claiming me as its possession. Even my eyes are red, a glowing crimson ring surrounding my golden irises.

A skirt brushes along mine. The season tree uses the cape to turn my head toward the innocent targets within reach. Three women and two men continue walking past me, puffs of breathy vapor coiling behind them. Hunger chokes me, and I start following the prey.

No! I press icy palms to my skull. *They are not prey.*

They're people. Ordinary people. With their thin, slumped bodies wrapped in layers of patched clothing, they curl their shoulders and duck their heads as another peal of thunder roars above us.

See them for who they are! I scream that thought like a banshee would, with a thread of melody that binds the shadow roots the tree has sunk into my mind. They writhe but remain contained, and I suck down a breath of frozen air. My knees tremble as my body teeters toward obeying the longing to give up, but I distract myself by focusing on my surroundings.

I'm in the middle of the city, on the edge of the slope that leads to the lower level. The buildings that used to be inns and gambling dens and music halls have become shelters for refugees or for those whose homes haven't lasted the winter.

Instead of drunk patrons or visitors looking for fun, guiders are beginning their dawn patrols. Putting out the night torches and replacing them with fresh ones. Streams of market workers set out from whichever building has become their home, bundles of wares under their arms or tied on sleds pulled behind them. They say goodbye to their wives and husbands in lantern-lit door-ways, and their children peek around their mothers' skirts or their fathers' trousers, eyes sparkling over the fresh snow covering the ground.

A girl runs out into the street, dropping and rolling in the powdery snow while her parents order her back inside. She's too young to have ever known a season other than winter. Her face glows, lit from within by a joy that bubbles out in a laugh.

I used to look at snow the same way. Marveling over how the snow catches both light and shadows, somehow always sparkling.

More children race into view, ignoring their parents' warnings about the blizzard bearing down on us all. They scoop the snow into balls and hurl them at each other, squealing and crying foul when hit, and a weight settles on my shoulders, reminding me of the game Alec was never good at.

Snowball fights.

I only won a few times until I saw through his anger over losing to the shame lying underneath. Shame, because he couldn't maneuver the way I could on my legs, which left him vulnerable. *Would he have kept playing for me?* If I hadn't lied and told him I didn't want to play such a childish game anymore? *I did it for him.*

The season tree speaks to my mind, crimson cloth sliding over my skin. *"Look what he has done for you."*

I wince as red taints my clear vision. Targets wink into being over their chests, and the children's voices fade, overpowered by the glorious rush of their heartbeats. My fingernails bite into my palms as I fight off the demand of an ancient hunger. *This isn't you.*

"Is it not?" The tree croons as if it knows something I don't. *"How many times did you wish for this city to die?"* The cape constricts around my leg, forcing me to step forward.

When you're cursed to sing so a monster can murder people, you wish for a lot of things you don't really mean. *I just wanted the killing to stop.*

I'm running again, my feet pounding the uneven cobblestones of the street, but everywhere I go, death follows. *Why did you do it,*

Alec? I remember the haunted look on his face, the fear and the regret, but none of that stopped him as he *chose* for me.

He chose *this.* Binding me to a monster far worse than him.

I trip and fall, rolling down the slope of the street. A woman crosses into my path at the bottom. As I crash into her legs, she cries out, thrown forward by my momentum into a guider. Their gazes pass over my face but never find me.

Still invisible.

I drag myself into the nearest alley, heaving but finding no relief from the sickness burning through me with more fury than any fever. Shadows embrace me with a welcoming chill, familiar and safe. For a few more breaths at least, as I survey the lower market to map my escape.

There's so many. I had expected guiders and a few dozen market workers determined to claim the best stalls, but not the crowd of a few hundred cluttering my path. *There's no way through without touching them.* The shaking in my hands worsens as my stomach knots itself around my unchanged truth. *I'm a threat to everyone here.* And I'm terrified of what I'll do if I stay within reach of their fragile souls.

Breathe. I inhale air so cold it burns and roll my shoulders back. *You can do this.* Run, so they survive. But as I step out into the weak light of dawn, I'm no longer a simple wraith.

I'm a predator.

People brush past me, and each glancing touch of their shoulders strikes like a hammer, the agony resonating into my bones. I hum a single note of Dovan's song to cover the sound of their heartbeats, but they only grow louder, my voice weaker.

They should all be dead. Rage pours into the well of my soul, drowning my heart's objection. *They stole everything from us.*

Yes, yes they—

NO.

I trip. My heart spasms between beats, and I throw out my

hands to the nearest stall beam. Rough wood scratches my palms, flashing a strobe of gray through my vision, but I bite my tongue. I will not let the season tree take my voice.

Forcing my head up, I scan the lower market. So many faces, at times obscured by exhaled vapor clouds, but none of them are guilty of harming me. Have they caused me pain? Yes. In the way an outsider feels pain. Born of a longing to share in the normalcy of their human exchanges. The small touches, the direct eye-contact, the comfort of companionable silence. Knowing you are seen. Knowing you are home. But my isolation is not their fault.

I yank the cape's crimson sleeve to steal the tree's attention. "I don't care what you do to me. I will not hurt them."

The edges of my gray vision pulse red with loathing. There's no shutting out the tree's arrogant whisper. "*You have been hurting them for ten years.*"

Of all the tactics a monster can use, the truth is the worst.

I clutch the beam of the stall as my legs give out under me. The cape withdraws, exposing my arms to the rough wood. Splinters scrape my skin. Little smears of blood mark the beam as I crumple to the ground. A stab of shock flinches through me at the color, at the deep red tone of my blood.

"*How many families have been wiped out or torn apart because of your winter?*"

All I can see are their faces. Every victim I sang to and every soul crushed by winter's decade-long hold.

"*How many orphans have you created?*"

The answer rips me apart. *Thousands.* There's no objection, no defense I can make that doesn't taste like a lie as shame presses in from all sides until I can't breathe.

"*Did no one ever tell you how winter chooses its embers?*"

I lock my gaze on the gate and hurl myself toward the next alley, but my boots slide out on a patch of ice before I'm halfway to my chosen shelter. I aim for another stall beam and collide with it hard enough to jar the breath from my lungs.

"Winter chooses its embers based on their capacity for destruction."

I cover my ears, forgetting that the season tree's voice is inside my head and can't be silenced.

"Broken things are the most destructive tools of all." Delight deepens the scratch of the tree's voice. *"With a single touch of your soul, winter knew you would bring vengeance upon this world."*

I'm trembling, my knees wobbling as the guilt the tree fans into flame tries to consume the foundation I've built through the rubble of my life.

Why did winter choose me? It's a question I've never thought to ask.

If the tree is right, then winter should have chosen Alec. *They would have been a perfect match.* Yet, it wasn't the soul of a cruel and destructive prince winter chose as its home, but mine. The soul of a wounded girl who wanted to add more beauty to the world.

I reach out to the half of the first season I still carry, the part that isn't consumed by rage, and sense a familiar loneliness. A desire to be seen, truly seen, instead of always being the season everyone dreads. *There is beauty and purpose to winter.* And I saw it. The elegant art of frost, the magic of snowflakes, the quiet peace of winter's white blanket. *I didn't see a weapon.* Maybe winter chose me because it was as tired of being used as I am.

Being broken doesn't make you a monster. The differences between me and Alec prove that, and I use the truth to fortify my heart.

Curling a fist, I answer the tree. "You speak of winter when we both know you mean yourself." The cape coils tighter in disapproval, but I'm not finished. "You are the monster. You are the destroyer, and you made a mistake when you chose me instead of Alec."

There's a hissing in my ears, the voiceless roar of the monster on my back, but I ignore it and hurry toward the gate. I haven't gone five steps before the cape constricts around my legs, and my run slows to a limp. I use my torso and shoulders, swaying side to side, as I pitch my weight forward to keep my stride from shrinking. Sweat stings my eyes as my breathing grows labored. Each step becomes a battle I win, but the outcome of the war is slipping away.

I'm not going to make it.

At least fifty men, women, and guiders stand between me and the gate. I touch winter's power, making a simple request, and a corridor of frigid air opens before me. Those in its path rub at their arms, grumbling, before they gather by the blazing firepits placed throughout the market. The guiders, who are used to such cold, stay where they are, tugging their wolf-fur-lined capes closer.

My path is clear. All I have to do is run. Run out into the wild wasteland of snow and my city will be safe. My muscles bunch, ready to spring, when a wave of power blasts from the cape. I'm thrown to the side as surprised voices remark on the sudden wind tearing through the market.

I hold my breath. I count my slow heartbeats, waiting for something to go wrong, but as the wind dies, the clouds above let out a low, rumbling groan. The spike in winter's magic throbs through my soul seconds before there's a—

Crack.

Icicles break free from the stalls near me. I lunge after them, only to be kicked in the chest by the pain of winter's power being torn away.

Please. I'm on my knees, once again begging a monster not to make me a tool of destruction, but my wordless wail becomes the icy wind the spikes ride upon, propelling them into the crowd. They cut across arms and legs before lodging in the ground.

Please, I will give you—I stop myself before I offer the season tree exactly what it wants. Watching my season, my magic harm people breaks something in me not even my father or brother could destroy.

I am a survivor.

But I don't want to bear the shame of surviving this.

That tiny admission opens a crack for the tree to slip through. The maddening itch of roots writhing in my veins and the ear-splitting pitch of alarmed screams—it's all too much. Until I catch a scent that straightens my spine and snaps all my senses to attention.

Blood.

My ears tune into the symphony of dozens of panicked hearts. Their pulses race from shock and pain, tainting the air with delicious and salty heat. I shiver as the warmth of their blood cools with a shift of my season.

Winter's power builds within my chest and surges toward my fingers. I curl them against my palms, hoping to bock the magic's escape, but the men and women in the market spread winter's wrath with every touch. Their words slur and their movements slow until they're barely moving. Ice frosts their hair and clothes, and their eyes cloud in confusion as they become statues.

"Behold, who you are."

My limbs start shaking, my teeth clench hard enough to shoot pain up my jaw, and my shoulders bunch as the tree tries to crush me with winter's betrayal.

No.

It's just one word, but I say it in my head, over and over until *no* becomes my pulse. A drumming chant that spreads to my soul until my whole being resonates with the song of a young woman who is no longer afraid because—*I know who I am.*

All my life I've been told I'm a disappointment, a coward, a softhearted child. I've been called *damaged.* Worthless. Banshee.

Monster. And for a long time, I let their words define me. *Until I met Dovan.* A good man who told me the same thing again and again.

"You're the bravest woman I've ever met."

Slowly, I slide my fingers under the sides of the cape that rest against my chest.

I'm not brave. That was my response to Dovan, because I couldn't understand how brokenness and courage could exist together. Not when bravery is supposed to be heroic. There was nothing heroic about my life. *I see it now.* The gift Dovan was trying to give me.

No one is strong every day. No one wins every battle. No life is safe from pain. No one is at their best all the time. We're all broken in our own ways. Scarred by others and by ourselves. Looking for meaning and for hope wherever we can find it. Failure isn't an unbreakable curse. Weakness isn't shameful. Fear isn't our fault. But where we lose, where we suffer most, is when we let them become our excuse not to try.

Bravery *is* trying.

Trying to make the best of things. Trying to make a difference. Trying to grow.

For my whole life, I've been trying to do one thing: survive. Surviving was all I could do, and there was no shame in that, but I'm ready to be brave in a new way.

I am no one's tool.

The icy points of my fingernails pierce the cape, granting me an unbreakable hold as I begin pulling. Pulling and ripping until I feel the scrape of roots retracting from the veins of my arms. I use the pain, letting it build in my gut before flinging my head back into a banshee scream.

The cape splits down the middle, freeing my head and back first, followed by my shoulders and arms. Winter coats my skin in protective layers of frost as I gather the cape into a ball and hold it away from my chest. The longer strips lash outward, desperate to reestablish their control, but the season tree can't find a place to anchor itself to me. A buzz of frigid power tickles my skin and I let go. As the cape falls, icicles snap free of the stalls and dive for each flapping piece, pinning the tree to the muddy cobblestones.

I bend forward, my hands barely finding my thighs to brace my upper body before I fall. I'm exhausted and I hurt everywhere but—

I am free.

Free, and standing on my own power.

The tree's faceless hood convulses at the center of my ring of icicle stakes, and I smile. *I did it.* I defeated an ancient monster. Now to fix the damage.

I straighten and raise my hands. With a cold rush of magic-thickened air, winter's anger recedes back into my chest, leaving the stall runners, the guiders, and early traders gasping but still alive. Their joints pop as winter's freeze leaves their bodies. They shake off thin pieces of ice and dart for the nearest pit fire, but their expressions remain haunted and full of questions. The wiser ones head up the hill to the next level of the city.

Good. The farther they are from me, the safer they will be.

A murmur of shock sweeps over the lower market. Everyone's pointing at the same place. I face that direction and my mouth opens in surprise. Dovan strides between the stalls, his expression bordering the line between irritated and stern, but his arms are full. He's carrying my brother. Alec's vibrant red curls bounce around his pale face as he waves at people, clearly enjoying himself.

"The crippled prince," a woman gasps beside me.

I wince at the title while my brother's smirk grows sharper, letting a little of his ruthless side show. *They shouldn't be able to see him.* But he is missing his possessed cape. *Does that mean he's no longer Red Death? Does that mean I am free?* I prod the bones above my heart, searching for the cursed magic that binds us.

"The heir returns," cries another voice, jarring me from my thoughts, but this man wears the white tree stump and dagger on his tunic. The symbol of the royal family. *Palace guard.* My muscles tense as he runs up the hill.

He'll go straight to our father. As if I didn't have enough monsters to deal with.

The rip of fabric tempts me to turn around, but I won't give the season tree any more attention. Instead, I meet Dovan halfway.

"Are you all right?"

"How did you get it off you?"

Dovan and Alec speak at the same time. Annoyance flickers across Dovan's face as he clenches his jaw and shifts my brother's weight, but Alec's mouth is open, his eyebrows raised in a mixture of surprise and curiosity.

I decide to answer Dovan first, but Alec interrupts again. "You shouldn't have been able to get it off."

I glare at him. "I took it off."

"You...took it off?" Alec quirks a brow, the dimple in his left cheek appearing. "Damn Wrenna. We should have tried this—" my brother's voice breaks off into a gulp as Dovan drops him.

My lips twitch, but before I can laugh, a bitterly cold wind whips through my hair, echoed by thunder. The storm above us has gone from snow cloud gray to coal black.

A streak of red flies toward those clouds, making Alec swear. I spin around but the cape has escaped. The world drops out from beneath my stomach, and I clutch Dovan's arm to anchor me to what's real.

"But I defeated it," I say, shivering, even with Dovan's spring heat as a shield.

"Only one thing can defeat the season tree, and it isn't you."

Alec's tone has gone as sharp as his dagger. "You should have trusted me."

I prepare to tell him what I think of that horrible idea when an outside force grabs the fabric of my soul and yanks me forward. Dovan snatches my arm, helping me stay on my feet, but I'm still being pulled. The tear between winter's two halves widens as the first season is summoned by the master it escaped. Winter's panic melts into mine, and snow spins from our gasping breath, ice cracking along our skin, and rage, rage burning through our veins.

No! I fight, jerking against the tree's invisible grip. *I do not— We do not belong to you!*

But the tree takes the part of winter my assassination set free. The winter that has been starving our world for a decade. I cry out, lunging after the chilly trail of stolen magic. *It's gone!* Dovan catches me as I fall, drawing me against his chest, but I can't look at him. I can't see my fear mirrored in his own face.

Ever since I learned I was the Ember of Winter, I've felt torn, caught between two halves of the most powerful season of all, but the connection to both was always there, even if I avoided winter's vengeful side. Now the side of winter I have feared belongs to the season tree.

A flash of silver falls through the air and crunches into the ground near my boots. Dovan and I both step back. The brush against my skirt tells me Alec has dragged himself to my other side. Together, we stare at an ice spike as thick as a spear and as long as my forearm. The opaque cylinder of ice vibrates from where it sticks out between two cobblestones, but the top is wide and flat, spike side down. *It fell from the sky.*

This time Dovan swears, but he's already moving as thunder booms. *"Find shelter!"* He shouts, but nobody listens. The lower market has gone quiet. Everyone's mesmerized by the magic being worked over our heads as the tree draws more ice from the storm.

Dovan marches toward the nearest guider, who's staring at the sky like everyone else, and shakes him. "Armory. Now! Gather everyone and bring shields. Go!"

The guider jolts into action, but my brother grunts. "It's too late for shields."

I follow his gaze back to the sky and my knees give out beneath me. As stone bites into my kneecaps, the noose of being powerless chokes my hope and crushes what I've achieved. *I thought I'd won.* A cold hand finds mine, but this time I don't recoil from Alec's touch. I hold on to him while the season tree hovers above us, arranging a thousand glittering ice spikes around its shadow-filled cape. They tilt, targeting individual people.

Dovan shifts tactics, grabbing those nearest to him and shoving them under the few stalls with roofs. "Clear the market!"

It's too late. The season tree answers our rejection with winter's fury, and the spikes fall. Where there should be screams, silence reigns. Nobody moves, as if their will to survive has finally been broken. Even Dovan stands like a statue, frozen by a familiar horror that renders him powerless.

He can't save them. Unless...

Our gazes meet, and my heart shatters because I know what he's going to do. *He's going to use spring.* All of spring. Vaporize the spikes as they fall. *But he can't change the season.* Not with my cursed winter still in power. All of that life bringing magic would be lost.

No, this is my burden. My battle.

As the wet *thwack* of ice piercing flesh sets off a wave of screams, chaos rolls over the market. People run in all directions, pushing, shoving, knocking each other down.

Dovan's irises blaze with green fire and the air around him shivers with heat.

I leap up onto wobbling legs, throwing my hands up as if I am powerful enough to catch every spike. *I have to be.* A shudder rattles through me as the season tree's vengeful winter meets my protective winter. The divided power ricocheting up and down my bones threatens to shatter me from the inside out because I am still the source.

All of winter was entrusted to me. I am its ember. No matter what form it takes.

I groan through my teeth. Cold sweat weeps down my skin and my eyelids close. There's only one thing I need to see, and it's not how many lives are in danger. It's how many have already died. The faces of three-hundred-and-sixty-nine men and women, all victims of my brother's game and my curse, fill my heart with the resolve I need.

No more.

Not. One. Life. More.

RED DEATH

38

I LOVE it when a plan works.

I make it my goal to never get too attached to plans, because like rules, the fun is in breaking them, in the chaos caused by their ruin. *But this one*—I shake my head as a smile forms.

She's doing it. Hundreds of spikes hang suspended in the air, lightning flashing off their icy points. They tremble, but not from the thunder roaring above the lower market. There's a battle going on over whose soul winter will serve.

The soul of the season tree. Or my sister's.

I know who I'm betting on. If people took bets on a death match.

The taste of copper fills my mouth seconds before the curse's ill-timed warning jabs my chest. I cough, spitting up black and red blood while my heart misses a beat. *Dammit.* I didn't think the curse would make its choice yet, but a fresh rush of screams has me focusing on Wrenna again. One of her hands is down, and she's dropped to her right knee.

She feels it too. The unraveling of our bargain.

Whimpers and frightened cries fill the moments between the thunder as the spikes begin falling toward the people they're meant to kill. It's such a pathetic sound, inconsequential to me, but to Wrenna, their gasps of fear matter.

I watch through the budding of rare tears as my sister transforms from almost beaten to damn near unbeatable. She forces her hands higher, and the spikes spin upward. Despite the weight of so much power and fury crushing down on her, she stands tall and steps forward, her fingers spread wide as if she's carrying all of winter. Well, obviously she is.

Confident she has this part of the plan handled, I scan the market in search of Dovan. *If his chest is still bleeding we have a problem.* A snort escapes me. *What* we? This plan is mine and mine alone, since I never share the glory of my wins.

A heaviness pulls at my stomach just as a lonely knot tightens my throat. I should sneer at such feelings. Laugh in their idiotic faces, but I can't help the ache for when Wrenna and I were a team. *Stop getting distracted.*

Being on the ground puts me at a disadvantage for locating one guider among many. Especially with the stalls and their tipped over wares blocking a lot of my view. Most of the traders have stuffed themselves under any available shelter—under stall roofs, under tables, or under carts—which seems smart, but the stall next to me has several holes in its roof where the spikes punched clean through. *At least the guiders are paying attention.* Shuffling people through the market into the closest stone building.

The dagger belted to my hip pulses with heat, the blade's unnatural hunger ten times as potent as what I usually experience. My arms shake, bowing under the strain of resisting the dagger's pull, but I force them to hold me up for a little while longer. *Not yet.* Timing is everything in this final game. I know what is to come, and I won't be strong enough to stop it.

But she will.

I'm sorry, Wrenna. She deserves better than another forced choice, but the game is set. I have no power to effect it anymore.

I blink hard, pupils narrowing as the dagger's power feeds into me, and my vision flickers. Gray and red and back to gray. It's enough for me to find Dovan. He and four other guiders are passing out shields. *They're preparing to run.* Get as many to safety as possible.

As Dovan waves at someone behind me, my nostrils flare, scenting blood. The wound that prophesies Red Death's kill bleeds down his chest. Cursing my lack of favor with fate would be pointless, so I save my breath and do what I always do. Focus on my target.

The west gate and the stairs on its right.

The cobblestones are rough against my palms, the lanes between stalls littered with discarded wares and a handful of bodies, but I drag myself onwards. After a dozen hand pulls, another bloody coughing fit forces me to stop. My head is pounding, my chest bruised from the curse's jab, and the truth strangles my *I can do anything* attitude.

I can't do this. Not without magic.

Sixty feet of debris-strewn market stands between me and the gate. Judging by the way my heart is losing beats, I'll be dead by the time I drag myself there. *Or she will.*

The cape lashes her arms, but my sister takes its beating and angles toward the gate. Each step is a battle won in a war she believes will cost her everything. *What will she think?* When she realizes who will pay that price?

I wish I could see her face.

I slap myself. The sting yanks me from the distraction of what happens when this is over. *It doesn't matter.* Not for me. Not if I can't walk. There is a solution that doesn't involve using the dagger or reaching out to the season tree that would gladly kill me at this point.

As I position my legs in front of me and straighten them out, I seize the thread of melody written in our blood that connects me and Wrenna as twins. The flood of her emotions and her physical state pours into me. Her heart is beating far too fast, her soul whipped between fear and guilt and anger while she struggles to stay upright. She's exhausted, but the icy core of her season pulses around her soul. A mostly untapped power, waiting to be used.

Interesting. She could shred the entire sky with a hundred thousand spikes of ice if she wanted to, or she could create a dome so thick nothing could penetrate it. But she's not. She's holding out for the right solution because she wants everyone to live. I suspect even I am included in that wish. *Predictable.*

Lucky for her, I excel at the wrong type of solution.

I'm also very good at stealing a particular valuable. *Magic.* The dagger might be too dangerous right now, and the tree a true enemy, but my sister is neither. *It has to be her.* I hate it, but we have no more time to waste.

Shifting my weight to my right hand, I reach out with my left. A strand of winter's magic unwinds from Wrenna's soul. It flows through the air before circling me. A wordless question pulses between me and winter, but I don't even need to answer. Winter already understands.

The first season guides the thread over my legs. I shiver, unprepared for the brutality of the magic's cold bite, but it's working. My calves twitch as I concentrate. I spent so many years wearing braces of steel that their cruel skeletons are scarred into my skin. Ice rods thick as my fingers form along my legs as loops coil around my ankles, my knees, my thighs. A quick glance relieves the concern my theft will weaken my sister.

Her steps have slowed, but she is still winning.

I have to stop her. She can't win this game.

She won't survive the cost.

Time to make my stand.

I roll onto my stomach and push against the ground, tilting my body into an arrow-like shape. But walking my hands to my boots proves to be a futile strategy since I don't have the strength to shove myself upright *and* maintain my balance. I fall on my face and break an ice rod. Winter helps me repair it, and I try again, and again, using anything near me for leverage. Cobblestones pummel me with each failure, but every winner knows victory is just one more fall away.

I need something to help me stand, something that's anchored unlike the hand cart I already tipped over. Swiping red curls out of my eyes, I notice the stall beam about three hand pulls away. *Idiot.* Sometimes the hard way isn't the way to go.

After pulling myself to the beam, I climb it, ignoring the sting of splinters digging into my palms. My body dangles under me until I'm high enough for the braces to take my weight, and then —I'm standing. A little wobbly, but that can't be helped. I let go of the beam but keep it within reach as I shift my hips and thighs into a sidestep. The braces hold. I almost throw my hands into the air as a wave of accomplishment sweeps through me, but now is not the time for celebration.

Two challenges down. One more to go.

The first twenty steps pass with only a handful of falls. My stiff gait grows more confident as my muscles recognize the familiar rhythm and start trusting the braces. Ten more steps and I'm halfway there. A cocky grin raises the corner of my mouth when thunder booms over my head, and an ice spike grazes my shoulder. Blood spills hot down my skin as I jerk to the right and bounce off a stall beam. I manage not to fall, scanning the sky every few steps for more attacks.

Thanks to Dovan, the path before me is clear of people. But

there's still twenty more steps to reach the wall, and then four dozen to climb to the top. A freezing wind blows at my back, communicating what I already know. *You need to go faster.* Unlike the dagger's magic, winter's won't remain under my power for long.

I can do this.

Risking a little more speed, I lean forward into each step. As I pass the final lane of the lower market and enter the open space before the gate, liquid trickles down my calves. My braces are melting, my hold on the magic slipping as it returns to my sister. *Not much farther.*

I'm near the wall when Wrenna cries out and five ice spikes come whistling at me. I throw myself forward. The ice bracing my legs shatters as I slam into the unforgiving stone of the wall. Pain sizzles along my side as two of the spikes scrape across my skin. I flip over, searching the sky for more, and the first real shudder of fear courses through me.

Two dozen crystalline spikes hang above me, vibrating, inching up and down without making any real progress in either direction. *Wrenna.*

She's crumpled on the ground a few strides from the gate. An ice blade has pierced her shoulder, and blood soaks her left arm as it hangs limp at her side. My hands curl into fists, a promise of a monster's rage, but for once, there's no curse good enough to express the hatred burning through me.

The tree will pay.

I glare that message into its faceless hood as the season tree acknowledges me for a mere second before circling my sister. I may be a cripple and by the tree's judgement, a dismissible threat, but not Wrenna. Even though her face is stained with tears and sweat, her hair whipping in the wind, she fights to keep her right arm up. To keep the season tree from killing us all. *She's not going to make it.*

Which is why I have to.

Her lips repeat the same pattern, a soundless oath that's been the backbone of every attempt she ever made to save my victims.

Not. One. Life. More.

I tear my eyes from her and reach for the stairs, ignoring the prick of guilt. I let the rage bury it. The stone steps dig into my ribs, my gut, and my thighs as I climb, but pain is my oldest friend. I don't care if I have to drag myself all the way to the top.

I'm going to end this. I'm going to give the curse what it wants.

A soul for a soul.

WRAITH

39

THE ICE BLADE stuck in my left shoulder hurts worse than a metal knife. If a fire iron burned cold, freezing the tissue around it and searing a wretched, icy path all the way to the bone, that would only account for a tenth of what I'm feeling. I bow my head, cobblestones pinching my knee as I sway, but by sheer determination, I maintain my control of the ice spikes threating the lower market.

No matter how bad this gets—my right fist cannot fall.

I search for a sign of hope to feed my courage, but in this fight, like so many before, there will be no rescue. The lanes around me are empty, and I can't find Dovan.

At least the ice missed my heart. A fact that's likely more of a mistake than a plan, but the tip splintered, scattering shards through skin, muscle, and bone. Each one throbs, their ripples of pain ricocheting off each other so I'm stuck in a loop of agony without beginning or end.

Just hold on. A bitter laugh bursts from my lips, bringing the salty sting of tears to my tongue. *Hold on for what?* I don't have a plan beyond putting as much distance between the season tree and my people as possible. *Will that be enough to save them?*

I don't know.

Velvet cloth slides against my hair as the tree circles me, the abrasive pulse of its power prickling my skin. *"You suffer needlessly."*

I twist away from the cape, jarring the ice wedged between my bones, and I gasp.

"You owe them nothing, just as I do not."

"We're not the same." I glare into its shadowed hood as the crimson cape finishes its circle and hovers before me.

"You fight for them, but they will never fight for you." The cape's sleeve curls around the blade. I whimper, and the tree's ripple of power turns soothing, lapping gently against my wound. The pain stops so suddenly I nearly collapse as the tension in my body no longer has anything to resist. *"You are their monster, little banshee. No matter what you do, they will make no place for you here."*

"Is this supposed to win me over?" I shake my head. "I've seen your plans. You won't be satisfied until everyone is dead."

"Plans can be adjusted." Another piece of the cape dares to caress my jaw, and I lunge for it with my teeth. The tree jerks the fabric away in time, its shadow filled hood angling down in disapproval. *"There are some lives I might consider worth sparing."*

My lip curls at the sour taste of those words and the pulse of longing behind them. Knowing that the tree finds me worth saving only for the destruction we could wreak together adds fresh fuel to my defiance. "I'm not interested in saving *some* lives. I plan to save them all."

"I am owed a debt of vengeance and they shall pay it," the tree's voice grows scratchy, *"but you could be my vessel."* The cape floats closer. *"Submit to me."*

"No."

The hood leans to the side. *"And if I offer you Dovan's life as a reward for choosing me?"*

That offer hits a little harder, like a kick to the chest, but I was already prepared to lose Dovan. Saving our world was our mission. *It still is.* My right arm has sunk during our exchange, allowing the spikes to fall a few feet before I force my fist higher again.

I lean into my answer as I tighten my hold on the spikes. "I will *never* choose you."

The tree hisses, the sound grating along my nerves like fingernails swiping glass, and tilts the ice blade to the left. Fresh agony knives through me and I scream.

"I know your weakness, foolish girl." Another twist, this time to the opposite side while also pushing deeper. My body jolts, and I bite my tongue hard, drawing blood. *"You won't last much longer."*

I shut my eyes, panting, and block out the season tree's poisonous voice. The cape releases the blade, and I sag forward as a wave of dizziness follows the temporary pause in our game. Every part of me aches with a question I can't ignore.

When will this be over?

My father thought pain would break me. He left bruises on my skin at first, and then he changed tactics to leave bruises on my soul. Even my brother as Red Death used pain to control me, but they were wrong. It wasn't pain that bent my will to theirs. Pain was never my weakness. It was the belief that I had no choice, no power to affect even the smallest of changes.

I've always had a choice.

Maybe not the choices I wanted, but it was my choice that kept my heart from hate. It was my choice to see the good in the world, a choice that kept a tiny spark of hope alive so I could dream of a future where I am whole, where I have purpose, and where I have love.

No one can take that power from me.

The storm rumbles as if in agreement and I open my eyes. The cape floats to the right, the lower length of its crimson train draping over the body of a young woman lying on the ground. Her open mouth voices a silent scream as she holds the ice spike imbedded in her gut. Bile rises to my throat as shame tries to wrap me up in its acidic folds, but—*this isn't my fault.* Her death is not my fault.

I fought for her.

I fought for them all.

Every victim of my curse. Every soul trapped in winter. I won't let shame corrupt that fact and weaken the strength I need to keep fighting, because I am not done.

The shadow-filled hood watches me, a sickening mix of pleasure and confidence pouring from it in waves. Two days ago, the sight of another life ended would have broken me. The tree would have won, as it expected, but I'm not that girl anymore.

I don't surrender to monsters.

I draw on my half of the first season and summon a frigid blast of wind.

The cape tumbles, blown back into the sky. Several strips lash out, torn edges coiling around more spikes before throwing them at me. My wind diverts the first three, and they slam into an empty stall. But the last two—*they're already too close.* In defiance, both halves of winter raise a wall in their path, but the ice isn't thick enough. The spikes smash through.

I could stop them. I could save myself from more pain. But that would mean letting go of the hundreds of spikes aimed at the dozen people making a run for a stone building behind the stalls.

It's better if I bleed. I can heal.

My muscles stiffen, bracing, when a shadow steps in the way.

Two solid *thunks* impact the shield being held over me by a man whose warmth coaxes extra beats from my curse-slowed heart. I choke on a sob because Dovan is here.

His gaze sweeps over me, snagging on my wounded shoulder, and his jaw clenches. A handful of emotions crack through his stoic guider mask, but love burns through them all. Telling me he's proud I haven't run and that he'll do anything I ask. All he says is, "Can you stand?"

Not—*you shouldn't keep fighting.*

Not—*you're too weak.*

Not—*I can handle this for you.*

I give him a soft smile but shake my head. "I need you to pull it out."

Plenty of other young men would go pale at such a request, but not Dovan. He slides the shield over his shoulder and inspects my wound before bringing his palm next to the blade. The ice steams from the threat of his spring-heated skin.

"Ready?" he asks, turning his body so his chest braces my right arm. The relief of not having to hold the ice spikes up alone and the tenderness of his instinctive gesture blur my vision. *Flakes, I love this man.*

After a deep breath, I give a sharp nod and he yanks the blade free. There's no point in stopping my scream as I flinch forward. Dovan casts the bloody spike aside and steadies me, gripping my right arm.

"Breathe," he commands in a soothing tone.

I rest my temple against his forearm and inhale deeply. The scents of leather, pine, and flowery spring comfort me, but while my torn flesh is on fire, while I try to pick up the fragments of my depleted strength, the season tree hurls a dozen spikes at us.

Dovan whirls, sliding his shield from his back and raising it in one smooth motion. He deflects most of them, but one spike shatters against the cobblestones. The second cuts across his arm. He grimaces but maintains his position as a third strikes something softer off to our left, followed by a cry. *Someone's been hurt.*

I haul myself to my feet, gripping Dovan's tunic to combat the wobbling of my legs. Hot liquid soaks through my left sleeve. I stare at the trickle of red leaking from my wound as pain continues to throb through my torn flesh. *It should be healing.* But the magic that has ruled my life isn't responding.

Wincing through a breath, I push aside what my lack of healing means. Whether or not my brother wrecked the banshee curse, my people are in danger, and I am tired.

I'm tired of the games. I'm tired of limited choices, but this one is mine to make.

"What do you need?" Dovan asks as I edge around his right side, once more spotting the cape between the clouds and the suspended ice. Red strips of cloth ripple and snap as they arrange the tree's army of spikes so most of them target us.

I swallow, but my mouth remains dry until a warm hand finds mine.

"What do you need?" He repeats his question. None of the doubts plaguing me appear in his eyes. He looks to me as a soldier would, knowing what we risk in this fight, and yet he's still willing to try, to follow where I lead.

I squeeze his fingers despite the pain ripping through my injured shoulder. "Be my shield?"

A tiny half smile softens his stern guider mask, and he leans in to kiss my temple. "Always."

The cape has finished gathering the spikes and unfurls like a bloody banner prophesying our doom, but I'm about to ruin the season tree's day.

"I have a question for you," I call up to it.

The cape ducks its hood as lightning splits the sky.

My right fist opens. Winter answers my unspoken call,

sending excited chills racing across my skin. "What good is a monster without teeth?"

Thunder booms as I thrust my open hand higher, taking hold of the season magic feeding the storm. Magic that winter entrusted to me, to be wielded not for destruction but for wonder. I pull, reclaiming what was stolen, and the tear between winter's halves heals. An electric charge leaps between the half I carry and the half that froze the world. The pressure builds and builds until my ears pop and the spikes shudder.

The cape lunges for me, but I'm already closing my hand into a fist.

Every single ice-spike shatters into harmless, sparkling dust.

The season tree flees back into the sky.

A lopsided grin teases my lips as fury deepens the shadows of the hood and makes the cape's strips writhe. "Tell me again how long you think I'll last? Because I promise you, I haven't even begun to fight you, and fight you, I will." I step forward, tall and strong, with Dovan at my side. "I will fight you in this market. I will fight you outside that gate. I will fight you in the snow."

The cape spins, flinging a fresh ice spike at me. Dovan pivots, catching it with his shield and exposing an interesting fact. This spike is half the size of the others.

I lift my hands, grimacing through the stabbing pain from my wound. "I will fight you through pain and broken bones and despair." My fingers meet the invisible threads of magic extending from the storm, reaching for me as I reach for them. "I will fight you until we are utterly spent or until we are both claimed by the banshee curse. Whichever comes first."

Lightning bolts across the clouds, barely missing the cape, and thunder echoes my promise.

"This city is my home, and you will not harm anyone else." I start walking, and winter follows with a frigid wind. Our combined power backs the tree toward the gate. "You will not use my season against me."

Three more spikes race for me, intercepted by Dovan's shield. They're even smaller, like frail ice twigs instead of lethal weapons. I smile and say the words I've been waiting to say my entire life.

"You will. Not. Win."

RED DEATH

40

I've always known how I would die.

Not that it bothered me. The clock began ticking when I made the deal with the season tree to save my sister's life. *All those portraits.* Hanging around the rotunda that imprisoned the tree—they showed me the truth. The banshee curse can't be broken. It must be paid. *A soul for a soul.* Every Red Death who came before me saw the same thing, the one price worth more than the others. The cost of an ending and a beginning. The lie in my one truth.

There was another way to save her.

I didn't even consider it that night when she was dying in my arms. Selfish, maybe. But we were both so young, just nineteen years old, and I wanted more time. We *deserved* more time. Ten years I bought us. Ten years of Red Death's violent games and Wraith's sorrowful songs. *At least I enjoyed it.* I embraced my new role while Wrenna suffered like she was still under our father's hard-handed rule.

I can still fix this.

Wrenna glimpsed the key to her freedom in those same paintings before the season tree tried to destroy them. I'm counting on her to remember and accept who I am.

I am a monster who lives for bloodshed.

It is only just I should die the same way.

A snickering laugh punches through my heaving breaths as I flop onto my back. I've completed my climb up forty-eight steps, dragging myself to the center of the wall's arched gate. The stone is grimy from patches of snow trampled under guiders' boots, but as the storm rumbles new threats, I sense a shift in power vibrate through the wall. *Almost time.*

I roll onto my side, careful not to tumble over the edge, and look down. Wrenna's irises shine pale blue with the full magic of her season as she stands, every inch of her a queen. The worries I've carried about what happens to her after I end the game slide from my shoulders.

She'll be fine. More than fine. *Especially with Dovan watching over her.* The guider positions himself at her side, his shield covered in ice spikes, and I'd be a liar if I didn't admit how right they look together. *He's no replacement for me,* snipes my darker self, but I refuse to give in to its bait. *He's good for her.* Even if he is the boring kind of honorable.

"What good is a monster without teeth?" my sister asks, a confidence in her tone I've never heard before.

She squeezes her raised hand into a fist. Clouds of diamond dust fill the air as the spikes the season tree would have used to kill our people explode. Then I glimpse the shared expression I thought we'd lost. She smirks. *Our* smirk. The one we shared before mine became a vicious sneer and hers vanished into the horror of what I'd done to save her. My heart clenches behind my ribs as I accept what this means.

She doesn't need me anymore.

Wrenna stands tall all on her own. Unshakable, even though she's broken.

The tree has lost hold of winter's vengeful half, and she taunts it like I would. Well, not exactly like I would. The words she chooses—*I will fight you*—ripple with the strength of her noble intentions, and nobody is bleeding or begging for mercy. Yet.

The season tree lunges for her, and the curse pierces my heart. But the pain of the invisible blade is pulling out, breaking the magical oath keeping her alive. The curse's magic, our only hope of beating the vile tree, grows dangerously thin. I turn toward the parapet that overlooks the snowfields instead of the city and dig my fingers into the cracks between its stones. My muscles burn, sweat freezes on my skin, but I have one more climb to make. And then I'll fall.

One.

Last.

Time.

My ears pop from the force of my sister's magic clashing with the tree's. They're locked in battle, equally matched for the moment, but I told the tree why it'd lose. *Love.* And I didn't mean hers.

As I wriggle onto the parapet and push myself up, tugging my useless legs so I'm straddling its sides, I find myself torn.

I have one regret.

She doesn't know. She doesn't understand, her own words cutting me again. *"What would you know of love? The only person you love is yourself!"*

A lie I needed her to accept without question. My sister and I had to become enemies. I broke her trust to protect this very future, and now there's nothing I can say, no proof I can offer, that she'll believe. But I will show her.

Everything I know about love, I learned from her.

I close my eyes. My heart beats faster, harder, ticking off the seconds I have left. I draw the dagger, hissing in pain at its furious heat, and point the blade's curved tip at my chest. A stone-splitting *crack* snaps through the market, but I can't let the fight between Wrenna and the tree distract me. I have my own battle to win.

The wind howls past me as it rushes back into the lower market to answer my sister's request for more power, uniting winter's split halves within her soul. This is the moment. We're on the verge of her first victory and my final betrayal.

I lay hold of the dagger's power, extending it to the weakening magic of our curse, and press the blade into my skin. My body jolts from the searing pain, and I have to plant my right hand to keep from tumbling over the wall.

The muscles of my left arm tremble as I push the dagger deeper. I drag the blade down the left side of my sternum to recreate the prophetic wound and mark myself as the victim. Once the weapon gets a taste through my blood of the ancient spirit it was created to devour, its hunger overrules the flimsy control the season tree has over our fate.

Reinstating the curse in full.

Through the twin bond we share and the bargain binding us, I sense my sister gasp. I feel her stumble, and I wish I was standing next to her. I wish I could see her face as the wound in Dovan's chest closes, replaced by mine, but the shock of what I've done breaks her concentration. Several hundred ice spikes adjust their aim, targeting the threat they should have focused on from the start.

Me.

Being underestimated is my true power. I allow myself a final sneer as the season tree's shredded cape focuses on me, but there's no Red Death without his bloody cape.

I extend my free hand, savoring my partner's spike in panic as the curse restores my authority. The tree fights, resisting my pull in darts of movement. *Oh, no you don't.* I fist my right hand around the invisible chord of magic strung between us.

Strips of red fabric lash out, throwing ice spikes at me, but the tree's aim is off. A few graze my skin while the rest miss me entirely. I clench my jaw, yanking the cape closer, and the dagger pours its power into my summons.

There's only one way this ends.

No matter how hard the season tree tries to resist, each desperate flutter of the cape brings the fabric closer to my fingers. For once, the tree is swearing. *I see you learned a few from me.* But the laugh dies in my throat when the tree stops fighting.

Blood-soaked cloth coils around my body, cloaking me and my view of the world in crimson once more. I gasp in pain as the tree attacks and almost lose my balance. Invisible roots claw at my skin, boring into me while its shadows writhe through my mind.

I slam the door between our minds shut. *Like we need to talk.* I've heard enough of its threats. But the tree is in my veins now, spreading like poison towards my heart, and I can't let the roots reach it. Even bound to the curse, the tree is too powerful for me to control. Once it takes my heart, the tree will rip my soul from my body if I don't finish this.

Now.

I risk glancing at my sister. Shock has stolen the glow of victory from her face, but the dagger skews my vision, allowing me to see her as she really is. Light-brown skin and kind hazel eyes and hair so dark it becomes the night to her snow. Her mouth moves in a silent plea, begging me not to say it, but the word is already forming on my tongue. Only this time it's born of love.

My love will pay the price she never could.

I am the last Red Death, the last partner of the season tree, and we will die so she can live the life she deserves.

A life free of monsters like me.

As a wicked fire rages through my right side, I watch the tree raise my right hand, reaching for my left—the one holding the blade to my chest—and the final tick of my clock echoes through my soul.

Wrenna screams as I lean toward my doom. She throws her season magic against mine, but no banshee has ever overruled Red Death's command. Not even as thick vines of frost come rushing up the wall to grab me, to keep me from falling.

I say the word that will cost me everything and end our game. "*Sing.*"

And then I hurl myself to the side.

I fall.

I give my soul for hers.

WRAITH

41

I'm running for my brother, and I don't know why.

The notes being forced through my throat should be enough for me to leave Alec to the punishment of the frozen ground. Let him shatter for once. *He made me sing.* Breaking my heart for the thousandth time, and yet I push my weary body toward the gate because—

He fell.

He's no stranger to falling. From the age of six, his legs have failed him. He bears many scars from falling at the worst possible moments into the worst possible things. Like thorn hedges and down flights of stairs or at the obstacle fields where his *nothing hurts me* mask was cruelly stripped away in front of the young court he was expected to rule.

He failed the simplest of drills with swords or spears. He was always last, always behind, eventually refusing to participate, but his absence didn't end their laughter.

Everyone laughed at him.

Everyone but me.

The melody of Alec's song turns sad, drawing out a memory, and a dull prick of pain crackles along my knuckles. *The only time I hurt someone was for Alec.* A visiting prince had made it his goal to humiliate my brother, and when one of his pranks caused Alec to fall in front of the entire court, including the king, I had to act.

I ended the prince's fun by ramming my fist into his gut. My brother repaid me by knocking me down, overshadowing his weakness with a violence that silenced the court and reminded me of our father.

"Don't you ever do that again." He warned before leaving me there alone.

His song shifts higher, speeding toward the end as another memory unfolds. I left crutches for him beside the door of our music room, but he never used them, preferring the risk of his legs collapsing than learning to rely on anything or anyone. *He always chose the hard way.*

There's no taking back what he's done. There's no making us right again. *I don't know if I can ever forgive him.* Not completely. But—*Alec was—he is*—my brother, and he would never let himself fall. Not if he was in control of his body. It goes against everything he has done, everything he is. Monsters don't lose. *So why is he losing for me?*

The flap of red cloth and the grunts of a struggle warn me I'm out of time. As the final notes in Alec's song leave my lips, I throw myself through the gate, arms outstretched and reaching despite the pain in my injured shoulder.

"I'll catch you." That's what I told him when I'd convinced him a cage of metal strapped around his legs might enable him to walk again.

He was skeptical at first, wary of looking weak for accepting my help, but he took my idea to a blacksmith and had the braces made. We locked ourselves in the music room when they were finished, and I noticed his hands were shaking.

I wanted to tell him it was okay if he fell. If the braces didn't work. But I held my tongue as he smirked, faking confidence, and waited as he strapped them on. He pushed himself up, and I opened my arms. Alec batted them away, the gesture so playful I almost missed the nervous wobble in his throat as he said, *"Don't assume I'm going to fall."*

The shadow of the gate's arch draws me from the past as I fly through it, and his full-grown body crashes into my right shoulder. My head rings, my legs tangle under me, and we both go down, our bodies bouncing and rolling in opposite directions.

New aches pinch my ribs, throbbing into my injured shoulder, but the silence is too heavy, too complete. My hand flies to my throat. *I'm not singing.* I finished Alec's song.

This is when the victim dies.

But he's not—he's never been the victim. Blood marks the snow in ropey lines and chaotic splatters as I crawl to his side. *Why would he do this?*

The dagger. He'd jabbed it into his chest seconds before he threw himself from the wall. Understanding spreads a chill across my skin.

He altered the curse.

That's why he made me sing his song. So he could play both monster and prey, Red Death *and* Red Death's victim. It shouldn't have been possible, but the impossible is just another game to Alec. *He's always known how to break the rules.*

I wasn't prepared for him to break them like this.

He lies so still on his side I fear he is dead. The coppery scent of blood hits my nose as I roll him over, revealing the dagger. A third of the blade is driven into his chest. His left hand grips the wrist of his right, preventing it from grabbing the weapon he meant to kill him.

I sit on my heels, Alec's words replaying in my mind. *"There's only one thing that can stop the season tree, and it isn't you."*

No, it was him. It was the boy I knew and the brother I loved and the monster who traded the souls of others to save me. *He wanted the tree to come to him.* He wanted its soul wrapped up in his. Unexpected tears sting my tongue with salt as the cape twists around his left arm, trying to crush his bones, and I hear him, telling me what was coming.

"There's nothing I wouldn't do for you."

A shudder wracks my frame as I realize what Alec has done.

He's ending the curse. *He's giving his soul.* To set mine free.

And now the season tree shall pay the cost with him. I sniff hard and tug the hood from his face before the evil spirit inhabiting its cloth smothers Alec.

A brush of warmth sweeps along my left side. I glance back and find Dovan standing just inside the gate. His worry wrinkle pinches his eyebrows together, but he doesn't come any closer, respecting a boundary that has shifted. It used to bind me to the city and force me to sing to Red Death's victims. Now I'm tied to my twin in a soul-shattering way.

Only one of our hearts will keep beating.

With a final rumble of thunder, the dark shadows of the storm pale, its anger softening into sorrow as perfect flakes of snow fall in a swirling dance. The snowflakes catch in my hair. They shiver on my skin and kiss the ground between me and my brother.

Alec coughs, his eyes rolling open but not quite settling on my face. "Your catching skills are worse than I remember."

Of all things, a laugh bursts through my lips. The sound of our joy cuts me and fails to lighten the weight of what's coming. After everything that's happened, it feels wrong to cling to this moment, but I do. I miss who we were. "I am a bit out of practice."

Alec chuckles weakly. "A bit? I almost broke my neck."

"You almost broke mine, actually."

"And here I was aiming to knock some sense into that nonsensical head of yours."

"I'm nonsensical? I wasn't the one who believed it was possible to kiss a dragon without bursting into flames."

We share another laugh, but it's softer, frailer because of what's coming. His chest flinches, his wrestling hands nearing the dagger. "I was eight. Kissing dragons seemed like a good way to..."

Die.

He doesn't say it, the word that is his future. A small act of mercy after a decade of cruel choices. Alec tilts his head, and the silly banter that used to be a daily practice for us disappears behind the dark hunger in his brown eyes. But the longing in his gaze isn't for bloodshed or for more power to control others.

"I never should have stopped trying to make you laugh." More confessions line his eyelids with moisture, but he doesn't speak them.

"Why did you stop?"

His jaw clenches as his shoulders twitch. Burgundy veins climb the right side of his neck, and when they reach his eye, the iris glows crimson. *The tree is infecting him.* A stab of fear pierces my heart, but I can't bring myself to touch him, to help.

Alec sighs. "I've done so many terrible things to you."

I hold my breath, worried a word from me will stop him from telling me the truth.

"I...made enemies to become feared." He grits his teeth. "You were my weakness. I couldn't have a weakness. I..." His right hand brushes the blade, and he lunges for me with a snarl. I jolt backward as Alec slams his skull on the icy ground, and the thick veins along the left side of his face thin to a normal size. *He's losing control.*

This might be my last chance to get answers. "Are you admitting the assassin who started all of this, who stabbed me..." Flashes of memory sharpen the pain biting like icicle teeth into my chest. Alec never admitted it to me, but we both know he never stopped wanting the throne. He was born to be king, and I was in his way. "Was she yours?"

Rare hurt cracks through Alec's emotionless mask. "I didn't send her, Wrenna. I never would."

"But—"

"Killing you was supposed to break me, and it would have."

I'm his weakness? I search his face for the lie that must exist behind his admission, but there isn't one.

"It was my fault. Everything. Is my fault." His voice fades into a gasp, followed by a shallow groan. "Even this."

The last piece falls into place, summoning a memory from when I woke up in that larger rotunda. *The paintings.* All those portraits. All those Red Deaths and banshees who like us were trapped by the season tree's curse until the banshee took his weapon. *Is that how the curse ends?*

With me stabbing my brother through the heart?

"I tried to spare you." Alec's soft voice is almost lost in the hush of falling snow.

But he fell—betting that the impact would push the dagger deep enough so—*I wouldn't have to kill him.* The curse isn't easily fooled. *Alec must have thought it could work.* Or he wouldn't have thrown himself off the wall. I wipe my sweaty palms on my thighs, leaving trails of frost behind as I grapple with a new horror. *If I hadn't tried to catch him, it might have worked.*

"I knew you'd try to catch me. I was counting on it."

"I shouldn't—"

"Yes, you should have. It's who you are." Alec's brown eye is fading to red, burgundy veins covering his entire face. His tree controlled right hand breaks free and closes around the dagger's hilt.

I throw my hand over his, pushing down as his corrupted fist yanks the blade.

Alec smiles at me. "I could always count on you to do the right thing."

I'm shaking, my skin soaked by a relentless stream of tears, and a gentle wind stirs my hair. A whisper of a divided season, half of which wants me to let go, promising an end to all the pain when I do, but winter isn't speaking to me. That whisper of power belongs to the evil spirit possessing my brother. Even though I know the season tree's offer is a lie, that it doesn't care about me and plans to kill everyone, the dagger slides upward as I weaken.

I don't want this.

I never wanted to be anyone's ending.

"Don't you dare let go." Alec's left hand covers mine, exerting slight pressure. "This is right."

"I don't—want to—kill you," the words stumble from my mouth as broken as my erratic heartbeat.

"Why? What future do you see for me?" His tone becomes harsh. "You said it yourself. I ruin things. I've ruined enough of your life." He cups my cheek, tracing my scar as if to prove his point, and the moisture beading along his eyelids trickles down his skin. Real, honest, tears. *I wish he had let them fall sooner.* Before it was too late.

"It's okay, Wrenna." Alec turns my head so I spot Dovan kneeling halfway between us and the gate, his expression torn between agreement and sorrow. A few dozen people stand behind him in the gateway, their faces pale, but they will never understand what is happening. What is being asked of me.

"There's your future." Alec tugs my chin, reclaiming my attention. "I don't belong there with you. I'm your past."

My hold on the hilt slips as his right hand jerks it up. I have no choice but to use both of mine to combat the tree's growing strength, while a quiet truth freezes my heart. *He's right. You know he's right.* Even if there was another way, even if we could break the curse without sacrificing another soul, Alec has no future anymore. He threw that away the moment he became Red Death. To be the monster who saved me.

But he can't do it alone. Alec isn't strong enough because his strength is stolen. Not earned, like mine. He's disappearing, the stubborn brown of his soul overwhelmed by wicked red and a hatred that will end every life if I don't end his first.

"Let me do one good thing for you." Alec's fingers leave my skin, and the thud of his left arm on the ground turns the wind biting cold.

He's stopped fighting, surrendering the future into my hands.

"Don't." I beg, my head shaking as my lungs seize. "Don't make me do this."

His typical Red Death sneer softens into a boyish grin as a flare of brown reclaims his irises. "Thank you for singing my song."

I cry out, unable to form words.

The dagger jerks, jarring my arms, as the tree tries to pull it out, and the brown of Alec's irises flickers like a dying candle. His tender expression mutates into the savage mask of a cornered beast. A monster who cannot be unleashed upon the world. I don't think or feel, I just move. My hands against his. Pushing the blade all the way in until the hilt cracks against his bones.

The blade has run through his heart.

WRAITH

42

Nothing happens at first.

The snowflakes swirl around me, their crystal edges sparkling as dawn spears low through the clouds. The dagger burns my skin, but I don't let go. I hold it in my brother's heart as his uneven breaths grow shallow, waiting and hoping. *Please be the last.* The last soul I will sing into the arms of death. The last face that will haunt me because I'm the reason.

I'm why they all died. But unlike the others, this death *was* my choice.

The old impulse to run, to flee from the pain that's too difficult to face, numbs my heart with the promise of escape. *You could be lost.* Out there, sheltered by the snowfields, I could disappear. No one would find me. No one would force me to do anything ever again. A shiver rips through my chest as I cry. *I don't want to be lost anymore.* Even if the price of being found means facing what I fear most, even then, *I'm not running.*

I stay.

I won't leave him. Not until his sacrifice is finished.

My breaking pieces anchor me to this moment as Alec begins to convulse. The red fades from his irises, from his hair, and his cape, transforming him into a pale ghost compared to usual vibrant self. Dull pain thrusts through my back as he arches away from the ground. Blood pools around him, but it's not flowing from his chest. While holding onto the dagger, I lift him to the side and find a gaping hole in the same spot as my pain.

The assassin's knife. Alec's body steals the wound that should have killed me, and it's not the only scar that's healing. The place he stabbed my arm, the cut on my cheek, and the injury in my shoulder I earned from battling the season tree, one by one they all vanish. Even the silver scars from the people I sang to as a banshee disappear.

I touch my chest, my face, my neck, my forearm, but my fingers meet with smooth, unblemished skin. *Like they never happened.* They tear open my brother's flesh instead, oozing tainted, curse blackened blood as my brother pays for the choice he made and the damage he caused.

He's reversing everything. Fulfilling our bargain as Red Death and Wraith.

I sniff hard and blink, and the gray of my vision flickers. All the colors the curse robbed from me come rushing in, painting my world once more. The fair ivory tone of Alec's skin next to the creamy brown of my own. The whispers of purple in the clouds above us. The pale ribbon of blue sky hugging the horizon. The strips of pine-green cloth and unraveling gold thread of my dress.

It is a ball gown, sewn for my wedding to the brutal northern prince, but I ran, as the assassin expected. If my brother had found me a few minutes later—

We wouldn't be here.

Me, kneeling in a pool of his blood, my hand keeping the

dagger in his chest as it drains the life from both him and the season tree. *He's dying for my future.*

I flinch forward as the final tether between our souls and the banshee curse snaps, drawing an invisible blade from my heart. The missing beats from my pulse kick in, pounding a normal rhythm through my veins.

I am restored. Physically at least, while my soul bears the stabbing of fresh sorrow.

Alec's head lolls side to side, lips twitching, as his lungs spasm.

Releasing the dagger, I take his left hand and press his palm to my cheek, but the words I want to speak get stuck behind a wall of conflicting emotions.

Gratitude clashes with guilt.

Horror rages against hope.

How can I squeeze it all into a few seconds? There's a lifetime of things I need to say, of things I need to do, and I will. I will live because my brother trades his soul for mine.

Alec's brown eyes are unfocused, but he winks at me. An incredulous laugh catching on a final gasp. "I. Lose."

He goes still.

"Alec?" His name strangles my throat like a fist because I know he can't hear me. I shake him, but—

He's gone.

Our game is over.

WRENNA

43

I TAKE my first breath of freedom. It stings, tasting of salty sorrow and copper sacrifice, but when I exhale, the magical demand to sing that I've served for ten years is gone.

I am a banshee no more.

I pull the dagger from Alec's chest. The blade shines silver, completely clean as if it absorbed his blood. There's no pulse of power, no brutal heat. There's nothing unnatural about it anymore. It's just a dagger. But even if the blade is clean, my hands are not.

Alec's blood coats the edge of my palms where they touched the wound he started but I finished. *You had to kill him.* That echo of truth rings hollow as a snowflake lands on my palm and sinks into my brother's blood.

There's one thing left for me to kill.

The air thickens with snow, but without my banshee wail, there's no wind to turn winter's defensiveness into a blizzard. I tip my head up so the snowflakes can slide down my face and mingle with my warming tears. *It's time.*

Time for winter to be free.

Time for the ice trapping our world to thaw.

Winter's chill lingers on my skin and wraps protectively around my heart, a gentle reminder of how we both survived what should never have happened. A curse that tore us into pieces and made us forget who we truly are. Teaching me to despair and winter to hate. Twisting the good and making us hard.

Winter is never softer than when it melts.

You're not a monster. You're the first season. You're—it hits me so gently. The truth of why winter matters. *You're when we rest.* When the land, the creatures, and the people rest from months of toiling. A time when families and neighbors gather, spinning hope in fire-lit tales. A season of remembering what's important because the cold isn't barren, for under the ice rests the most powerful force man has ever known. The seeds of new life.

Winter isn't the end of life but the journey to spring. The first season strips everything down to the bones and prepares the world to be reborn.

A fresh start. That's the gift winter gives.

I lean into the brush of flakes and icy air. *Thank you.*

A surge of power squeezes my heart in a bittersweet goodbye, and tremors rattle through me as the first season leaves my soul. They grow from fear into relieved anticipation, and my heart wrenches over the depth of winter's longing. To be born in full and then, to die. To fulfill its purpose and become a seed in the next ember's soul.

Frosty magic tugs at my chin. I follow winter's gentle nudge to find Dovan beside me. His warm hands grip my arms, lifting me up and helping me stand.

He takes the dagger, tucks it into his belt, and guides me a short distance from my brother's body. "We don't have to do this now. If you need to—"

"No." I cut him off. I glance from Alec to the people lingering at the gate, their eyes shining with hope. *They've waited long enough to know the freedom my brother died to give me.* I shudder as the smell of Alec's blood twists my stomach, as the knowledge of what I had to do, of what I'll have to live with, crushes my soul.

Dovan holds me, letting me breathe through this without telling me what to do or how to heal the wrongs that have been done. *There are so many.* I'm pierced by a jagged pain as I accept the fact that some of these wounds may never fully heal, but I know what I can fix. *The season.*

I didn't choose how my winter would be born, or how much death my brother's curse would reap, but I will choose what happens now. "Winter has had enough time."

There is no song rising from my soul. There is no dance. It's just me and Dovan, our arms wrapped around each other, as we sink to our knees. The frigid spark of winter and the roaring flame of spring brought together through our souls. We place our hands, his right and my left, on the icy crust of snow blanketing our world.

The rich copper tones of Dovan's skin shine as the evergreen power of spring flows from him, tickling my face with the promise of new beginnings. Spring spreads over the snowfields in a rippling wave of emerald magic. But the second season remains floating above winter's white armor, as if repelled by an unseen force.

Winter is still holding on.

Snowflakes spiral through the air, flashing gold with dawn and green with spring. I rest my head on Dovan's shoulder. Winter waits for me to command it, but my once-captive soul recoils at the idea of an order, of forcing the first season to surrender. If people deserve to choose their fate, then so do the seasons. Instead of a demand, I make a simple request.

Let go. I sink my fingers into the snow, my touch gentle and understanding as winter slides coils of frost around my hand. Protective. To the end. *It's okay. I'll be okay. You don't have to protect me anymore. You can let go.*

A sigh slips through the air, born of the soul of a weary season as it accepts its rest. A drop of warm water bounces off my cheek. The first of dozens, of hundreds, as the storm passes from the control of one season into the next.

Snowflakes melt into rain, gilded by the risen sun roaring golden victory over the night in the east. The rain soaks into my hair and my throat contracts against a laugh.

The first rain in a decade.

Dovan's grinning so wide his lips have broken through the strain of all the sorrow and responsibilities he carries. From behind us, a man lets out a wild whoop. A sound of pure joy that cracks the snow piled around the city. After ten years of knowing only one season, ten years of watching loved ones wither away—

It's over. Winter is finally over.

Other voices break out into laughing and song. I stare at my hands, at the sign of a different season being washed from my skin. Alec's blood drips away, spotting the melting snow, crimson fading into the faintest blush and then turning crystal clear.

My hands are clean, but my heart remains wedged under a suffocating weight.

Dovan draws me to his side as we stand, our feet finding the true ground that had been buried under snow for a decade. He kisses my head, his lips whispering truth against my temple. "Sometimes the right thing is the heaviest burden of all, but you don't have to carry it alone."

The knot in my throat tightens. One of the monsters in my life might be gone, but the other isn't. There are choices coming I'm not yet ready to face. Choices that could tear me and Dovan apart because of who we are. He's a guider without rank, and I'm the daughter of the old king. *I don't care.* I don't think he does either, but my father will.

I push those thoughts aside before they rob the joy from this moment.

Winter's shimmering white blanket breaks apart, revealing rich, velvet-brown earth. The thawing soil hums with the same thrumming pulse inside Dovan's chest. Spring echoes his determined heartbeat in powerful waves, spreading in all directions and retaking its kingdom. Everything bursts into life.

This is the future Dovan would have died for. Now, he lives to see it with me.

The long grasses billowing up from the earth, the orchard trees shaking their branches, unfurling new leaves from once frozen buds, and the wildflowers pushing their faces up from the dirt and turning toward the sun. One bows before us. Its golden center and white petals glistening with tiny drops of misting rain as it offers a taste of the sweetness to come. *A sugar daisy.*

Dovan picks it and tucks the bloom behind my ear. A shadow of grief over the loss of his mother, who loved these humble flowers, dims the light in his eyes. *He misses her.* His pain finds an echo in my heart, but what we've lost doesn't break us. Not when we're surrounded by life stretching itself awake after a decade of slumber.

We did it. We changed the season.

We *survived* changing the season.

I curl my fingers into his tunic, my chin tilting upward as I pull him closer, and he leans down to meet me halfway. Our third kiss. It's different from the others, missing the desperation and the impatience and the frustration. Those kisses said goodbye. This kiss says hello. A tender and relieved hello that's just happy to exist.

Someone blows a guider's horn, startling us apart, and we laugh. We're flushed and breathless and...whole. That's what this feeling is. Wholeness. Even in the wake of tragedy and an exhausting triumph, I spy a future filled with, yes, more kisses, but also, all the normal things I never thought we'd be able to share, and that gives me hope.

But the celebration has fallen silent as Dovan and I turn toward the gate. My muscles tense as a tall, imposing figure shoves through the crowd. Riffen's crown of flowers and thorns rests on his graying head, and dread knots my stomach.

The old king—*my father is here.*

I rub my arms as Dovan pulls me against his side, and a shard of hope breaks off in my chest, reopening old wounds. *What will he say? Will he understand? Will he accept who I've become?*

My father pays no attention to the miracle of spring's return, and he barely glances my way before falling next to Alec's body. Our people have recovered from the shock of his appearance and begin dancing again, rejoicing in the change in their fortunes, but my father throws back his head and cries. A keening wail like the ones I screamed after Red Death's kills.

The old king weeps as if his world has ended, cradling my brother against his chest. He never looks at me, never beckons me near, never calls my name the way he moans Alec's.

Like I don't even exist.

My eyes flood with tears as he decides my pain isn't worth his attention. I gasp and curl into myself, shivering as my lungs struggle against this suffocating sorrow, but I'm the only one shivering in a world that's warm once again. Dovan's arms circle my waist, providing support as my knees wobble, but his tender gesture deepens the ache in my heart.

Because it shouldn't be Dovan who's holding me up.

It should be my father.

If my father loved me.

I'm left behind as the palace guard helps my father carry Alec into the city. Separating me and my brother, as he always did.

I face Dovan's chest, fighting tears that should have no place here when everyone else is celebrating. *They're all coming to life while I'm dying on the inside.*

Dovan lifts my head, his pine-green irises contrasting with the copper tone of his skin and the ebony of his wavy hair. But it's not the handsome lines of his face thawing the chill from my wounded heart. It's the understanding in his eyes, the gentle truth passed from one orphan to another. "I'm not going anywhere."

A sob chokes my throat. There's too much sorrow breaking free, too much pain I've locked away for too many years. It won't be contained. *I don't want to be here.* Where everyone can see me fall apart. My heart longs for safety, for seclusion, for time to grieve.

I whisper the only thing that makes sense in this broken new world where I don't yet know my place. Except for one.

I belong with him.

In a house with too few rooms and too many orphans. A refuge where children tell silly stories and nobody crushes their dreams, where a stern-faced granny watches over them all, and where a good man lays his head, if he ever sleeps.

"Dovan, take us home."

Without hesitation, he bends down to hook an arm under my legs. My head settles on the slope of his shoulder as he lifts me into his arms. We're both exhausted, and yet he lends me his strength once more. I anchor myself to his heart's steady rhythm, and a tiny smile curls my lips, a stubborn star of hope shining through the dark sting of my father's abandonment.

Dovan's heart is *still* beating.

The first heart to outlive the song of a banshee.

AFTER THE SONG

DOVAN

44

Endings are like doorways.

I stand before mine, the rough wood faded from the sun and warped by the spring moisture. The boards' snug fit keep out most weather, but the storm I bring with me—the leather of my gloves creak as my hands shake, fisted at my sides. Years of training, years of survival and being the one who had to be strong, prevent me from entering my house while my heart is so raw. *They can't see you like this.*

Angry. Sad. And a little lost.

I tug off my gloves, needing to feel the air and find a spark of the season I once carried. Spring, more than any other human, knows me best, but my purpose as an ember is over. The connection gone. I'm glad spring is free, but I miss the season's companionship.

Instead of the warm brush of a spring breeze, the bitter memory of the pre-dawn hearing chafes my skin with cold. The guider council determined my fate while the sky was still black.

Their decision was just. I killed two of my own without an investigation or a trial. My gaze falls to the white bear embroidered across my chest. They decided not to separate me from the symbol that has embodied so much of my life, but my bear will never wear stripes like my father's.

I have lost the right to advance.

For three months, I've continued to serve my city and help people rebuild what the long winter left broken, all while not knowing my punishment. *They spared my life.* A gift of mercy for many years of honorable service and of gratitude for harboring the ember of spring. I'm still who I wanted to be, but nothing *more*.

"Do you regret the severity of your actions?" A member of the council asked before announcing their decision.

I've faced wolves and hunger and grief so heavy my soul should have shattered, and yet that question was more dangerous. The prickling awareness of their stern gazes, some blatant in their disapproval, others as unreadable as stone, failed to sway me.

If they were looking for a diplomatic response, or a twisting of the truth to make my actions seem heroic, they would remain disappointed. Could I have arranged my words in a way that put what I did in a better light? Yes. But I'd live or die on those words. My reputation fused to who I chose to be in that moment.

I study my calloused palms, thick and meaty from a better diet, but still scarred. There are kills I regret and kills I don't. And so, I gave the guider council the truth.

I did what I had to and I'd do it again.

To protect my people and keep my city from falling apart, I'd kill without hesitation. I'd serve until I collapsed. I'd give my blood until my veins were empty. Because I *am* a guider. Whether they allowed me to continue as one or not, my purpose will always be the same, but today's burden is heavier because of their judgement.

I sigh and scrape the mud off my boots on the flat rocks placed to the side of the door. One of the smaller stones puffs up, emitting a tiny, indignant screech. I jerk my boot aside and reveal a rain frog who gives me his grumpiest glare. *I could have stepped on him.* To the horror of our newest orphan. Zetta is ten and believes the perturbed frog is a cursed prince who can be saved by a maiden's kiss. Gran and I have tried twice to relocate the little thing, only for him to show up the next evening to Zetta's great delight.

"See! It's destiny!"

Now I'm more worried the blasted frog will go missing and break Zetta's heart. *She's known enough pain.* The bruises from her uncle have long since faded, but sometimes I catch her rubbing her arm where his hands left their mark. *If it wasn't for Wrenna*—if she hadn't recognized Zetta from her time as a banshee and told me of the abuse the girl was suffering, she'd still be stuck in that bastard's house.

With my boot, I nudge the frog away from the mud-scraping stones so someone else doesn't accidentally squash him, earning another sharp squeak. Having had enough of my hospitality, the frog buries himself, glaring at me the whole time.

What's done is done. I let those words sink deep. A saying that might as well be part of the guider oath. We don't believe in being stuck. Taking rest is encouraged, but wallowing in the shadows of the past? Wishing for other things and letting their absence turn your heart bitter? I inhale the crisp, cookfire scented air, and loosen the death grip I held on the future where I advanced to fill my father's boots.

Life is full of denials. I was denied the homeland of my birth, I was denied a full life with my blood family, I was denied achieving even more as a guider, but there are still good things.

I will see the good things.

A *splash* and a squeal of delight pulls me from my inner battle. When spring left my soul, the city of Riffen felt the cleansing wash of warm rains. Rains that have become an almost bi-weekly occurrence. There are puddles everywhere, some as wide as an entire street, and the children practice a new daily tradition.

Puddle dancing.

I glance behind me and watch a trio of children hop from puddle to puddle, splashing each other and speckling their clothes with mud. Nothing but pure joy brightening their rosy faces as the street echoes with their laughter. *This is what I was willing to die for.* To hear children come alive, confident in knowing they now have a chance. A real chance to live. No longer burdened by the threats of starvation or an endless winter. No longer trapped in death's shadow.

We are free.

A couple of adults pause on their way to the lower market to join in and make a game of who can cause the biggest splash. My lips twitch, starting to smile, when an old woman scrubbing clothes by the well belts out a wordless tune.

Chills scratch at my skin, waking a bone-deep longing for a different voice. The banshee who isn't a banshee anymore. *Wrenna hasn't sung anything since spring came.* Yes, we are free, but winning our freedom has left plenty of scars. My fingers itch for my sword, to deal out justice by its edge because I know why.

Why she's shielded herself behind a wall of silence.

Music was broken out of Wrenna's soul by her bastard of a father, by her murdering brother, and by the cost of their curse. She has taken her life back from them, but not everything they stole from her. *Not her music.* Not her future.

Not yet.

Like me, she was strong enough to do what had to be done. *She killed to break the cycle.* An action with a high cost she's still paying. Nights shattered by her screams. Days where grief hung about her like a shroud. Moments where I caught her wincing at any melody she heard. *I want more for her.* For us. If she feels the same as I do. But she's not ready. She's not ready to face the legacy her twisted family left her. Still, I see it growing in her hazel eyes, the hope of moving forward embodied by a single question.

What now?

The answer won't come easy. *It's a doorway.* One she must choose to open and walk through.

I face mine again, shoulders heavy. I tuck the loss of a full career as a guider away, letting the happiness of the children behind me propel me home. Opening the door, I step into a future that may not be everything I hoped for, but there are plenty of other hopes waiting to bloom.

Daylight reaches gilded fingers around me to bounce off the bright colors streaked and swirled along the walls. The sunflower yellows, the rose reds, the iris purples and primrose blues, these are a few of my good things. The burden I carry lightens, the anger cools, and the sense of loss gives way to being found.

I have come home. A gift I treasure because not everyone has. This house has lost many members over the years. *I thought it would lose me.* Yet here I am, a survivor of wolves, winter, and a banshee's song.

I touch the golden handprint visible amongst the colorful splatter and experience a giddy rush of raw joy. A deep, riotous laugh builds in my throat.

I'd never thought I'd see Sanaa's art displayed because of its dangers until one of the boys threw a bucket of sunflower dye at her. Once her hand touched the wall, smearing the color, everyone started laughing. It took some experimenting to be sure, but so long as she only swipes colors across a surface, never pursuing details or shapes, her art is safe. Capturing the purity of emotion without predicting anyone's future or exposing dangerous secrets.

I hang my lighter cloak on an empty peg and follow the narrow hall, picking up on a sour scent. The kitchen is silent, lacking our normal morning chaos. A dozen children, aged from six to Sanaa's sixteen, should be bustling about while Gran maintains order from the stove with her wooden spoon and a sharp look guaranteed to snuff out any sparks of mischief. *Something's wrong.* The aroma of salty herbs rising in swirls of steam from the large pot on the stove provides the next clue.

A wet slap draws me through the too-quiet kitchen toward the strip of hallway leading to the stairs on my left, a washroom across from me, and the back door. Pieces of split wood litter the space as the smell of sickness sharpens. Gran kneels on the scuffed wooden floor, scrubbing away the source of the sour scent.

I drop to my knee, reaching for the rag. "Let me."

Gran straightens. The wrinkles around her eyes and mouth curve down from what must have been an eventful morning. "It be clean enough." She slings the cloth into the bucket with another splash before lifting her crutch and using it to stand.

I rise as well. "How many are sick?"

"Six, seven," she shakes her head. "Ivan be too much like ye. Convinced himself to bring in the wood. His stomach be rebellin' now." Her gaze fixes on the stairs as her voice goes oddly soft. "That girl carried him up. She be carin' for them."

That girl. Even after three months of living with us, Gran has yet to call Wrenna by her name. "She'd love you with her whole heart if you'd let her, Gran. That's who she is."

A nod covers a flicker of something deeper in Gran's eyes. "She be a good soul." Gran gives me a knowing look before I can ask the question we've danced around for weeks. "But this house be not where she belongs."

"Then help her." The words slip out anyway, and Gran rocks

back on her heel, chin rising. A silent declaration that *this discussion be over.*

"Ye must be hungry." She limps past me, grabbing a fry pan from the pantry shelf and setting it down hard on the stove. The grating scrape of iron makes me wince as her knuckles whiten from her clenched grip on the pan.

"What of yer hearin'?" Gran shifts the conversation to me.

I bite into the sigh that escapes, folding my arms in front of me. "My rank will never change. It's...it's not as harsh of a judgement—"

"*Bastards.*"

As sharp-tongued as my Gran can be, she rarely swears. I'm torn between amusement or caution.

She turns around and wobbles a crutched step closer. Her bony fingers grasp the sides of my face as a fresh wave of sorrow blurs her image. "The guiders never did deserve ye, me stout bear cub."

She knows. She knows how deeply this hurts, no matter how untouched I may behave. Her maternal instinct has stripped me bare before her probing gaze. I allow the vulnerability to last for one sagging breath, and then I straighten, breaking the contact between our skin as the soldier in me takes over. "They did nothing wrong. I did. I accept—"

"They be hurting ye. Nothin' can be more wrong."

My eyebrows rise a little. "I killed two guiders, Gran."

"*Traitors,*" she corrects and smooths my tunic, her hands pausing above the white bear her son wore before me. "Yer council be fools for not givin' ye the reward ye deserve for rootin' out filth."

"They were just trying to survive. Like any of us."

"Not like ye." Gran thumps my chest with her palm. "Ye'd choose a starvin' death before lettin' another die of hunger first."

Her thumb runs over the bear's head above my heart. "Yer good, Dovan. Always be so good. Like me son were."

I press my hand over hers as her gaze grows distant, sorting through memories of the boy she raised into the man who saved me. "I miss him too, Gran."

"He'd 'ave done the same as ye." Tears gleam in her eyes. "Ye deserve more. From them ol' fools," she motions to the stairs, glaring, "and from that girl. How long she goin' a keep ye waitin'?"

My chin falls as I swallow another sigh. "I haven't told her everything yet."

"Why ever not?"

"She doesn't need my secret, Gran," I look her directly in the eye. "She needs yours."

Gran returns to the stove, snatching up the wooden spoon to stir the soup. "I know nothin' of what ye mean."

"Don't you?" My question comes out with the bite of a statement.

Gran's shoulders twitch as she leans harder on her crutch, stirring with vigor.

"You don't have to tell me how you knew details about the banshee curse no one has ever recorded, but Wrenna," I hesitate, trying to pick the right words. "She needs what only you can offer."

"And what. Be that?"

I lean in and kiss her temple as she frowns. "That even banshees deserve to have a normal life."

She snorts an uncomfortable laugh but pats my cheek. With a few terse orders, she sends me to the cellar to retrieve some potatoes, peppers, and herbs, and we settle into the familiar rhythm of making breakfast together.

We are alike in so many ways, but what we share the most is our desire to help others. Gran's approach may be rougher than mine, like a well-intentioned slap to the face, but sometimes that's what we need.

Someone to tell us to wake up and live.

Someone to beckon from the other side of the door.

Someone who's taken the same step before us.

And then I'll tell Wrenna everything. All the things I've kept tucked away. Moving forward together is a choice I hope she'll make, but it will be her choice.

WRENNA

45

THE OLD ONES say true happiness is found in being able to give. There was a time in my life when I experienced more unhappiness by that definition than anything else. I had so much to give. I wanted to be among my people, helping them, but no one at court shared my desire.

When the first wave of refugees from the Abrykarran Season Wars started arriving, I snuck out to one of the shelters with Alec's help. I gathered donations, cooked soup, sponged fevered heads, and sang songs to the orphans. Serving them freed my soul. But my father put a stop to it within a few weeks. He gave new orders to the palace guards and turned the palace into my prison, cutting me off from my people. Alec tried to cheer me up by bringing updates on how the refugees were faring, but it wasn't enough.

The few times they'd let me leave, guards surrounded me in a solid wall of armor and threatening looks. Nobody approached me because I was the daughter of the man they feared most. In the end, it didn't matter if I told them I was different. They feared the crown I would wear and the Ryvelt blood in my veins.

A clammy hand tugs at my sleeve. "What happened to the banshee?"

I blink away the haze of my thoughts and refocus on the plain walls of cracking plaster and simple pallet beds. Sunshine mixes with dust as it falls through the window to my left. The warm air smells of sickness and briny soup, and if I focus hard enough, I can still feel it. The buzzing pulse of spring's magic, a rhythm that will always match Dovan's heartbeat.

Even after three months, the power of his spring continues to exceed all records. We've reaped four harvests and planted a fifth, but none of the orphans watching me care about that. They'd rather be outside than stuck inside with fevers and stomach aches.

The boy named Ivan on the pallet I kneel next to has brown eyes. The same rich shade as my brother's, but I stuff the twinge of sorrow the color triggers behind the wall in my heart. "You promised to finish the story."

Zetta echoes Ivan's statement with a dramatic sigh as she flops onto her back. She's our newest rescue and has pale curls and freckled skin and irises as blue as the sky. She was the girl who angered her uncle by dropping a bag of potatoes because I bumped into her. *She couldn't see me.* I was still a banshee, and she wouldn't have joined our family if I hadn't run into her two months ago. *One good thing,* I tell myself, but my body tenses up as I try to apply one of Dovan's tricks—the gathering of good things.

It shouldn't be this hard to find peace. But who I was is an open wound that throbs anytime I'm reminded of my past.

"I say she lived," Zetta beams, her dimples showing. "She lived and met a handsome prince and kissed him madly."

A twinge of a grin tempts my lips, but I hold it back.

"What kind of ending is that?" Ivan moans, though not from an irritated stomach. "There's more to life than kissing." He rolls his eyes. "Girls always want mushy endings."

"What's better than kissing?" Zetta's fair skin flushes pink.

"Like you'd know. You're ten."

"I'm almost eleven. And I *will* know. If you ever turn into a prince." She bats her eyelashes at him. This time my smile escapes and I glance away to hide it.

"I'm going to be a guider, not a prince." Ivan declares, loud enough to cause the other three children to stir in their sleep. He grips his stomach but keeps going. "I think the banshee deserves more than a kissing ending. I think she'd fight, stopping those who'd harm—" he goes suddenly pale, and I snatch the large bowl from the floor and put it in his lap.

The sour sting of bile assaults my nose as he vomits the tiny amount of soup I'd spooned into him for breakfast. Some of it splatters along my sleeve and skirt, but I don't mind. Being with these children and serving them brings me peace.

I belong here. With them, in this old house we call home. There are fewer orphans living here now. Dovan and his Gran have been searching for couples who lost their children during winter to take them in. *I hope some of them will stay with us.*

I brush a lock of brown hair from Ivan's tan cheek as I ease him back onto his pallet. "Lie still." As I readjust the blanket around his gangly eleven-year-old frame, I spot the repaired guider's tunic half tucked under his pillow. It belonged to the guider who raised Dovan. *So this is the boy Dovan wanted to have his father's tunic.*

Dovan had gone to retrieve it from a chest during that night we met when I left him to challenge Red Death about the rules of my curse. A whirl of unpleasant memories closes in on me, but I employ another tactic, grasping at the one that warms my heart.

He kissed me. Not on the lips, but that was the first time he showed what he was feeling.

Ivan moans, breaking me from the memory. "But it's spring."

A complaint the children repeat every few breaths as if fevers only belong to winter. *It must feel like a curse to them.* Trapped in this room while they hear the vibrant bustle of life just outside the window, knowing they're supposed to be out there. Running in the sun and laughing and causing mischief in the markets. *They will run.* They will laugh and get into trouble.

Because this sickness isn't a curse. It won't last more than another day.

I cover the bowl to soften the acidic scent and carry it to the desk converted into a supply stand. Setting the bowl aside, I lift the pitcher. Fresh water splashes into a shallow basin, and I dip a cloth into the water, wringing it almost dry. I push the window open further before I return to Ivan. Warm air brushes my skin, reminding me of Dovan, and my heart quickens a beat. *I miss it.* The way our opposing seasons announced our presence to each other.

Since the season changed, we've barely touched. Keeping most of our conversations to the care of those in this house and the rebuilding of our city. But he was there in the days and weeks after Alec's death when the nightmares came and the grief left me hollow. Always giving but never asking anything in return. *He knew I needed time.* It's beginning to feel like too much time has passed, building a new barrier I don't know how to bring down.

I want more. More than his cautious support. *But how do I tell him?*

I'm ready. Two simple words chained to the bottom of my heart.

The street below catches my eye with a flash of vibrant colors. The sky-blue dresses and ocean teal capes, the cherry red tunics and salmon pink skirts, the purple alley shadows as dark as night and the lavender cobblestones as pale as the silvery blush of a new moon. The golds and coppers of rings and the dark browns of soft boots. All draped around a crush of people, whose colors of skin are just as varied. They come and go with cheery faces. Surrounded by the yeasty comfort of baking bread and the sugary perfume of flowers sticking out of window boxes and buttonholes in capes or ribbons in braided hair. *I'll never tire of seeing them like this.* My city, my people, come to life.

"Do you see her out there?" Ivan asks, his voice hoarser than it was.

I don't know why I started telling them a story about a banshee, watching their little faces get caught up in a tale I actually lived. With a few amendments. There are parts I couldn't tell a child. *It's easier to fictionalize the truth.* To transform our grief, our hopes, into stories. Stories are easier to move on from than the tough seasons of life.

"Is she with her prince?" Zetta asks, wistful yearning brightening her face.

I leave the window and return to Ivan, dabbing at his fever flushed cheeks with the damp cloth. "I...don't know."

"But it's *your* story."

I press a gentle kiss to Ivan's forehead. "Get some sleep. Maybe I'll know the ending when you wake up."

"Will you sing me to sleep?" Ivan's question isn't meant for me, but it slices my heart as Zetta starts to hum.

They used to ask me to sing. They stopped because I kept saying no. *I couldn't.* Every time a melody tickles my throat—*I see them.* All of my brother's victims, the souls he traded for mine. Their pleading faces, their wailing voices, their raging curses—all because I had appeared.

A banshee come to sing them to their death.

That's not who you are now. Accepting my past hasn't made

moving on any easier. It's why the story I told the children has no ending. I'm not living my ending. Not yet.

Dovan is standing in the doorway when I turn around. His skin shines a deeper copper from working under the spring sun, and his irises are a darker green since spring's magic has left his soul. The burgundy guider's tunic he wears fits him instead of hanging loose and stretches tight across his shoulders and chest. He's not skipping meals anymore, which means there's—*more of him to hug.* If we were hugging. Even with the distance he's allowed between us, one thing hasn't changed. He can still touch my soul with a single look.

A look that says, *I see how much you're hurting.*

I fuss with my sleeves, nervous and fighting tears as I break our stare. The stains of vomit stand out on the pale green of my simple dress and apron. My wavy hair hangs unbound to my waist, and my posture suffers from weariness. *I must look terrible.* And smell worse. But I'd give a thousand rose-scented baths and all the fine gowns in the palace to stay where I am. With a handful of ill orphans who think a banshee deserves a happy ending.

"I came to see if you needed anything before I go." Once again, Dovan avoids the question hanging between us. *You shouldn't be annoyed with him.* It takes two people to talk.

I ease toward him, lowering my voice as Zetta's humming trails off into a snore, "I have everything I need."

There's a tiny slip to his half-smile. "Then I'll see you at dinner."

My soul aches over how normal this is. Seeing him in the mornings, sharing a meal with him and the family who has adopted us both in the evenings. *We have so much time.* When we once had a single day.

Dovan starts toward the stairs and I touch his arm. He stops, waiting for me. *He's always waiting.* I should give him something. A sign of what I feel or an explanation for what I can't yet do. Let go or hold on. Put an end to this middle ground between who we were and who we might yet be. But the words and the emotions tangle in my throat, a song without the structure of measure lines, collapsing around itself before it's even begun.

"I...I need your help."

His eyes glint with a dangerous hope that also sparks in mine, but I'm not ready to let that hope become a fire.

I glance at the children. "I want to plan a surprise for them when they're better. Something outside. Somewhere nobody has gone since winter fell."

"The Pinewood isn't too far," he rubs his chin, his gaze thoughtful. "We'd need a wagon and a picnic lunch."

"Sounds perfect." My hand slips down his arm to his fingers. I hold on to them, trying to make this moment last a little longer.

Dovan studies my face, searching for the parts of me I don't share with anyone else. My lips tremble as whatever he sees softens his expression further. *Does he guess the truth?* That I am terrified of losing this, of losing him because I can't find the courage to move forward? I hold my tongue, dropping my gaze to his chest.

"It's okay," he whispers, his fingers weaving through mine. "You're going to be okay, Enna. And as I've told you before, I'm not going anywhere."

My breath leaves me in a stilted gasp as tears form along my eyelids, and I barely manage to keep from crumbling into his arms at the tenderness of his words. I squeeze his fingers, nodding my silent thanks.

His gentle smile feels like a hug for my soul, embracing me. All of me.

He leans forward just enough to unsettle my heart. A good kind of unsettled, filled with memories of how passionate he was when he kissed me goodbye, as Zetta would put it—quite madly. *Like there was no tomorrow.* Now, he holds back because we have more tomorrows than we could have ever hoped for, and he's protecting them all.

He kisses my forehead, his lips lingering against my skin. A timid wave of heat radiates from him, sweeping down my arms in a familiar embrace. It's a promise still unspoken, but then he lets go. He leaves, and the air cools in his absence.

I retrieve the sick bowl to take it downstairs for washing, only to find Dovan paused halfway down, his smirk flashing in the shadowed stairwell. "I almost forgot. Gran wants to speak with you."

A chill needles my arms. His Gran and I have mostly avoided each other. "When?"

"About an hour ago."

"Why didn't you tell me sooner?"

He shrugs. "You were busy doing important things. She understands."

About as well as my father might. If I appeared before him looking half-dead and stinking of vomit. "Dovan Alstad—" I chase him down the stairs, but my foot misses a step. The bowl flies from my hands as Dovan's quick reflexes help him both dodge the flying sick and grab my waist to save me from sharing the bowl's shattered fate.

"You all right?" He asks, his hands resting against my sides.

But he shouldn't be asking about me. We're not alone. *Please don't be*—All of Ivan's sick splattered across Dovan's Gran. From her black skirt, to her periwinkle blouse, to her wooden crutch, to the sour frown that only cracks with delight for Dovan.

He abandons me with an *everything will be fine* look, leaving me with the woman who knows what I was. She struck me for it. *She had every right to.* As a banshee, I brought death to her grandson.

I brace myself for a tongue lashing.

She blinks, her lined mouth twitching for a moment before

releasing the last sound I expected to hear. A rasping chuckle. A glimpse of warmth instead of icy disdain.

She waves off my apologies before I can even make them.

"Tea be waitn'." She beckons me down the hall to her left. Her crutch thumping on the wood as she moves. "But first, I be thinkin' baths be needed."

WRENNA

46

DOVAN'S GRAN lets me wash up first in the tiny washroom off the kitchen. A little water and soap, a clean black skirt and an emerald blouse, and my spirits revive, which is apparently great for feeding my nerves. My hands won't stop shaking. *If she's decided there's no room in her house for a banshee, she wouldn't invite you to tea.*

Would she?

The tea will be cold by the time we get to it. I set the kettle on the stove and stoke the fire, trying to be useful, before I check on the children again. *Still sleeping.* Their faces peaceful, eyelids fluttering as they dream. I leave empty bowls and glasses of water by each of them. Their skin is dry and cool, which means they'll soon be up and wreaking havoc through the house with the others. Until the guiders sort out the schools.

There's been no word. From the old king, from my—*father.* I shiver at the familial title as my stomach rolls. For the first few weeks after spring's return, the city seemed to hold its breath, waiting for the king to reassert his iron-fisted control, but he never did. Never even tried. Finally, a month after Alec's death, Dovan came to me with a message from my father.

"He wants to see you."

And as I looked up into Dovan's face, at the kindness and the understanding and the sorrow written there, I couldn't even form a response. My cheeks heat with shame at the memory, but Dovan didn't call me a coward that day, or the next week, or the months that followed as I hid here. He accepted my unspoken *no* without judgement and made sure my father couldn't violate my choice. *But I think Dovan suspects.* This wound inside me is a tear that won't heal until I face the monster who remains.

The washroom door is still closed when I return to the kitchen. It's a slanted, rectangular room with scuffed walls and broken tile floors and racks of drying herbs hanging from the ceiling. A skylight frames a perfect glimpse of blue sky and bathes the room in light. The table remains shoved against the wall opposite the stove until dinner, its bench and stools tucked under its scarred boards. A cracked vase holds a handful of white and gold sugar daisies, and I smile at them as they remind me of Dovan.

I move to the cupboard and take two mismatched mugs down when I spot something poking out of the shadows. I put the mugs on the table and reach back into the cupboard. A soft crinkling sound fills the air as I wiggle it closer, revealing yellowed parchment tied in a roll with a gray ribbon.

I rush to the stool and sit down, pressing the parchment flat against the table. Faded and moisture blurred ink flows through a series of repeating notes. They grip my heart, they churn my soul, they sting my eyes because—*I know them.* The turn of sorrow in their edges and the futile slump of defeat in their decrescendos rise into a wail. A cry for a victim that cannot be saved.

A banshee's song.

My tears stamp the paper with fresh sorrow as the washroom's door creaks open and Dovan's Gran crutches into the kitchen. For once, her slumped posture and stern frown make her look far more weary than cross, and the threads of time sewn into her skin point to an impossible revelation.

"I see ye be findin' it." She uses a thick cloth to grab the kettle as steam curls from the spout.

"How can you have this?" I choke on my next words, fighting through a flood of emotions. "This is a banshee's song. This is the voice of someone like me."

"It may be." She slips a thin cloth pouch of dried leaves and spices into the kettle.

"There's only one way you could have this." *If you were a banshee.* But no matter how badly I want to shout the accusation, it stays locked behind my teeth. *She knew how Dovan could save himself. She knew my curse was a trade.* Facts never revealed in any of the old stories.

"Ye be half right." She sits beside me, leaning her crutch on the table as her gnarled fingers trace the notes. "It be banshee music, but it be not mine."

I hang my head and blink away my foolish hope. *She's nothing like me.*

"Me gran was like ye be now." Cinnamon tickles my nose as she pours our tea. "A soul of two lives, belongin' ta none because movin' on be a frightenin' thing when ye've seen so much death and wrong."

I stare at the liquid inside my mug until its rich brown reminds me of Alec's eyes. A color that holds nothing but horror for me. I flinch as his dagger replaces the mug in my hands. Blood gushes over my skin. Metal scraping against bone. The air choking on a coppery scent. *Fresh death.* My heart races as I try to hold still. *It's not real. It's not—*

But it *was* real. So real I can't stop reliving the moment my brother died.

I killed him. I had to, but the burden I carry isn't growing any lighter.

The stench of salt and copper overwhelms me as I fling myself backwards from the blood spilling from my hands. The stool clatters to the ground a second before the mug shatters. Droplets of hot tea sting my skin, and with one blink, the blood is gone. *It was never here.* A shudder of weary relief wracks my slumped frame, but the daymare isn't over yet.

I'm backed against a wall. Nowhere to go but down, and so I sink into the swelling tide of memories. *So many faces.* So much anguish. Patches of hot and cold break out across my skin as I try to slow my breathing. A fuzzy figure reaches for me through the darkness of my nightmares, but I'm too tired to stand.

"I thought they'd be gone." Curling my knees into my chest, I bury my face in my arms. "I thought it was over."

A heavy blanket of despair tries to suffocate my heart, whispering a familiar fear. *It will never be over.* Desperate for hope, I remember how I got here. I ended a decade long curse, I killed my brother to destroy the season tree, and I helped change the season. I've fought the impossible and won. *But this?* It's worse than normal grief. *I don't know how to fight it.* Or if it can be defeated. *It doesn't play fair.* And there are no rules to protect me.

"Come child." Gran takes hold of my arms and pulls me to my feet.

Unable to stand the distance between us, I dart forward. I cling to her bony body and pretend that I am miles away. Here in her stiff embrace, my nightmares are nothing more than bad dreams. But the ache in my chest refuses to let me hide.

What I lived through isn't over.

"I wish I could forget everything," I mutter.

Gran strokes my hair. "That be untrue."

I bite my lip instead of challenging her. There are things I don't want to forget. Dovan's lopsided grin and all the truths he spoke into me. Alec's biting sarcasm and dramatic flair. *The music we wrote together. The future we dreamed of as children.*

I withdraw from her embrace, swiping at my wet cheeks. "Why must pain and joy always go together?"

"That be life, me girl," Gran guides me to the table, placing her own mug of tea in my trembling hands. "There be a balance to it. Ye'll see in time."

"It doesn't feel very balanced to me," I say as I sit.

"Ye have years ahead. Better years."

I tense, vision blurring. *She's right.* My future will be different now that I'm free of my curse and my monstrous family. But for most of my life, the future has been a threat and I'm—

"I'm afraid." It feels dangerous to admit that out loud, like I'm invoking a new curse, but I keep going. "I'm afraid of what comes next. I'm afraid of what could go wrong. I'm afraid I'll never find my way through the grief, and the pain, and the damage of what was done to me." Gran's wrinkled hands hold me steady as I sniff hard, all my secrets laid bare before her. "What do I do?"

"Drink yer tea."

"That's it?" I search her face. "That's your advice?"

"Fear be no shelter from what comes," she adds. "Nor be it a sage prophet." She shifts her weight, relying on her crutch. "It be simple, me girl. Life hurts. And there be nothin' we can do 'bout that. But then, life also thrives. So drink yer tea. Smell the flowers. Kiss me grandson, before he dies from pinin' over ye."

Heat creeps up my neck and spreads across my face. *I didn't think she wanted Dovan to be with me.*

"There be no tamin' life." Her stern expression softens with a kindred sorrow as she rubs the wedding band on her finger. "The future holds good and bad for us all, but—" she stamps her crutch on the tile and looks me in the eye, "—life be ours ta live."

I focus on my mug instead of her waiting, confident expression which reminds me of Dovan, but my mind is full of ghosts.

Countless horrors chill my skin and complicate her answer. *It's not that easy.* Not when the most common gift life has brought me is pain. Cinnamon stings my tongue as I take a sip, and a gentle, spicy heat spreads through my chest.

"Yer hair be the wildest thing."

I laugh at the absurd but necessary change in topic and run my fingers through the damp coils, snagging on endless tangles. "It's like my father's." I grimace and rub my chest where the sharp ache of the curse's pain used to be. *He hasn't held a funeral for Alec.* If he did, would he even invite me?

Gran's dark eyes glimmer with unspoken understanding. She moves behind me. Her fingers lift my hair, sifting through tangles and separating it into three strands. The familiar tug on my scalp as she begins braiding brings a lump to my throat. My mother braided my hair when I was a child until she died. Yet another tragedy looped around my soul and making it hard to breathe.

"Listen to me," Gran tilts my head downward as she braids. "There be nothing ye can do about what's past. It be what it be. A painful place. A broken place. Leaks into the present somethin' fierce." She leans around me to catch my gaze. "But it be not where we live."

The knot in my throat makes speaking difficult, but I manage two words. "I'm trying."

"I know ye be."

"I don't." I suck in a breath. "I don't know..."

"How ta make peace?"

I tug at my sleeve, torn between wanting this conversation to end and needing it to continue. "My brother, for all his evil—"

"Gave ye a gift," she interrupts, draping the braid tied with the gray ribbon from the old paper over my shoulder before hobbling toward the stool next to mine. She sits with me but doesn't speak. She knows it's my turn.

I glance at the song of another banshee and then at her.

Dovan's Gran is living proof a banshee can live beyond their curse. Maybe even thrive. "How did your grandmother make peace? How did she move forward?"

Gran's wrinkles deepen with her sad smile. "Unfinished business be the ruin of the soul."

A flutter of nerves has me toying with my braid.

"There be people ye need ta see, things that need speakin'. Until ye do, the past will be stayin' a wound and the future nothin' but a dream."

"My brother's dead," I whisper, torn between the relief that he's gone and the ache of missing who he was before his first kill.

"Yer father be livin'." She rises from the table as if everything is settled. "But livin' or dead be not what matters. What matters is ye get all that poisonous hurt out." She pats my shoulder. "Face it. Then let it be."

I shrug away from her touch. "You don't know what it's like."

"That may be true, but I do know this. The future be a big thing, me girl. Impossible to embrace it when yer arms be full of the past."

WRENNA

47

THE FOOT TRAFFIC thins by midday, giving way to carts drawn by teams of men. Fresh cut lumber or quarried stone fills most of them. Certain sections of the city fared worse than others during winter, but most of the rickety towers of shack houses have been torn down and replaced by proper housing with roofs that won't leak and walls that keep out the weather.

I pause at the mouth of the gate opening over the winding ramp to the lower level. The air is clear of wood smoke and storms. The pale stone of the buildings, spotted with dark roofs, bows before an ocean of green. Where once there had only been snow, miles of grasslands, of tilled fields, of orchards sprinkled with bursts of red, orange, and pink now stand. Our hope bearing fruit.

I tuck the basket closer to my side as a dozen guiders jog by. Several crack their stern expressions to smile at me, a few tap their chests with their fists, but most continue singing. A chant of duty, a melody of honor, as they climb toward the heart of Riffen.

We run, run to their call.
We fight, fight for their lives.
We stand, stand for them all.
We give, give so they thrive.

I stare after them for a moment, my throat thick with an old desire, my heart echoing their words, but I can't join them. I can't sing their song.

My voice no longer summons death, but it wakes my nightmares.

I lengthen my stride to put more distance between me and the guiders, then hurry down the cobblestone road between rows of stone houses. The basket grows heavier with each step as I try to keep up with all the *hellos* and *good days* being called after me.

My people see me.

Waving at me from windows and doorways, from benches on porches or as they pass me on the street. A gift they take for granted, but it means everything to me. Three months ago, I was nothing more than a shadow. A ghost. A wraith. Now I exist in their world.

I return their greetings, stumbling when I see it. The question written across their faces. The one Dovan and I keep avoiding.

Shouldn't you be somewhere else?

As the daughter of the old king, I am the heir to Riffen's throne. A princess who could be queen. *I have no desire to be locked inside the palace.* To be pulled backwards by my father's unbending will. *You're stronger than you were.* Yes, I am, but that doesn't mean I'm strong enough to face him and—stay me.

We're happy, aren't we? It's spring and we have food, and yet in their eyes and in my soul is a longing for more, the itch of things left unfinished.

I glance at my basket and focus on its contents instead of the weight pressing against my chest. A simple meal of hashed potatoes and mushrooms wrapped in flat bread with slices of fresh tomato and oregano leaves and a handful of raspberries for dessert. *Dovan was saving those for Sanaa's birthday.* It's in four days, and yet Gran tucked them into the basket before sending me to ensure he eats his lunch. *"Don't be lettin' him share it."*

Me, stop Dovan from being his generous self? Impossible.

The grin holding up my lips shrinks as the lower market opens before me. *This is where I first saw who he was.* Where Dovan witnessed how deeply a banshee can hurt in a crowd. I no longer fear my skin brushing against theirs, and so I walk among them, fully visible.

At least I blend in. With my ordinary but sturdy black skirt and simple emerald blouse with buttons and full sleeves. Most of the women around me wear similar outfits.

A few of the people leaving through the west gate are on horseback. A thrill of wonder ripples through me at the rare sight. The guiders rationed food during winter, but they also protected a core number of livestock in case spring returned. Horses are still carefully guarded. If they're letting a few riders leave, it means one thing.

Reopening the old trade roots.

It's time to see how the other kingdoms have fared. My heart sinks as I'm reminded of the damage my winter has done. *If any kingdoms survived.* I shake off the chill of despair and step into the sun. *Some will have survived.* Especially the cities near the sea where people could fish. There's a tremor of anxiety to the guiders handing satchels and papers to the riders.

What happens now? That question sweeps through the market in low waves. Voices talking not with hope but an apprehension that feeds the vacuum left by my father.

The warm breeze sweeps through the curls falling loose from my braid. A guider notices me, his marked stare drawing the attention of several others until everyone is staring. The market grows still. I stand, half in sunlight, half in shadow, my spine straight and shoulders squared, as I realize—*It's me.*

I'm the one they're waiting for.

They want me to lead them. A prick of shame pierces my heart. *But they don't know who I was.* What I was. They witnessed a strange storm, frozen by my hand, ice crushed by my fist, and then—*Alec fell.* And I killed him. *They saw it.* His blood on my hands. Their king clinging to my brother while rejecting me. *They must have so many questions.*

After three months of silence, I owe them an answer, but—*how do you tell someone your nightmare of a past and hope they'll accept you?* Because entertaining the idea of being queen, means facing them and sharing my story in full.

They're not Dovan. Some turn away with anger and disgust twisting their mouths. The winter they watched me end was born of my soul. All they have suffered and lost came through me. Not everyone will overlook that. All they'll see is the banshee I was. The banshee that cursed them with a winter that almost killed our entire world.

You could lie.

Lying would be another curse.

You don't have to tell them. I tighten my hold on the basket's handle, grounding myself to the feel of its rough texture. *Not today.* I breathe in and out. *You don't have to do anything today.* Except make sure one forgetful guider remembers to feed himself.

———

THE GUIDER's keep hugs the wall, its narrow structure cascading to the ground in four tiers. *Like stairs for giants.* Human-sized steps cut into its levels, disappearing into shadowed arches, and a guarded gate closes off a receiving courtyard. Unlike those at the palace, the iron bars of these gates bear no decorative design and are never closed. *They welcome visitors.* A steady flow of citizens, refugees, and guiders stream in and out, an obvious change overtaking many faces.

They go in uncertain and worried.

They come out calm and hopeful.

"Good day, your highness," the guider on duty at the gate bows, his face brightened by a generous grin.

"Good day," I echo his greeting with a bob of my head.

"You're in luck." He points at the right side of the keep. "They just finished a meeting. You'll find Dovan there."

I follow his direction to the keep and collide with a barrel-chested guider coming through the archway. We share an uncomfortable laugh, an exchange of *excuse me's* and *I'm sorry's*, and we go our separate ways. He stays in the sunlight while I enter cooler shadows.

The hall closes in around me like a cave tunnel. Jagged chisel marks mar the stone instead of smooth seams from blocks stacked together. Torches and skylights brighten the heavy darkness as rooms and other hallways break away to my left and stairs to my right. The air buzzes with voices of different timbres and the clopping thump of booted feet.

Guiders are everywhere, their pale bear tunics flashing in the dark when they pass the torches hanging from the walls every dozen feet. The guiders duck down halls, shutting and opening the doors of rooms filled with tables and maps, or barrels and shelved weapons. They gather in meeting rooms where laughter mingles with sterner tones and whispered worries.

I stop under the golden light of a torch and press a hand to my dizzy head. *It looked so small from the outside.* I hadn't expected a maze of halls and rooms plunging deeper and deeper. *You're lost.* I'm about to go back and find a guider to direct me when I hear a voice I will never forget. The voice that once owned my future.

My father is here.

WRENNA

48

I RETREAT from the room my father's voice is coming from, but even though every instinct is shouting at me to run, I stay. My hands tremble as I fold them around my arms. *I've always wanted to know why he*—a sob catches in my throat, threatening to reveal me, and I cover my mouth to silence the emotional spasm.

He broke me. My own father broke me. The answers I crave are in that room with him. I tug at my blouse, adjust the basket with Dovan's lunch, and smooth my skirt, and then, with a straight spine, I cross the threshold.

A long table with benches fills the room's oval center, maps covering every inch of the polished surface. Crates stacked along the opposing wall partially conceal another doorway. Through it, I glimpse a man's back, draped in the burgundy of a guider's tunic, and that familiar male frame eases the bands of anxiety crushing my lungs. I'd know that determined posture, those soft ebony waves of hair, those ever-burdened shoulders anywhere.

Dovan.

He moves around a desk, and I duck behind the crates before he spots me as my father breaks the tense silence. "You forget yourself, *guider*."

"Do I?" Dovan sounds bored, as if he's had this conversation a hundred times.

"I am your king. You will obey my command." My father's arrogant tone seethes with promises of torment and death. I shuffle sideways until I find a narrow gap that gives me a better view.

Dovan's grip on the map he holds tightens. "I serve the people of Riffen, not the king who abandoned them to winter's mercy." As he matches my father's threat without hesitation, I bite down on the urge to yell at Dovan. My father has executed people for far less. Yet he stands perfectly still, his sword sheathed at his side.

"I *need* to see my daughter."

I gape at his words, shocked.

My father paces across the doorway, his hands fisting at his sides. "I can't even get near her because of you and your friends." He pauses, body rigid as a rebellious grin raises my lips. Seeing the man who once ruled my fate being denied what he wants is good for my soul. "You can't keep me from her forever."

"You'll see her when she wants to see you," Dovan finally replies.

"You're committing treason by keeping her from me."

Dovan snorts. "Only you would call protecting someone you love treason."

"Oh, you *love* her," my father's tone turns mocking, and I picture his mouth slanted in the wicked sneer he taught Alec.

"I do love her, yes." My heart warms at Dovan's easy admission.

"Love is for children. For those too weak to take what's theirs. You don't deserve her. She's a queen, and you? You don't even hold rank among the guiders."

All warmth is snatched away by those words as my eyes water. *My father hasn't changed.* To him, my heart is a prize to be fought over where only the victor, drenched in innocent blood, would be deserving.

"Do not think I am blind to your ambition," my father's voice lashes out like a whip. "My daughter is vulnerable and easily manipulated, but her throne will never become yours while I live."

It's a ridiculous charge, made by a man who believes power is the ultimate virtue.

Dovan laughs, a bitter, almost regretful chuckle. "You don't understand her at all."

My father's hand grips his sword hilt. Dovan marks the movement and his expression turns to stone. "Very well. Since you demand an answer, I will state my intentions. I have no interest in the throne. What I feel for your daughter has nothing to do with the fact you share *royal* blood. Banshee, princess, or peasant, it makes no difference to me because she's more than a title. She's brave and kind and strong. Your daughter wants to do right by our people, and I will support her however I can."

The weight that was sitting on my shoulders eases. *He never doubts.*

"I love *all* that she is," Dovan adds. "Something you should've done long ago."

My father flinches as if struck, his light tan skin flushing before he spits out Dovan's name, "Dovan Alstad, the *hero* of the city. You speak of love, but you just want to bed her."

The map crumples in Dovan's hands as my stomach lurches.

"Do it then. Satisfy your lust for her pretty form and then leave her to my care."

How can he suggest something so horrible and say he cares for me in the same breath? *I can't*—I can't make sense of it. I'm hot and cold, shaking and sick, and yet through it all burns a righteous outrage. *How could he?* How could he think so little of me, so little of Dovan? How could he reduce my value to my physical appearance and degrade Dovan's love for me into nothing more than fleeting lust?

There's several quick bootsteps and a thump as Dovan pins my father in place against the crates hiding me from view.

"Get your hands off me!" my father shouts as he struggles to break free, moving them both to the side. I lean closer to the crates, but if my father turns, he'll see me.

"If you weren't her father..." Dovan's tone is low and rumbling with an anger that more than matches mine. The crates rattle again as he slams my father against them. "If Wrenna wasn't clinging to some small hope of reconciliation with a bastard like you, I'd kill you where you stand."

Dovan withdraws enough for most of his body to be visible. "Have you no shame? You dishonor her. With your every breath, you tear her down so you can keep her under your control. You're the one who is weak. You fear what she'll become, but I don't." He jabs his finger into my father's chest. "She will be a better ruler than you ever were."

I steady my breathing to temper the war of emotions raging through my soul, but I can't escape the memories of my father's bruising grip and his voice cutting me into pieces. *I was never enough for him.*

But I am enough for Dovan.

He spots me a second later, eyes widening ever so slightly, just before my father shoves him backward.

"How dare you!" My father smacks his palms into Dovan's chest. "You know *nothing* of my motives! The terrible sacrifices I've made for my children! If you cared about my daughter's honor, you'd get out of her way."

"I'd never stand in her way. I stand behind her, not before, and if she wants me to be more than an ally, to be closer than a friend," Dovan's gaze darts to my face, finding but never betraying me, "then I'll stand by her side until my last breath leaves my body. That is my promise to her."

I accept. Those words sing through my entire soul. The first melody that is entirely mine in a decade, and it doesn't trigger a nightmare. It whispers of a future where I'll never stand alone again.

"Then I've wasted my time. There's nothing left for me in this city." My father starts toward the door, and Dovan slides in front of me so I'm shielded from my father's view when he spins around. "You'll be the ruin of her, and she'll be the ruin of this city."

"No," Dovan meets my father's gaze, "she will be the saving of it."

My father disappears in the shadows of the hall, beaten by Dovan's unwavering confidence in who I am. Neither of us moves for a while. The silence rings with the echo of an argument I wasn't supposed to overhear, but every word forges a new strength inside me.

I don't have to wonder anymore. I know what my father and Dovan think of me, but only one of them is right. Only one of them has listened to the voice of my soul crying out—*this is who I am.*

The banshee who was stronger than her curse.

The princess who will be her *own* queen.

Dovan expels the remnants of his anger with a slow breath before facing me, his eyebrows pinched in the middle, his jaw-line clenched, but his pine-green irises burn with the passion of everything he said. He offers his hand instead of grabbing me. *Always giving me a choice.* I grip his forearm, letting him pull me to my feet.

"I'm sorry you had to hear—"

I stop him, my lips suddenly pressed against his. He sighs,

relaxing into me as I cup his face and pull him closer and give him the kiss we've been tiptoeing around for the past three months. His arm circles my lower back as he answers my physical declaration of love with his own. Our kiss is slow and passionate. It's a promise and a beginning, but there's something I must do first. Reality sinks along my shoulders and my heels find the stone floor.

Dovan caresses my cheek, wiping moisture from my skin before smoothing an errant curl that escaped my braid. "What was that for?" He sounds so unsettled the giggle tickling my throat almost slips out. The fierce, always confident protector of the people transformed into a flustered boy by a kiss. For once, he's the one who's melted.

Feeling playful, I nudge his shoulder. "It was your Gran's idea. She told me to do it."

He quirks a brow, mouth twitching with amusement. "I should suggest you two talk more often."

"Maybe I should have her plan all of our kisses." I raise my eyebrows. "Who needs a matchmaker when you have a kissmaker?"

He keeps his expression blank for a blink or two, but then he throws his head back in a laugh that shakes his whole body. Before long, we're both gasping for air, faces red with unrestricted joy. Tears sting my eyes, but I blink them away. *This is the first time I've laughed.* Really laughed. Since my brother died.

Dovan sobers as if he's thinking the same thing.

Sorrow has monopolized so much of my life. It can wait a little longer.

I clear my throat, swallowing the grief as I hoist the basket into view. "I brought you lunch."

He takes the basket and sets it on the table, but his gaze remains locked on my face as I crumble around the smile I'm trying to keep alive.

"Your Gran put Sanaa's raspberries in it. I told her you were saving them..." My voice trails off as he grasps my shoulders, drawing me against his chest. It's eerie how perceptive he is, because the moment his arms surround me, I fall apart. Grieving once more against the strong rhythm of his heartbeat.

I look up at him. "We're supposed to take turns with stuff like this." Leaving the full extent of what's in my heart unsaid. *I want to be the one who holds you, who comes to wake you from your nightmares. I want to be strong for you.* In all the ways he has been for me.

"Did you mean it? What you said to my father about standing by my side?"

Dovan's response begins in the way the lines of his face relax, as if my question holds no danger at all. "Every word."

This is it. This is when I should declare my heart as his, my future as ours, but I'm still not free. He senses my hesitation and waits, ever the patient listener. After failing multiple times to tell him what's holding me back, I decide to start with something easier.

"How many times has my father come to you?"

Dovan grunts, but he's quiet for a moment. "I've honestly lost count."

"That many?"

"It doesn't make him a good man."

I tighten my hold on Dovan's waist, using his heat to chase off the chill of that truth. "I'm sorry you had to...deal with him. He's not even your problem."

Dovan gently grips my neck, guiding me away from him so we can look at each other. "He's not yours either."

"I know."

"Do you?"

"I do. I just wish..." Tears glaze my vision as my chin trembles. I'm overwhelmed by the depth of his concern, but I don't know how to communicate what it means. For Dovan to suffer my father's verbal abuse and threats for my sake.

"Hey," he lifts my chin. "I'm your shield, remember?"

A breath blasts out of me. I nod and trace the white bear on his tunic because that's easier than holding his gaze or coming up with a response.

"I'm a guider." He pulls my hand up and kisses my palm. "If I'm not facing down a threat, I'm not doing my job."

That makes me laugh. It's a weak burst of joy, but I hold on to it with everything I have as he tugs me into his arms. "Thank you."

"You're welcome," he says as he holds me. His contented sigh warms me through and through because he loves this—me in his arms, our hearts beating next to each other, and I realize—*we've created our own song.* Someday, I will learn how to sing it.

"You can stay with me for a while," he offers, but it's also an admission of not wanting to let me go. "I don't report to the market for an hour."

Yes, burns on my tongue, and I almost say it, but I've been hiding for too long. For three months I've grieved in the shelter of Dovan's home. For three months, I have toyed with the idea that caring for our orphans and seeing Dovan twice a day is enough. That this is all the life I desire. *But we deserve more.*

After everything we've survived and everything we've done, Dovan and I deserve to grow. To try new things and step bravely into our future, because it will be ours.

Once more, I fortify my body with a deep breath and step back so Dovan's hands rest on my waist. His left eyebrow rises, but there's no question in his eyes.

"I need to face my father." My stomach knots at the idea, considering how badly the conversation between him and Dovan went, but the old king is the last obstacle before what comes next.

"You don't owe him anything."

A truth I will always love him for speaking, but there's another one I've overlooked. "I owe myself."

A hint of pride lifts his mouth into a half-smile.

"I have things I need to say, things I need to understand. I have to do this," I add, more to bolster my own courage than gain his support.

Dovan's fingers weave through mine, his firm squeeze yet another offer. "You don't have to face him alone."

I let out a nervous huff. "You don't get along with him."

Dovan smirks. Unflinchingly proud of that fact.

"My father would never answer my questions with you there." *If he answers them at all.* I don't want to dwell on that possibility. I pick at my blouse's hem as fresh tears come. The fabric is a deep green like Dovan's eyes, and when I glance up, I find him studying me.

"What do you need?" he asks.

"Don't go home tonight." It's as close as I can get to asking him to be there when it's over. To stand with me in the painful but necessary aftermath of what I have to do if we are to move forward.

Dovan nods and taps his fist over his heart in a guider's promise. "I'll come for you."

WRENNA

49

THE PALACE GUARD escorting me to my father wears a frown so deep his shoulders sag. I catch him glaring at me, but he doesn't say a word. The air shivers in the marble halls as we pass doorways and stairs leading up or down. Every fireplace is cold. Spring's chill is far gentler than winter's, but—*the fires should be lit.* The rooms made ready for the old king.

"There's nothing left for me in this city." My father's parting comment to Dovan sets off a shiver.

He wouldn't. My father would never leave. He'd never give up his crown or vacate a throne he held by violence and fear. He's too proud. Yet when the palace guard bows and abandons me outside my father's open door, his bedroom looks nothing like what I remember.

The sheer size of the room, with its high walls and vaulted ceilings, swallows me like a tomb as I cautiously enter. An office waits to the left through another door, and a bathing chamber to the right. Leaving most of the room for the king's personal things. None of which remain.

The walls are stripped of their paintings, the shelves left naked without their books, the racks for his armor and weapons stand empty. Even the velvet curtains for the tall windows are missing. Cases and crates line the floor at the foot of his bed while he carries clothing to the open case on the mattress. His movements are jerky and pinched as he slams its lid shut and snaps the leather belts tight to keep it closed.

My father hefts its weight and turns around. Our eyes meet. We see each other for the first time in three months, and the sole emotion that paints his face is the twitch of anger along his jawline. Anger, instead of joy or relief. He's biting back whatever lecture he feels I deserve. *Don't make this easy for him.* Straightening my spine, I dare to approach him.

"You came." He sets the case down, his body angled away from me as if I am unworthy of his full attention. "I didn't think you would."

"You're still my father." It's the truth neither of us can escape as I scan the cases. A few bear my mother's name, bringing the sting of sorrow. *We were happy once.* As happy as a ruling family surrounded by constant threats could be.

My father is clean shaven now, but he once wore a long beard in braids to please my mother after the custom of the high north. *He shaved it the day after she died.* A memory flickers like a weak flame, and I inhale sharply as I fall into the past.

I was nine when my stubby fingers tangled his beard into a mess of knots and pink ribbons, but he wore them with pride. He held court without taking them out and not once did he crack a smile, though plenty of courtiers did. It became our tradition. He never scolded me, never instructed a servant to show me how to do it right. For a solid year, braiding the king's beard was my job.

I let the memory go. Reconciling the man my father was with

the monster he became later is impossible without an explanation. I sift through the crueler memories that follow, trying to squeeze some sense from all the pain. Regardless of the curse Alec caused, our shattering began when our father changed. He was always ruthless with everyone else, but when our mother died, he treated me and Alec like potential threats. *I need to know why.* If it was just his buried grief or something more.

With a deep breath, I soften my posture. Relaxing my shoulders and easing my hands out of fists so I resemble the submissive young woman he knew before the curse.

My father stays silent. *Fine, I'll go first.* "Why was there no funeral for Alec?"

His gaze snaps to mine, shocked at my boldness, but then, I'm not the Wrenna he remembers. The Wrenna who trembled before him and tried to please him. It took me ten years of being cursed, and one day of falling in love with a good man, to figure out who I am and what I am worth. Things a father should have spoken to his daughter every night so she could never forget. How much she is loved. How strong she is. How capable she is of changing the world.

But he was never that kind of father.

The tension in his body tilts his chin higher and puffs out his chest. "You know damn well why."

The quiet but deadly tone of his voice and the flash of rage in his eyes used to be enough to silence me into compliance. *Not anymore.* I stare him down in a challenge the old me never could have made. "I've come to give you what you never gave me. A chance to explain."

"I don't owe you anything."

My lips tremble and I press them into a hard line. *He can't hurt you.* But he is, as he once again decides what I deserve.

He turns his back. "Go bother your lovesick guider. Leave me be."

My fingers curl into my palms. They're the same hands that controlled a storm, that *moved* a storm. *I can do this.* "I'm not leaving until you—"

My father spins toward me so fast I freeze. His hands spear through the air and close around my arms. "Until I what?"

I'm trembling, my confidence chipping and cracking. He has me under his power, and yet his grip doesn't become bruising.

"What do you want from me, *Enna*?"

I swallow hard as my stomach churns. *He never called me Enna.* Even Alec refused. They both thought the nickname mother gave me was too soft. *That was the point.* Nicknames are supposed to be soft and endearing, born of happier things. I study him, this king who is my father. *What new game is he playing?*

I don't see a player or a master of manipulation in his wet eyes and sagging mouth and wrinkled skin. I see a husband who lost his wife. A father who lost his son. A king who stopped caring about his people. He sighs, shaking his head as he lets me go.

"I wanted you to hold me," the words tumble through my lips. "I wanted you to listen. I wanted you to understand." I go on, through the tightening of my throat, through the hot sting of tears, and through the heartache boring a hole deep within my soul. "Why couldn't you love me for who I am?"

The bright gold of my father's irises darken into amber pits. I want to believe they're regrets, that some part of him is capable of understanding how cruel he was to me, but it's been too many years. Too many wrong decisions.

My father's heart is made of stone.

"I never wanted to be your heir. You broke my heart when you forced me to take Alec's rightful place." The corner of my father's right eye twitches, but I'm not done yet. "You abandoned him when he needed you most. You didn't even try to help him. You expected me to replace him, but I never could."

My father scowls at me. "You understand nothing."

"Then tell me."

His sharp gaze nicks my heart, and yet he is the one bleeding. A single, glimmering tear slips down his stony mask, proving he had a reason. *So why won't he explain?*

"Please," I edge closer. "Did...did you search for us when we vanished?"

He stands like a statue of uncompromised resolve, unmoved by the emotion wringing my voice into a mere whisper.

I spin away, heaving as the tears flood out. During the years of my curse, a tiny seed of hope took root in my heart. A belief that the family I'd left behind would search for me, and they wouldn't give up because they loved me and wanted to bring me home.

Some hopes never come true.

"I didn't need to look for you."

I face my father, but he's staring at the wall behind me. A large painting hangs there, but the canvas has been torn away. All that's left are a few curling strips in the corners.

"I never lost you." My father's admission tastes like another lie, but the truth is written across his face.

"You knew we were cursed."

"Someday you'll understand what it's like to work so hard to give your children everything. To see them growing in courage and cunning, the seeds you'd planted sprouting into all you hope, but then—" he cuts himself short. "It doesn't matter now. I failed."

"What do you mean you failed?" He bends toward the case he packed as if our discussion is finished, but it hasn't even begun. "Did you try to break our curse?"

"Only the banshee can break that curse," a darker edge sharpens his voice. "I didn't think you had it in you, but you proved me wrong. You're quite capable when it comes to killing."

I'd rather feel the painful bruising of his hands than hear the pride in his voice. I avoid looking at my clean palms as they itch.

They're never clean in my nightmares, and my father's compliment constricts my throat like a noose. "I did what I had to."

"Then you shouldn't be ashamed of it."

"Don't. Tell me. What I should be." I slash my hand through the air between us, as if I am cutting myself free of him. "You lost *any* right to shape my future the day you chose between me and Alec."

My father actually *smiles*.

"We were stronger than you. We wouldn't let you tear us apart."

He frowns, glancing at the frame behind me again. "That was my failure." And then his icy glare chills my soul. "I should have killed one of you myself."

What? There's no air in my lungs, no ground beneath my feet, no bones holding me up. I'm falling. My knees thud against the stone floor. "You're a..." I struggle to get the words out. They are sick and rotten and very deserved. "You're a monster."

"I told you what it takes to rule this kingdom." The amusement in his voice roils through my stomach as he savors his debased triumph.

No. I push myself up and stand on unsteady legs. *Don't let him win.*

My father stacks the last of the crates by his bed and takes the handles of two small cases in each hand. *He's leaving.* Striding toward the door.

I block his path and earn a brief flicker of surprise. "I'm done playing games. Answer my questions or don't, but I won't let you twist my mind to fit your warped reflection of who I am." I lift my chin. "I know who I am, and I'm not ashamed of the woman I'm becoming."

A sneer rips across his face. "You think the people of Riffen will want you as their queen when they know the truth?" He steps forward and I step back. "You caused the worst winter ever known. You aided in the death of hundreds through your voice." His chin falls as he draws a shuddering breath. "You killed your own brother to escape the consequences of your actions."

Without touching me, he drives a blade into my hope, cutting at its roots, and I gasp.

"I'll tell you what *your* beloved people will do," he whispers in my ear. "They'll treat you like the monster you are and come for your head."

I tuck my shaky fingers in the folds of my skirt. "We both know I'm not the monster in this story."

His lip curls into a snarl. "Move." He clenches his jaw as I refuse to obey, his fury twitching his shoulders. "Don't make me hurt you."

How easily blames me. As if his cruelty is *my* fault. It takes everything I have to hold my head up, to keep my shoulders square and spine straight. In the past, I would have cowered and begged for mercy.

I'm not that frightened girl anymore.

I blink away the tears and firm my chin. "Alec planned to kill you."

"As he should have," my father huffs a breath, exasperated. "Our city has survived because its rulers were never weak. I won't watch it fall with you."

The shock of each statement hits like a slap, but I stammer through a response, "I—I won't let Riffen fall."

"Only a weak ruler lets her people choose who will wear the crown."

"Wanting to give them a choice in their own future is not weakness." Strength kindles in my soul, fueled by all the years where my choices were taken from me. "It's doing what's right. We've been ruled by monsters long enough."

My father's head tilts back, nostrils flaring. "What happens when they reject you? How will you help them when they've stripped you of your power?"

I don't know what to say.

"You haven't thought that far ahead, have you?" My father drops one of the cases and grabs my arm. "I'll stay and help you on one condition. What happened to you and Alec must remain our secret."

The sudden change in his demeanor, from monstrous to caring, makes my head spin, but his offer is genuine. He wants me to succeed. *We have very different ideas of what success looks like.* His version is built on a lie.

Mine stands on the truth. The *whole* truth.

I wrench my arm from his grasp. "For most of my life with you, you made me a liar. I told so many lies I lost sight of who I was and what life, what real relationships should be like." The corner of my mouth dares to curve upward as Dovan enters my thoughts. The way he loves me, *all* of me. *He'd never ask me to do this.* To betray myself just to please my father. *Time to make myself clear.*

"I am *done* living under a lie." Heat flushes through me, burning through my glare as I step into my father's space. "And if that costs me the crown, so be it."

His eyebrows rise, an admission of either surprise or respect, but he offers no apology. He snatches the handle of the case he put down and marches from the room.

A rush of relief cools my skin because I stood up to my father. I endured his final attack without losing who I am.

"They won't love you," he says from the doorway. "Not when they find out you're a worse monster than I have ever been."

I hold myself together, long after he's left, but he never returns. Palace guards retrieve the rest of the crates, leaving the room empty except for me. Its lengthening shadows are but a haunted echo of the dark poison he leached into my soul.

I crumble to the floor and do what an old woman suggested. I let all the twisted hurt trapped inside my breaking heart come out. It floods through my eyes and heaves through my lungs. I weep, and I weep, until the last touch of sunlit warmth abandons me to the numbing caress of night. Only then, do I lift my gaze to the ruined painting my father kept staring at as he spoke of his failure.

I thought I had nothing left to break.

But the gilded frame once held the image of our family when it was still whole. It would be the only portrait of me and Alec with our mother, robbing me of a clear glimpse of her face instead of the fuzzy one in my memories. My father's last cruel trick. *He tore us apart.* Just as he ripped the canvas from its frame.

Some victories are more painful than the worst defeats.

WRENNA

50

IT's time to get up.

The bones of my legs ache from hours spent kneeling on the floor. My dry eyes scrape against their lids, and my back pops from my slumped posture. I'm so tired I could fall over and sleep for days, but my soul won't rest.

It can't rest.

After what I've survived, I'm still fighting, wrestling with what happened as I wait for an answer. *The* answer. The explanation I'm hoping will make everything okay. My best hope for one walked out of this room hours ago. *He left me*—as my father always did—

Broken.

Even broken things learn to stand, to walk, to move forward. Staying here in the dark lets him win. *He's won enough.* I sway side to side, bracing my palms on the cold stone floor as I unwind my legs and hiss through the prickling numbness in my feet. I massage my calves through the supple leather of my boots and flex my toes.

The glint of gilded torchlight winks along the pale marble. Someone must have lit the torches in the hall. A servant or a palace guard. *Alone, but not alone.* The life of a leader.

"They won't love you." My father's parting taunt hacks at the fragile bud of hope, but I take my first steps toward the light.

A palace guard waits outside the door, posture ramrod straight and alert. Thick streaks of gray in his black hair mark him as older than the guard who led me here.

"Did you light the torches?" I ask.

"It is my duty to protect my queen."

Queen. It shouldn't be possible for him to stand any straighter, and yet, my unclaimed title sharpens his stance with a proud expectation that unsettles my stomach. Riffen's fate is once more in my hands, but this time, the unknown future is full of new possibilities instead of certain death.

"Do the others share your feelings?" I wince at how foolish my question sounds.

He tilts his graying head toward me, and I glimpse a pair of kind blue eyes. "Those of us who stayed will serve you in our new future."

I offer him a nod, unsure of how to react to the news my father didn't leave alone, and start down the hall. The guard follows three steps behind, and I take comfort in his silent presence as I wander through the palace that was my home. *It's beautiful.* With ceilings made of glass, braided stone arches, glistening marble floors, and mahogany paneled rooms.

We wind up in the western wing. The floors reflect dim moonlight into my face, their once polished surfaces neglected. Cobwebs gather in the corners and a film of dust and soot from torches mar the glass ceiling. The shadows retreat in giant leaps as the guard fusses over the old torches until they light.

I slow as we pass a door with musical notes carved along its blackened surface. *Our music room.* A chill teases my skin with memories of whispered secrets and riotous laughter and bloodied gasps. The guard touches my shoulder, silently pleading with me to pick any room other than this one, but I can't.

This is where everything went wrong.

I twist the handle and push the door inward. Its hinges creak in grumpy protest and the charred scent of ash strikes my nose. A memory escapes, changing the brooding shadows into gilded sunlight. The ash vanishes, the harpsichord sits upright and unbroken, and—my heart swells inside my chest as I heave a breath and hold it, afraid of ruining the marvel before me. Because there we are.

Mother at the harpsichord, her hair crimson in the light, her dress simple and soft and deepest cobalt. *Her voice.* I forgot what it sounded like. Deep and airy but a little brittle. *Like mine.*

I sound like my mother.

I watch my rosy-cheeked younger self sing with a pang of envy. Before I was broken, I was full of dreams, my smiles bright as sunlight, and I wasn't alone. Alec skips through the room, a rabid bundle of energy as he charges unseen foes, slashes his paper dagger, and twirls on legs that have yet to fail.

We were so...*innocent.*

The guard squeezes my shoulder as I sniffle, breaking the spell. The memory fades, the past overpowered by the present. *I'm the last of my family.* I swipe at a tear as I enter the room and pick up a torn piece of sheet music. Ash clouds around my feet and spills from the fire-scorched song. *One of Alec's.* A defiant, dissonant string of swearing chords that rage against how our father betrayed him.

My eyes are watering, my hands shaking, and my heart fractures. *This was our home.* The place where my brother and I could be our true selves. I fold in half as I kneel and wipe the floor with my hands, sweeping back the ashy grime until I glimpse the pale tones of the marble underneath.

"Your highness, you mustn't. A maid can tend to that in the morning."

I peer up at the guard's face, at the deepening wrinkles of concern lining his forehead, but the only person who should clean up my family's mess is me. "It'll go faster if I have a broom."

The lowering of his eyebrows tells me he disapproves, but in a way that means *you've been through a lot and need to rest* instead of *this is beneath you.* He returns a few minutes later with a bucket of water, a few rags, and a broom.

I thank him and he bows, retreating to the hall where he'll stand guard. *Will he still serve me when he knows I sang three hundred and sixty-nine people to their deaths?* I push that thought away, focusing on the wet chill as I dip a cloth into the bucket and the sound of water splashing as I wring it out.

The soaked cloth splats against the floor. Ash puffs into the air, and I try not to breathe it in as I start scrubbing. The simple rhythm of cleaning, of stacking all the torn pieces of sheet music in a pile, calms my soul. My fingertips prune as I shuffle along on my knees, but for one blissful moment of peace, nothing else matters. There are no decisions to be made. No painful truths to accept. No past and future colliding.

I'm just a girl cleaning a floor.

———

A PRICKLE of awareness alerts me first. *You're not alone.*

I stiffen, the slippery friction of the wet cloth against the marble floor pausing as I blink, but my surroundings are fuzzy. My ears ring with all the songs absorbed into the wood-paneled walls of this room. Songs I sang. Songs I wrote. Songs that held me and my brother together. But their tethering melodies break, a shattered chain that no longer serves a purpose because one of us is dead.

A dull, knife-shaped pain twists in my heart, but I resist rubbing my chest. *It's just an echo.* Of a curse that was broken. *I'm free.* But freedom, I'm learning, is making your own chains and choosing where to tether your heart. It's my choice to be bound, and my choice is—

Here. Whispers my soul. Here, I bind myself. To this room, to this city, to one person more than anyone else.

The guider who always finds me.

Worn boots scuff the floor, and I glance up. Dovan's care-lined eyes bore into mine. I sit back on my heels, chilled by the clingy wetness of my skirt and sleeves. *How long have I been cleaning?* Hours have passed, judging by the moonlight making the window glow silver. *I didn't even hear him enter.*

Dovan kneels down and sits cross-legged in damp ash as if everything about this fire-destroyed room and my manic scrubbing in the middle of the night is normal. He gives me a knowing look that doesn't berate me or list off better ways to handle my grief. "Do you want to talk about it?"

I drop the cloth into the bucket with a splash and dry my palms on my blouse. "My father left."

"I know."

My chest grows tight, the air hard to breathe. "He would have stayed if I had agreed to lie to everyone about where I've been and what I've done." I pick at the wet wrinkles of my skirt, and Dovan reaches out to take my hand. "He twisted my words and tried to break me. He thought I was the same, but he was wrong."

"That's because you're not the girl who runs away anymore." He bends forward and kisses my hand, glancing up at me with pride. "You're the queen who stays."

For the first time, I don't recoil from my title. Not as Dovan's unwavering faith pours into me, filling every crack, because he knows what I've overcome. What it took to break my curse and face my father.

"I hope you at least told your father off." Amusement tugs at Dovan's mouth.

"I did," I say as I hold my head higher. "Even Alec would have been proud of me."

A dull ache throbs through my chest at the mention of my brother. Saying his name was a mistake because I know exactly how he would have looked, with his red curls and dimpled smirk. *He would have clapped.* Very slowly. And swung the door closed so it hit our father's ass on his way out.

A strangled sound comes from my tight throat. *I shouldn't think of Alec this way.* He was a monster, but I'm beginning to wonder if my heart will ever let him go. Not the Red Death version or the murderous prince. But the boy who slept by my bed so he could slay any monsters that dared appear.

As I rub my sternum, I notice the blood stain that will never come clean.

"This is where I almost died." Where winter began and a curse took control. It marked the end of the life we knew. One violent moment cost us both so much, but this is also where what comes next begins.

A new life, rising from the wreckage of the old.

But it still hurts.

Dovan's grip tightens until I feel his pulse against my cool fingers. He doesn't tell me the past will stop hurting or that what my father and brother did will stop being a part of me. He leans forward and wipes a new string of tears from my face. "Some wounds take a lifetime to heal."

I see that truth written in the grief haunting his eyes. A month after the season change, Dovan shared his most painful loss with me after I'd had a nightmare. He bundled me up and took me to the roof to look at the stars.

That was the night he told me how his father died.

They were on a mission to meet a refugee band, and raiders attacked. Dovan had to choose between saving his father or the children they were trying to get to safety. An impossible choice, and yet he made it. *He was only sixteen.* And that boy who let his father die lives inside the man who's with me now. *But at least he knows why his world was shattered.* Giving him what I don't yet have —peace.

"What is it?" Dovan asks.

My chin trembles. "I'm afraid."

"Of what?"

"You've never blamed me," I force myself to meet his gaze. "My winter stole so much from you—"

"Wrenna—"

"—your father, your childhood—"

"No, it wasn't—"

"It started with *me*." I jerk my hand from his, and he stops trying to interrupt. "I was the Ember of Winter. I was a banshee. And I'm terrified my people will never see me as anything more."

"Then we'll show them."

"How? As much as I hate admitting my father could be right about anything," I shiver and wrap my arms around myself, "my story can't be told. Anyone who hears it will stop listening the moment they find out how many lives ended because mine didn't."

The corner of Dovan's mouth tugs upward and I glare at him. "There is a way, and it won't require a single word."

"That's not—"

"—possible?" Hope sparkles in his pine-green gaze. "If I were thinking of a normal portrait, it would be."

"You can't mean—"

"Sanaa." He confirms. "I'll ask her to paint you."

My pulse quickens as I consider Dovan's solution. *It could work.* Sanaa's art is magical, telling the full truth of her subjects. *It would show my people everything.* They would see me, all of me. Nothing hidden or twisted for harm or gain. Just the raw, honest truth.

A ripple of unease steals my train of thought, casting it in a direction that quickens my pulse. *I've already been painted.* In a family portrait that hangs in tatters in my father's room. *What if* —I glance at the doorway, seizing the answer to my deepest question that's so simple I overlooked it.

The painting.

I'm scrambling, my body fighting my skirt to stand.

"Wrenna?" Dovan calls after me as my boots screech against the stone floor, and I race from the room.

WRENNA

51

I'm running.

Back to the portrait hanging in my father's abandoned room. Dovan and the guard call after me, their footsteps echoing as they follow. The light of their torches pushes the darkness in front of me away, but I don't slow down.

My boots squeal as I skid to a stop before the painting. Moonlight and shadows caress its dusty frame, washing out the colors painted on the strips. I stare at them, my chest tight. I'm afraid to move closer as my father's words repeat over and over in my head.

"That was my failure."

"I should have killed one of you myself."

What could cause my father to say such terrible things? What could convince him that killing one of his children would've been better than what actually happened? I shiver, wrapping an arm around my middle, because I'm standing before the answer. Our ruined portrait is the symbol of my father's failure. The way he looked at it, with hatred and fear, as if commissioning it was his greatest mistake. *It can't be a normal painting.*

Soul art.

The very thing Dovan wants to use to tell my story. *What if it already did?*

Soul art reveals every moment, every truth of its subjects, through the capturing of a still but living image. *My father knew me and Alec were cursed.* What if the painting showed him? Before my brother found the dagger, before my father chose me as his heir, before the assassin stabbed me.

What if my father saw what we'd become in its prophetic colors?

What if he tried to prevent that future from coming true?

It would explain everything. Why my father ripped the crown from Alec. Why he tried to drive a wedge between us. Why he wanted me to be a monster. A chill nibbles my skin as I stumble forward. *It has to be.* Nothing else makes sense, but the moment I touch the nearest shred of canvas, a quiet, shattered gasp escapes my trembling lips. *It's not moving.*

The colors are long dead.

I flip the strip over in my hands. I snap the flimsy piece of canvas straight, twisting it in every direction, but—*There's...nothing.* The damaged painting has no story to tell. No answer to give me and help me heal. No truth to reveal, no explanation for my father's cruel choices.

Nothing.

"No." I claw at the frame, reaching for another strip.

"Wrenna, stop."

I ignore Dovan and wrench the painting from the wall. The frame breaks on the floor. A piece strikes my leg so hard I cry out, but Dovan is there. Supporting me through the throbbing pain and pulling me against his chest. He doesn't let go as I struggle to break free so I can run my hands over each fragment of canvas.

One of them must have the answer.

"Wrenna, look at me."

I resist until Dovan's palms trail up my arms and cup my face. His hold is so gentle I could escape with the slightest effort and finish examining the painting, but I'm frozen, my energy utterly spent. And my chest is heavy with what only one of us has the courage to speak.

"The answer isn't there," he says, his palm sliding down to rest above my heart. "It's here."

My next breath breaks me and I slump against him. "I just want to know why. Is that so wrong?"

"No, it's not wrong. It's human," he draws me closer, and my head settles along the slope of his shoulder, my forehead tucked near his stubbled jaw. "But I've seen the question *why* rob people of all the good they can still do." His sigh warms my cheek. "*Why* is a monster best left unfed."

A monster I feel roaring through me, twisting and turning my soul toward bitterness and fear and building a wall around my heart. It will become a new curse if I let it. "But if I understood what changed, *why* he changed, I'd know if...if it was my fault. Something I said. Something I did or didn't do. Maybe if I'd tried harder. Maybe if I said no—"

"Stop." The sharp tone of Dovan's voice startles me. "There was nothing you did or didn't do, nothing you said that made them cruel. They *chose* to be monsters."

"I made choices too."

He huffs an exasperated breath. "Yes, but that doesn't make *their* choices *your* fault. Don't carry their guilt. You have burdens enough."

But guilt is all my brother and father left me. Guilt and gnawing questions. The broken and empty frame on the ground taunts me. Its painting might have been the answer I needed once, but I arrived too late to claim it.

"Do you know why you're the bravest woman I've ever met?" Dovan's question draws a thin smile to my lips. "Because you *hold* on. Longer than anyone else. Longer than you should."

My smile fades.

His hand cradles the back of my neck, tipping my face toward his, but I can't meet his gaze. "Your brother is dead. Your father is gone. They did terrible things to you, and you did what you had to, so you could survive them."

He's cutting me open, exposing my wound and drawing out its poison. It flows from my eyes. Clear, honest pain. "I loved them."

"There's no shame in that."

Isn't there? I loved two monsters. A murderous brother and a cruel father. They used me and betrayed me, trapping me in their bloody games, but I still love them.

Dovan rests his forehead on mine. "You're waiting for an answer that isn't coming."

I push against his chest, but his arm tightens around my waist. *I don't want to hear this.*

"You can't make sense of what's been done."

My breathing becomes ragged, my body trembles, my soul screaming for him to stop, but the word never leaves my lips because—*I need this*. The hard truth Dovan speaks scrapes me raw, and yet, I feel lighter as the deadened husk of my old life peels away.

"It's time to let them go," he brushes a strand of hair from my tear-stained cheek. "It's time to live *your* life. Not the one they wanted for you."

I look up into Dovan's face and all I see is love. The kind that walked through snowfields to find the lost. That goes hungry and loses sleep. That never stops trying, that refuses to surrender, that fights on even when brokenness begs him to be still.

A love that stays.

A love that knows.

A love that's helped him make the hard decisions when he had every right to demand an explanation.

"It's *your* choice, Wrenna. It always has been." Dovan guides my head to his shoulder, stroking my back and holding me close.

I breathe in his warmth, taking slow, steady breaths to calm the chaos of my soul, and in the quiet, I hear what Dovan means but isn't saying. A truth unlocks deep inside me. Through all the death and misery of the curse, through all the joy and pain of my life, it has been there, waiting for me to listen to its song. A quiet melody etched in my bones.

The answer you need isn't an explanation. It's a choice.

I grip Dovan harder as a relieved sob shudders through me. My choice is the key.

I stand between two different futures. I've been living a cursed version of one my entire life, but the other is unknown, and yet I'm not afraid because Dovan's right.

It's time to put the past behind me. It's time to make less of my brother's and my father's choices and more of mine. For too long, I've allowed their mistakes to own me. *No more.*

I'm done living under the shadow of their choices.

What they did to me is not more powerful than what I can do.

I can choose. And I choose to let go.

WRENNA

52

The gravestone is far simpler than I expected. Gray and chipped like a broken tooth, with no clan crest, no fierce beast or gentle spirit crowning its humble head. A wretched guardian for a dead prince. *Doesn't even stand upright.* The stone lies in the mud, splattered by the recent rains. The name, a mere scratch, is barely readable. *Alec Navadon Ryvelt, the fourth.* There's no date, no description of who he was or if he has a family who'll miss him.

Our father did this.

He robbed Alec of his right to rest next to our mother in the royal graveyard. Left him to decay in a field guarded by naked thorn bushes and a crow perched on the spindly arm of a tree that has yet to bud. The bird croaks at me, flapping its shiny black wings and clicking its beak. I draw my arms around me as a chill snakes up from the ground. My mind has been so preoccupied with why I've come that I didn't notice.

Nothing is growing.

There's no grass, no flowers, nothing but cool, dark soil, pockmarked with puddles that look bitter enough to spit the rain back at the sky. I shiver as I realize what's wrong with the gravestone. *There should be three names.* One of them might explain why spring's magic has failed here, creating a lopsided circle of barren earth that spans a hundred feet.

Alec, Red Death, *and* the season tree are all buried here.

And they're still killing things. Even in death.

The ground slants down from the city, and the cruel irony of the steep ascent to the palace stabs my chest. *A climb to the throne.* One my brother couldn't have made without using the power of the dagger to walk. With his choice of burial site, my father laughs at Alec, mocking the boy who would never be king.

The crow *caws*, blinking dark brown eyes as it cocks its head toward my feet. A shovel lies between me and the grave where I dropped it after I arrived. The bird's beak opens in a threat as its wings flick outward.

"I'm not here for him." I've come for what Alec will never have.

But knowing I'm right to desecrate my brother's grave doesn't make my hands shake any less as I pick up the shovel and begin digging. The soil is wet and soft and gives easily.

It took a week to convince Dovan's Gran painting my portrait wouldn't expose Sanaa as a soul artist. Her exact words were, *"Have yer minds be gone from yer heads?"* Her way of calling our plan crazy. I expected her to knock some sense into us with her crutch, but Dovan convinced her to trust us.

We moved their entire household into the palace so no one would wonder why Sanaa was coming and going from it. The painting would take place at night, and we chose a room without windows and only one door, which Dovan guarded. Sanaa wore a cloak with the hood up to further protect her identity.

Soul artists were treated worse than season embers by the four kingdoms. Hunted, enslaved, and kidnapped by those hungry for power, the gift of a soul artist's all-seeing art was used to cripple enemies and secure tyrant dynasties. No protective measure was too much if it meant keeping Sanaa safe.

I spent the following week standing tall through the night as Sanaa painted my story with layer after layer of colors. She asked me to focus on what I wanted my people to see, and I did. *Everything.* I repeated that word over and over, fighting down the fears it raised, blocking out my father's cruel voice, and corralling the hope it dared to soar. When Sanaa finished the portrait, we covered it and placed it in the ballroom.

"Are you ready?" Dovan asked as we lingered over the final plans for its reveal.

"Is anyone ever ready to bare their soul when they could be rejected?"

"They won't reject you."

"You can't know that."

"I don't have to know it." He cupped my face with his hand. *"I have faith. Faith in them and in you."*

The plan was simple. Dovan and a few dozen guiders we trusted would bring small groups to see the painting, starting with the lower quarters and working to the heart of the city. Then they'd be asked a question. *Will you have Wrenna Ryvelt as your queen?* Their answer would be recorded: a single tally in the right column of a ledger for *yes* or the left for *no*.

The shovel jerks as it hits a rock, but a mere stone is hardly an obstacle compared to what I've already faced. I roll it away, wincing at the scrape of metal on stone.

Our plan had one problem. The painting would show them my past and my present, but also my future. All the things I haven't lived through yet. Sanaa tried to limit the painting, but soul art is a wild magic and won't be tamed.

The portrait would need a protector. It couldn't be Sanaa, couldn't be Dovan, or anyone who'd be tempted to use its prophetic knowledge against me. That's when Dovan's Gran surprised us by volunteering to bear the burden of my future and guard it with her silence. A curtain would serve as the barrier she would control, lifting and lowering it as needed.

For the next three months, my people came and went from the ballroom, leaving their answers behind. I observed from the hall a few times, which was a mistake. No matter how they entered— nervous or confident—they always left *different*. Witnessing the full truth of who I am *changed* them. I tried not to dwell on if it was a good or bad sign.

Until everyone had cast their vote, I *was* queen, and my city needed me. I started going to meetings. I met with the leaders of the guiders and the palace guard, the heads of the merchant guilds and the market quarters, the farmers and the refugee coordinators. And they gave me records that backed up their opinions. They shared the flaws *they* saw in our city.

But I wanted to see everything.

During the days of those three months, I walked from house to house, business to business, shelter to shelter, conducting my own surveys, getting a feel for each part of the city and its strengths and struggles. During the nights, I combed through the official records, looking for discrepancies and jotting down ideas for solutions. I began assigning tasks. Some leaders were skeptical. Most were annoyed I didn't do what they suggested, but when I showed up and dirtied my clothes and blistered my palms to fix the problems I'd discovered, their complaints fell silent. Their irritation changed into respect and a willingness to work beside me.

Dovan once told me I loved this city, and he was right. But that love was starved. It was never nurtured until now, and as it bloomed, a new fear crept like frost over my heart. *I want to be their queen.* More than I've ever wanted anything, but I've given our future into their hands. *Whatever happens, I have no regrets.*

Dovan met me at sundown every night. We'd cross off the households who'd visited the ballroom that day from the city map, and as the number of those left dwindled, I started searching. Two important things had gone missing from the palace after the season changed. My brother's body and the crown of Riffen. Nobody knew where my father had buried Alec, and most assumed he'd taken the crown with him when he left. They were wrong.

I know my father.

I know how cruel he is.

I knew where the crown would be.

A guider on patrol stumbled across my father's last wicked secret. Dovan relayed what she'd found to me, which is why I'm here, disturbing my brother's grave. Not to bring his body back to the royal cemetery, but to reclaim what isn't his or mine. Not yet.

The shovel *thuds* against wood. I kneel along the rim of the hole I've dug and swipe the loose soil aside to reveal the shape of a simple coffin. The odor of decay sours the air. I hesitate, overcome by a fresh stab of disgust. Burying my brother here wasn't just about my father's disappointment in Alec.

This is about me.

The girl he broke who became a woman he couldn't control.

He still thinks I'm too weak to face the hard things. That I'd find out what he did with the crown and run, because reclaiming it would be too painful. A spark of rebellion burns the chill from my heart. I claw at the dirt, digging my fingers deeper until wood splinters against my skin, and then—something cold and smooth like stone. An oval with flowers and thorns.

I lift the crown from my brother's grave. It will never be his, but it could be mine. I use my skirt to clean the grime away before setting it on my cloak. The crow flaps over, landing on the gravestone and eyeing the coffin with a hungry look.

I shovel the soil back into the grave before the bird gets any ideas of feasting. *Alec doesn't deserve to be food for crows.* A tired sigh escapes as I wipe sweat from my forehead. My brother deserved to answer for his crimes, and if he had lived, he'd have been executed. *By me.* Maybe that was the real reason he fell from the wall. To save us both from his public trial.

Maybe he didn't want my first act as queen to be one of death.

It's a tradition for the new ruler of Riffen to hold an execution after being crowned. A tradition I intend to break if my people choose me.

I drag the flat of the shovel over the grave to smooth the soil. The moon glows like a silver crescent to the east, rising as the sun fades, and for a moment, I glimpse my brother's mischievous smirk. A final farewell for the boy who was both my brother and a monster.

"Thank you," I whisper to his grave, "for giving me a chance." I lean against the shovel. My gaze returns to the city, but a part of me will stay with the twin I couldn't keep from destroying himself. "You were right, Alec. They are my future, but they could have been yours."

Could have been *ours.* But our dream of ruling together died long ago.

I sniff, blinking my vision clear as I grab the crown and swing my cape around my shoulders. The metal feels fragile in my hands, like a new dream that isn't quite solid yet, but the sound of a rider approaching draws my focus.

Dovan has come as he said he would. The serious set of his expression tells me the tally is complete. A wave of anxiety unsettles my stomach. The moment I've been waiting for has finally arrived, and I'm to meet my fate in a simple gown marred with sweat and dirt. *My father would be horrified by my common appear-*

ance. Alec would be proud. As am I. I'm not ashamed of the work I've done, both in my city and inside my heart.

Dovan guides his horse sideways and offers me his hand. I take it, and he pulls me up behind him. Together, we ride for our city.

Time to find out if I will be queen.

WRENNA

53

SHADOWS DRAPE the ballroom as me and Dovan enter. Our boots click on the polished marble, creating a slower counter-beat to my faster pulse. *Breathe.* The air tickles my nose with the pungent aroma of a forest. Naked beams and planks of pine have replaced the once-elegant glass ceiling I shattered, and guilt squeezes my heart over the damage I caused when the season tree tried to possess me.

The memory of my banshee shriek, of the jagged glass falling, and my brother's bloodied face assaults me, but I unclench my hands and fix my gaze straight ahead to the sole source of light. Two torches in full golden flame. They flicker from iron stands on either side of my covered portrait. Fear escapes my tight hold and stabs an icy blade into my chest.

You will never be queen.

The thought causes a misstep as I wrangle my spinning mind under control. *Even if I don't become queen, I won't stop loving my people.* Or helping them.

Dovan touches the small of my back as we slow before the painting, a gentle reminder he's with me whatever happens. He flashes his *I'm never wrong* smirk at me while I clutch the folds of my emerald skirt.

His Gran waits to the right of my portrait, her dark gaze sharp as knives. She's seen my life replay hundreds of times, but her grim expression reveals nothing. No emotion, except for how heavily she leans on her crutch. *She must be exhausted.* But she stays for me.

The woman, who would have traded my life for Dovan's, guards my future.

She shares something with my brother I never can, that made walking a challenge for them both, and yet—*how different they are.* Proving it's never our circumstances or our wounds that define us. It's our choices. Alec chose to be a killer while she chose to be a protector. *Think of all the orphans she's saved.* Raising them with a stern but generous love, giving them a home, and one of those orphans stands beside me. How different would Dovan have been without her influence?

She gives me hope.

"Ye be ready?" she asks, her words sharp and cold. But her eyes soften as she senses my dread. Crutching forward, she takes my hand and then Dovan's, pressing them together between hers. "Life be about learnin' what ta let go of. Not this. Never this. Do ye hear me?"

Dovan's fingers tighten around mine and I respond with a squeeze.

"Good." A wry grin plays with her wrinkles, showing a few of her chipped teeth. "Best be getting' on with it. Sanaa be makin' a feast." She catches herself, waving a hand through the air. "It may be a consolin' feast." She winks at Dovan as she crutches past him, but spots me watching and frowns. "Girl, how long must yer future be a waitin'?"

Dovan clears his throat, a lousy attempt to conceal his chuckle. Their light-handed manner should give me hope, but it only heightens my fear.

Fear of all I could lose.

I focus on how Dovan's hand cradles mine in safety and warmth. *I won't lose this.* Not Dovan or his Gran or Sanaa and the other children. *We're a family now.*

A closed ledger sits on top of a small table beside my portrait. The tally. My people's answer to my question. My fingers tremble as I lift the cover. A red ribbon marks the end of the tally where the final count waits, but I want to see it all. Every page and every mark.

At first, my hope feels the cracking of their rejection. Most of the marks are in the *no* column. Despair punches me in the gut as the ledger blurs, spotted with my tears. *They didn't choose me.* The painting wasn't enough.

I'm still a monster to them.

Dovan grips my shoulder as I hiccup and try to sniff back my pain. "Look closer."

The steady heat of his presence gives me the courage to continue. I blink hard, and the page comes into focus. There are *yes* and *no* votes in the same lines. Page after page, the same pattern plays out with the *no* votes crossed out. "I don't understand."

"They changed their votes," Dovan explains. He flips the ledger to the end where the final count is written. I stare at the numbers, my pulse pounding in my ears, my breath caught in my throat. The first is in the thousands, the second a few hundred.

I slump onto the little table. *Why would they vote one way and then another?*

"It started a month ago," Dovan continues. "Those who'd voted against you came back saying they wanted you as queen."

"Why?"

A tiny smile tugs at the corner of his mouth as he sets the saddlebags he carried in with him on the table. The left bag contains the crown I will wear. He stopped to clean it at a well we passed because he knew I'd be wearing it, but he reaches into the right one and retrieves a small box tied with string.

Dovan holds it out to me. "This is why."

I cradle the box as I untie the string and lift the lid. Ink scrolls a familiar melody over torn measure lines. My gaze leaps to Dovan's, unbelieving, because there is no reason for him to have this song. *He wasn't there.* Yet as I study his face, the nervous twitch of his half-grin and the boyish longing in his eyes, my objection unravels. He wore the same look when we met after I fell through that storage shed buried in the snowfields.

He saw me. Before the curse chose him.

An impossibility he still hasn't explained. *It was more than seeing.* Dovan *knew* me. He admitted as much on the day he was supposed to die, and this song is the proof.

Only one thing can overpower the rules of the banshee curse.

The very thing that broke it.

Love.

I raise the song's ripped fragments between us. "How do you have this? I wrote it in the backroom of the Mermaiden fourteen years ago for—"

"A boy crying in a corner. A boy with no home and no family and even less hope." He finishes for me while I gape at him in shock. "I was ten, just another orphan fleeing the war in my country. I had no one. I was nothing." He edges closer, his hand cupping my face, and his thumb caresses my cheek. "But you heard me. And you saw me."

I lean into his touch, letting his words guide my memories to the inn. To Ioana shouting directions at those who'd come to help, to all the cots filled with children who'd never see their families again. Some were sick. Some were frightened. And others, like Dovan, kept their eyes down and their faces to the wall.

His silence echoed. Even then, his soul was louder than all the voices in the room.

I lift my fingers to his cheek and trace the proud rise and fall of his bones. As I match the man he is to the boy he was, that scared orphan transforms into a guider with unshakable confidence. "You weren't nothing. You could never be nothing, Dovan. Not to me."

He kisses my palm. "But you were the daughter of a king. You weren't supposed to notice someone like me, and yet you wiped my fevered head, and held my hand, and told me why life is still beautiful even when it's hard." The love shining through his gaze unfurls like a flower he's kept tucked away in secret, waiting for this moment, and as it blooms, it reveals the boy whose heart I stole with a song.

My chin trembles as I suck in a breath that lights my soul on fire, because the banshee curse didn't bring us together—I did.

I stayed with him that night. My father was holding a dinner for the north prince, and my attendance was expected. But I couldn't leave the Abrykarran boy.

I couldn't leave *Dovan.*

He'd dreamed of his family's slaughter and had screamed so loud that the other orphans and even the adults were afraid of him. His vibrant green irises had already alienated him, marking him as dangerous. A child suspected of harboring season magic when the four kingdoms were warring over who would own the embers. *They wouldn't sit with him.* So I did.

The dim grief in his eyes brightens into gratitude. "You cared more about an orphan's welfare than about protecting yourself from your father's wrath."

Wrath is a mild description. When my father noticed my absence, he left his dinner and hunted me down. *He found me singing to Dovan.* And after yanking me from my stool, he ripped my song apart and dragged me to the palace. Alec met us when we arrived, and our father broke three of Alec's ribs to punish me before making me play hostess for the rest of the night.

With a shiver, I force the memory away. It wasn't the first time my father had tried to crush my dream of helping people instead of ruling them with an iron fist.

Dovan rubs the chill from my arms. "Do you know why the painting failed to convince them you should be queen?"

I shake my head.

"It showed them who you were and the hard choices you had to make, but the past wasn't enough. They're afraid, Wrenna, and it gave them no comfort until you started meeting with them. Helping them. Leading them. You made them feel seen and their concerns, no matter how small, important. You, being who you are, changed their minds."

"I'm just trying to help." Moisture lines my eyelids as the warmth of his praise sooths the ache in my heart.

"That's the point. You're thinking more about them and their needs instead of what they can do for you. How they can make you richer or increase your power." He brushes a tear from my cheek. "You don't give a damn about crowns or titles or keeping up old barriers between the high and the low. You're nothing like your father or your brother or the rulers we've known. You're the banshee who wept over every victim. You're the warrior who saved a city from the season tree. You're the princess who put herself at risk to sing an orphan to sleep and I love you for it. *All of it.*"

I start to cry, but these tears aren't born of my failure to believe what he's saying. They are burning with hope. For so long, I wouldn't let myself accept I was strong in ways others weren't. That I had value despite what had been done to me.

Broken as I still am, I have something good to give.

"I never lost sight of you." His fingers curl into my sides, drawing me close. "Not before the curse, not even after. I searched for a way to break your curse, and I would have done *anything* to free you."

Tears stream down my face as I listen, and my heart swells inside my chest, aching over lost time and yet rejoicing over the time ahead of us.

"All I wanted." His breath hitches as his emotions overwhelm him, turning his gaze glassy and softening his stern jaw. "All I hoped for, was to spend my last day with the woman I loved but could never have." And so he walked into the snowfields six months ago to meet a banshee, knowing I would be his end.

"Don't you know?" I wrap my arms around his neck. "You already have me."

An invitation for an epic kiss if ever there was one, but we're not in a hurry. There's no threat of death hanging over our heads. This is our beginning. The orphan and the banshee, the guider and the queen, a story we will write together.

We kiss like it's our first time. Nearing each other slowly, savoring every angle and soft caress. For a moment, we're not weighed down by grief or by the responsibilities we carry. We're young and in love and full of hope.

After we break apart, Dovan's a little breathless as he says, "There's something else I've been waiting months to do." He draws the crown from the saddle bag. "May I?"

I straighten my spine, lifting my chin and throwing my shoulders back, before nodding once. All while breathing through a bittersweet rush of joy and sorrow that causes a fresh cascade of tears and the ghost of a grin. I brace myself as he lowers the cool metal onto my head only to be surprised. *Not as heavy as I expected.* But I think that's wise, since a ruler's true burden is carried by their soul.

Dovan kneels as he places his fist over his heart. "*My* queen."

I suppress a giggle because he put extra emphasis on me being *his* queen. The pride in his voice burns through me, fueling my confidence. I pull him to his feet, and we face my portrait. Still covered, its mysteries and dangers remain hidden.

I never looked at it. *Dovan's Gran would have whacked me if I'd tried.* My lips quirk in amusement at that, but these past few months I've been too busy to consider sneaking a peek.

And now? As a banshee, my future was always the same. I would sing and watch another person die. That loop has been broken and so many things are now possible. *Maybe that's the true gift of the future.* That it is unknown. A course uncharted, a story not yet written, a song to be discovered.

The painting may hold my past and my present, but my future is mine.

I will sow its seeds through every choice I make and reap a good harvest someday. One, where the laughter outnumbers the tears, where the wrongs have been made right, and where hope always wins.

"Together?" Dovan asks, plucking a torch from its stand.

"Together," I repeat our promise as I grab the other torch, and we set the painting on fire.

We hold hands as it burns, and I recall the advice of a wise old woman.

Life is about learning to let go, but it's also about knowing what to hold on to.

ACKNOWLEDGMENTS

What a journey this book has been. It all started the night before Thanksgiving in 2018 when a banshee cursed to serve a murderer woke me up with her story. I thought this book was supposed to be a simple novella, but these characters had other plans. It became a story I needed to tell. A story about being shattered and powerless and how to find a way through all the damage other people can do to our bodies, our minds, and our hearts.

And then 2020 happened. I was hit with what I thought at the time were severe food allergies, and I burned out so badly I couldn't write anything for three months. I've never felt like such an utter failure before, but with rest, I was able crawl forward again. (To the writers reading this, never look down on small progress. Small progress is what finished this book. Don't give up.) This book demanded so much of me. I could not have finished it without the people who came alongside me through the grueling three-plus years of writing and rewriting. So here's my list of gratitude to the people who helped me get here.

First, to Jesus, if he couldn't redeem pain and brokenness, this book wouldn't exist.

Mom and Pop, thanks for believing in me as a woman and as a writer, especially during the hard seasons where I doubted everything. Thank you for loving my stories (even when Pop always resisted my need to rewrite things. In his eyes, every draft was perfect, and I love him for that.). Thanks mom, for never tiring of my manic walk and talks where I used you as a soundboard to figure out tricky plot things and my annoying characters. Thank you for praying over me when I was too tired to pray for strength myself.

Sarah Delena White it was your banshee Sadika from Halayda and Rothana that made me fall in love with and start researching banshees. So, basically, I can blame you for everything. (Kidding, lol.)

Selina Gonzalez, thanks for everything, friend, and I mean everything. All our chats, the feedback that was always helpful, the logic slaps for my illogical spirals, and the friendship. (Thanks for putting up with my very random brain and all my frog spam.) You were one of the first people to read the early draft of The Soul Crier, and I still remember crying with joy over the email that you sent after staying up late to finish reading. Thank you for also reminding me to take care of myself too, not just work.

Janeen Ippolito, this book would not be what it is without you. Although, your first round of edits made me mad. "What do you mean, 'the ending is wrong'?" Lol. But you were right. That original ending was so very wrong for these characters. You were also right that 50,000 words was too short for a story as complex as this one. You were the perfect editor for this project, the editor I needed to wrangle this story into shape. Thank you for being so patient and understanding as I missed deadlines and had a gap of over a year between edits.

Laura Pol, just thinking of how grateful I am for all the ways you loved on this story and me over the past three years makes me tear up. You were always this story's biggest fan. Your comments and shared videos kept me going through so many hard rewrites.

Noelle Nichols, thank you for the writing sprints! They helped me gain momentum when I was stuck several times.

Katie Philips, although you were not my editor for this book, much of what I learned from you on a different book stuck with me as I worked on this one.

All my alpha/beta readers, especially Rae, Heather, Olivia, Heidi, and Angie, thank you for the feedback at various stages and the excitement and continued support for this book.

Kayla Grey, thank you for looking over the opening chapters when I was panicking they still weren't good enough.

Lindsay Franklin, thank you for all the advice as I struggled with parts of Wraith's trauma and healing journey. It meant everything to talk with someone who understands.

Jenny Zemanek, thank you for the stunning cover! Being able to look at it through all the trials of getting this book done kept me going.

Jesse Rivas, for the perfect tree-based insult of "axe-bait."

To my coworkers, especially Chris, Spencer, Carmela, Alfred, Lena, Roxy, Latoya, April, and Devin, who have continued to ask me how the book is coming. Your excitement was a surprise and a blessing. Alfred, you cracked me up when you proclaimed, "She's writing a book" to visiting managers, even if I did just want to go hide in my office afterwards. I hope you guys enjoy this book.

To the writers of the Realmmakers Consortium, thank you for the friendships and advice and encouragement.

To the coffee/writer group, you ladies are all awesome. Thanks for the encouragement and for the blurb help.

To everyone else who has expressed excitement and sent messages or left comments on my posts throughout these three years, know that each one meant everything. So often I was at a low point and doubting I'd get this book done when one of you would send such a message.

To all the family and friends who have prayed over me and this book—thank you!

And finally, to you, dear reader, thank you for giving this book a chance. I hope you remember that you always have the power of your choice, and that no wrong thing ever done to you is the end of your story. Healing is hard, and although some hurts may never fully heal, there is still joy and purpose to life. There are good things to come. And we are not alone.

Be kind to yourselves.

WHAT I'M WRITING NEXT

"*She could set me free.*
If he didn't unintentionally kill her first."

And so begins the ambitious writing adventure I've dubbed Project Faebies. The main characters in this four book high fantasy series have been chatting in my ear for months, keeping me sane as I finished edits for The Soul Crier. I am SO excited about this story. Here's a little more about it.

———

Noxar Draven, leader of the Hand of Death, Prince of Shadows, and executioner for the shadow queen harbors a deep hatred for the way his fae-kind run their world, but for all his feared power, he's as powerless to change things as a magic-less human.

Tempest is a half fae and human rebel on the run, but when she uses lightning to save another half and kills her fae lord, she finds herself facing the death wager. A fatal challenge designed so her magic will fail. It's how the fae do executions. What she doesn't expect is to be saved by the most lethal and feared fae of all, the shadow queen's favorite prince, Noxar.

Forced to be reluctant allies, Nox and Tempest must team up

not only for their survival but for the chance of changing their world.

The best way to stay up to date on how this project is going is to sign up for my newsletter. All subscribers will get to see updates, teasers, background world/character info, and timeline announcements for Project Faebies first. Sign up at https://www.beckygaines.com.

ABOUT THE AUTHOR

Becky Gaines lives in the desert of Southern California with her family where the sunsets are epic and the lizards plentiful. When not working or plotting new stories, she loves rereading her favorite books (especially Red Rising by Pierce Brown and Six of Crows by Leigh Bardugo), adding new songs to her next book playlist, watching Grimm again, and scouring the internet for new frogs to obsess over (even if nothing will top the grumpy cuteness of the black rain frog). If there's a thunderstorm nearby, you will find her enjoying the rain and swearing when the thunder shakes the house, all while wishing storm powers/storm magic were really a thing.

You can find Becky on Facebook or on Instagram, where she's most active, under the name @beckygainesauthor.